Book #1

HOME BY MORNING

HOME BY MORNING

by

ALEXIS HARRINGTON

The characters and events portrayed in this book are fictitious. Any similarity to real persons, living or dead, is coincidental and not intended by the author.

Printed in the United States of America.

Published by Montlake Romance
P.O. Box 400818
Las Vegas, NV 89140

ISBN-13: 9781612182056
ISBN-10: 1612182054

DEDICATION

For the lads

CHAPTER ONE

October 1918
Powell Springs, Oregon

As the 9:10 train chugged into the station at Powell Springs, Jessica Layton strained to see through the smudged window.

Home. This was her hometown, even though she'd once sworn never to return.

As the train stopped, the sounds of cheers rose. Jessica peered through the dirty glass at a crowd of people milling under the morning sun. Saturdays were always busy in town, but this was something more.

Flags waved from hands, from poles, and from building fronts, and placards of a stern-looking Uncle Sam stared out over the happy mob. Some carried placards painted with slogans such as BEAT BACK THE HUN!

Children laughed. Women smiled and waved handkerchiefs, while horses, wagons, and humanity all jammed together for a good look at a spectacle coming down the street.

Clutching her black leather bag, Jess stepped down to the railroad platform just as the local grange band struck up a rusty but loud rendition of "Stars and Stripes Forever," almost blasting her back onto the train.

Despite her ambivalence at being back in familiar surroundings, her heart flooded with nostalgia she had not anticipated, enhanced by the tang of autumn in the air and the scent of the clean, fresh breeze after she'd been confined in stuffy Pullman cars for a week.

Her sister was supposed to meet her here, but her telegram to Jessica had said nothing about a parade; of Amy, there was no sign.

She paid an ancient porter to have her luggage sent to the hotel, then managed to make her way through the spectators, jostling and bumping like chickens in a crowded coop. Jess looked up in time to see her sister go by, waving and smiling at everyone as if she were a queen on a sedan chair instead of an ordinary citizen on a sturdy farm wagon. A few other people Jessica didn't recognize sat on the wagon beside her. Astonished, Jess found herself waving back, although she was sure Amy didn't see her. The parade's route took it past the depot, around the horse trough that now featured a clumsy replica of the Statue of Liberty, then turned left up Main Street.

She leaned over and asked the woman standing next to her, "What's this all about?"

When the woman turned, Jess recognized Susannah Braddock, her face glowing with a happy grin. "Jessica!" With her was a tall, rangy man of about thirty, and two young boys.

"Susannah, you look wonderful." Actually, Jess thought she seemed thinner and a bit weary around the eyes. She still wore her glossy black curls long and unfettered by more than a pair of tortoiseshell combs. Her dark hair and eyes gave her a slightly exotic look.

"It's so good to see you," Susannah said, then gestured at the street. "This is a Liberty Bond parade to raise money. Mayor Cookson's son, Eddie, is already in uniform and he's the guest of honor."

"Really?" Little Eddie Cookson, old enough to be a soldier?

Susannah clasped Jess's gloved hand. "I'm glad you're back, even if it's just for a while. We really couldn't spare the time to come to town today, but it's been weeks since I was here and it's good to get away from the farm. Anyway, the boys wanted to see the parade." She nodded at the two youngsters, who had wormed their way to the front of the group to watch the passing spectacle. Then she turned toward the man who accompanied her. "Jess, this is Tanner Grenfell. He and his two nephews came to work for us a couple of years ago."

Tanner, a sandy-haired, wiry man of medium build, tugged on the brim of his hat. "Ma'am."

"We'd just be lost without him, now that Riley is away at war. Tanner's a wonder with the horses. Even Cole says so, and you know he can be pretty picky."

Jess knew, perhaps even more than Susannah realized.

"Now, Miss Susannah—" Color rose in Tanner's face, but Jess could tell that he basked in Susannah's praise. In fact, he looked at her with a genuine devotion that Jessica did not miss.

Singing "Over There," school children peddled past on bicycles with crepe paper streamers woven in the spokes. They led the rest of the floats, which included a woman pounding out "You're a Grand Old Flag" on a piano from the back of a farm wagon, assorted mounted riders, and a squeaking Conestoga full of suffragettes. All the music clashed, but from farther down the line of onlookers, Jessica heard a swell of cheering that drowned out the discordant notes and just about everything else.

"Here comes Eddie!"

"I see him! He makes a grand soldier!"

The most elaborately decorated float of all came rolling into view, draped with bunting and several American flags. Nailed to the sides of the float were more Liberty Bond posters. The applause and shouting around Jess grew even louder. She would never have recognized Mayor Cookson's son, a blushing, reedy boy of about eighteen, who looked bashful and very young despite his stiff army uniform. He stood with several others who'd been chosen for the honor of sharing the obvious grand finale of the parade. People rushed forward to shake his hand and wish him luck in Europe. He touched every hand extended toward him. The applause and to-do made him redden all the way to his cap. He must have been warm in his olive drab, because even from Jess's vantage point she saw a sheen of perspiration gleaming on his features. Squealing girls on the sidewalk, abandoning decorum, threw paper flowers and the last of the season's roses from their yards. He grinned sheepishly.

Sheriff Whit Gannon, on horseback, marked the end of the parade, and the onlookers poured off the sidewalks into the street to follow along and continue the festivities.

Tanner and Susannah began moving toward Eddie's float, following Josh and Wade. Susannah called back, "Jessica, you'll have to come out for dinner while you're home!" Then she and Tanner disappeared into the crowd.

Jess mingled with a few people who stopped to say hello and welcome her back to town with warm greetings and expressions of hope that she'd come to stay.

Jess, unprepared for their enthusiasm, didn't have the chance—or the heart—to tell them she would be here only for a few days on her way to Seattle.

Then from up the street, a wave of alarmed, concerned voices reached Jessica. The back end of the parade stuttered to a halt and Sheriff Gannon nudged his horse through the crowd of confused spectators to reach the spot. Taking advantage of his breaking trail, Jess followed, sensing urgency in the tones of raised voices. Someone was hurt or ill.

"Granny Mae! Someone get Granny Mae!" a dominant voice ordered, and Jessica swallowed hard against the tight knot in her throat, recognizing the voice's tone. Cole Braddock. She'd known she'd have to see him, but thought she'd be more prepared.

"It's Eddie," someone else said. "He just toppled right off that float, like he passed out or something."

Jessica pushed around someone who stood in her way in time to see Cole hoist Eddie onto his shoulder and carry him toward Granny Mae's café on the other side of the street. She followed close behind, her grip still tight on her black bag.

As she went through the door, the familiar redolence of spices and savory aromas hit Jess's nose.

Jess worked her way through the crowd that filled the tiny restaurant and caught a glimpse of Eddie, who was now on his feet, but unsteady.

Then her gaze shifted to Cole. In that moment, everything else around her faded to a blur and memories rushed over her like a swift-flowing river. Her focus fixed on him. The way he still wore his hair cut to chin length, the straight nose and firm mouth, the set of his shoulders.

"Mae!" Cole yelled. "Where the hell is Mae? Eddie Cookson passed out and fell off his float in front of my shop."

Eddie, looking pale and stunned, had a gash on his forehead from the fall. Automatically, Jess's attention shifted to the patient. "Let me look at him." Cole's eyes fell on her and a shiver rushed through her. His cold stare hardened into that of a stranger's as he assessed her from hair to hem before dismissing her.

"Someone call me?" A weathered, slat-sided woman emerged from the kitchen in the back room. Her gray hair was pulled into a messy knot on the top of her head, and her long face bore more lines than a peach pit. She carried a raw beef roast on the end of a big cooking fork. "What in blazes are all you people doing in here?" Casually, she wiped one hand on the waist of her blood-spattered apron.

Cole turned his back to Jess, pivoting Eddie with him. "His legs just gave out, Mae. He folded up like a paper umbrella."

"Maybe I only tripped over my own feet," Eddie said, half-heartedly.

The old woman made a cursory examination of the young soldier. "Bring him on back so I can take a closer look at him." Then, without regard for his privacy or dignity, she trumpeted, "He probably just needs a good healthy dose of Epsom salts to clean him out. It's amazing what trouble backed-up bowels cause." Mae, Eddie, and Cole headed for the kitchen.

"God in heaven, she can't mean that," Jess murmured. Ignoring the small, flyspecked "No Admittance" sign posted next to the kitchen doorway, she pushed her way through the swinging doors.

By the window, Mae gave Eddie Cookson a quick once-over while Cole steadied him, then she mixed two heaping tablespoons of white crystals into a glass of water. "It doesn't taste so good but you drink that all down in one—"

"Eddie Cookson, don't you do anything of the kind!" Jess interrupted, striding toward the trio. This close, he looked even younger than he had earlier despite his military trappings. Reaching out, she tipped his chin toward her and saw what the old woman plainly did not. Glazed eyes. Sweaty pallor. Damp hair. This could not be dismissed as "backed-up bowels." The wound on his forehead trickled blood down the side of his face and his skin was oddly clammy under her touch. "How do you feel?"

"Well, ma'am, except for a headache that I've had all day, I was fine this morning when I woke up. Then after the parade, well, next thing I knew I was on my face on the ground. I just feel...alloverish."

"That's what the salts are for! Alloverish!" Mae continued to stir the salts and water, now with fierce agitation.

Jess refrained from clenching her teeth too tightly. "No, they are not. This isn't a digestive problem. He needs medical attention, Mae." She knew that many physicians with medical school educations also subscribed to the blanket practice of purging, but she opposed the idea. She pointed at the can of Epsom salts. "That will just weaken him."

Mae turned, her high-cut nostrils accentuating her sneer. "Oh, chicken feathers, *Doctor* Layton. I was dosing and tending people before you arrived on this earth."

"That's not a good reason to keep doing it." She took Eddie's chin again and turned his face toward the old woman. "He needs a more thorough examination, not to mention a dressing for that gash."

Mae exhaled a gusty sigh. "I didn't back down from your father, missy, and I'm not about to let you tell me my business. Didn't you see that sign at the door? Customers aren't allowed in the kitchen."

"But the *dog* is?" Jess pointed at a flea-ridden, brindle-coated mongrel, lying in a pool of sunlight, gnawing on a bone. The animal sat up and scratched vigorously behind one ear, releasing a flurry of loose hair. "Where food is being prepared?" she added, with a shudder of revulsion.

Granny Mae gave her a sour look and thrust the glass into Eddie's hand. "You drink this down. Now."

In utter frustration, Jessica turned to Cole. "For heaven's sake, Cole, you don't agree with her, do you?" He smelled of wood smoke, horses, and burnished metal from hours spent at his blacksmith forge, just as she remembered.

Eddie waited for a decision. "My throat feels like it was scraped with an old rasp, and my head…"

Cole's hard expression eased and finally he shook his head. "No. You should see to him, Jessica." His tone was grudging.

Granny Mae straightened, huffy and insulted. Jess swore she could hear those old joints creaking like a rusty wheelbarrow left out in the weather. "Not in my kitchen, she won't. You can just take all this somewhere else." She snatched the glass from Eddie's hand.

"Oh, damn it, Mae—"

"That's fine, Cole." Jessica eyed the dog again and the raw meat on the table. "It's not sanitary in here, anyway."

Mae turned up her nose and made an inarticulate, irritated noise.

The three walked back through the café, past the curious diners.

Amy had arrived and stood beside a table, her hands folded in a single, tight fist.

With no time for more than a cursory kiss on her sister's cheek, Jessica was all business now. Patients came first. "Amy, can you think of anyplace I can use to take care of this young man?"

"Maybe Mrs. Donaldson will let us use her kitchen. She's been so kind while I've been boarding there."

Cole stepped closer. "No. I have the key to the doctor's office between the blacksmith shop and the bank. It's just standing empty, waiting for the new doc to get here." He fished around in his tight front pants pocket and produced a brass key.

"That would do very well," Jess said, conscious of the stiffness between them. "Thank you, Cole."

His tough gaze bored through her, then softened a bit and he nodded. "All right, buck up there, son," he said to Eddie. "Think you can make the walk back across the street?"

"Yeah. I didn't mean to cause so much trouble. I don't know what happened."

Cole waved off his protests and steered him outside.

An unwanted picture paraded before her mind's eye, one of Cole standing over his black and fire-reddened forge, shirtless and wearing only a heavy leather apron while he wielded a hammer. With each stroke of his hammer, sparks, like tiny fireflies, bounced off the hot metal he shaped on the anvil. As powerful and elemental as his task, she saw him as a beautiful incarnation of homely and lame Hephaestus, the god of fire and metalwork, and armorer to Olympus immortals. Oh, yes. Blond, muscled, rugged—that was Cole Braddock. Faithless—that was also Cole. Would she ever get him out of her head?

Jessica turned and picked up her bag, then said to her sister, "Amy, after I see to Eddie I'm going to the hotel. Meet me there for lunch?" She smiled. "We have so much to catch up on." She hurried after Eddie, whom Cole was helping across the street. Amy trotted along beside her.

"That would be wonderful," Amy replied. "I'll ask Cole, too. The hotel dining room is so nice." She glanced back at Granny Mae's café. "We probably ought to stay away from Granny for a while, anyway. She wasn't too happy when we left."

— — —

Outside on Main Street, people were mostly back to their usual business, and foot traffic had tapered off.

"I'm sure sorry to bother you, Dr. Layton," Eddie said, not for the first time, as he sat swaying slightly on the first chair inside the door as though the very essence of his strength had drained away.

"If you hadn't been at the café, I would have done what Granny Mae said."

God only knew what else Mae would have prescribed, Jess thought as she dabbed at his forehead. She might have tied onion slices over his ears and had him stare at the moon as it rose over Mount Hood. She sat in a chair across from him, her bag at her feet. He winced while she applied a stinging antiseptic, but cleaned up, the wound wasn't as bad as she'd first thought. "I'm glad I was there, Eddie."

"I guess it must be just a cold but—" He put his hands to the sides of his skull as if to keep it from splitting open. He smiled weakly and Jess noticed that he still looked pale and hot-eyed. She could hear congestion in his sinuses and chest, making his words sound as if he had a bucket over his head. Suddenly a fit of coughing overtook him, a spell so violent that Jess half-expected to see his lungs on the waiting room floor.

She frowned. "That's a nasty cough you have."

"Yes, ma'am," he gasped. "It came on fast. I swear everything hurts, every muscle in my body. And I'm freezing cold. I'm going home to rest, but maybe you could give me something for these aches?"

Jess leaned back and considered him. It could be something as minor as a bad cold. Or something worse. Amy, who'd rushed off to a meeting of the Liberty Bond Committee, had said there were some medicines in the back, but there had been no time to investigate, and Jess knew she had aspirin tablets in her bag. "All right, let's start with a simple treatment." She flipped open the latches and pulled out the glass-stoppered bottle. Rummaging through a side pocket, she also produced an empty envelope and counted them out. "Here are ten tablets—take two every four to six hours."

He took the packet from her extended hand and gobbled down two pills before she could even search for a glass of water. “Thank you, ma’am. I mean, Doctor.”

“Can your father give you a ride home?”

“He’s busy in his office.”

She nodded. “All right, then. Let’s see if we can find you a better place to wait for him.” She walked down the short hall that led to an examination room and an office. In the latter she found a horsehair sofa in decent condition that would be more comfortable than the straight-backed wooden chair in the front.

“Eddie,” she called, “you come sit back here.”

He struggled to his feet. “Just for a few minutes—I’ve had lots of marching drills at Camp Lewis, and I can walk home once the aspirin starts working.”

She didn’t think that was a good idea but didn’t bother to argue. “All the same, I’ll get word to your father. I have some errands to run, but I’ll see to it that you get home.”

Jess left him slumped on the sofa, and a nagging worry pulled at her. Still, she told herself, he’s a strong young man in the peak of health. But it seemed strange he should react so swiftly to a cold. It didn’t make sense.

Weaving through people on the sidewalk, she saw the mayor coming her way. He strode along purposefully.

“Jessica! I mean Miss—Dr. Layton. You’re just the person I’ve been looking for.” Horace Cookson was a heavyset man in his mid-forties, a dairy farmer by occupation, who bore a rumpled, homespun dignity. His shirtsleeves were rolled up to his elbows, the bottom button of his vest was missing, and his tie was askew. He had the look of a man who was always either one step ahead of or behind himself. Every weekday morning he rose in the dark, milked his cows, then put on his dress clothes and came to town.

"If it's about Eddie—"

"I heard about your set-to with Granny Mae over him. He'll be fine, won't he?"

"He's resting in the doctor's office, but he's going to need a ride home. He said he'd walk, but really, he's not up to that."

The mayor nodded, plainly unconcerned. "He's strong and young. He'll be fine and I'll see to it that someone gets him—his mother will make a fuss over him. But right now, I'm interested in talking to you. Please," he said, gesturing in the direction of Powell Springs's tiny city hall at the end of the block. "Will you come on down to my office for a chat?"

Jessica frowned slightly. "What about? The county isn't still insisting that I owe them property taxes—"

He waved off the suggestion. "No, no, I'm sure that's not the case. Anyway, I don't have a thing to do with tax collection. No, we have another subject to talk about."

"We do?"

"Please—come and join me for a short meeting," Cookson asked again and held out his hand in a gesture of invitation.

Jessica glanced around, baffled and looking for an escape. There was none. "Well, all right." She followed him, dodging a woman pulling along two children who clutched small American flags in their fists. There was a bright, holiday atmosphere on the street.

When they arrived at city hall, Cookson whisked past his secretary. "No interruptions, Birdeen," he said to the dark-haired woman sitting at a switchboard outside his door. Birdeen Lyons held dual jobs as the mayor's receptionist and Powell Springs's telephone operator, although as far as Jess knew, telephones here were not as common as they were in other places. Powell Springs was still a small town, and only a house or two per block had one.

"Sure, Horace."

Breezing into his untidy office, he pushed a pile of papers off the chair next to his oak desk. He motioned to Jessica to sit. "I don't have any tea or coffee here, but I could send out to the café. It would only take a minute."

"Thank you, no." She glanced around. On the wall behind the mayor's desk, she saw the same war bond poster that was in nearly every shop window in town. Next to it hung a small, framed photograph of Eddie, looking stiff and proud in his army uniform.

The mayor sat down in his chair and turned to face her. "You'll have to forgive me for herding you off the sidewalk. Believe me, I wouldn't have done it if this wasn't urgent."

Jessica nodded and waited for an explanation that was more urgent than giving his sick boy a simple ride to the family farm. His round face, though kind enough, gave away nothing.

"This morning when I heard you'd arrived in town and then tended to my son, I called a special meeting of the town council."

She straightened in the chair, on her guard. How had word of her arrival gotten around so quickly? Then her brows met over the bridge of her nose as a thought occurred to her. "For heaven's sake, did Granny Mae actually complain to you about it? Is that why I'm here?"

"Now, now, don't let Mae ruffle your feathers. She's a fine woman and a fixture in this community. She's been here since Methuselah wore knee pants, mixing potions and delivering babies."

Now now, there there... This was so typical of the kind of patronizing attitudes she'd endured since deciding to pursue medicine. "Mayor Cookson, my *feathers* are not—"

"Mae is a fine woman," he interrupted, "and she makes a chicken stew that would put my mother's to shame, rest her soul. But I think we can agree that she is not a medical doctor."

Jess's mouth, which she'd opened to continue her defense, snapped shut. Then she went on cautiously, "Well, no, she isn't. That was why I stepped in."

"And I'm glad you did. We need a *physician*, and we've been without one since Doc Vandermeer was taken by the influenza last spring."

"I understood that you've found one." Amy's last letter to her had mentioned that.

"Yes, Frederick Pearson. A presentable young graduate, as far as I can tell from his letters." He shuffled through another few stacks of papers on his desk. "Well, I don't see them right now. But presentable or not, I'm still not certain when he'll be here. We've been expecting him for a while. With the war on, most of the doctors and nurses have gone overseas."

She already knew that. In fact, she wasn't sure how *presentable* this Pearson could be since the army had drafted every physician who was even semi-competent. The only ones left were quacks without degrees and a few females like herself, in whom the army was not interested. "How does this involve me, Mr. Cookson?"

He folded his big farmer's hands on his desk blotter. "It was a short meeting. After some argu—I mean jawing, the council voted that I should ask you stay on in Powell Springs until Dr. Pearson arrives."

Jessica stared at him. "I'm sure this wasn't a unanimous decision."

He shifted. "Well, not exactly. To be honest, there was a little doubt because you're, well…" He paused. "Well, a woman." Jess lifted her brows slightly and felt her cheeks grow warm. "But your father was an upright man—you know, well thought of. And most folks in town have known you since way back." He brightened here. "Adam

Jacobsen spoke up in your favor, and pretty enthusiastically. Of course, the opinion of Powell Springs's minister, and a man so active in the American Protective League—well, he won over the others."

The APL—she would expect that of Adam. Jess remembered him as a whiny little pip-squeak of a child who tattled on everyone to his own father, the minister before him. The American Protective League, an outgrowth of President Wilson's Sedition Act, had over two hundred thousand volunteer members who made it their business to spy on their neighbors, report men they considered to be draft dodgers, stick their noses into everyone's activities, find treachery where none existed, and harass people for not buying Liberty Bonds. They could have others arrested for expressing a critical opinion of the war, and viewed everyone with suspicion. So Adam's endorsement was unexpected and probably unwelcome.

"But I'm only staying a little more than a week, just to see my sister. I have a research position waiting for me in Seattle."

"Hmm, yes, that might be a problem, since we don't know when Pearson is arriving."

"Not 'might be.' It *is* a problem. I'm expected in Washington, and I have to go. I don't practice clinical medicine anymore."

He leaned forward, his expression earnest and open. "Dr. Layton…Jessica…I know this is a hell of a lot to ask of you, but you managed the situation with Ed so well. Granny Mae just isn't qualified to take care of medical problems. She's helped me pull a calf or two over the years, and I suppose she can handle little things. But some people around here have started to worry about what will happen the next time a real emergency comes up. Poor old Elvin Fowler just sits on his porch all day long now, since he broke his leg and had no real doctoring. It's my job as mayor to see that the citizens of Powell Springs are taken care of."

He caught her gaze and held it fast. "And I think your pa would want you to help your own hometown in its hour of need."

"But—" Jessica tightened her jaw, feeling guilty and outmaneuvered. Yes, of course, her father would want her to help. In fact, she knew he'd demand it. She didn't want to stay in Powell Springs *or* jeopardize her new job at Seattle General Hospital. Still, clever Mayor Cookson had known exactly what to say to bend her resolve. "Well, I—" she began, crumbling under the weight of duty, "I suppose—I've been given six weeks' travel time, I guess I can stay for a month." Then with more vigor she added, "But whether or not Dr. Pearson is here in thirty days, I'll be leaving."

He sat back in his chair, and a shadow of either satisfaction or relief crossed his weathered face. "Sure, of course, I understand."

"Maybe I could use the empty office I borrowed this morning, since my father's house is no longer available."

If he detected the note of bitterness she'd been unable to keep from her tone, the mayor didn't let on. "That's exactly the spot I had in mind! Of course, we've already hung Pearson's shingle on the place, but that won't matter. We'll get you set up right away, don't you worry about a thing. I don't want to give you the impression that you'll be busy—after all, you're here to visit Amy. We'll pay to put you up in the apartment that we fixed up for Pearson. In fact, we'll pay *all* the expenses." He stood and reached a hand across the desk. "Glad to have you back, Doctor."

She shook his hand, already doubting her decision. "Only for a while, though, Mr. Cookson. Only for a while." She stood up. "And you'll see to Ed? I left him in the clinic."

"Sure, sure, just as soon as some of this business is taken care of." He nudged the piles of papers. Jessica never would have guessed that the administration of such a small town could be so time-consuming.

CHAPTER TWO

Cole Braddock held the mare's hoof between his knees and nailed her shoe in place. Jeremy, the youngster who worked for him after school, had started the job, but Cole redid his work. The boy was still learning, after all, and he was bound to make his share of mistakes. Cole would have had him fix the problem himself, but he'd sent the boy home to tend his ailing mother.

In the rafters, a row of house sparrows cheeped and flapped. Roscoe, Cole's black-and-white sheepdog, yipped a comment and dropped to his backside to watch to proceedings.

Amy had asked Cole to accept the lunch invitation, and damn if he could come up with a good excuse to get himself out of it. She'd looked up at him with her long-lashed green eyes and that expression that made him feel as if she hung on his every word, and he'd given in. Having lunch with her and Jess was the last thing he wanted to do. Why had Jess Layton come back? Each strike of hammer on nail emphasized the question. *Why?* Of course, he'd expected that she'd want to visit her sister, but damn it—

Seeing Jess again got him all riled up in a tangle of feelings, the chief one being anger. She was still beautiful enough to make a man look twice. Yet she appeared more fragile than he remembered, maybe a bit weary. For a moment he wondered how she'd been.

Then he thought of all that had passed between them and anger settled on him again. He pounded the nail until the horse made a grumpy noise and turned her head to the side to glower at him.

He stared at the brown equine eye and drew a deep breath. He was acting like an idiot. "Sorry, Molly," he mumbled around the nails he held in his mouth.

He was *lucky*: soon he'd make Amy his fiancée, a wonderful woman, a woman who possessed all the qualities a man could ask for in a wife. Pretty, sweet-tempered, an innocent charmer, a good cook, eager to be a mother.

Everyone loved Amy.

She didn't challenge him or try his patience to the breaking point before letting him off the hook, as Jess had. His plan to marry her was definitely a smart one.

Then, after the wedding, he'd have all the good things in life that Riley had—well, except for joining the army. On that topic, the two brothers had been divided. Cole had wanted to enlist as soon as Congress had voted to declare war. He'd wanted to go to France and help topple Kaiser Bill. But Riley, who was two years older and had always gotten what he wanted, had enlisted first.

Oh, and didn't Pop just love to brag about his soldier son?

Cole took another nail out of his mouth and fitted it into Molly's shoe. He could hear Pop's rusty voice, going on and on about Riley's exploits, many of which he dreamed up in his own imagination. But the old-timers down at Tilly's Soda Fountain didn't know that, or maybe they didn't care, and on days when his frozen joints thawed enough to let him saddle a horse and mount it, Pop would ride over to drink whiskey poured into a soda glass and tell the boys about Corporal Riley Braddock. Two years into Oregon's passage of prohibition hadn't done much to change the sale of alcohol at Tilly's, only how it was served.

Supplying horses to the Allies and the U.S. Army wasn't a glamorous job worth free drinks at Tilly's. But it was a big one, and Cole knew that his sister-in-law shouldn't have to face it alone. When America entered the conflict, it sent 182,000 horses with the armed forces. Though miles of barbed wire had made a mounted cavalry impractical, the horses were needed to haul equipment and supplies. Animals were just as vulnerable to mustard gas and machine guns as the men, and replacements had to be shipped overseas. Whenever he thought of what they were sending the poor beasts off to, it made his stomach turn. A man knew he was walking into danger as a soldier. A horse didn't.

Concentrating on his task and mulling over his thoughts, he didn't hear another horse and rider approach until Roscoe barked a short greeting and danced up to meet them. Cole looked up to see Pop riding in on Muley, a long-eared gelding who was nearly as old as his rider.

His father climbed down stiffly, his one knee almost completely locked. He wore his ash-gray hair cut short, and his weathered face bore a history of every hot sun and stormy day the old man had ever seen. "So. Came back, did she?"

Immediately on guard, Cole dropped Molly's hoof and straightened. "Who?"

"*Who?* Ben Layton's doctor gal, that's who. The one you almost got hitched to. They're yapping about it over at Tilly's. Heard she stole away one of Granny Mae's patients, and you helped her do it."

Cole groaned inwardly. Those old farts at Tilly's were worse than a bunch of church women with their gossip. And leave it to Pop to hurry over here to talk about it. "Yeah, Jess took care of Ed Cookson. He's got a bad cold or something—flopped right over into the street. But she didn't 'steal' Mae's patient. Mae isn't a doctor."

Though Cole stood a head taller than his father, Pop still tried to make him feel like a ten-year-old with a withering glare from his coffee-bean eyes. "You got the right woman now, a fine woman, so don't go getting any ideas about the doctor gal."

Cole couldn't hide his irritation. "Jesus, Pop, she came home for a visit. That's all. Whatever was between Jess and me was over a long time ago. Anyway, Amy told me she wrote about going to a job in Seattle."

The old man tied Muley to an upright with gnarled hands and hobbled over to a stool that stood next to a bucket of nails. He eased himself to the seat with a loud grunt and continued, "Well, I remember how you moped around like a calf looking for his mama when she told you she was going back to New York."

"That was *a long time ago*."

With his gift for beating a subject to death, Pop went on as if Cole hadn't spoken. "By God, the house was like a damned funeral parlor for months, between Riley's wife's droopy sulking over him leaving and your moping. So you just let Ben's doctor gal ride on. She's fine to look at, but too smart for her own good. Always was, with all that book learning. That's a bad thing in a woman, too smart." He went on for a few minutes, declaring his opinions about women, horses, and a number of topics in between.

Cole suppressed a sigh. "Pop, isn't it time for your medicine? You know Susannah likes you to take it at the same time every day."

He made an impatient gesture. "Bah, medicine! That stuff tastes like turpentine and it don't help at all. I'm still as stiff as John Brown's body." But he heaved himself from the stool and shuffled over to Muley. "I'll just amble back to Tilly's. The medicine they serve works better."

Cole watched his frail, stubborn father climb onto his gelding's back. He could easily imagine Pop having a few too many and toppling out of the saddle. "Take it easy with the whiskey, Pop. It's a little early in the day to start on that. Maybe you should let me drive you home when you leave."

"The hell I will. I was on a horse before I could walk, and I ain't giving it up now. Come on down later, though, and have a drink with me and the boys if you want. Those speechifiers will be having their meeting in the park across the street from there. Should be entertaining."

"I still have work to do."

"Suit yourself." He wheeled Muley around and rode through the big open shop doors.

Cole released a pent-up sigh and went back to shoeing Molly. Pounding the last nail into place, he dropped the mare's hoof and patted her flank. "There you go, honey. Try not to throw that shoe again, okay?" Molly replied with a satisfied nicker. Untying her, Cole led her to the paddock outside and turned her loose.

He was pitching straw into an empty stall when Jessica's face rose in his mind. Usually, physical work pushed troubling thoughts out of his head. At least for a while. He must have moved fifty hay bales the day he got Jess's telegram. Now it wasn't helping. He put the pitchfork in a corner. Anyway, there was no putting it off. He had to meet the women for lunch.

"Roscoe, you're in charge," he said to the sheepdog. "Keep an eye on things for a while."

— — —

Jess hugged her sister when they finally met again at the hotel. Amy still bore the faint vanilla scent that she remembered, and her small, fine bones made her feel like a bird in Jess's arms. They were alike in many ways—each sister honey-haired and green-eyed—and yet as different as if they'd grown up in separate homes.

They took a table near the window in the hotel dining room, and while they sipped tea, waiting for Cole, Amy said, "Jess, I just had a wonderful idea. It all came from your treating young Eddie. There's no need for you pay for a hotel room when there's that perfectly nice furnished apartment over the doctor's office. It even has a brand-new hoosier kitchen." Amy lifted her chin. "I decorated it myself. Of course, it's probably nothing like what you had in New York, but it has electricity and indoor plumbing, and it's ready to move into."

Then, with scarcely a break for greeting Cole, who arrived looking freshly scrubbed but still smelling faintly of his blacksmith shop, Amy went on. "I was just telling Jess she must stay in that apartment over the doctor's office. Don't you agree that's a fine idea, Cole?"

Cole stared first at Amy, then Jessica.

"That's all right with you, isn't it, Cole?" Amy asked. "You said yourself it's just standing empty."

"Really, that's not necess—" Jess began.

Cole settled into a chair. "Well, yeah, I suppose if it's just for a few days—"

Amy beamed. "Good, it's settled then," she said before Jess could mention she'd agreed to stay on for a month. "I can keep an eye on both of you that way. The two most important people in my life." Her voice had a teasing edge but Jess puzzled over her sly expression. "Jess, we'll have your things moved over. I guess—Cole, can you arrange for someone to get her trunks and such?"

A waiter came to take their orders, and when he was gone, Amy went on as if there'd been no interruption. "You can have her things moved right after lunch, can't you, Cole?"

"I can manage," Jess put in hastily.

"With 'trunks and such'?" Cole asked, his tone flat. "Are you going to haul them over on your back?"

"Hardly. I'll hire someone, just like I did to get them to my hotel room. It will take more than one person, anyway," she replied, bristling. She did not want to owe Cole Braddock a single thing. "I've gotten by on my own for quite some time."

"Now, Jessica," Amy said, "you don't need to pay anyone. Cole's practically family, after all."

"I'll take care of it." That grudging note was back in Cole's voice.

Amy gave them both a satisfied look.

Jess bit back a sharp comment and managed a tight smile for her sister's sake. She had never been an adept liar. Feeling railroaded, she capitulated. "Thank you, Cole. I'd appreciate your help. And it will be for more than just a few days. Mayor Cookson has asked me to stay on until Dr. Pearson arrives. I have a few weeks before I'm due to take up my position in Seattle, so I agreed to stay for a month unless Dr. Pearson gets here sooner."

"Oh—um, Jess, that's so nice!" Amy said, turning to Cole. "Cole, isn't it nice?"

Cole pushed his food around with the edge of his butter knife. "Yeah, it's dandy."

Amy looped her arm through his, giving it a quick hug. "I was sure you'd agree." She shot Jessica another sly smile then continued, looking into Cole's eyes. "Goodness, if Dr. Pearson doesn't come, you know, if he's decided not to, maybe Mr. Cookson will ask Jess to take his place. The mayor would probably think that's a fine idea."

Cole didn't think it was a fine idea at all. Frustrated and still smarting from months of wounded pride, he said, "I don't think we should hold Jessica back from her new opportunity. It's what she wants."

It was hard enough to sit here with the two women, one he'd been practically engaged to, the other he was now thinking of marrying—eventually. Amy sparkled like dew on spring grass, and Jessica…well, Jess was like a ruby: rich, darkly gleaming, and complex. Those qualities had drawn him to her years ago, and ultimately, she had used them to push him away. He glanced up and saw Jessica's cool eyes on him. Those eyes—he'd always felt as if she could see into his heart, that she was the only one who could. The thought only increased the tension at the table, but Amy chatted on, apparently happy to have her sister with her again. He couldn't begrudge her that when it was so little to ask for.

"But Jess! Having you stay here, as you'd planned to long ago, would be perfect," Amy said.

‘"Amy, you know that won't happen," Jessica said. "I wouldn't have agreed to do this if Mayor Cookson hadn't brought up Daddy's name. The man practically invoked his spirit to get me to say yes."

"I'm not surprised. You two spent so much time with your heads together over those science books and specimens when we were children, he never even noticed me."

Jess tilted her head a bit and smiled, puzzled by the comment. "What—"

"And you'll just keep working in the space you used for Eddie."

"Well, yes, Mr. Cookson said the town council will pay for everything while I'm here."

Cole's head came up. God, wait till Pop heard about this. If he hadn't already—Tilly's was a clearinghouse for news, more efficient than the newspapers. The old man would be on his back day and night about not getting mixed up with "Ben Layton's doctor gal," even though Amy was always around the ranch house and he didn't object to that.

But now Jess would be next door to his smithy every day until she left, and that wouldn't be for another month.

"Of course, that's the ideal arrangement, even if it's not as fancy as you're used to," Amy said, and added to Cole, "and you'll get a paying tenant."

Jessica considered her sister, surprised by this tidbit of information that the mayor had neglected to give her. Cole owned the building? She'd thought he had the key just because he was a business neighbor.

If only he weren't still so attractive, she thought irritably. He'd slicked back his chin-length wheaten hair, but compared to the neatly barbered men she was accustomed to seeing, Cole looked downright untamed. She could not imagine him sitting in a stuffy drawing room. He was a man who had spent his life out of doors, trying to bend the elements and nature to his will. He'd frequently succeeded, even with her. She took a sip of water, hoping to swallow the aching knot of banked anger and regret that had formed in her throat.

Trying to drag her thoughts from her growing doubts, she said, "Amy, New York may have some beautiful homes and elegant neighborhoods, but you know I lived in a rooming house. I think I'll have more privacy here than I did there. And having an office certainly will be better than trying to treat patients at the hotel. Anyway, Mayor Cookson doesn't believe I'll be very busy."

"I think you'll be busier than you expect. A couple of people have already taken me aside and asked if I thought you'd see them while you're home. And that was before the mayor talked to you."

Jessica shrank from the idea, and her thoughts turned to Eddie Cookson. "I suppose you might be right."

"I'll come over and help you get organized—oh, no, wait, I've got that bandage-rolling session with the Red Cross in the school lunchroom. And the Liberty Bond Committee has the to-do in the park. Rats, it's going to take the rest of my day."

Amy was a just a font of good deeds.

She chatted on, bringing Jess up to date on who'd gotten married, who had died, who'd been lost in the war.

As they talked, a man of medium height and dark hair passing by stopped to look at them over the short lace curtains.

Amy waved, but his gaze shifted to Jess and lingered. He smiled and hurried on.

"Who was that?" Jessica asked. He looked familiar but she couldn't place him.

"You remember Adam Jacobsen," Cole put in, flicking his gaze briefly into her eyes. "He's the minister now that his father is gone."

"Yes, remember, Jess?" Amy asked. "I wrote to you that old Reverend Jacobsen died last spring."

"Oh, yes, I guess you did." So that was what Adam looked like now.

"I've been working with him on the Liberty Bond Committee," Amy rushed on. "It's a very important responsibility, let me tell you. The money is so desperately needed. Adam has been an absolute wonder with that—I swear he could squeeze cash out of a rock. He manages to get practically everyone to buy bonds."

Jess did not want to talk about Adam Jacobsen. "I saw a couple of Liberty Bond parades in the East. They drew huge crowds, tens of thousands," she added. "I even saw Mary Pickford riding in one of them."

Cole's brows lifted. "Really? We might not have Mary Pickford, but we do have Private Eddie Cookson."

"Who is sick," Jessica said with a frown. "I hope his father collected him from the doctor's office and took him home. I understand he's training at Camp Lewis."

"That's right," Amy said. "He came home yesterday morning on a few days' furlough. His father pulled a lot strings to get him here. Eddie went door to door personally, raising funds. Adam went with him—I don't think they missed a single house or business. Poor Eddie. Maybe the excitement was too much for him. I wouldn't have expected him to faint like that, but I hope his father didn't take him home. He's supposed to make an appearance at the bond rally picnic in the park this afternoon. Everyone will be there. He's the cornerstone of our program."

"I think he should be home in bed."

"But—but—he can't! We have very important plans, plans that require his participation." Amy looked at the clear sky beyond the window. "Even the weather has cooperated. It's a sunny day, and we don't get many of those at this time of year. I fretted about that all week. You know how rainy October can be here. We need Eddie."

Cole finished up the last bit of the trout he'd ordered. It felt like a rock sitting in his stomach. "Adam Jacobsen should be able to manage without Ed."

Amy sat back and folded her hands. "I just think of Riley and know we have to do all we can. We've all been so worried about him, fighting in France, haven't we, Cole?"

Jessica said, "I'm surprised your brother was drafted. I thought the Braddocks' contract to supply horses to the war would keep him home."

"It would have," Cole said, his expression hard, "but he enlisted."

"And left his wife to run the farm? I suppose that was your father's idea," Jessica said. She'd never been fond of Cole's father, whom she considered a bully.

"No, Riley really wanted to go."

"As I know you did." Amy patted Cole's hand. To Jessica she said, "But of course, they couldn't both leave. Anyway, Susannah dotes on Mr. Braddock and tries to keep him from gallivanting around the countryside. He's a little crusty and gruff, but down deep, he's an old dear. Besides, she has Tanner Grenfell helping out. And Cole has taken on extra work." Amy's eyes glowed with pride and a new complacency Jess had not seen in her before as she beamed at Cole.

Cole, declining coffee and dessert, bade both women a stiff good afternoon and went back to work, pleading an overload.

Amy took her sister's hand and squeezed it. "I'm so glad you came home, Jess. I was afraid you might not. I suppose this might be awkward for you, Cole courting me."

Awkward didn't begin to describe how Jessica felt.

One afternoon more than a year earlier, she had made a vow. On that grim day, with the telegram trembling in her shaking hands and tears streaming down her face, she had sworn that to even visit Powell Springs would break her heart all over again. Yet here she was.

But except for dear but dotty old Great Aunt Rhea in Nebraska, who sent unintentionally hilarious letters about strange lights hovering over her farmhouse and little gray men stealing her chickens, Jess and Amy had only each other left in this world for kin. And she'd learned that family ties ran deeper than she'd have believed.

She forced herself to give Amy's hand a reassuring squeeze. Just as she'd forced herself to come back. "What's done is done. If he and I were meant to be—he—*we* wouldn't have broken off our—our *understanding*." What else could she call it? There had been no formal agreement between them, no engagement. That would have happened when she returned home, if not for that telegram.

She managed a smile. "I'm just glad I was able to visit you, and that Powell Springs is close enough to Portland to let me stop on the way to Seattle."

Her sister uttered a nervous little laugh. "Yes, that is lucky, isn't it? And having you to keep me company gives us a chance to catch up. Cole has been so busy with the horses and the smithy. But then, I've had my work with the Bond Committee." She lowered her voice. "I'm certain he's going to propose any day now, and I want a short engagement. We'll have the wedding in Reverend Jacobsen's church with all of our friends, and I'll have Mama's wedding gown altered to fit me. Of course, we won't have time for a real honeymoon. But later, when everything is more settled, we'll take a trip. After the ceremony, we'll just have a room at the hotel for our wedding night." A faint pink stain colored her cheeks and she dropped her gaze to her plate. Obviously, Amy had worked out every detail in her imagination.

Jessica couldn't reply. Memories flashed through her mind, of Cole's lips on hers, his hands searching the sensitive places on her body while they lay in the wildflowers beside Powell Creek so long ago…She would make certain she would *not* be here when Cole married Amy. She swallowed hard and busied herself with stirring more sugar than she wanted into her coffee.

Amy took a sip of hers and set the cup back on its saucer. "You're really happy about going to Washington?"

Relieved to change the subject, Jess said, "Yes. I'll be working in Seattle General Hospital's research laboratory. It's a wonderful opportunity, especially now with so many male doctors in Europe for the war."

"Do you mean you won't see patients?"

Jess lifted her chin a bit. "No. Not anymore."

"But I thought—"

"There is so much progress being made in the area of disease treatment and prevention, I decided that research would be the most important work I can do." Jess tightened her grip on her water glass. "Just think of how much Edward Jenner did for humanity with his smallpox vaccine, or, or…Lister, with his use of carbolic acid to prevent infection. And ether for pain-free surgery. Someone had to discover those advances."

"Well…I suppose. I just thought you were interested in the *practice* of medicine."

An involuntary shudder ran up Jessica's spine. "I was. I used to be."

"But you treated Eddie."

Jess shrugged. It had been an automatic response. She would get over that in time. "It was an emergency. I had to step in."

"When you didn't come back here after you finished your schooling, I expected you to stay in New York, but I guess even Seattle will be nothing like boring old Powell Springs. You know, we just got electricity in town in the last few months, and not very many of us have indoor plumbing yet. I think Daddy's house was the first to have either."

Jess looked up at Amy. "You've been getting along all right at Mrs. Donaldson's?"

"Cole thinks she's a busybody, but really, she has such a good heart. She's made me feel welcome. Of course, I miss our own home."

"Amy, I wanted to keep the house. But I had no idea how much debt Daddy had run up for the practice until he died. You know he always gave away free care to half the county. And darn few patients of the other half stopped to think that he should be paid." She sighed, remembering the mess. "Dr. Vandermeer wasn't any better. When I found out that he hadn't covered the property taxes, I couldn't afford to do anything but let the county take it to pay—"

"That's all right, Jess. Cole will build me a fine new house on property that adjoins the horse farm." Amy laughed again. "Mrs. Donaldson gets weepy every time we talk about my leaving." She leaned forward. "Of course, you've been gone for such a long time, and from what I read in your letters, well, I told Cole you were probably enjoying the theaters and libraries and such."

Jessica searched her memory for things she might have said about her mostly nonexistent social life. Once or twice she might have written about going to the theater, but the rest of the time—"That's not why I stayed there. It was—" She faltered a moment, then cleared her throat and smiled.

"I know, your work," Amy said. "I imagine Daddy is spinning in his grave. After all, you promised him you'd take over his practice."

Jess stared at her. What a nightmare of a notion. Yes, at one time, that had been her plan. But now? To come back to Powell

Springs and have to see Cole Braddock around town, *as Amy's husband*, perhaps even have to treat him as a patient? After everything that had happened?

Jess might be able to visit with a facade of grace, but she would have to be a saint to come back to Powell Springs to live. Surely her father would understand that from wherever he watched her now. "I think the town can get along without me. And if Cole… proposes, you'll be busy planning your wedding."

"I certainly will." That vaguely smug expression slipped across her face again.

CHAPTER THREE

The man sat on the edge of Emmaline's thin, sagging mattress and began dressing. She watched as he pushed his arms into the fine fabric of his shirtsleeves. He'd stayed longer than usual, and he checked his pocket watch, once, and then again.

"Where does your wife think you are, Frank? Out selling your tractors?"

He glanced over his shoulder at her. She propped herself up on one elbow and turned her gaze to the shaggy five acres just outside the window. It was wild and overgrown, with straggling rosebushes and a wall of blackberry brambles that all but surrounded this shanty.

"I'm not married. You already know that, Em."

She laughed, but there wasn't much humor behind it. "Don't worry. Even if you really are, there ain't much chance that she'd find out about me." Facing him, she ran a hand through her long hair. "'Less you told her."

"I'm not married," he repeated. "If I was, I wouldn't..." He let the sentence hang unfinished.

"Yeah, I know. You wouldn't be here. Don't be too blamed sure of that. Married men come by here all the time. They don't have to offer excuses but some do. Others are full of complaints. And believe me, I've heard 'em all." She shrugged a bare shoulder.

"I imagine they're the same ones my husband told to some other woman after he run off and left me without as much as a so-long-sister."

Standing, he pulled up his trousers and buttoned them. "How long has he been gone?"

She sighed slightly. "Five years, now."

"And you've never heard from him?"

"No, and good riddance, I say."

"But you're still married to him?"

"Not by my reckoning. He don't know where I am anyhow. For all *I* know, he could be dead. It wouldn't surprise me. He was the sort who made a lot of people mad."

He looked in the peeling mirror over her dresser and combed his hair with his fingers. He was young, quite a bit younger than her own forty years. "What line of business was he in?"

"Lambert?" Now her chuckle was harsh and incredulous, and the bedsprings screeched beneath her. "Lambert's notion of business was turning a quick dollar whichever way he could, legal or not. He was sure his one big break was just around the next corner, and that I was holding him back. So he took off, and I was stuck over in Parkridge with two kids and a cardboard suitcase."

He turned his back to the mirror and fixed her with an expression of faint horror. "You have *children*? Where are they?"

Damn, she hadn't meant to mention the youngsters. She tried not to even think about them, it gave her such heartache, though it was impossible not to. She got up and grabbed a faded dressing gown from the end of the bed to wrap around her body, suddenly feeling naked. "Well, they're not around here, if you're wondering that."

"But do you ever see them?"

She pressed her mouth into a tight line. "You're just full of questions today, ain't you? That's my private business and it's got nothing to do with you or anyone else."

She was amused to see Frank actually turn red, all the way up to the ears. There was something about him that didn't figure quite right. She knew his name, Frank Meadows, and that he lived nearby in Twelve Mile where he sold John Deere tractors. At least that's what he'd told her. She'd never once seen him on the street when she rode her tired, swaybacked mare into town for supplies. Twelve Mile was a decent-size place, but not so big that she wouldn't expect to run into him once in a while.

Still, in the line of work she'd been forced to take up, she'd become a fairly good judge of men. He was kind and well-mannered for the most part, but she couldn't imagine him in his job, chitchatting with farmers about crops while he stood in a field, ankle-deep in mud and manure, wearing his nice clothes and smelling of bay rum. And he was so closemouthed about himself, she figured he was married, no matter what he said.

"I didn't mean to pry, Em." He dug into his pocket to fish out five dollars, which he left on the battered dresser.

It was more than she asked from him, but she wasn't about to turn it down. Although the place was as neat as she could manage, it was still a tiny, two-room shack furnished with castoffs that she'd cobbled together. It had no ceiling, and above the open rafters overhead were bare shingles, patched here and there with water-stained tar paper. She didn't suppose the moss that furred the roof helped to keep it from leaking. In winter, this place was as cold as a witch's tit. The owner let her stay here rent-free, and had been one of her customers, a doctor from down in Powell Springs. He'd used it as a hunting cabin when he was younger, he said.

He'd made some improvements, such as buying her a new stove, and had promised to fix up the place. Then she'd gotten word that he died. Nobody had come to claim it, or throw her off the land, so it was hers now as far as she was concerned. But the house was still a dump.

She reached over and snapped up the money, putting it in her pocket. "Yeah, well, no harm done."

Still standing beside the bed, she lifted the thin quilt and dingy top sheet to look at the state of the bedding beneath it. Deciding it would stand another use, she reached for an atomizer on the windowsill and spritzed the coarse, graying bottom sheet with five-and-dime rosewater. Then she made the bed for the next man who came knocking on the door of her shack. As much as she needed the money, she hoped no one else showed up. She was tired and had a headache.

"I got me a rabbit stewing on the stove, if you'd like to stay to eat." The words were out before she realized she'd uttered them. She never asked anyone to stay. But sometimes the soul-stripping, confounded loneliness of her existence ate at her.

Again, that astonished look crossed his mild features, more pronounced this time. "Oh no, I've still got—a busy day. Sales calls to make. I just dropped in for…well, I've got to be going." He grabbed his coat and reached for the doorknob.

She nodded and fingered the cash in the pocket of her dressing gown. "All right, then. See you next time, Frank." He regarded her silently for a moment, as if he were about to say more. Instead, he pulled the door open and stepped outside.

Emmaline waited until she heard his horse and buggy travel down the long path that hid her place from the main road. As she stood there, she caught a glimpse of her reflection in the dresser's milky mirror. She couldn't remember when all those gray strands had begun dusting her red hair. The sound of the wheels faded away, and she sat down at her tiny kitchen table, looking at the money he'd given her until the sun worked its way through the gloom of the tall trees surrounding her little spot on Butler Hill.

CHAPTER FOUR

"Good Corporal Braddock, do you have a match?"

Riley Braddock glanced to his left, the direction from which the request had come. It was pointless, though. With a black, cloudy night overhead, it was so damned dark here in this wet, miserable trench he doubted that a cat would be able to see anything. He was surrounded by men from his battalion, but he recognized this voice by its liquid vowels.

"Whip, that you?"

"It is," Remy Whipperton Fournier, III, replied. "I managed to roll one dry smoke but I don't have any matches."

"I'll check." Riley patted his pockets and rummaged through the pouches on his cartridge belt. His fingers closed on a small metal canister. Opening the lid, he extracted a single match. "Here you go."

Whip's hand fumbled with his own in the darkness until it found what he was searching for. "Thanks." The match flared for a moment, and Riley saw the man's genial face in its glow. "Damn, but I hate it up here," was his languid complaint. "This is hardly what I expected my Grand Tour to be like. You never know when the Hun is going to lob a shell at you, and there goes your head, rolling down the trench like a croquet ball. Or floating past, if it's raining."

Riley smiled. "At least it probably won't happen at night. But I admit I liked it better back at that farmhouse we left yesterday.

The food was a hell of a lot better than that monkey meat and canned salmon we get here."

Whip pulled on the cigarette, creating a small orange beacon. It highlighted his grin, as broad as a cantaloupe slice. "The scenery was far nicer, too. That old man's young wife—ooh-lah-lah." Whippy was a drawling Southern gentleman from Baton Rouge with a wry sense of humor. The fluent French he spoke made it easier for him than the other boys to communicate with the locals, though Riley had the feeling that most found his particular dialect offensive to their ears.

"Don't you ever think about anything except women, Fournier?" another voice asked from the dark.

"I certainly do. I think about keeping my body and soul together."

"What about the countryside? Didn't you notice that grove of *live* trees?"

"Gentlemen, I agree the landscape was pretty, too, except for that unfortunate yard ornament every French villager seems to have."

"You mean the manure pile by the front door?"

Whip let out a gusty sigh. "Yes, I just can't get used to that."

"Just as well," came another voice that sounded like Steven Collier's. "If the French were as fussy as Americans, they wouldn't let us in with our cooties. At least they don't mind the lice. And we don't smell much better than those dung heaps."

"Well, damn, Lieutenant, I suppose that's a *little* comfort," Riley said, only a touch of humor in his chuckle.

Fournier continued in his lazy molasses accent, his train of thought not derailed. "I imagine if I had a stunning paragon like your Miss Susannah waiting for me back home, I'd be thinking about her instead. She's a beautiful, angelic creation on God's mortal earth. Let's see her picture again, Braddock." He sucked on the cigarette once more.

Automatically, Riley put his hand over the pocket that held Susannah's photograph. "You just keep to your own business. Besides, it's too dark here to see anything."

"And just what is this place again?"

"Jesus, Whippy, where have you been?" Riley posed. Fournier was a nice guy and even a good soldier when he had to be, but he never seemed to have his mind on the right subject. He was college educated and should have been an officer, but he'd refused the commission. Too much responsibility, he'd said. That he'd avoided getting his head torn off, as he joked, sometimes amazed Riley. "This battle started back on September twenty-sixth. We're near Verdun, somewhere between the Meuse River and the Argonne Forest. I guess. It's hard to tell in the dark."

"Ah, yes, the Argonne. Where all the fighting has been going on." With one last drag, the hot coal of his cigarette disappeared. Riley heard the sound of a heel grinding it into the mud. "Well, I'm off to the latrine, boys," Whippy said. "Be sure to come get me if the Hun starts up. I don't want to miss anything."

Their battalion had just trekked several hours in the rain, winding their way through communication trenches, blown-out roads, and snarled traffic of vehicles, horses, and men that seemed hopelessly locked. They'd come loaded down with supplies to reinforce another front-line battalion. Moving at night helped them avoid the enemy's snipers and lookouts, but the weather wasn't fit for any living thing except the frogs and rats that infested this hole.

Riley sat with his back against the trench wall, which had been fortified with sandbags and slim tree branches. His army-issue Springfield rifle stood upright on its stock, also resting against the wall. Somewhere down the line he heard soft singing, beautiful soft singing, a harmony of wistful voices.

There's a long, long night of waiting
Until my dreams all come true;
Till the day when I'll be going down
That long, long trail with you.

Riley swallowed the sudden knot that had formed in his throat. He wished that Whip hadn't mentioned Susannah. He hadn't seen his wife in sixteen months. God, it seemed like a lifetime. The abject loneliness and isolation he often felt, despite being surrounded by thousands of men, were not problems he'd expected when he left home. How can a person feel isolated in a crush of humanity? But he did.

He closed his eyes and pictured Susannah's long, black curls, her soft cheek, the sweet curve of her hip under her chemise, the way she looked at him with those dark chocolate eyes when they were alone. He imagined her, thigh-deep in tall summer grass, smiling at him, beckoning him with a glint in her gaze that made him come to her and wind his hands through her hair. Then she'd pull him down with her, down, down, where no one would find them.

If he really concentrated, he could still remember the scent of her—cherry bark and almonds. He caught himself sniffing hard enough to bring him back to his present circumstances.

The trenches smelled like—well, there was no way to describe it. So many things contributed to the stink: thousands of shallow graves, cooking, overflowing latrines, unwashed bodies, rotting sandbags, all mixed with stagnant mud. Sitting here in the dark, there was no way to see the brown rats he knew crawled through these trenches without fear. The filthy rodents were often the size of house cats, since they didn't lack for food. They gorged themselves on the human remains that littered the countryside. Some campaign veterans swore the rats could sense impending German shellfire and so scampered away until it was over.

Why he'd originally believed that war would be a glamorous, noble experience escaped him now. Nothing about running a horse farm had prepared him for miles of barbed wire, machine guns that could reduce a village to rubble in a matter of minutes, and the unspeakably inhuman savagery he'd witnessed. But then, none of these men had been prepared for what they saw. Hell, at least he could have waited to be drafted, like some of them had.

Sometimes…just for a minute…he would wish that he'd let Cole win the argument about which of them should go and which should stay behind. Cole had wanted to come over here.

Of course, Pop had been beating his tambourine, insisting that both of his sons would bring honor and glory to the Braddock name. There had never been a question in Riley's mind that he should enlist. But Pop's cranky nagging hadn't worked on Cole, and Riley was glad for that. There had been resentment between them, Riley and his brother, over the turn of events. But someone had to help Susannah with the contracts, and his father was in no shape to do that.

And those days of eternal summer, golden and lambent, that he remembered so well—they were why he was here in France. They were why he and the others were fighting an enemy that would crush their freedom under a cruel heel of tyranny.

So they'd all been told, anyway. But he didn't believe it anymore. If he died, what good would freedom be to him?

He tipped his head back to look at the sky. There wasn't much to see.

At least it had stopped raining.

CHAPTER FIVE

After lunch, Jessica walked down to the telegraph office to send a wire to Dr. Martin at the hospital in Seattle explaining her revised plans. She handed her note to Leroy Fenton, Powell Springs's elderly head telegrapher.

"Seattle, eh? I've been getting some news from those parts—looks like there's a bout of the grippe going around up there."

"There is?"

Leroy adjusted his sleeve garter and continued. "They say it might have started at Camp Lewis and spread to some civilians who went there to watch a review of the National Guard Infantry." He shrugged. "The docs up there say we have nothing to worry about, though. Other camps have had it, too, but they've got the situation under control. That'll be three dollars, Miss Jessica."

Jess had heard about a few of those outbreaks herself—some doctors diagnosed it as pneumonia—but she'd also heard of the overcrowded conditions in the temporary military camps. Disease found easy pickings under those circumstances. Still, the mention of Camp Lewis drew her thoughts back to the Cookson boy.

"In war, more men die of disease than wounds," she said, searching her drawstring purse for the cash to pay Leroy.

"Do they?" He looked at her message again, then dropped his voice and glanced around, as though there were someone else in his office besides the two of them. These days, that was not an unreasonable fear. A casual comment could get a person in trouble. "Then I'm glad I'm too old to go."

She patted the older man's arm and smiled. "So am I, Leroy."

Then she left the office and stood on the sidewalk for a moment, anticipation and dread thumping in her chest. Taking a deep breath, she headed for the hotel.

— — —

Cole stopped at Jessica's hotel room door and pulled off his right buckskin glove, his knuckles hovering over the wooden panel. Although Amy had drafted him for this job, he'd gotten himself in even deeper and he was determined to make the meeting as brief as possible. If Amy hadn't asked, he would be back at his forge now, or helping Susannah and Tanner with the horses.

Another guest passed him in the hallway, and Cole didn't want to be seen lurking out here like some kind of big bad wolf. He rapped sharply on the door.

He heard her footsteps cross the floor. "Who is it, please?"

"It's Cole." She opened the door a crack to make sure, then swung it wide. "Expecting the boogeyman?"

She had changed into a slim, fawn-colored dress with a collar so wide it touched her shoulders and tiers of skirting that were edged with black trim. It enhanced her curves and made him look twice.

"No, I've just become more cautious over the years. No one needs to lock their front doors here, but Powell Springs isn't like New York."

As if he needed reminding. "I didn't think it was. Is this everything?" He gestured at two trunks and a few suitcases stacked against the wall in her hotel room. Women never traveled light, he thought, and while practical, apparently Jessica was no exception. But then, to be fair, she was on her way to Seattle to…continue her career. Of course she'd have all her possessions with her.

Although the door was wide open, Jess fidgeted, letting her hand wander from her large hat, to her cuffs, to the simple gold chain hanging from her neck. "Yes, I'm sorry I couldn't have them brought down before you got here so you wouldn't, well—" Her gaze darted to the bed.

It wasn't a small room, but the iron bed was the most obvious piece of furniture within its walls.

One winter night, more than two years earlier, he had lain with Jessica on a bed similar to this one.

Her father's funeral had taken place that afternoon, and she had been stoic, organizing the gathering after, greeting neighbors, comforting the sobbing, inconsolable Amy. When everyone had finally left, she'd put her sister to bed with a strong sleeping powder. Only then had Jessica's numb composure cracked. She had cried in his arms until he thought her heart would break, and his as well. They'd spent the night lying on her bed, still dressed in the clothes they'd worn to the funeral, while a fierce January wind howled around the corners of the house and seeped in through the window casings. His shirt front had been wet with her tears. In those cold hours of darkness they had never been closer, not even during their brief, desperate moments of hungry passion stolen in summer wildflowers.

It had been the last time he'd seen her cry. It had been, he realized, the only time.

She set her purse on the bureau and draped some dresses over her arm. "Didn't you bring help?"

"Help—what for? If I can't manage this load, I might as well hang it up and spend my days with Pop at Tilly's."

She lifted an eyebrow but said nothing more.

He carried the one trunk down the hall and to his Ford TT out front. The truck had created a ruckus in the house when he bought it last year. Riley had insisted they couldn't afford it, when Cole knew full well that they could. His father had declared that he'd shoot the thing between its headlamps before he'd let it near the horses. Pop still eyed it with suspicion but admitted grudgingly that it served a purpose, especially when it came to hauling. With so much work to be done, Cole had made good use of the vehicle.

Jessica followed him with her purse and the dresses. When they went back for the second trunk, she repeated, "You'll need help for this one. It's heavy."

He gave her a dismissive wave. "I can control Bill Franklin's Percheron, so I think I can handle this. That horse weighs twenty-five hundred pounds."

"Really? Do you haul it around on your back?" she asked sweetly.

He frowned at her and bent his knees to lift the trunk. It didn't budge. He tried again, his muscles tight and burning with the effort. He got nothing but the sound of joints popping in his shoulders. He glanced up at Jess, then tugged at the edges of his gloves and grasped the leather grip on one end of the leather-bound case. Pulling hard, he barely managed to shift it three feet.

"Jesus, what's in this thing?" he demanded, out of breath and feeling as if every vein in his head was about to explode.

"Medical books."

His frown turned into a scowl. "Why the hell didn't you tell me that?"

"You said you could handle it just fine. I'm sure it doesn't weigh as much as the Percheron, does it?"

"How did you get this up here?" He lifted his hat and resettled it more firmly on his head.

"It took three men and a small boy. I *hired* them at the railroad station." She looked very pleased with herself.

By God, but she was sassy. She always had been. How could a woman with such a serious mind and occupation be so sassy? But that had been part of her allure—a mingling of opposites within the same person. Studious and disciplined, but rebellious and daring, knowing yet innocent. Amy was unworldly and uncomplicated. Though he'd known Jessica longer, Cole had never quite figured her out. It was irritating, but it had its appeal. When she wanted to, she could have a man stepping all over his own feet.

"All right, I'll have to get someone to help. You go back to the office."

"I'm going to stop at Wegner's Laundry first."

He dug around in his back pocket. "Here's the key. I'll see you over there after I find another man to—after a while."

He wasn't certain, but he thought he saw an evil gleam of satisfaction in her smile as she left.

— — —

"Don't you worry, ma'am, we'll deliver these to you later this afternoon, pressed good as new." Clarence Wegner took Jessica's creased, wrinkled dresses from her arms. After days of sitting in her luggage, they'd been crushed beyond wearing. He prattled on in a friendly, interested manner. "It's good to see you again after all this time. I'll bet you're glad to be home. Looks like we might see your sister getting married here one of these days."

"Um, yes, Mr. Wegner…"

"It's a shame that Riley Braddock is off in France. But here's hoping he'll make it for the wedding. My brother was best man when I married Mrs. Wegner and…"

Jessica struggled to concentrate on their conversation. While the sky was clear, it was a cool day. Despite the open door, though, the air in the laundry was stifling and humid. She could see through the gap in the purple drapes meant to separate the working part of the place from the storefront. Steam poured out of the laundry tubs to combine with the hot irons and the mangle. Cooking smells floated in from somewhere. Maybe from Mae Rumsteadt's café down the street, or maybe there was something on the stove upstairs. Jess knew that Clarence Wegner and his wife lived in rooms over their business.

In her mind there suddenly rose a vivid memory of the stench of boiling cabbage and rancid pork fat trapped in dark, stifling hallways connected by dark, stifling staircases. Children wailed in the summer heat, and their mothers carped in strident tones or moaned with despair. A cacophony of voices raised in anger, pain, or helplessness, drummed through the thin walls of the tenements. It didn't matter which building—in New York's poor neighborhoods they were all alike. Hell on earth. There was a little girl with a broken arm in one room, a stringy-haired new mother barely clinging to life with childbed fever down the hall, and still another lying shrunken and hollow-eyed on a stained, bare mattress with only a ragged quilt for cover, a tumor the size of a lemon in her breast.

The heat.

The rats.

The poverty.

The hopelessness.

They haunted her dreams, but Jess hadn't remembered it all quite so clearly since she'd left New York for her sabbatical in Sarasota Springs.

"...all right, Miss Layton? You look a little peaked."

Jessica was jerked back to the counter at Wegner's Laundry. "Yes, I'm sorry." She pressed her hand to her forehead. Her dress was stuck to her back, and her heart felt as if it were pounding as hard as the grange band's bass drum. A suffocating feeling of panic overwhelmed her, and she struggled to hide it. "It—it's quite warm in here, isn't it?"

"Oh, sure, summers are real hard in this business, although that new electric fan helps." Mr. Wegner's own face gleamed with a sweaty luster as he pointed to a spinning blade in its wire cage. "But come next month—from November to March, we'll be warm as toast."

She reached into her bag and withdrew a handkerchief. "Well, I—I must be running along." If she didn't get out of here, she was afraid she'd faint. Or worse.

"That's fine. I'll send a girl around when—"

But Jess had already edged out the doorway and was on the sidewalk. Pausing under Wegner's awning, she dabbed at her temples with the square of linen balled in her hand. She was relieved to be outside where it was much cooler, but was troubled by the panic she'd felt.

When would the memories leave her in peace? she wondered. Had they become so deeply etched in her mind that they would play again and again, like scenes in a moving picture? No, she asserted, it wasn't possible. She'd feel better when she got to

Seattle—she'd get a fresh start and new memories to shut out the old ones.

Drawing a deep, steadying breath, she pushed the damp hankie into her skirt pocket and made her way back down Main Street. When she reached the office, she saw that Eddie Cookson was gone.

Good. At least someone had come for him. He really needed bed rest and decent nursing care.

CHAPTER SIX

"Boy, now what are you up to?" Shaw Braddock reined his horse in front of Cole's building.

Damn it, Cole thought, his hand tightening on a suitcase grip. He'd hoped that Tilly's and the excitement of the Liberty Bond doings would keep his father busy until Cole had gotten Jessica's rigging moved into the new office space. Maybe he hadn't heard that the mayor drafted her to fill in for Pearson, and that she'd be living in the doctor's quarters. Now, here Cole was, with Jess's trunks in the Ford, parked in front of the office. On the sidewalk next to him was Winks Lamont, whom he'd hired to help move the box of books. It wouldn't cost him much more than the price of a couple of beers, since the simpleminded old rummy spent most of his time at the end of Tilly's bar cadging drinks. On the other hand, he wasn't worth more. Winks smelled like an overripe cheese left in an outhouse during a heat wave.

"I thought you were hobnobbing down at the saloon."

"Did that already. I'm on my way home. It'll be dark soon." The old man waved in the general direction of the home place. "We put some pressure on those slackers in the crowd, too, the ones who claim they can't join the army just now. They all have thin, whiny excuses. 'My ma needs me,' 'I can't see so good,' 'I got to tend the stock.' Your brother didn't say any of that stuff. He just went, like a *man* should. It ain't a matter of convenience. This is war."

Cole clenched his jaw. "Maybe those men aren't making excuses. They're probably telling the truth."

"Bah! Anyway, you still haven't told me what you're doing with this junk."

"Jessica is going to stay here for a month."

The old man eyed him from Muley's tall back. "Oh, she is, huh?"

"Yeah," Cole answered, hefting the case from the truck. "Horace asked her to stay for a while, and the town is paying the rent." He shrugged. "It's better than having the place go unused while we wait for the other doc." He put a hand on the tailgate and vaulted into the truck bed. "Come on, Winks, grab the other end. Let's get this thing moved and be done with it."

"That's the trouble with Horace Cookson," Pop began, "always letting his mouth get ahead of his brain. We don't need that doctor gal, always too smart for—"

"Shaw, how good to see you again." Jessica emerged from the office. She carried a basket with her and crossed the sidewalk. "Would you care for a doughnut? I bought them at the bakery." She flipped open the napkin covering the pastries and lifted the basket so that he could reach it.

Cole glanced up from the trunk. The old man actually looked sheepish. He'd always been a pushover for sweets. "A doughnut..." Derailed from his complaining, his attention shifted.

"How have you been?" she asked, nodding at the swan-neck deformity of his fingers as he took a treat. "It looks like that arthritis is still giving you trouble."

"Well, it don't get better with age, does it?" Pop snapped, taking a big bite.

She smiled, ignoring his cranky behavior. "No, but it can subside—I mean, it can improve sometimes, especially when the weather is good."

His scowl deepened and he swallowed. "Ditch water, girlie! I already know that." Then to Cole he added, "What did I tell you? Doctors ain't no help, and the new ones don't know any more than the old ones."

"It's too bad that you won't stay active and get out more often," she went on. "Amy mentioned that you spend a lot of time in the parlor, making Susannah wait on you. The condition gets worse if the patient just sits." Jess had always been good at that, putting the old man in his place.

"*Sits!* By God—"

Winks's hoot of laughter gurgled with phlegm.

Cole turned away to hide his grin.

Pop poked the rest of the doughnut into his big, rectangular mouth as color rose in his weathered face. "That's what I tell 'em at home, that I'm as good as ever. But they try to keep me nailed to my rocker." Crumbs and powdered sugar flew. "They say I'm too old and stiff to do anything else. Susannah is trying to turn me into an invalid with all her fussing and coddling. Huh! I can still whup ass and I'll prove it to any man who's willing to try me. And that goes for you, too, youngster!" he said to Winks, who was not much younger than Pop.

He wheeled Muley around and took off at a trot toward the farm, which was probably joint-jarring for both horse and rider.

Jessica waved as the old man left, amused and relieved to be rid of him. She knew he'd never really approved of her, and after she'd left Powell Springs the first time, he'd been downright rude during her visits home. But she wasn't going to lurk behind the lace curtains covering the office's bay window and listen to him criticize her.

She turned and caught Cole actually smiling at her. It was a familiar smile that pulled at her heart. "Pretty good, Jess."

"He's still a rough old cob, isn't he?" She watched the dust stir around Muley's retreating hooves.

"Yeah, well, he didn't get better with age, either. He treats us all like ten-year-olds, and tries to run the world."

"But now I'm worried that I've brought down the roof on poor Susannah. Maybe Amy too, for telling on him."

He took hold of his end of the trunk and lifted it. "Don't let him fool you," he said, his shirt clinging to his torso. "He's a glutton for their attention. And Amy can sweet-talk him into just about anything. She can sweet-talk anyone. It's part of her charm."

As she watched Cole and Winks finesse the trunk through the narrow doorway, her gaze landed on the back of Cole's neck, where his sweat-damp hair curled below his collar. Unwillingly, she let her perusal slide down his lean, broad back, then lower to the seat of his jeans, just before he disappeared into the darkness of the office.

She lifted her chin, refusing to let herself fall into a trap of self-doubt and second-guessing. The past year and a half had been hard enough.

"Do you want to unload these books?" she heard Cole call from the back room.

She walked inside, through the tidy waiting area and into the examination room, where he waited with Winks. His expression was not quite as hostile as it had been earlier in the day, but the brief smile she'd seen outside was gone now. It was as if a cloud had covered the sun, leaving a chill. "There's no point. I'm not staying, you know."

His eyes lingered on her before he turned back to the trunk. "Yeah. I know." Reaching into the front pocket of his tight jeans, he pulled out a silver dollar and handed it to Winks. "Here you go, you old horse thief. Don't spend it all in one place."

Winks practically leaped on the money and showed off his foolish, almost toothless grin. "Thanks, Cole." He nodded at Jessica and left them standing there, alone again and awkward.

"He's probably on his way to Tilly's right now to drink up that dollar," Cole said. His shirt was unbuttoned to the center of his chest, revealing a glimpse of a suntanned *V* which she knew would fade over the winter but never completely disappear.

"Maybe if everyone around him is drinking, it will dull their sense of smell. I attended autopsies on bodies pulled out of the Hudson River that were less…aromatic."

He actually chuckled again. Then he considered her with a tense, searching look. Why didn't it feel different now, after everything that had happened? For one brief moment, she expected him to open his arms to her and if he did, she would be sorely tempted to cross the narrow strip of flooring between them and walk into his embrace.

The sound of footsteps echoed somewhere in the back of her consciousness, but she could not break eye contact with him. The very air seemed thick between them.

"Oh, here you are." Amy appeared in the back office doorway. "I managed to break away from the bandage rolling and—" Eying them, her smile faded. "Is everything all right? Did you get moved over?"

"It—yes. It went just fine," Jessica said at last. "I should reimburse you, Cole, for the money you paid Winks."

He took a step back and waved her off. "Forget it." He looked at both women. "I've got to get back to work." Then he turned and walked out.

"Well, that was odd," Amy said, watching him go.

Jess turned away, inhaling the commingled blend of her sister's vanilla fragrance and the equally familiar scent of Cole.

— — —

Although her attention was fixed on getting settled, the sound of more music drew Jess to the sidewalk to watch everyone moving toward the park. Standing there, she had the sensation of being watched herself. She shrugged slightly, as if to shake off an invisible hand, but the feeling persisted.

Finally, glancing to her left, she noticed Cole leaning against the door frame of his shop, his arms crossed as he viewed the passing crowd. Her focus shifted. The people seemed to fade into a blur, the music and noise grew muffled—there was nothing and no one except Cole Braddock. He wore no shirt, just the heavy leather apron that covered him from chest to knees. His shoulders and arms were corded with muscle that bespoke years of swinging a hammer and hard physical work. His handsome face was smudged and gleaming with sweat, as if he had just stepped away from his forge for a moment.

He looked at her full on, and she felt as if a lightning bolt had shuddered through her body. She forced herself to turn her eyes from his, but the sensation of being watched persisted. Eyes on her, considering her.

He was Amy's intended, she reminded herself. He had betrayed Jessica. He had proven to be fickle and faithless—

"—so glad to run into you, Jessica. I was hoping to see you."

Jessica jumped at the sound of her name being spoken, and turning around, she saw Adam Jacobsen. "What? Oh, Adam! Yes, it's been a long time."

He'd grown into a taller man than she'd expected. His wide brow and full face were offset by large, dark-lashed eyes. Still, she could see traces of the child he'd been, especially around the jaw and chin, and his nose had acquired an arrow shape that seemed to point to his mouth. Dressed in his Sunday best, he carried a clipboard under one arm. He leaned a bit closer to be heard over the crowd around them. "I'm glad you decided to accept Mayor Cookson's offer to stay with us for a while."

"I understand you had a say in it," she replied, not completely comfortable with that fact, or with him. Why would he, of all people, have lobbied for her to linger in Powell Springs? Late in their teen years, he'd once caught Jess and Cole in the tall grass by the creek and had run to blab the news to his own father, who in turn had reported her to Ben Layton. The elder Jacobsen had built an entire Sunday sermon around the sin of lust and the dangers of leaving young people unsupervised.

Shortly thereafter, Jessica's father had shipped her off to college with the intention of giving her something besides Cole Braddock to occupy her mind.

"You were just the right candidate to take care of our folks till Dr. Pearson gets here."

She lifted a brow and smiled slightly. "I think I was the *only* candidate."

He flushed and shifted his clipboard. "Well, yes, that's true. But you know a lot of the people around here. I felt it was a good idea."

She noticed that the paper on his board held a list of local townspeople. Some of those whom she'd seen along the street to watch the earlier parade had check marks beside their names, as if he was taking roll. Nodding at the page, she asked, "Making notes?"

"Oh—this." He turned the list toward his jacket. "I'm just keeping track—that is, I want to be sure everything we planned is going well. The committee, including your sister, worked so hard on this."

Right, she thought. Still the little sneak, but worse now. A self-important sneak for the American Protective League. She wondered if her name was written with the others.

Jessica caught sight of Granny Mae, who glared at her and then walked back inside the café on the other side of Main.

"Ah, well, I'd better get down to the park," Adam said. "That will keep us busy for the rest of the day." He turned and gave her a sincere smile. "I'd really like to see you again, Jessica. Maybe even in church. It's good to have you back."

He headed off, full of purpose. When she glanced back at the door to the smithy, Cole was gone.

— — —

Later, Jess sat at her kitchen table with her coffee when she heard the office door open below. Another patient? she wondered. So much for Horace Cookson's prediction of a slow month here.

"Telegram for Dr. Layton!"

Hearing this, she abandoned her cup and hurried down the stairs. In the waiting room she found a boy she didn't recognize. He wore a wool cap and knickers, and his shirttail hung out on one side. "I'm Dr. Layton."

"Sign here, ma'am. Mr. Fenton said this is a 'mergency." He shoved a pencil and a receipt book into her hand. When she'd scratched her initials on a blank line and handed back the book, he ran outside, jumped on an old bicycle, and peddled down the street.

Jessica closed the door and stared at the Western Union envelope as if it contained a snake. In her experience, telegrams usually brought bad news.

She knew she had to read it, and with no little trepidation she tore open the flap. Pulling out the hastily folded note, she saw that it was from her soon-to-be employer.

> *Dr. Jessica Layton*
> *Powell Springs, Oregon*
> *--URGENT--*
> *Your help needed at Seattle General Hospital immediately. Influenza ravaging city. All medical resources stretched to breaking. Mortality rate high. Please come with greatest haste.*
> *Signed,*
> *Thomas Martin, MD*

She sat down in the nearest chair and reread the message. Leroy Fenton had said something about an outbreak of sickness at Camp Lewis. It had spread from a few people who'd reviewed the troops there to consuming all of Seattle? This was serious, and she knew it. Although she'd promised to stay in Powell Springs for a month, this new development changed everything. She would have to catch the next train north on Saturday and put the town's healthcare back into the hands of Granny Mae.

There was nothing else to be done.

— — —

Adam Jacobsen sat at his desk, the very desk his father had used before him. Pencil in hand, he stared at a blank sheet of paper. The daylight was fading, and he'd been sitting here for a good hour now, trying to create a meaningful sermon for Sunday's church service. Wads of crumpled paper surrounded him, the result of false starts and boring discourses.

Though he had followed his father's vocation, Adam sometimes caught himself questioning the older man's view of God and religion. He wasn't altogether convinced that angry exhortations, threats of fire and brimstone, and thundering sermons were the only ways to keep people on the path of righteousness. He had been raised to believe that they were; the Reverend Ephraim Jacobsen had ruled Powell Springs's souls—and his son and wife—with an unflinching determination to root out evil wherever it might try to hide.

"The enemy is clever and takes many forms," he would say, "but God will not be outwitted—or disobeyed." Adam's mother had dealt with the rigid view by becoming increasingly distant, both emotionally and at last, literally. Five years earlier, she'd gone to Colorado to care for her aging mother and had never returned, not even to attend her husband's funeral last winter. Only in letters had they maintained contact with her.

Adam had embraced his father's precepts of a terror-inspiring deity and the certainty that heaven had appointed Ephraim Jacobsen as one of its soldiers, complete with official induction papers—the Bible—dictated by the Almighty and taken down by one of His angel-scribes. He had also inherited his father's unwavering patriotism and the ironclad belief that President Wilson's decisions came directly from God.

Now that his father was gone and his responsibilities had fallen to Adam, he was torn between pastoring styles, if only a bit. But whenever he stopped to think about his slight deviation from his father's teachings, a shiver of panicky guilt ran through him.

This week, the topic he'd selected for his sermon was marriage. It was no random choice. Adam was on the downside of his twenties, and still he had no wife. Nettie Stark, the sturdy and outspoken woman who had come to keep house for him and his father three years earlier, reminded him about it on a regular basis. Oddly, though, nothing had brought his marital status home to him more forcefully than seeing Jessica Layton in the window at the hotel.

Their paths had not often crossed when they were younger—she was exactly the type of female his father had warned him against. And she'd been mixed up with Cole Braddock, who came from a family of rugged, bronco-busting ranchers. They managed horses, the elements, and women with equal ease. But he'd always kept an eye out for her over the years. He'd catch sight of her on her rare trips home, and the image of her was imprinted on his mind. Now her courtship had ended, Cole was probably going to marry Amy Layton, and Adam was reminded of a particular truism in the Book of Genesis.

It is not good for man to be alone.

Truth be told, Amy, and not her sister, was much more the kind of woman he might have envisioned as his helpmate. Yet part of him had always secretly yearned for Jessica even while he'd reported her wantonness to his father. (He had never forgotten stumbling upon her and Braddock down by the creek. The image had been seared upon his memory…their urgent hands all over one another, her skirts hiked up above her knees, his shirt unbuttoned, Adam's own arousal and fear as he'd turned to run away.)

He'd found it in his heart to look beyond that adolescent indiscretion and forgive it. Her choice of professions had redeemed her in his eyes, and he admired that choice, though Ephraim had not. But just as Adam was called to save souls, she had been called to save lives. They had both followed in their fathers' footsteps. He saw a sort of compatibility in that, especially since she'd defied convention to administer to the sick. Female physicians were such a rarity, he'd never even heard of another besides Jessica.

Forgetting for a moment the blank paper under his hand, he looked around the room and thought that the house seemed more empty every day. It was silly, he supposed. Nothing had changed all that much; before his father died, they'd lived here for years, entrenched in their routines. The parsonage stood across from the church, with a green, park-like expanse between them. It was a modest home, comfortable, but definitely intended for a small family rather than one man alone.

Then there was that other, even more shamefully urgent matter.

It is better to marry than to burn.

And burn Adam did. He'd never envisioned or wished for the life of a monk. For that reason, among others, he had urged Horace Cookson to ask Jessica to stay in Powell Springs. He wanted her. If luck and God were with him, she might make him a fine wife.

— — —

Lieutenant Steven Collier emerged from platoon headquarters, which had been set up in the front yard of a bombed-out farmhouse. "Back to the front lines again tonight, boys." He flopped down next to Riley in the trench and looked at the rest of their platoon.

"What?" Riley demanded. "We just got here and it took us hours. We were only relieved last night." They were in the reserve trenches at the back of the action. From somewhere in the rear, he heard a harmonica wheezing "My Old Kentucky Home."

Whippy, unperturbed as always, had the makings for a cigarette balanced on his lap.

"But, Sir, I was hoping to get a bath," Stoney said.

"*Here*?" Whip asked, without looking up from his cigarette papers. "You're dreaming, son. The only way to get a bath in this place is to stand in a rainstorm." He looked up at the heavy gray sky. "Your chance appears to be coming momentarily."

General grumbling and muttered swearing ensued.

"Yeah, yeah, I know," Collier said. "That's the word from platoon headquarters, though. We're moving out late this afternoon."

As the war had ground on and casualties were counted in the millions, men spent more and more time at the front lines.

"I guess I'd better write that letter to my folks pronto." Stig Ostergard had a blond head the size of a pumpkin, and finding a helmet to fit him had been a challenge. He was a nice young guy from Wisconsin, engaged to a pretty Swedish girl who spoke no English.

"Right. No lollygagging back here in the rear forever. We have a duty perform, and Fritz is waiting for us."

"Hey, my family has a dog named Fritz. I see him sometimes when I'm on patrol," Stoney said. Everyone looked at him. He was a very green farm boy from Ohio. Until this trip overseas, he'd never traveled farther than fifteen miles from home. Riley worried about him these days—he seemed to be coming loose at the seams. They'd lost a few others in the last months to shell shock. The victims ended up either gibbering idiots or stone-silent zombies. Or they'd just sit and rock themselves and cry. None could follow orders or do anything but huddle in the trenches, or shoot everything that moved, including allies. A couple had even managed to get their rifle muzzles into their own mouths.

"Freedom has an enemy named Fritz, kid," Collier replied with all grave sincerity, choosing to ignore the odd remark. "You fight this war, and you'll never fight another, and neither will your kids or your grandkids. This one is going to end 'em all. This one is going to make the world safe for democracy. And it depends on us. The world is depending on us."

The grumbling died away.

"Sergeant?" Collier prodded Riley.

He nodded. "All right, you heard the lieutenant. Draw your water and chow rations. We need to be ready to go in a couple of hours."

Whippy hauled himself to his feet, his deed accomplished. "First the British, then the Yankees, and now this. It looks like the Fourniers are fated to carry a gun and defend the honor of their country in every generation."

"What country did the Fourniers defend against Yankees?" Kansas Pete asked.

"Why, the Confederate States of America, of course. You do remember the War of Northern Aggression, don't you, Pete? I believe they still teach it in schools."

"The what?"

"The War Between the States."

"Oh, hell, Pete never went past third grade," Stig said.

"I did so! I finished seventh grade, for your information, smart aleck."

"In any event, gentlemen, here we are." The cigarette dangled from the corner of Whippy's mouth. "*C'est la vie.* I hope."

The men were exhausted. Nobody slept much as it was, and it was no secret to anyone that casualties were running sky-high.

Both sides were losing men in vast numbers. Riley was beginning to wonder about all the star-spangled rhetoric they'd been given. Would the world really be a better place for losing millions of lives in this horrible bloodbath? And that didn't count the men who'd had arms, legs, or arms *and* legs blown off. Was it true that no price was too large, no sacrifice too great? Would there be any kids or grandkids left after this was over?

Riley was a sergeant now, and the complexities of the world order were too vast for him to settle. But the questions, the doubt about his presence in this conflict and the exact nature of what they would actually gain for their "sacrifice," hummed in the back of his head like a murmured conversation, pitched too low for him to grasp. Sighing, he hoisted his rifle and went in search of a place to sit for a while.

In the two or so hours they'd been given, the men took the opportunity to shave, wash up a little, and write letters home. Riley sat in a dugout that was as gloomy as a cave, and except for the light provided by a couple of dim, bare bulbs, was almost as dark. He didn't have time to send a note to everybody in the family, so he addressed his to Susannah to tell her as much as he could about his well-being and to ask for things from home.

"Aren't you going to write to your mother, Whippy?"

Fournier stood in front of a small mirror that hung on a wire from a peg driven into the dirt wall. A basin of water stood on a camp stool next to his knee, and he'd stripped down to his undershirt. "Yes, but it offends my dignity to look this disreputable. I'll scratch a note to her after I finish here." Riley heard the scrape of his razor and then a sharp intake of breath. "Jesus," he muttered, "I swear I don't know how they expect a man to shave in light like this."

He wiped the rest of the lather off his chin with a somewhat clean towel and faced Riley. A spot of blood revealed the nick on his chin.

"Hey, soldier, where's your identification tag? You know we're never supposed to take it off."

"You aren't going to pull rank on me at this late date, are you, Braddock? I met a lovely Gallic mademoiselle who wanted a keepsake from our enchanting evening rendezvous."

"You gave her your tag?"

Whip turned on that lazy, cantaloupe grin again. "Along with the best part of me."

Riley started laughing. He couldn't help himself. This Southern eccentric was the only fun part about the whole miserable war. "You're amazing. You give away cheap jewelry and 'the best part' of yourself, and here we are close to getting our asses shot off."

"Exactly so. That's the perfect reason for doing it." He dragged a comb through his roebuck-colored hair.

Riley shook his head, still laughing. "I hope you also gave her a French letter so that she didn't get a longer-lasting souvenir from you."

"Why, I rather believe that the seed of my loins would go far toward improving some of the stock I've seen here. However, a gentleman is always prepared." He pulled a small, wrapped packet from his gear to wave at Riley. "I didn't want a lasting souvenir either. What is it the chaplains are preaching? One night with Venus and three years with mercury. I don't fancy acquiring a social disease, and the treatment sounds even worse."

Riley shifted the writing tablet on his knee. "Well, you'd better get another tag and hold onto it. The ambulance drivers will want to be able to put a name to you in case they pick you up."

Whippy made a graceful bow. "I'll see what I can do, Sir."

Riley finished his letter to Susannah and gave it to the post, then tried to catch a nap. After what seemed like five minutes, he felt a hand shaking his shoulder as he sat with his back against the dugout wall.

"It's time, Braddock." Riley looked up to see Lieutenant Collier standing over him.

Rations were drawn, and as the October daylight dwindled, the doughboys climbed the dugout stairs and started their way back toward the front. They passed mud-caked men turning their shovels to a trench bottom, others working to repair a broken telephone cable, and a foul-smelling corpse in a German uniform lying face-down in a stagnant puddle. Overhead, a Hun airplane buzzed through the sky. Enemy air strikes had been especially brutal in this latest offensive; the Germans sought to gain and hold control.

Trudging along, Riley couldn't help but wonder what the French countryside had looked like before this war started. It had to have been different from this. For miles and miles around, the earth was pockmarked with shell craters that reminded him of a photograph of the moon he'd once seen in an old periodical. This place looked just as desolate. The trees were broken, leafless, and lifeless. At night, they could easily be mistaken for men. If ever there had been rolling fields of lavender or tomatoes or grapes, any real vegetation, they were gone now. In his memory rose a picture of the home place, green, peaceful, dotted with beautiful horses. God, just to see it again…

In the distance, a shell blew three men out of a trench.

He put his head down and plodded on. Right now, his main goal was to keep himself and his men alive so he could return to the world that he was supposed to be improving.

CHAPTER SEVEN

Jessica unpacked in the apartment over the office and hung her freshly pressed clothes in the wardrobe. Nothing sounded better than a bath. A bathroom of her own—it would be heaven. In the rooming house where she'd lived, the bath had been down the hall and every boarder was assigned a scheduled time to use it. If she missed her slot, as she often did because of work, she'd had to sponge-bathe using the sink in the corner of her room. And the past week on the train had been even more Spartan—she'd had to make do with the most minimal of washing. She sat on the bed and looked at her surroundings. The apartment was unsophisticated, with its quilt on the bed, clean, quiet, and homey, just like all of Powell Springs. Amy had done a good job of decorating.

She was tired from her trip and the long day. More than anything, Jess knew she was exhausted by what had happened in New York. She didn't like to think about it, but the memories swamped her like engulfing waves of a winter-tossed Atlantic Ocean. They came to her at times when she wasn't expecting them, or as they did today, when Amy had asked her about those years. Often her dreams were haunted by sounds and images so vivid, she'd wake with her heart galloping in her chest, expecting to find herself back in the midst of what she'd left behind in the East. Even the month she'd spent resting in Saratoga Springs had not helped. A month wasn't long enough. It would take more time, she told herself. Time to recover, time to forgive herself. She might never forget, but as the weeks and months passed, and she settled into her new position in Seattle, surely those images would fade. She clung to that hope as a lifeline. If the wire from Seattle was any indication, she'd have an entirely new set of experiences to deal with.

She lifted her arms to remove her hairpins when she heard a tapping at the door. It was so faint, she thought it was coming from another room down the hall, only here, in Powell Springs, there was no other room down the hall—at least not with an occupant.

No, there it was again, and she realized it came from downstairs.

Going to the door, she saw the silhouette of a man's figure through the twilit lace curtain. "Who is it, please?"

"Dr. Layton?" The question sounded more like a croak. She peeked around the edge of the curtain and discovered Eddie Cookson weaving drunkenly on the stoop. Immediately, she unlocked the door and pulled it open.

"Eddie! What in heaven's name are you doing here?" She took his arm, steered him into the waiting room, and pushed him into the nearest chair. He was still dressed in his uniform, but he looked far worse now than he had this morning. "I thought your father came to get you!"

"He had to milk the cows. I told him…to go on…it's only a couple of miles. I thought I could walk."

"But you left here. Where have you been all these hours?"

"I wandered around…the truth is, I'm not sure where all I—" A fit of coughing overtook him before he could finish the sentence.

"Dear God," she muttered.

Jess hurried down the hall to retrieve her stethoscope and thermometer from her bag in the office. After poking the glass tube into Eddie's mouth, she had him unbutton the top of his wool tunic so she could listen to his heart. It beat like a labored horse's. She went into the back and grabbed her white apron from the hook where she'd hung it earlier. Then she searched through the stoppered bottles and vials in the glass-front cabinets, hoping to find the ingredients she needed. Her throat closed when she recognized her father's handwriting in faded brown ink on some of the labels. Others bore Cyrus Vandermeer's scratching.

Atropine sulphate...morphine sulphate...quinine sulphate... camphor...gum tragacanth...Yes, they were all here, thank goodness. Rummaging through other shelves, she discovered apothecaries' weights, a mortar and pestle, a pill roller, and a pharmacopoeia for the dosages, and piled them on a work table. She'd not had to compound her own medicines for a while, but fortunately she hadn't lost the skill.

Meanwhile, she heard Eddie's hacking cough in the other room and her mission increased its urgency.

In a few minutes, she'd manufactured twenty pills and poured them into a square of paper, which she folded shut. On a corner of the packet she wrote hasty instructions.

Take one pill every two hours.

She came back to the waiting room and found her patient slumped down farther in the chair, the thermometer chattering between his teeth. God, he seemed to grow worse before her very eyes. Jessica had seen and experienced her share of influenza—acute onset was often a distinguishing characteristic—but she couldn't recall anyone in robust health like Eddie fading so quickly. She tucked the packet of pills into his hand.

Taking the thermometer from his mouth, she read 103F degrees.

She remembered the telegram she'd received from Seattle General Hospital and her stomach dropped with a cold heaviness. "People have been ill up at Camp Lewis, haven't they?"

He made a feeble gesture. "Some troops came in on the train. A lot of them were sick with something. Things are pretty crowded up in camp. We've got lots more men than we have room. We're practically one on top of the other. But the camp medical officer said there was nothing to worry over. I didn't think anymore about—" Another attack of coughing interrupted him.

Jessica wasn't as sanguine as that medical officer. Working in public health, she had stayed up to date on epidemics going around. But she had purposely insulated herself from outside distractions since she'd left New York. In Saratoga Springs, she had not read a newspaper or even glanced at a headline. In that green and peaceful place, she'd wanted to shut out the war and the world, to forget. Now her self-imposed isolation was coming back to haunt her, and she knew she'd made a huge mistake.

She stood and put a hand to his forehead. Fever raged in him, and her concern grew. "Take those pills I made up for you. They should help with the cough and the aches. I wrote the instructions on the packet."

He nodded his thanks, plainly losing what strength he had left.

"How will you get home? Is your father still in his office?"

"I don't think so. I tried to walk back…" he repeated.

Hiding her irritation at Horace Cookson's lackadaisical attitude about this, she said, "I'm going to find someone to take you back your place. You wouldn't be able to walk across the street."

She waited to see if her words registered. "You stay here," she added sternly, then pulled open the door.

The sun sat golden-red on the western horizon, and night would come soon. As in most small towns at this hour, people were at home eating dinner, and traffic had dwindled to a scant trickle. Even Granny Mae had closed her restaurant for the day.

The unpaved street was dotted with the remnants of the day's activities—bits of crepe paper and handbills, a ribbon or two, and a few tiny American flags that had gotten away from small hands. She looked around, hoping to see someone, anyone, who could give Eddie a ride. But the only place that showed any activity was Tilly's Saloon down at the end of Main. There she saw an automobile and a few horses and wagons outside.

She marched down to Tilly's, past the darkened windows of the hardware store and Bright's Grocery. Her white apron flapped around her skirts. Yanking open the screen door, she stepped inside. Several customers stood at the bar, a few with a foot resting on the brass rail at the bottom. She had a confused impression of various bottles lined up on the back bar interspersed with mounted antlers and stuffed trophy heads of elk. Paintings of nearby Multnomah Falls and Mount Hood, along with a photograph of Teddy Roosevelt, mingled with signs that warned *No Credit—Don't Ask, No Minors Permitted,* and more of the standard Liberty Bond posters. A few small tables lined one wall where old-timers like Winks Lamont and Shaw Braddock sat sipping their whiskies. The hum of conversation and smoke hung over the scene.

It certainly wasn't Delmonico's, was her wry, initial thought. That elegant New York establishment had entertained such luminaries as Mark Twain, Charles Dickens, and any number of American presidents and captains of industry. At Tilly's, spittoons stood wherever they'd been kicked to, and the floor was covered with sawdust and peanut shells.

From his post behind the bar, a flustered Virgil Tilly saw Jess first. He reached for the towel slung over one shoulder and wiped his hands. His expression of mild horror would have been amusing under less dire circumstances. "Um, Miss Layton, ma'am—"

When he spoke her name, all eyes turned toward her and goggled. Conversation ceased.

"No offense, but this really isn't a place for a lady—"

Not bothering with preliminary chitchat, Jess interrupted, "I need a man with a wagon or an automobile who can take Eddie Cookson back to his farm. He's in my office, and he's too ill to walk that far."

"What's the matter with him?" Winks asked.

"He has influenza."

Several customers weighed in on the situation.

"The grippe? He was all right earlier when he rode in the parade."

"Yeah, he was smiling and shaking hands right and left. He didn't look sick to me."

Another said darkly, "Hey, I think heard about this thing. My wife had a letter from her mother last week. She lives in Philadelphia and she said the grippe is mowing folks down like wheat under a hailstorm. They're fine one minute and dropping over the next. The coffins are stacked up on the sidewalks, they can't bury them fast enough. She said the dead people turned blue *before* they died."

"Blue—God almighty!"

"Yessir, blue as ink. Some as dark as a midnight sky. She said they die gasping and gurgling like someone who's drowned.

Others dropped dead on the streetcar or on the sidewalk, just like that." He snapped his fingers, then added in a suspicious tone, "They think it came from Spain."

Everyone spoke at once. "I heard about that—the black plague! It happened over in Europe."

"They said it was the rats."

"Wait a minute," Jess tried to intervene. "That was hundreds of years ago. This is just influenza, not the plague—"

The conversation continued as if she hadn't said a thing.

"I seen it." A man sitting at the end of the bar spoke up. "I seen people, blue in the face and gasping for air."

"Where'd you say you was from, mister?" Shaw Braddock asked him.

"Nowheres in particular. I spent some time over in Troutdale and Parkridge a few years back, but I been traveling since then. Then I got to hankering for this part of the country again so I come back." The drifter wore a hat pulled low, but what Jess could see of his face she remembered well. Not that she knew him. But she'd seen scores of men just like him back East—shabby, unshaven, and as ragged as a burlap bag nailed to a post to flap in the wind. His few belongings were tied in a grimy pillowcase that sat on the floor at his feet.

"You got folks around here?" Winks asked.

"Maybe. I haven't seen 'em in a long time and I'm hoping to find 'em."

"And you say you've seen this influenza?" Virgil pressed, refilling his whiskey glass.

He nodded his thanks. "Yup. I shared a boxcar out here with a man who was sick with it. He lost enough blood from his nose to fill a gin bottle." He bolted the drink in one gulp and wiped his mouth on the back of his hand.

"Jesus!"

"It sounds bad. The plague—good night, nurse! I don't want no part of that."

"Neither do I. It's catching."

But the man's audience edged a bit closer, obviously eager for more gruesome details. The possibility that he himself could be contagious either didn't cross their minds, or they were willing to risk it to hear the story.

If ever there was a case of an exaggerated whopper, Jess figured this had to be one. Aunt Someone confided to Somebody Else about a distant cousin's appendectomy, and by the third or fourth telling, the appendix had grown hair and teeth and turned into an undeveloped twin the cousin had carried around for thirty years. Unfounded rumor became concrete fact. Now influenza patients were turning blue-black, hemorrhaging, and dropping dead. There was cause for concern, yes, but the Seattle telegram hadn't reported anything so sensational.

"It's *not* the plague. It's just the grippe," she insisted. But one point had been raised with which she agreed. "Yes, it can be contagious. Still, that doesn't guarantee the one who gives Eddie a ride will come down with it."

No one jumped forward to volunteer.

"Even so—I had it last winter and I was in bed for a week," another man said. She didn't recognize him, but he seemed strong and healthy enough. He must have had an exemption from military service. "I can't afford to catch it again."

"You might have immunity from the case you had last winter," she said. She wasn't sure that was true, but she was desperate.

"By God, doctor gal, you sure make it sound like an attractive proposition," Shaw observed tartly. "'You could get sick and die, but maybe not.'" He cracked a peanut, popped the nuts into his mouth, and threw the shells on the floor. "If even half of what this feller, here—what's your name?"

"Bert Bauer," the ragged man answered. He signaled Tilly for a refill, complaining, "Got me a hell of a toothache."

"If even half of what Bert, here, says is true, I imagine we're in for a heap of trouble. That doesn't mean we have to go galloping up to meet it."

Surprised and annoyed by what she saw as their lack of compassion, Jess advanced from her spot just inside the door. The sawdust and litter crunched beneath her shoes. They had made a great fuss over Eddie as their one of their own in uniform with their patriotic posturing, but now they dithered over their drinks and muttered among themselves. She glanced at the Liberty Bond poster on the wall and an idea hit her.

"Here this soldier came down from Camp Lewis, where he's been training to go off to Europe to fight for America, and now that he needs you you're turning your backs?" She knew it was hypocritical, given her opinion of the war, but she also knew how these men's minds worked. And it wasn't Eddie's fault that he'd been drafted. They muttered some more and wouldn't meet her eyes, but still no one offered to help. "What shall I tell him when I go back to my office? That his friends and neighbors wave flags for him but leave him to fend for himself? I'm only asking you to give him a ride home. I'd do it myself if I had the means."

No one spoke, and the silence fired her temper. "*Will no one help this boy?*"

"I will."

Jess whirled and saw Cole standing on the other side of the screen door behind her. He pulled it open and stepped into the saloon. The whole place seemed to sizzle with his presence, and she caught a brief whiff of leather and hay that overrode the typical saloon smells.

"I came to get the old man," he said, nodding at his father. "But I imagine he'll keep until we get Cookson taken care of. I've got the truck outside. I just have to take Amy home first."

Glancing beyond his shoulder, she saw her sister sitting in the front seat of the Ford parked next to the sidewalk. As much as she wished to avoid him, Jess couldn't refuse his help. He was the only one who had offered. "Thank you, Cole."

But he wasn't looking at her. His hard gaze was fixed on the group in Tilly's. "I'll meet you back at the office," he said at last, then turned and walked outside.

Before she left she frowned at them, too.

"I'm ashamed of all of you."

— — —

Cole jammed the truck into first gear and made a wide U-turn to take Amy to Mrs. Donaldson's.

"Was that *Jessica* I saw storming out of Tilly's?" Amy asked, aghast. "What on earth was she doing in the saloon?"

His chuckle was on the grim side. "Making those guys look like jackasses. She walked down here to ask someone to help Eddie Cookson. He's sick and needs a ride home. No one would do it."

Amy gripped the edge of the seat as they bumped over a wheel rut and clutched her hat with her free hand. "Sick—with what?"

"Jess says it's influenza, and none of those men would help."

"Good heavens, why not?"

Cole had stood on Tilly's porch long enough to witness the main part of the confrontation. "They don't want to catch it."

"That's—it's unpatriotic."

He told her what he'd overheard.

"The plague! That's not possible, is it?"

"I don't know—your sister said no. Of course, now that story will probably be all over town by morning. You know how those guys spread gossip. They're worse than a bunch of old women."

"But—but how could they refuse to help? Eddie is a U.S. Army infantryman, a soldier." He caught her outraged expression from the corner of his eye. "We gave him a parade," she added, as if that said everything.

"That's basically what Jess told them, only she was more direct. That's her—high-minded, outraged, plainspoken." Yeah, that was his Jess. Then he reined in the thought. She wasn't his anymore. She had seen to that.

"Now what's going to happen? And what about your father?"

"Pop can cool his heels in the saloon for a while. He won't care. I'm going to drive you home, then go back for Eddie."

"You see, Cole? You *are* a hero." She hugged his arm, making him pull the wheel toward the right. "If you'd gone off to France, who would be here to do this good deed?"

Yeah, a hero, he mulled sourly, straightening the wheel as they chugged down quiet Russell Street, with its rows of tidy homes and fenced yards. He didn't feel like much of a hero.

He pulled up in front of Mrs. Donaldson's neat, two-story house. Through one window, he could see the woman setting the dining room table. "Looks like I got you home in time for dinner."

"It's been such a busy day, I'm just going to have a little bite to eat and put my feet up."

He jumped out of the truck and came around to help her out. In the cool, pale twilight they walked up to Mrs. Donaldson's porch. He saw the older woman retreat to the other side of the front door. He just knew she was standing there with her ear pressed against the panel, listening.

"She's spying on us again," Cole said in a low voice.

"Shh! I think she's just a romantic at heart," Amy whispered, smiling. "She's never really gotten over losing Mr. Donaldson."

Cole snorted in derision. "Donaldson died twenty years ago." He was more inclined to believe the old lady was just a nosy snoop, but he didn't say so. He knew that Amy was fond of her. He took Amy's gloved hands in his and gave her a chaste peck on the cheek.

"Thank you for helping Jessica."

He wanted to say that he wasn't helping her. He was helping Eddie. But that would have only created a tense moment. And he wasn't sure it was true. He shrugged. "What else can I do? I'd like to think that someone would give me a ride if I was too sick to walk."

"And that's why you're my hero." She gazed up at him shyly.

He cringed at the notion of being anyone's hero.

She gave him a searching look, her own expression uncertain. "Cole, is everything—well, is there anything you want to talk about?"

"Me? No, why?"

"Lately I've had the feeling that something is troubling you. Something we should discuss." She gazed at him as if she were trying to read his thoughts. The scrutiny made his throat tight, and he looked away.

He kissed her cheek. "You worry too much." He sighed and rubbed the back of his neck, trying to squelch the hollow feeling in the pit of his soul. "Everything is fine. Or at least as fine as it can be, considering. You go in. I've got to get Eddie Cookson home. I'll talk to you tomorrow."

"Well, if you're certain—"

He made a shooing gesture at her.

She smiled then, apparently reassured, and pushed open the front door. Mrs. Donaldson let out a loud squawk and Cole caught a glimpse of her holding her nose.

"Mrs. Donaldson!" Amy exclaimed. "Oh, dear, are you all right? Here, take my handkerchief. The bleeding will stop—"

He jumped down the stairs two at a time, and with colossal self-control, didn't laugh until he was back in the truck.

— — —

Jessica was waiting for Cole on the sidewalk when he pulled up in front of her office. He recognized her expression. He saw worry in her face, and she looked tired.

"He's ready to go?"

She shook her head. "I don't know, Cole. I'm beginning to think I should keep Eddie here in one of the patient beds. He's doing so poorly. He has a high fever and he's becoming delirious."

He shut off the engine and got out of the Ford. "Can you cure him?"

"No. There's no cure for influenza. The body has to heal itself." She paced a short path, back and forth, her arms folded over her chest. She was talking to him, but it seemed as if she was outlining a course of action to herself as well. "I can make sure he gets his medication every two hours. Beyond that, there's not much I can provide except good nursing. But I'd like to keep an eye on him. If an emergency comes up, someone would have to bring him into town again. That is, if the crisis was even recognized. I don't think he should be shuttled around like that." She told him about Eddie wandering for hours without ever getting home.

Just then, a crash came from the waiting room. They ran inside and found Eddie Cookson collapsed on the floor. In the fall, he'd overturned his chair and a wrought-iron coat tree, which had cut a gash in the oak flooring.

"Jesus," Cole uttered. The change in Eddie's appearance was almost unbelievable. This was not the boy-soldier who'd smiled and waved from his parade float earlier in the day. Or even the one Cole had helped carry over here earlier. This young man looked as if he'd already been through the war—and lost. His eyes were inflamed, his face was the color of one of Shaw's old red bandanas, and he was shivering like a wet dog left out in the snow.

Jess grasped his wrist. "His heart is galloping."

Eddie looked up at Jessica with bleary, unfocused eyes. "Mother? Can you make the hammer stop banging in my head? It—" His rambling was interrupted by another bout of coughing.

"I've got to get him upstairs and into bed."

Cole nodded. This was just plain bad. "Come on, Ed. We'll get you fixed up." He hoisted Eddie to his feet. Between the two of them, they practically dragged him up the stairs to the patient room situated across the hall from Jess's own apartment. Cole lowered Eddie to one of the narrow iron beds while Jessica looked in the cabinet that stood in one corner.

"I don't know if I have gowns or pajamas in here." She rummaged through sheets, bedding, and other linens. "Aha! Here they are." They managed to wrestle their patient out of his hot wool uniform and into a pair of white cotton pajamas. All the while, Eddie coughed and mumbled in a disjointed ramble, complaining about the bone-deep pain that had overtaken his body.

Cole had never seen anything like it. Judging by the expression on Jessica's face, he wasn't sure she had, either.

Once they had him in the bed, Jess forced a pill down Eddie's throat. Her hair had come loose from its pins, and blond tendrils hung around her face. "The morphine should help the cough and aches."

"What else can you do for him?" Cole asked, and sat on the empty bed in the room.

"I'll examine him to try to figure out just which systems are involved." She glanced up at him. "I mean how much of his body is affected. Do the Cooksons have a telephone?"

"I don't know. We do at the farm since we're on a main road, but Birdeen only works days, so there's no one to put the call through. There's been talk about getting a night operator, but it hasn't happened."

She pushed her straggling hair out of her face. "All right. If you could get word to his family that he's here, it would be a big help." Her words were fractured by Eddie's hacking, Watching him, her expression took on a pale look of dawning horror.

"What?"

"Oh, God..." She stared at the shivering, muttering man in the bed.

"*What?* What's the matter?"

She told him about her conversation with Leroy Fenton and the telegram she'd received. "I was going to leave for Seattle on Saturday's train. I supposed Powell Springs would survive until Pearson gets here. But if this epidemic is as contagious as it sounds—Cole, this boy probably talked to nearly every person in town in the past two days. Who knows how many people were exposed? Who he shook hands with, breathed on? The children and the older folks around here will be coming down with it too."

"So all those men down at Tilly's who didn't want to help—"

"They might get sick anyway, along with a lot of others."

"And us?"

She sighed. "Yes, although we can try our best not to. Go downstairs to the back office right now and wash your hands with hot, soapy water, and don't touch your face until you do. I've got to contact the hospital in Seattle and get some information. Maybe the Red Cross too."

He stood, making the bedsprings screech. He couldn't help but admire her decisiveness. The same take-charge, resolute attitude that rubbed some men the wrong way—and which had drawn him to her as a strong-willed equal—was alive and well.

She followed him down the steps and waited while he washed up, then she washed her own hands.

"Will you need help taking care of Cookson? Should I get Granny Mae?"

"God, no," Jess muttered, wiping her hands on a clean towel.

"Can you handle this alone?"

She bent a look on him. "What do you think I've been doing all this time in New York, Cole?"

New York, New York, *New York*. He frowned, sick of being reminded of why everything went so wrong. The tension of war-time life, compounded by Pop, compounded by so many things, came alive in him. What had Jess found there that kept her from coming home as she'd promised? What had happened that caused her to break off their courtship? The question, which he'd managed to push to the back of his mind, had come roaring to his waking thoughts since she returned to Powell Springs. "That's what I've wondered for two years. What *have* you been doing there?"

Cole moved closer to Jess. His face, suddenly flushed and almost angry, was nearly in hers as he stood there. For a moment, she thought he might either shake her or kiss her. But apparently he expected an answer. The tension between them was like an electric current, snapping and dangerous. Unprepared for the sudden turn of the conversation, or the feeling that hot honey was running in her veins, she backed away, highly annoyed that he would raise the subject at this moment. She turned and with nervous, brittle energy began cleaning up the table she'd used to compound Eddie's pills.

"I've got a very sick patient upstairs, and you're supposed to go tell his family where he is. Why in the world are we talking about this now?"

"You keep bringing it up, Jess. You keep telling me how swell it was in New York. In your letters you told me you had too much important work to do to leave. I just want to know what was so damned special about it that you gave up everything here."

She spun around to look at him. "I never said it was 'swell.' But, yes, the work was important. You can't know—I can't explain how much—how desperately—" She stumbled to a stop and took up her chore again. Her heart seemed to be pounding as hard and fast as Eddie's had when she'd listened to his chest.

"Then why didn't you stay there if it meant so much? Why did you leave it for a different job?"

"*Why* should you care?" she countered. "You'll marry Amy and have a happy home. What difference does it make now?"

For an instant, she thought he would pound his fist on the table, but instead he put up his hands and took a deep breath. His face fell into the unpleasant, stony expression she was growing accustomed to. "It doesn't make any difference. I'll go talk to Horace." He walked away then, his boot heels resonating on the pine flooring. That was followed by the sound of the front door closing.

A moment later, she heard the truck engine turn over, and Cole drove away.

CHAPTER EIGHT

Jessica spent a very long night taking care of Eddie. She dosed him with the pills every two hours. Some of them even stayed down. But if they were of any help, it was minimal. She didn't go to bed, but instead sat up in a chair in her apartment with both doors open so that she could hear him. Not that it would have been difficult—his cough was so harsh, it sounded as if it could lift the roof off the second floor. During those moments when she sat in her kitchenette, drinking coffee and trying to think of some treatment, she composed wires to Dr. Martin at Seattle General and to the Red Cross office, which had opened the year before in Portland. Although she had to explain to Dr. Martin why she would not be coming to Washington as soon as he'd asked, she also asked for some up-to-date information from him regarding the influenza that stood poised on her hometown's doorstep.

At least it gave her something else to think about besides Cole and the effect he still had on her.

She drank her coffee bitter and black. Sugar and cream were hard-to-get luxuries these days; in fact, it was considered a badge of honor to do without, and a mark of shame to consume anything that should be going to the troops. Her hands shook with fatigue and caffeine as she worked to stem the tide of self-reproach that kept trying to engulf her.

How could she have cocooned herself so tightly that she'd been out of touch with the events taking place around her? How had she not heard about this sickness invading the civilian population?

She knew the answer, but it was no comfort, and it was not an excuse she could accept.

Yes, thoughts of those helpless people in the tenements still haunted her. But her fate had been decided years ago. By becoming a physician, she'd also made a tacit agreement to accept the good with the bad. Dealing with human suffering was part of her profession. Not every life could be saved. And even for those that could be, not every outcome was positive.

Only—only there had been so *many* that weren't...

Still, kicking herself would do no good. She had to take up her calling where she'd left it and do her best to learn all she could about this epidemic.

The pale streaks of dawn seemed to come late due to the heavy, lead-gray sky that threatened rain. At about seven o'clock, Jess heard sharp knocking on the front door. Not knowing what to expect, she ran down to answer it. She recognized Helen Cookson, Eddie's mother, standing on the other side of the glass.

Helen's fine-boned face looked drawn and wilted. Her hair, shot with silver threads, was pulled into a bun, and Jessica imagined she'd had no more sleep than she herself.

"I came as soon as could," Helen said, her voice quavery. Out front, Horace Cookson was wrapping the reins around the brake of their farm wagon. "How is my boy?"

Jess stepped aside and let her in. "His fever is higher than I would like, and he has moments of...confusion."

"Confusion?"

"Delirium," Jess conceded. "I'm giving him medication, but I'm not sure how much it's helping. Mostly what he needs is good nursing and rest."

"Cole said it's the influenza." Helen's tone gave it grave importance.

The influenza.

"Yes." At least she hadn't said *plague*.

Horace, dressed haphazardly in overalls and a blue-striped work shirt, walked in. These clothes seemed more suited to him than the boiled shirt and crooked tie that went with his mayoral duties. "Had to milk the cows first. The cows can't wait."

Helen gave her husband a tight-lipped look. "Can I see him?"

"Yes, of course. Eddie's upstairs."

After she was out of earshot, Horace turned to Jess and dropped his voice to a confidential tone. "Helen's got herself in a downright conniption over this. I sure appreciate you looking after the boy for us. Even though it's only influenza, I knew he'd be in good hands with you."

"I'm sorry I had to send Cole Braddock out to your place last night, but I thought you should know about the situation."

"It's just the grippe, though," he reiterated. "That's not such a bad thing, is it? Not for a young man like Ed. We've all had it at one time or another. Had it myself last spring. In fact, so did Cole, now that I think about it. I remember because Susannah had to practically tie him to his bed to keep him from working. She said the sooner he got well, the better off they'd all be. Most of us did get better." He hitched his brows, then added, "Well, Doctor Vandermeer didn't, and Eph Jacobsen, but they were getting on."

"Except this might be worse than the usual illness."

"Bah, I heard they've had an outbreak of some kind of Spanish flu on the East Coast, but they're all jammed together back there with machines and smoky factories and such. Well, you know that better than the rest of us." He gestured vaguely with his big farmer's hand. "This is God's country out here—clean air, simple living, wide-open spaces."

From the second floor came the bark of Eddie's wretched, gurgling cough, an unnerving, hopeless sound. It had continued most of the night, preventing him from getting much rest. Horace turned his gaze to the top of the stairs, and a shadow of concern crossed his eyes. "Ed's strong, he'll be back on his feet in no time." But his tone had lost some of its conviction.

Jess squared her shoulders, as much to ease the tension and fatigue in them as to give him courage. "I certainly hope so, Mr. Cookson. I'm doing everything I can for him."

"Helen made up a bed in the back of the wagon so we can take him home."

"We probably don't want to move him just yet," she said, using the calm tone she saved for delivering dire news. "I'd intended to have Cole give Eddie a ride home last night. But after he collapsed here in the waiting room—well, I think it would be best for him to stay here for a while, at least until his fever breaks. In the meantime, you'll want to contact his cantonment at Camp Lewis to let them know where he is." She was careful not to add that she didn't believe Eddie had reached the crisis point yet, but she sensed that Horace at last understood the seriousness of his son's illness.

Keeping his eyes on the stairs, he said, "I…oh…sure…I believe I'll go up and visit with him for a moment." He shuffled off toward the steps.

Jess nodded and sat down in a nearby chair, fatigue weighing on her shoulders. She knew that Horace would be in for a rude surprise.

Eddie, so vital and healthy yesterday, now had a dusky-blue tint to his nose, ears, and lips. And chances were good that he might not recognize his own father this morning.

— — —

"Then next year, I could plant nasturtiums and climbing roses so they trail over the porch railing." Amy moved back and forth across the front yard of Cole's not-quite-finished house, explaining to him her plans for the landscape. She had already taken him on a tour of the interior, showing him her finishing touches on the painting, which she'd generously offered to undertake, despite the fact that they had no formal engagement between them yet. She'd started with bare walls and floors and transformed them into a real home. It had stood unfinished for nearly two years, waiting for its originally-intended mistress to see it completed. "I can get all the cuttings I need from the ladies on my committees. Won't that be pretty?"

"Uh-huh."

While Roscoe bounded around the brush, Amy pointed here and there, her lavender skirts brushing through the yellow grass, picking up seed tops along the way. Her honey hair was caught in a loose knot on top of her head and gleamed like a thoroughbred's. Now and then, a breeze kicked up to snag a few strands that had escaped their pins. The sun, which had hidden behind a gray veil of clouds all day, had emerged for the last hour of daylight, casting lambent gold over the west-facing sage-and-cream-painted house, and over her. Amy was a very pretty young woman, with a heart to match.

Not for the first time, Cole pondered the fact that he'd never really noticed her when Jessica had lived in Powell Springs. Amy had always been there, a shy girl who had stayed close to her mother. Then when Lenore Layton died, she'd clung to the Layton housekeeper. He didn't remember much about her except that she had played with her dolls, hated getting dirty, and had turned beet-red whenever he'd looked at her. Jess, on the other hand, had liked poking around under rocks to see what lived beneath them, or collecting bugs and pond water to bring home to her father's microscope. For all that she was smart and learned, Jessica had never been a stuffy bluestocking. She'd been protective of Amy, but it wasn't until Jess left that Amy had seemed to bloom.

Once her sister was gone and her father had died, she had made friends with Susannah, and it hadn't been unusual for him to come in after a long work day and find Amy Layton as a guest at the Braddock dinner table. She had plied him with questions about the horses and the farm, and hung on his every word. He'd had to admit to himself that he was flattered by her attention.

Everyone loved Amy.

How could he not?

She walked back to his side, her face radiant with joy. "Cole, this is such a beautiful house. It's a shame to let it stand empty now that it's almost finished."

He had chosen a good place to build the two-story home. It backed up to a tree-covered hill, where it would be sheltered from sharp winter winds and get the summer sun for a garden. Its wide, wraparound porch would be a comfortable place to sit on mild evenings and watch the sunset. He tried to forget that he had once pictured Jessica sitting on the porch with him.

Slinging an arm over Amy's narrow shoulders, he smiled down at her. "You've done a great job of putting it all together. I'm just an old cowboy at heart. If it was up to me, I'd probably bed down on a cot next to the stove in the kitchen."

"Goodness, I'm sure it will never have to be like that!" she said, laughing. "You'll need decently cooked meals, and *someone*," she added archly, "to sew your shirts and keep the house cleaner than our housekeeper did. You know, poor Jessica was never good at any of those things. Oh, did I mention Mrs. Donaldson let it slip that she's making a brand-new quilt for me as a gift for my hope chest?"

"Speaking of gifts," he said, "I picked up a little something for you in town today." He reached into his shirt pocket and pulled out a tiny box.

"What is it?" she asked, as delighted as a little girl.

"Open it and find out."

She took the box from him and opened it to reveal a pair of small cameo earrings. He'd seen them in the jeweler's window after he'd left Jessica and was heading for the post office to pick up the ranch's mail.

"Aren't they beautiful," she said, her tone oddly flat as she stared at the carved profiles lying on the black velvet of the box. "But—but why?"

He realized she'd seen the small box and expected a ring.

He shrugged, a surge of disquiet rolling through him. "No reason. I saw them and thought you'd like them."

She smiled up at him. "Oh, I do like them. I'm so lucky. What woman could ask for more?"

He hugged her to him and inhaled the vanilla fragrance of her. She was so delicately made, she felt almost like a child in his arms. Maybe if they'd been married already, this heavy, unnamable emptiness wouldn't be sitting in his chest like a rock. Again. Still.

She drew back and looked into his eyes. "Life hasn't seemed normal since America entered the war. I know you have a big job to do with Riley gone. But *nothing* and no one stands in our way now."

Her meaning was so obvious, he almost expected *her* to propose. Why couldn't he just do what was expected of him?

He swallowed, trying to dislodge that knot in his chest. "Sounds good to me." He kissed her then, a sweet and tender touch of lips. Beyond hand-holding, it was the only intimacy they had ever shared. More than this would seem somehow, well, a *defilement* of Amy. Her aura of simple virtue stopped him from going any further. He couldn't even imagine it. "I guess we should go. Susannah has dinner waiting for us. Besides, after rolling bandages and organizing a parade, you're probably done in for the day."

He took her arm and steered her back toward the ranch house, a quarter-mile to the west across the flat, green expanse of pasture. Split-rail fences rimmed the area, where sleek, healthy horses bowed their necks to nip the grass. The dog trotted ahead of them. It was a peaceful scene—the pale, hushed twilight, the soft nickering in the herd, the house in the distance.

Amy was right—nothing stood between them now.

Not one thing. Not even the secret hand on his heart.

CHAPTER NINE

By the time everyone was assembled at the table, Cole was starving. It was a fair-size group Susannah had to cook for. She had Cole, his father, their foreman, Tanner Grenfell, Tanner's two young nephews, Wade and Joshua, and tonight, Amy. Before the war began, when the crew was bigger, they'd had their own cook in the bunkhouse. Now there was more work than ever and fewer people to do it.

Somehow Susannah managed. She had the same steel-cored resilience that Jessica had. No one asked how she did it all. She simply did what had to be done. But even Cole had to admit, the strain was beginning to show. Some mornings she appeared at the breakfast table with purple shadows beneath her eyes, or her long black curls tied back hastily with a strip of leather. Cole often heard her pacing the hallway long after everyone was in bed, or puttering in the kitchen. He didn't believe she'd slept an entire night through since Riley left. One day he'd passed her bedroom and it caught his eye that she'd moved their silver-framed wedding photograph from the dresser to her nightstand, as if she might bring him closer.

They were well into a savory meal of fried chicken when Pop blared across the dinner table, "Well, Mrs. Braddock, what does our war hero have to say for himself in that letter?" With the mail that Cole had brought home was a letter from Riley to Susannah.

Susannah sat at her place, scanning Riley's hasty scribbles written on water-stained paper. "He says it's been raining for days on end…his clothes are never dry and in the trenches they stand ankle-deep in water and—and worse…they're sleeping in the wet. Lord above, he keeps saying they're eating monkey meat. That can't be right."

"If a man's hungry enough, he ain't too picky about where the meat came from. I remember one time I et a rattlesnake because we didn't have anything else on the trail. Shot it myself and—"

Cole interrupted. "I've heard about that meat. It's not really monkey. The troops just call it that. It's some kind of lousy-tasting canned French stuff they bring in from Madagascar."

"He's a sergeant now. He's been promoted."

"Hah!" Pop said, thumping the table. "I knew he'd do it!"

Susannah's brows drew together slightly as she paused to read part of the letter to herself. Then she continued, her voice trembling slightly. "H-he'd like me to send him some clean socks and soap. The Germans are attacking them with poison gas, and lots of men have been blinded or killed. *Ohh*…he s-says the man next to him was hit by a shell and—" She broke off and refolded the letter to put it in her apron pocket.

Cole saw her swallow hard, and her brown eyes were bright with tears. Obviously there was more in Riley's words that she either could not or didn't want to share.

"Damn it, never mind that boo-hoo girlie stuff. What about the battles? What's *he* doing? Is he giving it to the Huns? If I was over there, I'd teach them to *par-lee-vooz*, by God," the old man declared.

"Pop, leave her alone," Cole warned, irked by his father's tactlessness.

"Well, the boys at Tilly's count on me to bring 'em full reports."

Susannah handed a bowl of mashed potatoes to Amy, who looked even more distressed than her future sister-in-law. Discord bothered Amy.

Pop went on, oblivious to the tension around him. "Sleeping in the wet—hell, that's nothing. I herded cattle through gully washers and Montana blizzards that blew so hard the cows froze stiff on the hoof. By God, one time the snow was flying so thick the dumb beasts was about to walk right off a cliff. And I've slept out in weather that wasn't fit for the herd or me, with nothing more to keep warm than one blanket and a bottle of whiskey. Cow camp ain't for sissies." He took a big bite out of a drumstick and continued talking around the food. "But I didn't whine, I just kept—"

Susannah put down her fork and glared at him. "I don't suppose that while you were on a cattle drive you had to worry about being blown to the hereafter by a howitzer or stabbed with a bayonet?"

Pop paused with his jaws in mid-chew. "Well, I never knew when I might come acrossed a wolf or an angry mountain lion—"

She folded her hands on the table, so tightly that her knuckles were white and her fingertips red. "And *if* one came along, did it have poison gas that it fired at you?"

"Gas—"

"Did you miss your family while you were out there, not knowing if you would see them again?"

"Naw, that was years ago. I didn't have no family back then, but—"

"I hardly see any comparison, then, Shaw. I'm sorry I can't give you something better to tell those fools at Tilly's. Maybe your stories about cattle drives will interest them. Excuse me." She backed her chair from the table and left the room. Tanner watched her go, then turned a sour look on the old man. They heard her run up the stairs and through the upper hall. In a moment, a door slammed overhead.

"What the hell was that all about?" Pop groused, plainly amazed.

"Are you happy now?" Cole snapped. Susannah had coddled Pop for a long time—spoiled him, as far as Cole was concerned—but obviously she'd reached her breaking point. There was so much work to be done on the ranch, and he knew she worried about Riley, despite the brave face she put on, and Shaw Braddock was as ornery an old crank as a body was likely to find.

Amy sat with her hands in her lap, looking at her plate, her cheeks flushed with embarrassment. Tanner tried to appear busy with his dinner, but all he really did was push the food around on his dish. Wade and Josh stared wide-eyed at the adults until Tanner elbowed them and nodded at their own plates.

"What did *I* do?" Pop asked. "I just want to know how the fighting's going and what Riley is up to in France. I didn't expect her to have the fantods like that." He sopped up some gravy with a biscuit, but his own face was red to the ears, and he wouldn't look anyone in the eye. "Bah, that's the trouble with women—they get all stirred up."

"Yeah, there's something about having a husband at war in a foreign country that bothers them," Cole replied with a knife-edge in his voice. "That's why I should have enlisted instead of Riley. He has everything to lose. I didn't have a thing."

Beside him, Amy uttered a horror-stricken noise, jumped up from the table, and flew to the kitchen. Her muffled weeping could be heard in the dining room.

"Shit!" Cole muttered, and threw down his napkin. He jabbed a finger in the old man's direction. "If you weren't my father, I'd make you bed down in the stables tonight!" He stood and walked out of the dining room as well, leaving just Pop and the hired hands at the table.

— — —

It took some doing, but Cole was finally able to calm Amy and convince her of what he'd meant by his remark at dinner. That he'd had nothing to lose by enlisting *before* he began courting her.

They rode in Cole's truck, not speaking. Only the sound of bouncing springs and creaking metal joints broke the silence as they bumped over the rutted road toward town. It was easier than driving a wagon at night. The vehicle's headlamps lighted the road ahead.

Finally Cole said, "Pop is a mean-spirited old bast—son of a gun. Sometimes I think my mother died just to get away from him."

Amy tightened her jacket around her. Evenings had taken on a definite chill now that summer was leaving them. "Maybe he's the way he is *because* she died. She's been gone for a long time, hasn't she?"

"Yeah, I was eight years old. Your father said something was wrong with her heart, probably from the day she was born. It just quit one day while she was standing in the yard hanging the wash."

"Oh, then she was young."

"Yeah, younger than I am now. She was twenty-seven."

"And Mr. Braddock never remarried. He's probably pining for her, and it's made him bitter and less sensitive to the feelings of others. Maybe he envies us, and Riley and Susannah, for our closeness."

Cole didn't believe her theory, but Amy was always justifying the actions of others and looking for the good in people. If it wasn't there, she manufactured it. "Maybe. Anyway, I'm sorry about that ruckus at dinner."

She touched his elbow briefly. "So am I. It was so silly of me to—how did your father put it?—have the fantods. I felt terrible for Susannah, and then when I imagined you in harm's way with nothing to lose, well…" She turned away to look out at the field zipping past in the purple dusk. "I know it's not patriotic to say this, but I'm glad you didn't enlist. I'm glad you stayed in Powell Springs, where you're safe."

Cole didn't answer. That word popped into his head again and repeated itself all the way into town.

Slacker.

— — —

Horace Cookson's prediction that Jessica wouldn't be busy with patients turned out to be a poor one.

Word of her presence and location spread quickly, and those who didn't trust Granny Mae, or weren't satisfied with her doctoring, began appearing at Jessica's office door on Sunday morning after church.

She treated a variety of ailments, most of them minor. That was a good thing, too, because she'd had no time to really get acquainted with the space and was working primarily from her doctor's bag. It was also fortunate that Horace had been so desperate to find a physician that he'd sweetened the invitation by outfitting the office with a telephone, decent equipment, and a few supplies. Some, she noticed, were from her father's own practice. Along with checking on Eddie Cookson, whose mother seemed capable enough of providing most of the nursing care he required, Jessica strapped a sprained ankle, lanced a boil, and diagnosed a pregnancy, all by two o'clock in the afternoon.

It was almost ten o'clock when she stood in her nightgown breathing in the scent of the soft, clean air. Between Eddie's harsh bouts of coughing, the night was hushed and clean-scented, and a light breeze wafted the lace curtains, bringing in the smells of the season's last hay, mown from the fields beyond the edge of town. It was much quieter in Powell Springs than it had been in New York. There were no noises in the street, no racket of clanging fire engines or wagons and trucks rolling by at all hours.

After she brushed her hair the required one hundred strokes, the gently stirring curtains called her to the upholstered chair by the window. She switched off the overhead electric light and let the moon cast shadows across the floor. As she braided her hair, she looked out at quiet Main Street. The shop windows were dark and if she listened hard enough, the occasional shift of the wind would carry the sound of slow-moving water in Powell Creek. Putting her elbows on the windowsill, she rested her chin in her hands and drew in a deep breath to smell the freshness.

It was nighttime in a small town. Her town.

Even more peaceful than she had remembered at moments of longing for home, it tugged at her heart. This was a very nice apartment, she thought, looking around at the dimly lit shapes. It was certainly nicer than she'd expected. Pearson should be very comfortable here. She knew she would be for the short time of her stay.

She'd had a long, busy day, and fatigue weighed down her limbs. But at least it wasn't the utterly consumed feeling she had grown accustomed to. In New York, she'd known nights when she could barely drag herself up the stairs to her third-floor room.

Despite her exhaustion, though, there had been sleepless hours when she ached inside for the world's broken heart, and would vow to work harder the next day to mend it. But no matter what she did, the world still wept.

Yawning, she crossed the room and climbed into the comfortable, welcoming bed. Sleep approached to enclose her in a soft embrace.

Here, the only broken heart was her own.

CHAPTER TEN

As Cole predicted, it didn't take long for news of Eddie Cookson's influenza to make its way around Powell Springs. By Tuesday afternoon, people had left flowers and notes for him on Jessica's front stoop and in her waiting room.

Then the patients began trickling in, complaining of sudden sore throat, fever, cough, and headache. None was yet so ill that she'd had to put anyone in the other bed upstairs, but she worried that it was only a matter of time. Nearly everyone got the same instructions: go home, get into bed, and stay there. She had the druggist compound more influenza pills for her to dispense and recommended the application of Vicks VapoRub for chest congestion.

Jessica's wires to Seattle and Portland yielded helpful but daunting information.

The Red Cross sternly advised that everyone in town should wear fine-mesh gauze masks to block sneezes and coughs. Their volunteers were making them and they could sell them to Powell Springs for ten cents apiece. She got Mayor Cookson to authorize the funds and placed an order. She also told the mayor the rest of what she'd learned—anything that drew people together, such as church services, theaters, schools, meetings, and parades, should be cancelled or closed. He agreed with her (convinced in part by the alarming condition of his own son, she was certain) and sent a formal public announcement to the *Powell Springs Star*, the town's semiweekly newspaper. The editor thought the proclamation important enough to print an extra edition, which had happened only twice in the periodical's twenty-year history.

The Red Cross asked Jessica if she needed a nurse sent to help her, but she declined. She'd not reached that point. Dr. Martin at Seattle General Hospital made the same cautionary observations, and also mentioned the possibility that an effective vaccine was in development but not yet available.

Helen Cookson took a room at the hotel and remained in town to help care for her son, for which Jessica was most grateful. It gave her a chance to sleep, wash, and change her clothes. Soon the small clinic smelled of sickness, camphor, and Vicks VapoRub.

Now that she had a little help, Jessica was able to escape for a while to meet Amy for lunch at Brill's Confectionery. The shop had a very limited menu—mostly phosphates and sweets—but they'd both heard that Granny Mae was still crabby over the business with Eddie so they avoided the café.

As usual, Amy was neatly dressed and pressed, with shoes that matched her gloves and bag. Her honey-blond hair was curled and swept up into a fashionable hat. Jess was certain only that her own face was clean, her teeth brushed, and her hair combed. But given her last twenty-four hours, she was satisfied with that.

Over egg salad sandwiches and iced tea, Amy stabbed at the newspaper announcement with her index finger. "Mayor Cookson can't mean this! If the bond committee can't meet, how will we raise funds?" In a most uncharacteristic display of temper, she thumped the small marble-topped table with her fist, making the silverware clatter. "It's not fair! No one but poor Eddie Cookson is really sick, and he's practically quarantined in your office. How can anyone else come down with the grippe?"

The counter girl stared at them.

Amazed by her outburst, Jess said quietly, "Shh, people are already getting sick." She revealed some of the information she'd received. "I asked the mayor to ban large public gatherings like church services and to close the schools. I imagine places like this and Mae's might be next."

"*You* did! Jess, how could you? You know how important this is to me."

"For heaven's sake, Amy, this is disappointing, I know, but—"

Her sister's face took on a pinched, suspicious expression. "No, you don't. I've been expecting Cole to take me to the hotel for dinner and propose—" Tears glistened on her lower lids, and she dabbed at them quickly. "I've dreamed of my wedding day for years, and just when I think he's about to ask for my hand, something happens. His work, the ranch, now this. You can't begin to feel, to know, how disappointing it is."

Jess fixed her with a sharp look for several seconds. "I know very well how it feels. You might remember who *I* expected to marry before you—" She broke off the sentence, fearing she would say something she might regret.

Amy stared at her with a flash of guilty comprehension and then dropped her gaze to her sandwich, her cheeks blazing red. "Yes, of course," she mumbled.

They ate in silence for a few moments while Jessica smothered the fierce resentment that had flared within her. In the days since she'd come back to Powell Springs, she'd struggled to put on her best face and keep her hard feelings in tight check. Amy was her sister, her only family, she told herself, blood was thicker than water, things just hadn't worked out between Jess and Cole. She'd conjured every excuse and tired bromide she could think of to get through the days.

But the unvarnished fact was that Amy, sister or not, was planning to marry the man Jess had once expected to have as her own husband. A man who had told her he would no longer wait for her. And though it was probably her imagination, Jess thought that Amy seemed unbearably smug and triumphant about the turn of events.

Pushing her resentment back into a dark corner of her heart, she spoke at last. "I'm sure the ban on public gatherings won't last long. Just until we know if Powell Springs is in danger of a real epidemic. Things have been bad everywhere else."

Her dignity recovered, Amy replied stiffly, "Then I'll pray that Eddie not only gets better soon, but that he'll have the only serious case of influenza."

— — —

Late the next afternoon, Jessica had just sent an order to the druggist's for more influenza pills when she heard someone open the front door. Worried about what might be coming next, she was surprised to find Adam Jacobsen standing in her waiting room holding a bouquet of pink and yellow chrysanthemums.

"Adam! You must be here to visit Eddie." She assumed so, since he was once again Sunday-dressed and didn't seem to be ill himself.

He smiled at her. "Yes. Well, partly."

"And you brought him flowers. How thoughtful."

He stepped closer and handed her the mums. Over the sickroom odors, she caught the faint whiff of hair tonic. Holding her gaze with his dark-lashed eyes, he said, "The bouquet is for you, Jessica."

Though the blooms themselves had no fragrance, the flowers and stems were damp and smelled fresh and green in her grip. Dumbfounded, she stammered, "Me—I—"

He glanced at the floor and looked almost sheepish. "I saw them growing in the yard and they reminded me of you. Golden and blushing pink."

As if on cue, Jessica felt her cheeks grow warm. She hadn't blushed in years. It was an awkward moment, but one that also was a balm to her female ego, somehow. No one had given her flowers in, well, she couldn't remember how long it had been, and now they came from Adam Jacobsen, of all people. She barely knew how to respond. "It's very kind of you. Thank you, Adam."

"I wanted to thank you again for agreeing to take care of our folks for a while." He shifted from one foot to the other. "And I came to see Eddie, of course."

"You know, you probably shouldn't. You'll expose yourself to his contagion."

"That hasn't stopped you from tending to him."

"But I'm his doctor."

"And a noble one at that."

She laughed, thinking he must be joking. Amy seemed closer to noble, knee-deep in her good deeds. "Really, I'm nothing of the sort—" But in his face she saw that he was serious.

He glossed over her objection. "Just as your calling requires you to deal with difficult situations, so does mine sometimes. I'm sure Eddie could use a little spiritual comfort right now. I hear he's pretty sick."

Her smile faded. "He is. He might not even know you're there. He's been delirious a lot of the time."

"It doesn't matter, God is with him. Eddie isn't alone in his darkness. I just want to remind him of that."

Jess could think of no answer to that statement. If Adam was determined to visit her patient, she wouldn't stop him. She gestured at the stairs. "He's up there. His mother is sitting with him."

He nodded and turned to climb the steps.

Jess went to find a vase for the mums, her firmly established opinion of Adam Jacobsen a bit discomposed.

— — —

Midnight settled over the clinic, a lonely time that, in Jessica's experience, began the hours that could bring a new life or take one too weary to survive. These were the hours when the rest of the world dreamed in sleep, or wept in the darkness from loneliness or despair or regret.

Helen Cookson had gone back to the hotel just an hour earlier, and now Jess examined Eddie with growing alarm. Air that should be in his lungs seemed to be escaping into the outer tissues of his failing body, puffing him up like a balloon. Whenever he moved he made a crackling noise like crumpled cellophane. What in the world kind of influenza was this? she wondered desperately. His breathing had become more labored than ever, and the cyanosis—the blue pallor tinting his skin—had grown darker and more pronounced. Muted light from the bedside lamp only made him look worse.

But there was something else, something new. The smell. This wasn't the odor of an unwashed body—Jess had experienced that plenty of times. And it wasn't just from sickness. This was the smell of putrefaction.

Jessica's heart sank.

She reached down to straighten the sheet across his chest and he opened his fever-bright eyes.

"I'm going to die," he croaked in a froggy whisper. It was the first time in the forty-six hours since he'd collapsed in her office that he'd seemed almost lucid.

Jess grasped his hot hand where it lay on top of the blanket. "Do you think so?"

His nod was almost imperceptible, and Jess knew the truth nearly as well as he did. A few times she'd seen people as ill as he was who felt the very life draining from them and knew their time had come.

"I'll get your mother—"

"No," he said, struggling for every breath and word. He kept his grip on her hand. "Stay with…me. I don't…want…to be alone with him."

"Him?"

"He's come to take…me. See?"

Jess felt the hair rise on her scalp as she looked around the room. "No."

He lifted a heavy arm an inch or two and pointed. "Sitting down there…end of the bed…waiting…for me to die."

Again she looked, though she knew she would find nothing. Jess ought to get his mother—the hotel was just a couple of blocks down the street. But she didn't want to leave Eddie. If he died alone, she would never forgive herself.

She thought of the telephone downstairs. The hotel had one, too. But without an operator to connect them, it was just a useless gadget mounted on the wall, like a stopped clock with no key to wind it.

Disentangling Eddie's hand from hers, she went to the window, looking for any living soul on the street below. It reminded her of two nights earlier when she'd hoped to find someone to give him a ride. There had been no one around then, and that had been at six-thirty. Now at midnight, even Tilly's was about to close.

Feeling helpless and cut off, she lifted the sash and stuck her head out to gaze up and down the dark street. There was no one. Only a stiff night breeze carrying the scent of rain. Its first drops hit her in the face. The fresh air was a relief but didn't solve her dilemma. Then, just as she was about to lower the window, she saw movement, someone on the sidewalk below. Straining to see into the darkness, she waited for the figure to step into the square of light cast from her own window.

Cole Braddock. Wishing it was someone else, she was also grateful to see *anyone*. And she knew he would take action.

"Cole!"

He looked up, his eyes shadowed by his Stetson. "Jessica? What's the matter?"

"Please—will you go down to the hotel and get Mrs. Cookson? It's an emergency! I can't leave Eddie alone."

He gave her a short nod and took off a trot. She watched him go, all long legs and lean torso, as he faded into the darkness. Only fleetingly did she wonder why he was in town and on the street at this hour. Returning to the bed, she took Eddie's hand again.

"Your mother will be here in a minute." But he'd slipped back into the shadowy world between life and death, and this time she didn't believe he would come out again.

CHAPTER ELEVEN

Time lost its meaning as Jess sat beside her patient's bed. It crept by while she waited for Helen, and she worried that the woman wouldn't have a chance to say good-bye to her son. But time flew in terms of the moments that were left to Eddie on this earth. With each gurgling rattle, Jess watched the shallow rise and fall of his chest. His breathing had become irregular, stopping for several agonizing seconds before commencing again with a gasp. Outside, rain began to fall in heavy, spattering drops.

"Hold on, Eddie," she urged, squeezing his hand, "hold on. You can't leave us yet. You have to wait for your mother. She should be here any minute." She had no idea if he could hear her.

At last Jess heard a frantic knocking on the door downstairs, and then the rattle of a key in the lock. She ran out to the landing to look over the railing and saw that Cole had let Helen in with his own key.

The poor woman was soaked to the skin. She had obviously thrown on her clothes in a hurry, wearing only a light dress, her bedroom slippers, and no coat. Her hair was plastered to her skull and swung in a wet, braided rope down her back.

"Is he…?" Helen couldn't finish the sentence.

"He's still with us. Go up."

Helen bounded up the stairs, grief already etching her face. Jess patted her shoulder and came down to the clinic to give the mother and son privacy.

In the waiting room, Cole stood by the door, his long frame limber and easy. He was drenched too, and his thin tan shirt stuck to his torso. Though he still wore his hat, his ruddy-fawn hair curled at the ends from the dampness.

"He's dying?" Cole asked quietly.

Jess nodded.

That someone in the prime of life could be taken so quickly was astounding to Cole. "He's only been sick for two days."

Jess whispered, "I know. It's frightening. I wanted to make sure his mother had a last chance to see him, but he didn't want me to leave him alone." She poked at some loose strands of hair framing her face. "H-he said someone is sitting at the foot of the bed, waiting to take him when he dies."

Cole stared at her. "Did you see—"

She shook her head and shrugged. "So I couldn't go for her." She lifted her chin. "I'm grateful for your help. What were you doing out there at this hour, anyway?"

They spoke in hushed tones. "I was just catching up on some chores next door."

"At midnight."

"Well, *you're* awake." And beautiful though she was, she looked as if she'd been up for days. Her white bib apron was stained, and purple smudges underscored her eyes.

"But I'm working."

"So was I." It was a partial truth Cole told her, and he knew she realized it. There was no end of work to be done these days, but he had come into town because he'd gotten bored and restless just staring at the ceiling over his bed. Like Susannah, he hadn't slept a whole night through for weeks. His sister-in-law had a good reason; he wasn't sure of his own. Tonight, instead of tossing and turning until the bedding was a wad at the foot of the mattress, he had gotten dressed and come to the shop.

She searched his face, looking for a better explanation. When they'd been closer, Jess had always been able to tell when he was hiding something from her. He didn't know if it was her woman's intuition or the sensitivity of her vocation. Or just that she knew him so well. He glanced away from her inquiring gaze.

He settled in a chair and Jess sat as well, in an unspoken agreement to keep a deathwatch.

"Have any others gotten sick?" he asked.

"A few, but none as critical as Eddie. Yet."

"You think it'll get worse?"

She nodded. "That was why I followed the Red Cross's recommendation about banning public gatherings. Amy was pretty unhappy about that." She sighed. "She was unhappy with me, too."

He took off his wet hat and turned it in his hands. "I know. She told me she even went to Cookson's office, asking him to make an exception on the ban just for the Liberty Bond Committee and the hotel dining room."

"She did?"

"She came by the shop yesterday afternoon to tell me about it."

"What did he say?"

"He refused. I guess you convinced him to stick to his guns."

"She mentioned that she's been waiting for you to, well..." There was a question in her voice, one that asked for an explanation Cole was not prepared to give.

He shifted in the chair and crossed his ankle over his knee, distinctly uncomfortable. "Yeah, I know. With one thing and another to do with this war business..."

"So she said. I was kind of surprised."

"About what?"

"For a man so eager to get married, I would have expected you to propose to her by now." Her green eyes glinted slightly.

He hadn't forgotten how direct Jess could be. He simply hadn't experienced it lately, and he resented being put on the spot, so he deflected her attack with one of his own.

He uncrossed his ankle and leaned forward, elbows on his knees. "Yeah? Once upon a time, you were eager to get married too. How is it that you can't explain why you wouldn't come home?"

She pulled in her chin like a turtle retreating into its shell and fiddled with her collar. "I don't see any point in discussing that now."

"I think you owe me that much, don't you?"

She sat up a bit straighter. "I don't owe you a thing. You never proposed to me, either. And you're the one who changed... everything."

A question sat in his mind like a burning coal, one that his wounded pride had never allowed him to ask. One that Amy had hinted at but never really expressed. But now, with death waiting to claim a soul upstairs, perhaps waiting to claim others, he reined in his ego. "Was there another man?" They were already speaking in low voices. This question came out in a whisper.

She stared at him, her mouth ajar. "What?"

"Amy mentioned that you told her you made the acquaintance of a doctor's son. Someone named Stafford, Stanton—"

"Dr. Stavers? Yes, I knew him and his family. They were kind enough to ask me to their home for dinner. I went to the theater with them a few times."

"And the son?"

"Andrew?"

He sat back and studied her. "Well? What was he to you? Is he why you didn't come back?"

She rested her forehead against the palm of her hand. Reaching into the pocket of her dirty apron, she pulled out a handkerchief to swipe at her eyes. He couldn't tell if she was laughing or crying.

"Oh, God, there was *never* another man," she said, finally. "There was poverty. There was squalor. And misery and ostracism. I treated immigrant women worn out from hunger and constant childbearing. There were children who died from something as simple as a cold because they didn't have the strength to fight the infection." The words tumbled out, and her expression reflected anger and helplessness. "I saw rat bites on babies who were too weak to nurse, and women with black eyes and broken faces because of the beatings they got from drunken husbands or customers they met in dark alleys. I visited old people who'd been left to die in the corners of filthy, airless rooms barely big enough for four people, but were jammed in with twelve. A lot of the rooms had no windows because they were partitioned off from other rooms so the greedy men who owned those firetraps could make even more money. They were dark, stinking boxes of suffering humanity."

He listened without flinching, but he clenched his jaw so hard he felt a muscle twitch.

"If you haven't seen it with your own eyes, haven't experienced it, you can't understand." Her hands were wrapped around her hankie in a tight knot. "The dogs at your ranch have better lives than those people. That's why I stayed. How could I turn my back on them?"

"But you finally did," he said at last, his throat tight. "Why?"

Jess turned her face and looked at the bouquet of mums that sat on a small table between them. She didn't answer. In the silence, broken only by the soft patter of the rain outside, they heard muffled, wordless sobbing coming from upstairs.

"Oh…dear…"

Cole glanced up, listening. "It's over."

Jess nodded and rose from her chair. "I'll keep him here until morning. By then Fred Hustad will be open and the Cooksons can make arrangements with him. He's still running an undertaking business from the back of his furniture store?"

"Yeah. Do you need anything from me?" He wanted to help her if he could, wanted to do *something*.

To Jessica, it was a loaded question. She could have requested a dozen things from him, none of which was hers to ask for any longer. *Yes, oh, yes, please hold me, comfort me, take these nightmare memories from me, help me to feel alive again, make me laugh again, the way you used to.*

She realized she was leaning toward him, trying to close the gap between them and looking at his mouth. He bent toward her, too, as if unseen hands pushed them both from behind. Her field of vision was filled with his face, the straight nose, the mouth that was neither too full nor too thin, the square jaw and his eyes, fringed with lashes that she'd always envied. He smelled of leather…

The sound of another sob slashed through the quiet, breaking the dangerous spell, and she pulled back.

"No. I'm fine," she lied.

— — —

Adam Jacobsen laid Eddie to rest the next day with no one but his parents to witness the burial. Jessica wanted to attend but she was busy seeing influenza patients, and those who were still well had taken to hiding behind their doors as much as possible. Almost as soon as she had put clean bedding on the mattress upstairs, she had another patient to occupy it, a six-year-old boy, and his mother for the other bed in the room.

With Amy's help, she strung a sheet between the beds, hoping to reduce the exchange of contagion. But Anna Warneke wept so pitifully over not being able to see her child, Philip, that they took it down again. Jess conceded that it probably didn't make much difference anyway.

That night she kept watch over the two, catching naps when she could. Although Philip was certainly sick, he seemed to be doing better than his failing mother, which baffled Jessica. Influenza was known to strike down the very young and the elderly, not people in the strength and prime of their lives.

Anna was not yet thirty years old.

Eddie had been just eighteen.

At lunchtime the next day, Amy and Jess sat at the small kitchen table in her apartment to bolt down quick cups of coffee and sandwiches.

"Here," Jess said, pushing a pitcher of cream to her sister.

"Wherever did you manage to get this?" Amy asked, completely transported by the sight of the cream. She poured enough of the forbidden luxury into her cup to turn her coffee a light beige.

"Horace Cookson. He told me he'd bring me cream and a little butter from his dairy every day. He's grateful that I took care of Eddie, but I'm not sure I deserve this after what happened."

"Take it anyway," Amy said, sipping the coffee with an expression of profound bliss. "You did everything you could, and it's a small gift. It probably makes him feel better."

Below, the door opened, ringing its overhead bell. But the women needed no such signal. The visitor's cough was loud enough to announce his arrival. Jess started to rise, but Amy put a hand on her arm and went to the landing.

She heard Amy call down, "Oh, Mr. Driscoll, Dr. Layton will be right with you. Please, have a seat."

Before Amy returned to her own chair, the bell rang again. "Dr. Layton will be down in a moment, Mrs. Lester." She came back to the table and said quietly, "You have to eat your lunch, Jessica. You look worn out."

Jess *was* worn out. She had turned her office into a round-the-clock clinic. A few people had called on the telephone, begging her to make house calls, but it simply wasn't practical. She had no transportation, and when someone came to pick her up, she found patients waiting for her when she returned. They came night and day. Even when she was able to lie down for a few hours, nightmares of indigent, gray-faced patients and dreams of Cole interrupted her sleep.

She poured a quick dollop of cream into her own cup. "Amy, goodness knows I appreciate your help, but this isn't going to work. We two can't treat all of these patients alone, and we need more room. There are people who have no one at home to take care of them, and they can't be left to fend for themselves. They need to be fed and washed and tended. I have to do something more. Has anyone heard from Pearson?"

Amy shook her head while she swallowed. "Not a word, as far as I know."

"The Red Cross offered me a nurse a few days ago and I told them I didn't need one yet. Now it's already too late, and I could kick myself for turning them down. I telephoned their office in Portland and they have their own epidemic brewing. They're not willing to spare anyone. Will you ask every woman you know if she can pitch in?"

"Yes, although I think some of them have sick families of their own to look after. I hate to suggest this but..." Amy said and trailed off.

"What?"

"Granny Mae isn't running the café now that it's closed under the mayor's orders. I imagine she's probably available." Delicately, Amy nibbled the last crust of her sandwich.

Jess rested her forehead on the palm of her hand. "I know. She's already crossed my mind. I'm not in a position to refuse, but I don't know if she'd work with me."

"Oh, I think she would."

Jess glanced up. "You mean she'd probably *revel* in it, getting the chance to try and show me up?"

A shadow of chagrin flitted over Amy's expression. "Well, yes, probably."

"I don't care about that. I can't. It's the least of my problems."

Her sister dribbled a little more cream into her cup. "Anyway, I know she's already seeing some people who've gotten used to going to her for medical help. You might as well join forces."

The coughing from downstairs and across the hall made Jess swallow her lukewarm coffee in one unladylike gulp. She had work to do. "I'll go talk to her as soon as I get a free minute."

Standing up, she walked to the sink to rinse her cup. "I just hope that old woman doesn't gloat."

— — —

It was late in the afternoon when Adam Jacobsen, clutching his bouquet of chrysanthemums and box of chocolates, walked toward Main Street and Jessica Layton's office. The flowers were the last ones in his yard, and Nettie Stark had picked them herself for the dining room table. He'd grabbed them right out of the vase.

He wondered briefly if the gift of the chocolates might seem too forward, like he was rushing things. After all, he'd brought Jessica the first bouquet just a couple of days earlier. Another was probably all right, but was it too soon for candy? He hadn't had much practice in calling upon a lady. He did know that Jessica's time would be short in Powell Springs if he couldn't win her over and make her stay permanently—as his wife. Ultimately, he'd gone to Bright's Grocery, which was allowed to remain open for business, and bought a Whitman's Sampler. Seeing the bouquet Adam carried, Roland Bright had asked several probing questions, trying to learn who the presents were for. Adam had evaded his curiosity.

He mulled over the procedure of courting Jessica as he walked along, imagining a future with her. Powell Springs was a town of tidy homes and large yards, with trees that had matured enough to offer shade in summer. It was a good place to raise a family. Of course, if he could win Jessica's hand, she would have to give up her work. A woman couldn't devote herself to her own husband and children, and hold the kind of demanding position she had now. By that time, Pearson would be here anyway.

A few children, given an unscheduled vacation from the new school year, played in their yards and on the damp streets. They waved to him as he passed, and he waved back. Gray clouds scudded overhead, and a stiff breeze rustled the leaves of oak, maple, and locust that had begun to turn and drift earthward. It happened every season, it was part of the cycle of life.

But this year the change seemed ominous to him. He felt a dread in the air.

Some houses were quiet, with blinds drawn tightly, although it was only late afternoon. Adam knew without being told that sickness lay behind their doors. His father probably would have said this scourge was God's punishment of an evil world. He supposed it was true, but these were areas of thought where Adam sometimes felt the slightest tremor in his conviction. His father had been unswerving in his certainty of God's plans. But what sin had Eddie Cookson committed to deserve the punishment of an agonizing and untimely death? How were the guilty chosen? Or were they chosen at all? He kicked at a stone in his path. Maybe souls were captured in God's dragnet regardless of their innocence or guilt, like unseen and unsuspecting insects crushed beneath a heedless boot.

The thought was not only depressing, it was frighteningly sacrilegious, so he shook it off. Despite his occasional questions, he held the unwavering belief in the promise of heaven and that paradise was the reward for the righteous. Just as fervently, he believed that the guilty should and would be properly and unflinchingly condemned to eternal damnation.

When he reached Jessica's office, he noticed a few wagons and an automobile or two parked in front. He glanced briefly at his own reflection in the window glass to make sure his tie was straight, then opened the door. In the waiting room, he found a scene he was not prepared for.

The small space was packed with sick people, at least ten or fifteen of them. Every seat, more than he remembered seeing here before, was occupied. Some patients even lay on the floor under thin blankets. Others listed on their chairs, plainly lacking the strength to sit upright. All of them were shivering and coughing violently.

Stunned, Adam let the bouquet drop to his side.

"Mr. Jacobsen," a man called from a seat in the corner. Adam saw Wilson Dreyer, who sat beside his wife, Lily, propping her up. She was Powell Springs's librarian and Adam barely recognized her. She looked as horrible as she probably felt. "You aren't sick too, are you?"

"Um, no, Mr. Dreyer. I was just…" Just what? How could he explain his arrival with the trappings of a man who'd come courting, especially under these circumstances?

Some of the others who noticed him looked up with glazed, fever-bright eyes.

"If you're waiting to see the doc, get in line. I've been here for an hour already," said another man whom Adam didn't know. "But I'm ahead of them," he said, indicating a pair on the floor. The man looked like a drifter, with ragged clothes, several days' growth of beard, and shifty, reddened eyes. One side of his jaw was swollen considerably. Adam made a mental note of him—with the war on, they couldn't be too careful about strangers these days. Spies, the American Protective League told its members, were everywhere.

"Watch your manners. He's our minister," Wilson Dreyer snapped. "And I don't know who you are."

"I don't give a damn if he's the King of England. He can wait like everyone else. I got me a rotten tooth that needs pulling, the dentist ain't in, and the barber won't touch it."

Over the racket, he heard the sound of staccato heels on the hardwood floor. Jessica emerged from the back room, looking harassed but tightly controlled. Her sleeves were rolled up to expose pale, slender arms, and she had on a wilted bib apron, like the kind grocers and soda fountain clerks wore. A stethoscope dangled from her neck. But even in this chaos she was alluring.

"Oh, Adam, it's you," she said. "I thought I heard the bell." She glanced around the waiting room. "There are a lot of people ahead of you."

"No, no, I'm not sick. I, well—" He gestured slightly at the flowers and candy, trying to be discreet. "I didn't realize you were so busy."

Seeing his gifts, her cheeks flushed slightly. "It's very nice, but—" She stopped and considered him. "Come to the back."

"Hey—what about my bum tooth? I was here before him," the seedy man complained, jerking his head in Adam's direction.

"Yes, and I'll be with all of you just as soon as I can." She turned and nodded toward her back office.

"I'm sorry," Adam said, once they were out of the others' earshot. "I guess this isn't very appropriate." He held out the candy and flowers. She took them and put them on the work table.

Smiling, she said, "It isn't that I don't appreciate the thought, Adam. It's just that, well, it's been a…trying day. I had to send Amy home. She's a big help, but she's not used to dealing with this much bedlam."

He felt heartened that he hadn't seemed to offend her. Then from overhead, a child's thin cry reached him. He glanced up.

"I've got two patients in the beds upstairs, but I need more room. I can't use this office to treat all the people who are going to need me. And I can't go to their homes."

"You need a hospital."

She nodded. "Yes, ideally, and Powell Springs doesn't have one. I need more help, too, but I'm working on that part. You're on the town council. Do you know if there's a bigger space available around here? Like—like the grange hall, or a meeting place?"

He thought for a moment. "What about the high school gymnasium? The schools are closed anyway."

"That would be perfect!" She gazed up at him with such a grateful expression that he felt a foot taller. "I hate to bother Mayor Cookson with this—can the town council act without troubling him? Do you think you can arrange for that?"

"Don't you worry. I'll take care of it." Buoyed by Jessica's attention, Adam believed he could manage anything.

— — —

"Well, well. So now you want my help, eh, *Doctor* Layton?"

How was it that some people could make her title sound like a filthy epithet? Jessica wondered. She had dashed through the rain to climb Mae Rumsteadt's stairs with some trepidation. Her uneasiness was not without merit, she realized. She clenched her jaw as she stood in the woman's parlor, feeling most unwelcome. Mae lived in rooms above her restaurant that were cluttered with mismatched furniture and stacks of newspapers. Jess could see a length of clothesline strung in the small kitchen, from which hung bunches of drying herbs and other plants. The smell of rosemary and sage were especially strong.

"I need *every* pair of hands I can get," she said. "People are getting sick and I'm asking for volunteers. I need women to provide nursing care." Jess was practical but not without her pride—she didn't want to give Granny Mae the impression that she was the only person who could help.

Mae's high-cut nostrils usually made her look as if she wore a perpetual sneer, and right now Jess swore she could see all the way up the woman's nose to her frontal sinuses. Her jaw was set, and her smug expression made Jess sorry she had come.

"Well, I don't know," she drawled, plainly enjoying her position. "I'm already taking care of sick folks, myself. You're not getting every patient in town, you know." She crossed her bony arms over her flat chest.

Ignoring her coyness, Jess continued. "Adam, that is, Mr. Jacobsen is arranging for me to use the high school gym as a temporary infirmary. We need the space, and it will be easier to treat people if they're grouped in one spot. We just need to get some people to help us set up."

Mae smoothed the sleeves of her faded house dress and brushed at her apron. "I suppose that might work. I'm not saying I'll do this, mind. I still don't hold with a lot of that folderol you school-learned doctors use. Just because you didn't hear about something at college or read it in a medical book doesn't mean it won't work. I've seen my share of ills and cures in my lifetime, and *I've* got books, too. Handed down to me by my grandmother and great-grandmother. A lot of the remedies came straight from the Indians. They know plenty about healing and natural cures. Like the Bible says, 'The Lord hath created medicines out of the earth: and he that is wise will not abhor them.' There's a reason that kidney beans have their name—they're good for kidney troubles!

Drinking nothing but cold water stops diarrhea. And a good soak in urine will cure ringworm. I told your father and Cyrus Vandermeer the same things time and again, but would they listen to a word I said? Oh, no, they just…"

And on and on. Jessica rubbed her forehead with the fingertips of one hand. She was bone-tired, she had not even been invited to sit down, and the woman was going off on the same tired diatribe Jess had heard so many times before. She whipped her hand back to her side, her arm stiff, and caught Mae's faded blue gaze as surely as if she'd gripped the old lady's dress lapels.

"Granny Mae Rumsteadt, in the name of humanity! I need help, not someone who wants to argue about who's right! I left five patients in the waiting room to come over here, people I haven't even examined yet." One of them was Bert Bauer, the drifter she'd first seen at Tilly's who'd reported the story about a man with a nosebleed. At the time she'd thought it was an outrageous lie, told for the chief purpose of cadging free drinks. Now she knew better. "People in this town are getting sick, and a lot of them, a great deal of them, might very well die. Before I came over here, I checked on Anna Warneke—she's taken Eddie Cookson's place in the bed over my office. She has turned as blue as a new pair of Levi Strauss's denims and she's bleeding from her nose—"

"Did you put a penny in her mouth? Everyone knows a penny in the mouth stops nosebleeds."

"Oh, really? What about the blood oozing from her eyes? Have you got a cure for that in one of your great-grandmother's damned books?"

Mae gaped at her, the tirade interrupted. Apparently, Jessica had finally made an impression on her. "She's b-bleeding from her *eyes*?"

Desperate and out of patience, Jess went on, full of righteous anger. “If you won’t help with nursing, would you at least cook for the sick? They need soup and bland food. Even *I* need to eat.”

The sharp angles and planes of the old woman’s face softened a bit. “Well, I can see you look a little peaked yourself.” Lowering her jaw, she said, “All right, I’ll come. And I’ll cook too. I’ve got some beef bones simmering in the stockpot downstairs right now.”

Jess closed her eyes for a moment and drew a long breath. “Thank you,” she answered hoarsely.

CHAPTER TWELVE

"Let's get this materiel unloaded," Adam Jacobsen ordered from behind a white gauze mask. "Careful with the medical instruments."

Materiel, Cole groaned inwardly. Oh, brother.

Under a sky heavy with dark clouds, Cole once again found himself helping to move some of Jessica's equipment, this time to the high school, three blocks from her office. Jacobsen had appointed himself foreman of this operation, and Cole sizzled under the man's arrogance. He stood at the school's front door, full of importance, with his clipboard, on which he occasionally scribbled a note, tucked under his arm. Several wagons and a car or two were parked in front of the school, loaded with supplies.

It wasn't that Cole minded helping out. In fact, he was amazed at how quickly Jessica had managed to galvanize the town, getting donations of bedding, cots, and other necessities. And there were plenty of volunteers helping with this trail drive. Even Susannah and crusty Mae Rumsteadt had pitched in, although Amy was at home nursing a headache.

What Cole minded was Jacobsen himself. When a man marched down the street in Powell Springs with a bouquet and a box of chocolates, he might as well be waving a red flag and firing a shotgun. People went to their windows to watch. Word got around.

And the word going around was that despite the turmoil of sickness and deaths, Adam Jacobsen had found time to begin courting Jessica. More than one person, including Pop, had taken the trouble to mention it to Cole. He knew he shouldn't care, that it was none of his business. But the notion grated on him like a file on a blister, just as Jacobsen always had. Although the epidemic was shaking the town to its very foundations, or maybe because of it, people were eager to talk about Powell Springs's latest romance. It had raised a few eyebrows, but for the most part, people seemed to approve of the pairing.

"Cole, *please*—wear the mask I gave you," Jessica called from the doorway before she ducked back inside.

"Yes, Braddock, put on your mask," Jacobsen added. Cole sent him a venomous glare. The man broke eye contact first and pretended to shuffle his papers, which pleased Cole enormously. He knew it was childish. Just the same, he wished he could have five minutes alone with God's self-important goody-goody.

White gauze masks had arrived the day before and were being distributed around Powell Springs. Just about everyone here was wearing something over their noses and mouths—masks or handkerchiefs—but Cole wasn't sure they'd really do any good. To keep the peace, he reached into his shirt pocket, took out the mask, and tied it on. Then from the back of his truck, he hoisted a box of sheets to his shoulder and climbed the front steps of the school.

He walked through the hallway that led to the gymnasium, a trip he'd already made several times. The big room, which had barely been used since last June, smelled of the fresh floor wax it had received over the summer. It was a hive of activity now, with people setting up cots, making beds, and unpacking supplies. Jessica was overseeing the tasks in here.

"Where do you want these sheets?" he asked. She stood on the gleaming wood near a teacher's desk that had been brought in for her use. The exercise equipment that usually stood in this space had been pushed to one wall.

"Give them to the ladies down there," she replied, indicating a few women on the far end of the gym. "They're organizing the bedding." Looking at him over the top of the mask, she continued, "I really appreciate you being here, Cole. You've been very… helpful during this whole business."

He shifted the box and backed her into a quiet corner. "I hear Jacobsen has been helpful, too. Everyone seems to know how helpful he's been."

Her gaze darted away from his—it was odd trying to talk to her when all he could see were her eyes. "Yes, Adam arranged to get this space for me. His position on the town council is very fortunate."

"I'm not talking about the town council, and you know it." He dropped his voice to a low, angry tone. "What are you doing with him? We didn't like him when we were in school. No one did, and he's not especially high on anyone's list now. But you're letting him bring you candy and flowers?" He took her elbow and the heat of her skin radiated through her sleeve.

"I didn't *let* him do anything, and I haven't encouraged his attention. It was just an innocent gift." She pulled her arm from his grasp.

"Bullshit, Jess. There's no such thing as an innocent gift when it comes to him. He's still a snoopy tattletale, and now he's one for the government too."

She pulled down her mask, revealing lips that were full and softly coral, and her eyes narrowed. "Honestly, Cole! Are you suggesting that he seduced me with chocolate to worm some kind of information out of me? To make me inform on my patients?"

He felt his face grow warm. "Hell, no, I didn't mean—"

Her brows snapped together. "Do you realize how ridiculous and truly insulting that sounds? That he isn't even sincere about his courtesy to me? And that I would so easily submit to such maneuvers?"

"That's not what I meant!" Sweat and stale air built up behind the piece of gauze he wore on his own face, and he yanked it off. Without it, he could smell the spicy fragrance of her hair and skin, despite the antiseptic odors. It was so familiar. He'd dreamed of it often—and recently.

"No? Then what are you talking about?"

A knot of frustration and raging jealousy burned like acid in his gut. "People are saying that he's courting you." It galled him to even utter the words.

She put her hand to her throat in mock horror and gazed at him with wide eyes. "Why, my stars and garters, the shame of it all! A respectable woman being courted by a minister. Whatever is the world coming to?"

"Is it true?"

"Why is this your business?" she demanded, dropping her hand.

He frowned. "I just don't understand why you'd want to have anything to do with that pissant."

She pressed her lips into a prim, tight line before answering. "My personal life is none of your concern. Not anymore, and you know why. Good God, you sound more like Shaw every day."

Taken aback by the comparison to Pop, he was about to blunder on when Susannah's approach interrupted the scene. She and

Jessica exchanged looks. Susannah's long, dark curls were pulled into a thick tail. She wore a split riding skirt and boots, and Cole knew she'd spent the dawn hours working with the horses.

"Cole, did you bring the bed linens? We're putting all that down here." Susannah pointed to a group of assorted china cabinets they were using for storage. Each bore a sign that read "Courtesy of Hustad's Fine Furnishings."

Swearing under his breath, he turned abruptly and walked away, wondering why life had become so damned complicated.

— — —

By that afternoon, patients had begun occupying the cots in the gymnasium. The volunteers hung sheets to create separate men's and women's sections, and there were patients on both sides. Granny Mae brought over a kettle of beef broth from the café, as she had promised, and it sat on a wood stove in a nearby classroom, ready to feed the hungry.

But most of Jess's patients were too ill to eat. The sickest of Powell Springs's citizens straggled into her makeshift infirmary, delivered from the backs of wagons and cars. A couple even wobbled in on foot. And they all came with an astounding variety of symptoms. Some she would expect with influenza. Others, such as hemorrhaging from the nose, mouth and eyes, petechial hemorrhages—bruise-like marks under the skin—ruptured ear drums, and of course, the frightful omen of cyanosis, ranging from gray-blue to indigo, were particularly horrific and baffling. The sounds of coughing, groaning, retching, and incoherent rambling echoed off the ceiling and walls of the big, open room. Every news dispatch she'd managed to get reported that this was influenza, and that it was mowing down people all over the world, but she swore that some of the symptoms resembled those of typhoid and cholera. She had never seen anything like this.

As for the rest of the globe, well, Jessica's own world had shrunk to this one, the town of Powell Springs.

Now, as night fell, she sat for a moment at the teacher's desk in the corner and massaged her temples, contemplating the miserable panorama of cots and sickness.

Granny Mae, dutifully wearing her mask, perched on a stool beside shivering six-year-old Philip Warneke and sponged his brow.

"Mama," the boy cried weakly, his dark hair damp and his eyes fever-glazed. "Want Mama."

"Hush, now, young man. Your mama is resting, and that's what you need to do," Granny said.

Jess supposed that what Mae told the child wasn't a complete lie. Anna Warneke was "resting" in the cloakroom, wrapped in a sheet and tagged, waiting with two other victims to be taken to Fred Hustad's undertaking business. She had died shortly after being moved to the school. Philip was an orphan now. His father had been killed in France last June.

Touched by the child's pitiful circumstances, Granny had taken charge of him. An asafetida bag hung from her neck, containing the most foul-smelling of mysterious concoctions and long believed by many to ward off disease. Afraid to ask what was in it, Jessica was grateful for her own mask, which helped block the fumes. If she weren't so desperate for Granny's help, she would have made her remove the vile thing and bury it behind the school. But she knew that would spark an argument and the woman's possible decampment, which Jess could not afford.

For the time being, an uneasy truce existed between her and the tough old lady, and she was glad for that. How long it would last, though, was something she had no time to think about. The rest of her masked volunteers, frightened but biddable, followed her directions without much question. One and all, the patients' chests had been slathered with Vicks VapoRub, had a piece of flannel stuck to the salve—to help it penetrate to the lungs, Granny said—and been dosed with the morphine pills made up by the druggist.

What could Jess do for these people with such puny weapons? She felt as if she were fighting a swarm of locusts with a flyswatter. Nothing in her training or experience had prepared her for this. But then, what modern physician had had to deal with a plague in recent times?

Given everything she'd read, and what she'd seen here with her own eyes, she was ready to concede that this influenza was more than an epidemic.

It was indeed a plague.

— — —

It was nearly eight o'clock by the time Jess walked back to her office. Although Powell Springs was a quiet place at night, now it almost seemed abandoned, as though everyone had left suddenly to escape an oncoming and unseen invader. She tightened her coat collar around her throat, trying to hurry her tired steps as a chill wind moaned through the trees and swirled dead leaves around her. Streetlights were few and added little illumination to dispel the feeling of gloomy emptiness that hung over the town.

At last Cole's smithy came into view, and her own office beside it. She flogged her draining energy, as if pushing a spent horse toward a finish line, and reached her door. Out of breath and her heart thumping, she rooted around in her pocket to find the key.

No sooner had she gotten inside, locked the door again, and begun climbing the stairs, than she heard someone knocking.

"Oh, please no," she muttered. For a moment, she was tempted to skulk here in the shadows, then tiptoe all the way upstairs where she wouldn't be seen.

The knocking continued.

With a weary sigh, she turned and went back down the steps. In the darkness she could see only the shape of a tallish man through the door's glass pane. "Who is it?" she asked.

"Jessica, it's Adam. I've brought you some dinner."

She twisted the switch that turned on the light and opened the door. Adam stood there, bearing a wicker hamper. Beyond his shoulder, she could see his horse and buggy tied to a hitching ring at the curb down the street.

"How thoughtful of you!" A snippet of her earlier conversation with Cole ran through her mind, but she pushed it away. She was hungry and tired, and Adam had brought her something to eat. Cole had not. "Please—come in. I just got here myself, and I dreaded the idea of having to cook. I'm not very good at it on the best of days."

He stepped inside and closed the door, bringing the smell of fresh food with him. Jessica's mouth watered. "I stopped by the school first, but you'd already left." He lifted one side of the lid and peeked into the basket. "Mrs. Stark put something together in here. Roast beef, I think. And if I know her, probably some other things, too. I hope it's still hot."

"I don't care if it's cold, it smells wonderful. I haven't eaten since early this morning. Thank you, and please thank her for me, too. It's been a very long, hard day. But probably for you as well?" She took off her coat, and he hurried to put down the hamper to help her, brushing the small of her back as he did so. He hung the wrap on the coat tree.

"I visited a couple of families. They're frightened and grieving."

She could understand that. She was frightened too, though she dared not show it to those counting upon her.

"I offered what comfort I could," he said. "I tried hard to make them understand that when God takes our loved ones, there's a good reason we mustn't question."

Yes, what consolation that must be, Jess thought tartly. It should make little Philip Warneke feel much better about being an orphan. Adam had brought her dinner, so she didn't give voice to the observation. But she'd always resented the type of religion that Adam's father had taught, which allowed no room for inquiry or exception to interpretation. Although Adam didn't seem quite as inflexible as Ephraim Jacobsen, she detected pronounced similarities of thought.

She lifted the hamper lid and pulled out a napkin-covered dish of sliced roast beef. "Would you like to join me?"

"No, no, I brought this for you."

She dug a little deeper and found plates, silver, and napkins. "Hmm. It would seem that Mrs. Stark had other ideas. There are two place settings in here, and a lot of food. Even peach crisp with a pitcher of fresh cream."

Adam wore a sheepish expression. "I guess she remembered that I haven't had dinner."

She looked at him with raised brows. "Then I guess you should."

It was such a transparent maneuver she could think of no other response.

He smiled and straightened his tie. "All right."

Since it would be unthinkable to invite Adam upstairs to her kitchen table, they moved some waiting room furniture to the back office to create a little dining area on a small table between two chairs.

"We didn't leave you with much, did we?" Adam commented.

This part of the place looked picked over and disorganized, as some of her equipment and one of her cabinets had been moved to the high school.

"I'll probably be spending most of my time at the infirmary, anyway."

Jess had to stop herself from falling upon the food and ripping at a piece of beef with her teeth. But she managed to devour the tender pieces she carefully cut up with her silver, ate a mound of Mrs. Stark's wonderful mashed potatoes, and savored a buttermilk biscuit. At last, when her hunger began to wane, she relaxed and small talk sprang up between them. Eventually, conversation grew more specific.

"Did anyone else come to the infirmary after I left?" Adam asked, his napkin tucked into his shirt collar.

"Yes, several people, desperately ill. I felt guilty leaving them."

"Who were they?"

She put down her fork, and again, Cole's angry accusation swept through her mind, putting her on her guard unwillingly. "Adam, you know I can't tell you that. It would violate physician-patient confidentiality."

He finished a biscuit dripping with melted butter. Jess noted briefly that Adam hadn't placed the same dietary restrictions on himself that the rest of the country was expected to endure. Cream, butter, beef—many people were doing without these. "I didn't realize it was a secret. I saw some of those people myself before I left."

Strictly speaking, that was true. He *had* seen some of her patients and through his own work knew many of those who had succumbed. She nodded. "I know. But it's part of my training and I can't let it go. Just as you wouldn't tell me if someone came to you and, say, admitted that he'd committed adultery."

"No." His gaze slid away from hers and he shifted in his chair. "No, of course not. Although I'm not sure the comparison is equal."

"I suppose it isn't. But it's still sensitive information."

"Tell me about your work," he said, shifting the subject. "I know you're planning to go to Seattle. I suppose after New York, Powell Springs must seem pretty tame and backward to you." While Jess dished up the peach crisp, he poured coffee for them both from the Thermos bottle Mrs. Stark had included in the hamper.

She spread a napkin on her lap. "A lot of people seem to think that I'd feel that way, but I don't. It's not backward." For a moment, her thoughts misted over and she remembered the beauty of the area. "New York was a lonely place. I missed the slower pace of life here, the sight of rolling farmland settling down for winter, or waking in the spring, the peace. In fact, under different circumstances, I'd rather be here than anywhere else." The response popped out of her mouth before she had the chance to stifle it. She hadn't even admitted it to herself, and yet she knew it was true. Nothing had brought that fact home to her more poignantly than the soft, quiet nights, even during her all-night vigils with patients.

Adam leaned forward eagerly, so close to her that Jess drew back in her chair. "Really. And what would it take to keep you here?"

She wasn't about to reveal to him, of all people, the secrets in her heart. He seemed nice enough, but..."Nothing. I have a job.

As soon as this flu epidemic is under control, or if Dr. Pearson gets here, I have to go. I'm expected and needed in Seattle."

He covered her hand with his own where it rested on the arm of her chair. His palm was slightly damp. "You're needed here, too."

"I have been over this with several people, Adam. I've talked about it with Horace Cookson, too. I'm sure Dr. Pearson will do a fine job for Powell Springs. As for Granny Mae, she's always had her followers, and they're free to go to her if they want."

He tightened his grip on her hand. "I'm not talking about doctoring." He drew a deep breath and exhaled a stale smell of roast beef and coffee in her face. "I'm talking about a different life, with a husband and children. A woman's life."

Jessica felt her eyes widen. "Adam, what—"

At that moment, the front door swung open, ringing the overhead bell, and shut again. The sound of boot heels on the flooring suggested the presence of a man.

"Jessica?"

Oh, no…

Cole walked into the back room, bringing with him the clean scent of the night. With his appearance in the doorframe, the atmosphere in the room changed. Jess started, and Adam tightened his fingers on hers.

Cole carried a small wooden crate. "Jessica? I saw your light—" His eyes fell upon Adam and the cozy dinner scene, and his expression hardened. "Sorry. I didn't realize you had a caller."

"Adam was kind enough to bring dinner to me." Realizing that Adam still held her hand, she snatched it from his grip with some difficulty, her spine as stiff as a celluloid collar.

Cole glared at him. The feeble overhead light shadowed his eyes. "Uh-huh. There seems to be no end to your good works,

Adam. Susannah had the same idea. Well, sort of the same idea, since the only spooning she mentioned has to do with the bread pudding in here."

"Don't you knock before you barge into a room?" Adam demanded.

"I didn't realize I was interrupting anything. I guess that's your buggy parked halfway down the street, then, huh? Afraid someone might recognize it?"

Annoyed, Jess throttled her napkin, but Adam stood up. "What are you implying, Braddock?"

Cole's grin was sardonic. "Why, not a damned thing. I came to deliver Susannah's pork chops and pudding, and that's all *I'm* doing. How about you?"

"Your mind has always been in the gutter, hasn't it," Adam snapped, his face splotched with color. "When we were boys, and even now, a grown man, you still—"

Although Cole was egging him on, Jess was surprised by Adam's quick, rude anger. "That's all, both of you! I'm not going to put up with your bickering. This day was hard enough."

Adam sat again, plainly trying to recover his dignity. "I apologize, Jessica."

Cole gave her an even look that asked the same question he'd posed earlier in the day. *What are you doing with him?* But he only put the box on the work table and said, "Susannah was worried about you."

"I appreciate it. Please let her know."

He tugged at the brim of his Stetson and turned to leave. "See you around." He gave Adam a lingering glance but said nothing more. The sound of his steps retreating to the waiting room was followed by the opening and closing of the door.

"I've sometimes wondered how your sister got involved with a man like him, so earthy and lustful." Their eyes met, and he seemed to remember that Jess, too, was once *involved* with Cole. The memory of the embarrassing summer day by the river so long ago hung between them like a photograph. That sweet, desperate summer day…

After an awkward moment of silence, Jessica began stacking their dishes. The moderately pleasant rapport between them had fizzled, and Jess wished for nothing more than to be rid of Adam so she could go upstairs. "I should wash these before you take them back to Mrs. Stark."

"No, no," Adam said, taking the plates from her and putting them back in the hamper. "I don't expect you to do that. It wouldn't be much of a treat if you have to work for it."

"Thanks. I still have patient chart notes to make."

"I'll get out of your hair, then." He picked up the hamper and she walked him to the door. Facing her in the doorway, he shifted the hamper from one hand to the other. "Jessica, about what I said earlier…about staying in Powell Springs…"

"Oh, Adam, I don't think—"

Before she could finish the sentence, he pulled her to him with his free hand and planted a passionate beef-and-coffee-flavored kiss on her mouth. His tongue sought hers and Jessica made a muffled noise and managed to push herself away.

"*Adam*!"

"I'm sorry, but I—you—" He rushed on, as if he might lose his nerve or she might interrupt before he could have his say. In the faint light, his face was more animated than she'd ever seen it. "You don't know how long I've thought of you, wished for you. Every time you came back to town, I thought—I hoped—but always, always there was Braddock. Now—" He put down the basket with a clatter of dishes. "Jessica, I'm not wealthy, ministers aren't meant to be wealthy. But I would be a good husband and provider to you and our children. You would still be able to serve mankind and God, in a whole new way. As my wife." He was slightly breathless after his declaration.

Jess stared at him, flummoxed. She supposed he'd been courting her, with the flowers and chocolate, but she hadn't anticipated such an abrupt proposal. In fact, with everything else that had been happening, she hadn't given it any thought at all. She wasn't sure how to refuse without being downright rude. Marry Adam Jacobsen? "This is such a bad time," she began.

He nodded. "I know this must seem sudden to you, and maybe not appropriate, given the present circumstances."

That was an understatement.

"But, Jessica, lovely Jessica." He brushed her hair with the back of his fingers. "This plague only makes the situation more urgent. What if…what if this is the end?"

A shiver ran down her back. "The end. Of what?"

"What if the world as we know it is finally breathing its last? We already have war and pestilence."

The end. No, no, that would mean there's no hope. That everything I'm doing here, everything I have ever done, is futile. That I can't make any difference at all. Her pulse began to pound in her temples, and images of sick, ragged human scarecrows, lodged in tiny, airless rooms—the same ghosts that haunted her dreams—filled her mind. She scarcely heard what Adam was saying.

"…famine, and I would want you with me. Even if it's not the end, I don't want you to leave Powell Springs. I want to spend the rest of my life with you. You don't have to give me an answer now. But please, promise me that you'll at least think about it."

Dumbstruck and feeling dizzy by the grim pictures parading through her head, Jess could think of nothing to do but stare with her mouth open. He grinned and leaned forward to kiss her again, but she pulled back.

"All right, then. I'll leave you for now. Tomorrow I'll come by the infirmary to see you and to comfort the afflicted."

Jess watched him walk away, terrified not by his horror story that the end of the world was coming, or even so much by his proposal. Terror ripped through her heart that this pestilence, as he called it, could steal more lives than anyone had imagined.

And perhaps her own sanity.

CHAPTER THIRTEEN

"Another whiskey, Cole?" Virgil Tilly asked, holding a square bottle of amber liquid.

"A short one." Cole stood at the end of the bar, upwind of Winks Lamont. Next to Winks, Bert Bauer hunched over the counter, nursing a beer of his own. Shaw Braddock sat at a table next to the stove, dealing himself a game of solitaire and scowling at the cards. When he thought no one was watching, he peeked under the seven face-down stacks to see what they hid.

Winks gripped his glass between two hands. "You must have done some fast talking to keep Cookson from closing down this place, Virgil. 'Course over to Bridal Veil, that town went dry by choice." He shuddered, as if the very idea was enough to give him the jimjams. "Just about everywhere else is shut up tight, except Bright's and Main Street Drug."

Virgil fiddled with a display of cheap cigars that sat on the bar near the beer tap, his ever-present bar towel slung over one shoulder. "Poor old Horace has been moving in a fog since his boy died. He hasn't said anything about closing me, and I'm not going to mention it. Leave well enough alone, I figure. He just asked me not to serve food." He went on to name several other people who had died in the past few days.

As critical as circumstances were, all of this was just background chatter to Cole, who stared into his glass and saw the image of Adam Jacobsen at that happy little picnic with Jess. They'd both frozen like two raccoons caught in the headlamps of his truck when he walked in on them. And, Jesus, but Jacobsen had been touchy and defensive, as if he'd been caught with another man's wife.

Cole had gone straight to see Amy afterward, hoping to cool his indignation. But she was still struggling with the headache she'd had for two days, and that only gave him something else to think about. She'd been working too hard, and now she'd worn herself out. People caught influenza when they were worn out. Mrs. Donaldson had made her promise to see Jessica the next morning, and had her lying back in a parlor chair with a cold cloth on her forehead. The woman clucked and fussed over her, so he knew she was in good hands.

Worse, now, though, he felt more awkward around Amy than ever, and he sensed that she knew it. She'd peered at him, as if through her female intuition—that mysterious ability no man understood—she could read his thoughts.

He shouldn't feel awkward. Everyone loved Amy. Everyone except—

"Cole, what're you looking so hangdog about?" Pop piped up.

There was the eternal question. If only he could get rid of the feeling that he'd made a horrible mistake, a life-changing, God-awful blunder. How could the old man read him so well, yet seem to know so little about him? Cole retreated behind a good excuse, one that he even believed himself. "People we know are dying, Pop. People we've known for years, and anyone could be next. I'd say that's pretty damned gloomy."

For a change, Pop didn't make some tactless remark. He nodded solemnly and went back to cheating at solitaire.

"You ought to go see your woman. That'll make you feel better." This advice came from Bauer, unsolicited and out of the blue. The man had been fairly quiet since he appeared in town, keeping to himself. There was something about him, though, that put Cole off. "Give us another couple of beers here, Tilly," Bauer said.

Virgil pointed at the sign that warned he didn't run tabs for anyone. "Can you pay for more than the nickel beer you already ordered?"

Bauer slapped a dollar on the bar.

Tilly cast a suspicious gaze at both him and Winks. "Where are you two getting your money? I haven't heard about anyone hiring around here."

"Well, I guess you don't hear everything, then. Winks and me, we got jobs."

"Yeah? Doing what?"

"Digging graves in that cemetery behind the school. Seventy-five cents each." He wore a smug expression.

Everyone in the saloon stared at him, as if waiting to see if he was just making a bad joke. Even the stuffed elk heads appeared to look over the scene with their glass eyes.

Bauer's brows rose, lifting the brim of his battered hat. "What? Fred Hustad hired me to help Winks. Those dying friends of yours need to be buried, and the undertaker's got more business than he can handle. It's damned hard work, I'll tell you. Some of those stiffs smell worse than Winks, here, even through the coffins. At least the graveyard is convenient. We just move 'em outside from the infirmary. Hustad doesn't have time to embalm all of them. He's getting five, six a day."

"Jesus Christ," Cole muttered, disgusted. He hated to think that anyone he knew was put in the ground by Bauer. At least Winks had the good sense to keep his attention fixed on his beer, and added nothing to the conversation.

"Oh, regular nabobs, now, huh?" Virgil remarked with a hint of derision, and filled two glasses from the tap. "Lighting your cigars with ten-dollar bills, drinking champagne out of some woman's satin shoe?"

The jab obviously went over Bauer's head. "Speaking of women," he went on expansively, "are there any around here who know how to show a man a good time?"

Virgil brought the foaming lagers to the bar. "Yeah, there's one, way up on Butler Road. But you'd have trouble finding her place in the dark. You'd better go during the day."

"Which way on Butler Road?"

Cole knew Em, and he didn't think she deserved to be burdened with a creep like Bauer, with his mean, red-rimmed eyes and pointed, ratlike face. But he kept that to himself. While Virgil gave Bauer directions to Emmaline's place, Cole drained his glass and turned to his father. In his mood, it wouldn't take much more of Bauer's yapping to make Cole punch him in the mouth. "Come on, Pop. Let's get on home. It's been a long day."

The old man griped, "*Now,* damn it? I'm winning this hand!"

"Don't worry, you can win at home too if you cheat like that."

"Cheat!" Pop blustered some, but unbent his creaking joints and got to his feet without further argument.

— — —

Early the next morning, while a chill east wind drove raindrops against the walls of the building, Jessica stood in the back room of her office gathering some medicine bottles to put in her doctor's bag. The bell rang over the front door, and she heard Amy's voice.

"Jessica?"

Thank God, Jess thought, her sister was better. She needed her help, and Frederick Pearson was still only a name with no tangible presence. "Back here, Amy. I'm just about to leave for the infirmary. There's some coffee in the pot on the hotplate." But when Amy appeared in the doorway, Jess took one look at her and knew she wasn't better. Not at all.

"You can't work. You look terrible." A woman who was always so careful about her appearance, today Amy wore her damp hair in a ragged tail tied with a piece of wrinkled ribbon at the back of her neck. She'd wrapped an old shawl over a dress that she saved for doing hard jobs like laundry and housecleaning, and her stockings both had runs in them. Dark smudges gave her eyes a sunken, bitter look. At odds with her shabby dress was a pair of expensive-looking cameo earrings.

Amy wilted into a straight-backed chair and stared at her shoes in a blank, fixed way. "I'm not here to work."

Jessica frowned. Her sister's appearance was downright alarming. She stepped over and took Amy's wrist between her fingers to feel her pulse. "How do you feel?"

"I have a headache, but mostly I'm just so tired. I barely slept last night."

Jess pulled a thermometer from her bag and poked it into Amy's mouth. "I don't wonder why. You've probably worn yourself to a nub," she said. "You've been busy with your committees and helping me. I'm sure it's just too much."

Amy took the thermometer out again. "No. I could handle those things. It's the worrying that has me undone and I've come to have my say."

Baffled, Jess asked, "Your say—what are you worried about?"

Her sister slanted an odd look at her. "Cole. And you."

She got an icy feeling in her stomach. "Why?"

"He came to see me last evening. He's unhappy that Adam Jacobsen is courting you."

"Oh, well," Jess said, quietly relieved, "you know they never liked each other."

"No, Jessica. It was more than that."

She considered her sister and crossed her arms over her chest. "What then?"

"I know he's jealous about Adam."

The icy feeling was back. "Jealous! Oh, now Amy, I don't think so. We—he—" She was irked with Cole for putting her in this position. "Cole made the decision to end our *understanding*. I didn't."

"I know, but I think he regrets that decision. And I *know* you do—I've seen the way you look at him. I'd hoped that it was over between you." Her eyes, at the same time bright with fever and anger, narrowed into slits of rancor.

Astounded by the accusations and Amy's dudgeon, Jess pressed her lips into a tight line. "It is over. He broke it off between us and began courting you. Your imagination is running away with you because you're sick. Please put the thermometer back in your mouth."

"You always got everything you wanted, didn't you?" Amy went on, ignoring Jessica's direction. The pitch of her voice climbed with her agitation. "You got all of Daddy's time and attention. I was the boring daughter with more homey interests. I remember you two in his office, staring into a microscope for what seemed like hours at some disgusting blob on a slide. As far as he was concerned, I was just someone who lived under the same roof. When Mother died, I might as well have been part of the furniture. He was proud of *you*, he bragged about *you* until he died. But after you left, Cole got tired of waiting for you and he finally noticed me. He realized how much more I could offer him as a wife. At least I thought he did." Vitriolic resentment poured out of Amy like the long-simmering infection from a lanced abscess. "I should have known you'd try to lure him away, even though I've loved him since I was twelve years old!"

Jessica's heart thumped in her chest, giving her a sick, breathless feeling. Her mouth was dry with shock. This woman was not her sister. She had never heard Amy utter a harsh opinion about anything or anyone. "Maybe Cole shouldn't marry at all," she replied coolly, trying to maintain her composure. "Have you thought about that?"

"No! It's not true. He should marry me. He gave me these earrings! I wish now you had never come back."

"I'm sure you do. You probably didn't spend any sleepless nights worrying about *my* feelings before you beat a path to Cole." Jessica hadn't meant to blurt that out, but she wasn't going to let Amy use her as a whipping post.

Amy stood up and threw the thermometer on the floor. Shards of glass and gleaming beads of quicksilver skittered around their feet. "You didn't deserve him. You went off and left him. I gave him a chance to understand how a real wife should behave, a doting, obedient, loving wife."

"A real wife," Jess repeated with no little asperity.

"I'm going home." A sudden burst of coughing interrupted her tirade. When she recovered her breath, she added, "Mrs. Donaldson might not be a blood relative, but I'd rather have her take care of me than my own kin."

Jessica reached out to stop her. "Amy, wait. I want to at least go back with you to—"

Amy threw off her hand. "Thank you, no. I will manage myself." She rearranged her shawl like a queen adjusting her robes, though the ends hung limp and uneven. She walked out to the waiting room.

Jess followed her. "Amy, don't be foolish. You could be ill, and I don't want you walking home alone in this rain."

A glassy-eyed, wild-haired stranger spun to face her. "I don't answer to you, Jessica. I am my own person."

Both distraught and insulted, Jess watched her sister open the door and walk down the street toward Mrs. Donaldson's house.

— — —

Emmaline heard a knock on her door and caught a quick glance in her filmy mirror before she went to open it. As if her appearance mattered to *them*. They slapped their money on the bureau or the kitchen table and didn't pay her much notice as a person. Truthfully, she didn't notice them either, unless they were too awful to blank out. Or unless they were worth remembering, like Frank Meadows, or Cole Braddock, who hadn't visited her since that brief spell when he was between sisters. But in a tiny corner of her heart, the part that remained untouched by everything that had happened to her, she still had her pride. She straightened the sash that held her worn dressing gown closed and lowered her eyelids in a practiced expression of sultry interest.

When she turned the knob and pulled open the door, though, her eyes flew wide. The man on her porch had a face she would never forget. And one she'd never expected, or wanted, to see again.

"Hi, there, little lady. I hear you entertain gentlemen." Lambert Bauer stood there on her stoop, grinning at her with an idiotic leer that she supposed he thought was irresistibly virile.

"Gentleman! You—*you* a gentleman, Lambert?"

He peered at her, slack-jawed with surprise and looking worse for wear. His clothes were muddy and he had a few days' worth of patchy beard growing on his narrow, angular face. Time had been no friend to his features.

After gawping for a moment, he found his voice. "Emmaline? Well, by God, Tilly didn't tell me he was sending me to my own wife for a roll in the hay! What do you think you're doing, a married woman turned whore? I've been looking up hill and down dale for you."

"Why?"

The question seemed to amaze him. "*Why*! Because. You're my woman. That's reason enough." He might as well have said that she was his saw or his pocketknife—just another possession. He gripped her forearm with a dirty hand.

"You mean you're down on your luck and broke again."

"No, that's not what I mean." His whiny, mimicking words dripped with sarcasm, but she could still read him. "Who are you to talk, anyway?" He gestured at her and her little shack. "What the hell do you think you're up to, turning into a trollop?"

"An abandoned woman has to earn a living. No one died and left me a gold mine or a big inheritance."

He didn't look the least bit ashamed or seem to realize he had a thing to do with her present circumstances. "Well, I'm sure not going to pay you for my husband's rights." He began to push his way inside. "I'm getting what I came for, so you just go on in there and—"

In an instant, she recovered from her paralysis and pulled her arm away. Memories flooded back, of beatings and cheatings, of arguments and belittling, threats and intimidation. In a surge of anger, fear, and astonishment, she grabbed the loaded shotgun she kept beside the door. She was a fair shot, too. Living in this remote place, if a customer turned mean or a coyote got into her tiny henhouse, no one was going to come to her rescue.

She aimed the double barrels at him. "You get off my porch and keep on going, Lambert. I ain't your wife anymore. You slapped me around for years and then left me in Parkridge. Our marriage ended that day. I'm long done with you."

"Is that so?" He straightened, full of righteous indignation. Far too much for a man on the business end of a gun. "Well, I've got news for you, missy. You can't just decide—"

She raised the weapon to her shoulder and pointed it at his weaselly mug. "You git, and don't come back here again."

Popeyed, he finally backed down the two rickety steps that led to her door and stood in the yard. His mean face was flushed with rage, but he kept his gaze on the barrels of the shotgun. "I know my rights. I didn't get no dee-vorce papers and you're still my wife. I'll bet that thing ain't even loaded."

With hands that were much steadier than her insides, Emmaline aimed at a pinecone hanging from a ponderosa branch above his head and squeezed the trigger. The blast flushed out dozens of birds, and sulfurous blue smoke filled the air. A shower of pulverized seeds rained down on him, making him jump as if he'd been hit by lightning.

"*Goddamn* it!" He danced around like a man who'd stepped in a hornet's nest. "Are you crazy?"

"Want me to blow off your hat next?"

"You've gotten pretty sassy in the last few years. Well, this isn't over, Emmaline!" He thumped his chest with his forefinger. "I'll be back, and I'll bring the county sheriff with me."

"Whitney Gannon? He visited me just last month. Give him my regards." She blasted a branch off the same tree, which missed him by an eyelash when it crashed to the ground. Lambert swore a blue streak, and she got a lot of satisfaction watching his skinny shanks trot him down the drive that led to the road.

"This ain't over!" he shouted again from the edge of the property. He launched this last threat from behind the safety of the overgrown blackberries and weeds before he took off down the road.

Em slammed the door, threw the slide bolt, and sank into the closest kitchen chair. Her heart galloped in her chest so fast and hard, she felt it was all her ribs could do to contain it. Her hands turned cold and shaky. Tremors spread through her limbs, and she shivered on the hard chair. A faint wave of nausea rolled through her. Oh, God…dear God…

She reached for her pack of Lucky Strikes on the table—one of the few luxuries she permitted herself—and lit a cigarette with a hand that held a shaking match. Drawing deep on the tobacco, she sought to calm her frazzled nerves.

Lambert Bauer.

How—why—after all this time, why would he turn up around here? *Why* wasn't it over? What could he want with her now? And damn that Virgil Tilly for sending him to her place. Of course, he hadn't known the connection between her and Lambert.

What about the kids? Lambert hadn't even mentioned them. Did he know about the boys? She raked a trembling hand through her hair. No, he couldn't. No one knew about them. Only she and one other person knew where they were. Not that Lambert had ever been a father to them. What kind of man could leave a wife with two little boys and still call himself a father?

It was the hardest thing she'd ever done, letting them go, but it was a decision she'd made with love. Most of what she earned went into a bank account in Twelve Mile to pay for their keep. Sometimes she let herself dream of a day in the future when the three of them would be together again. But Em was nothing if not practical. It wasn't likely to happen, and pretending that it might only made her heart ache.

She stared at the sagging iron bed on the other side of the room. She'd made that bed many times.

And she'd learned to lie in it.

— — —

Over the next few days, Jessica tried every remedy she could think of to treat her patients. In desperation she employed plasters, elixirs, tonics, extracts, and distillations of various sorts. She also dispensed aspirin, over Granny Mae's objections that it was poisonous. Though everyone received the same diligent treatment and conscientious nursing, some lived, but many died. For all her training and experience, Jessica had no idea why. She'd never seen anything quite like it, but she took to heart each life lost or saved.

Those who clung to life, she silently cheered on, seeing each as a victory over death. Those who did not survive gave her a gloomy sense of defeat. Death vanquished her frequently.

Adam spent much of his time at the infirmary, visiting each sickbed, offering comfort and prayers to the afflicted. She heard him recite the twenty-third psalm so many times, it seemed to have worn a groove in her tired brain. More often than not, though, when she looked up, she caught him watching her expectantly, as if waiting for her to accept his proposal, right then and there. In the midst of this pandemonium, he arrived each day with some small gift for her, a handkerchief, a volume of poetry, a lace doily that had been his mother's. None was too personal, yet given the circumstances, she found his attention annoying and inappropriate.

Added to all this was the memory of her recent horrible conversation with Amy. Jess tried to console herself with the reasoning that her sister's words had been flung in haste, and that she was overwrought. But even that wasn't much comfort.

Late one afternoon, she decided she had to get away for a few minutes, away from the rows of cots with their tossing, delirious occupants. She'd had about five hours of sleep in the past three days, and those hours hadn't been contiguous. "I'll be outside, Mae," she said quietly.

The old woman nodded as she sponged Helen Cookson's brow with a damp cloth. Horace had delivered her in his wagon when she collapsed at home. Mae stepped in to care for her. Jess didn't mind. She had enough patients of her own. In any event, some of Mae's hostility had withered after she'd seen for herself the influenza's devastation of bodies—the ruptured eardrums, the broken ribs, the hemorrhaging, the indigo pallor.

Still wearing her stained apron, Jess stepped out the back door of the school and massaged the tight muscles in the back of her neck. She pulled down her mask and took a breath of clean, crisp air, trying to clear the sickroom stench from her nose and lungs. The rain had stopped earlier in the day, and now the sky was sharp, crystalline blue, the color that only autumn could produce. Boiling kettles of laundry stood in the grassy area to her left, filled with soiled bedding and gowns. To her right, a galvanized stock tank burned the contents of chamber pots that had been carried outside and set afire with kerosene.

But the universe continued about its business, the sun rose and crossed the sky, and the earth settled down for the peace of winter, completely untouched by the doings of the humans who lived and died upon it.

The moon did not care that men were making war on each other in the trenches in France.

The stars that would appear in a few hours had no concern for those whose lives were being snuffed out like candle flames by an organism no microscope could see.

As she stood there, she wished she'd gone to the front door instead. From this spot she could see the old graveyard that had been here before the school was built. The two were separated only by a baseball field and the low, wrought-iron fence that enclosed the place where so many were now being laid to rest. Every family member she'd ever lost slept beneath its turf—her grandparents, her mother, her father, who'd been her rock and her inspiration. She'd never realized that Amy had so resented it…

As if pulled by an unseen hand, Jess left the back porch and strode across the grassy field toward the cemetery. In a distant, less populated area of the acreage, she recognized Winks Lamont and that dreadful Bauer man, both plying shovels to move mounds of dirt beside a large willow tree. Only their upper torsos were visible as they worked in the graves they dug. Nearby sat three coffins, waiting.

Traditional funerals, with mourners and dignified, elaborate ceremonies, had by necessity turned into assembly line affairs. Those families who wished for a few words to be spoken over their departed loved ones often could not attend because they were sick themselves. The dead had to be buried as soon as possible because it would be so easy for them to stack up, as they had in other cities. So they were put in the ground, their location noted, and plans for more formal rites were put off till some time in the future.

Jess averted her gaze and made her way down the rows to a granite headstone that was newer than many of those here. Just two years old.

Benjamin Andrew Layton, MD

Born July 3, 1860

Died January 15, 1916

Beside his grave was her mother's. She missed her mother, with her wry humor and loving common sense, but losing her father had affected Jessica most. Fallen leaves fluttered over the graves, driven by a brisk wind, and she wished more than ever that she could talk with him. What would he do, faced with this catastrophe? Was there a treatment, a remedy that she'd overlooked? With her crushing responsibilities and no one to turn to, she had never felt more alone in her life.

Her legs shaking with fatigue, Jessica dropped to her knees beside her father's grave. "Daddy," she murmured, reaching out to touch his headstone as if it were a shoulder. "Daddy, I don't know what to do. I don't know how to help these people. They're dying horrible deaths, no matter what I try." She talked to him for several moments, telling him of her trials with the epidemic. Then, more haltingly, she whispered the private things in her heart. She rested her forehead on the hand that gripped the stone, and as she spoke in a hushed, almost prayerlike tone, tears spilled down her face.

"I hate Cole for giving up on me. But, God help me, I still have feelings for him." There. Amy had not been wrong about that. Jess had admitted it, if only to the silence of a grave. But just as it would not repeat her secrets, neither did it give her the counsel she so desperately sought.

"Jessica!"

Hastily, she wiped her tears with the back of her sleeve and looked up. Cole, of all people, trotted toward her with quick, long-legged strides. She frowned. Didn't he realize he was intruding on her privacy? Despite his other failings, it wasn't like him to be so dense. As he drew closer, though, she saw that his face was the color of cold ashes.

He stopped on the opposite side of her father's headstone. "It's Amy. I drove her here in the truck. She's got it, Jess, she's got influenza."

CHAPTER FOURTEEN

Cole paced the front end of the gymnasium while Jessica and a couple of other clucking, fussing volunteer nurses put Amy to bed in a recently-vacated cot. Though the walls and high ceiling echoed with the harsh, wheezy coughing of those patients who languished behind the curtained-off area, to Cole's ears Amy's hack seemed louder and worse than the rest.

He hadn't been here since the morning he'd helped Jessica move in. Now fully occupied with the sick and dying, the place had the quality of a waking nightmare. God, just the smells of sickness, disinfectant, camphor, and eucalyptus were enough to drive a person out into the street. He'd tied his bandana over his face, more to filter out the odors than to protect his own health. And with the coughing he heard the same awful sound he'd heard the morning that Eddie Cookson died, a peculiar crackling noise some of the patients made as they moved. Before she'd gotten sick herself, Amy had told him the cause was air trapped in the patients' tissues.

" '...restoreth my soul...' "

Adam Jacobsen's voice drifted to him like a distant sound picked up on a windy day.

" '...the shadow of death...' "

Cole winced at the words.

" '...thou has laid me in the lowest pit...thou hast afflicted me...' "

Damn, why didn't Jacobsen just invite Death to drop by and pick up another goner? Cole wondered, disgusted by the man's choice of prayers. He rubbed the muscles in the back of his tight neck. If a person wasn't dead yet, listening to Jacobsen might just send one over the edge.

Cole chafed at his feeling of helplessness. It wasn't in him to just sit by in the face of trouble. He'd always taken action, determined to do *something*, even if it turned out to be the wrong move. From his limited vantage point, he watched for Jessica to emerge from Amy's cubicle, guilt and regret nibbling at the edges of his determination to keep his head.

Amy would get well. She had to. If she didn't—

No, she would. Then...what?

— — —

Jessica stared at Amy's nearly lifeless form, which looked as bruised and disfigured as a flower that had been crushed under a wagon wheel. Right now, at this terrible, frozen moment, all of her training and expertise drained away, leaving her as stunned and horror-stricken as every other person who had watched a loved one hover near death.

And worse, all that training seemed worthless, because she didn't know what to do to save her sister. The genteel girl of her childhood, one so different from herself, now lay here, ravaged by a disease over which Jess had no power. She folded her hands into a single tight fist and put them to her mouth. "Oh, my God... why? Why Amy?"

"You'll do everything you can, Jess. Just like you've done for everyone here."

Her eyes hot and her throat aching with unshed tears, Jessica had forgotten that Cole was standing on the other side of the cot until he spoke. He'd pulled the bandana off his face, and his voice was low and rough with emotion.

She looked up at him and thought she saw her own guilt and wretchedness reflected in his eyes. Her first instinct was to reach for him in this time of unspeakable calamity. "I should have forced her to come here as soon as I suspected she was ill. But I let my pride and hurt feelings get in the way of my better judgment. We quarreled about—" She stopped then, remembering who she was talking to, and her anger shifted.

"About what?"

"About you," she blurted.

"Me!"

"She said you changed your mind about your feelings for her, and that it was my fault. Mine! We both know it's because you can't really give your heart to *anyone*!" She wanted to lash out at someone over the unfairness of everything—the all-too-human blunders and bad choices, the twists of fate and timing that had put the three of them, inextricably bound, in this situation. It was so much easier to hurl blame than to accept the unthinkable.

It worked. What color remained in Cole's drawn face drained away, emphasizing the faint stubble of his russet beard. He looked as if she'd reached across the bed and slapped him. But Jessica didn't feel better for her outburst. Rather, it sapped what little strength she still had. Just as he opened his mouth to respond, her brief anger fizzled, and she sank to her knees beside Amy and took her hot hand. A garbled sob tried to work its way up Jessica's throat, but caught there, unuttered.

"*Dr. Layton*." Adam Jacobsen appeared from behind the partition of sheets. "Everyone can hear you," he said in a disapproving whisper, "and I'm sure you don't want to create a scene." He glowered at Cole, but Cole didn't flinch.

She felt Adam's grip on her shoulders, pulling her to her feet. "There's nothing more you can do for Amy right now. You should go home."

He tried to turn her away from the bed, but Jess, fixed on a single thought, held fast. "Are you out of your mind? I can't leave her and the rest of these people!" Everything—the room, the scene, even the colors of things—had an unreal, dreamlike quality.

"You can't do anything else for them right now, either. I'll walk you to your office. You need to rest."

Jess pulled away from him, but his hands tightened. She found no comfort in his touch. In fact, she shrank from it and his offer to help. "Adam, let me go. I don't want to rest."

"You're not thinking clearly."

She tried to twist away again. "Adam—"

Cole stepped around the bed and pulled Jess out of the man's grip. "Now who's making a scene, Jacobsen? The lady said no. Go back to herding people into the valley of death, or whatever you do, and butt out of this. It's family business."

Adam's face reddened with resentment, and more than ever his arrow-shaped nose seemed to be on the verge of touching his mouth. "*You're* not family."

"Any way you want to look at it, I'm closer than you. So back off!" Cole didn't raise his voice, but there was no arguing with the authority it carried. Even though Jessica's emotions were a jumble of terror and irritation, she felt a sense of relief at Cole's intervention.

A muscle jumped in Adam's clenched jaw. His mouth flattened into a tight, white line, and he spun around and walked away.

When he was out of earshot, Cole said, "Jess, you really ought to go home, even for a little while. The women will see to Amy. You've said yourself that good nursing is what these people need most."

She looked at her sister, moaning in her delirium. It was a hard choice to make, but she was tired. "Yes, I suppose. But only for an hour or two." For a brief moment, she wilted against him, grateful for his strength. Then she saw Fred Hustad and Bert Bauer come in through the back door to collect the dead from the cloakroom they'd turned into a morgue. She knew there were five sheet-wrapped bodies in there.

Straightening at the sight, she whispered, "Cole, please—if—no matter what happens, please don't let that horrible Bauer man take her. I've seen how he treats the—please don't let him—and Winks is just—" She shook her head, unable to finish the sentence. She'd heard rumors that Bert Bauer had been seen at saloons in Twelve Mile and Fairdale, paying for drinks with pieces of jewelry he claimed to have "found." There wasn't much question as to where he'd gotten the goods, although no one had actually come forward to identify a family heirloom that should have been buried with its owner or returned.

His gaze followed hers to watch them carry a corpse outside. "It's not going to come to that. She'll get better."

She reached out and squeezed his wrist with more strength than he would have believed she had. "*No*. You have to promise. I need you make the promise and not break it."

He looked her straight in the eyes. "I—don't worry. I'll take care of it." His voice sounded as tight as her nerves felt. Satisfied, she let herself lean against him again, just for an instant. In Jess's dull confusion, she thought she felt his lips brush her forehead. What a nightmarish world this had become—she had to contemplate having Cole bury her sister because the only other people available to do it were a greedy ghoul and a simpleminded alcoholic.

He steered her around the partitions and past the beds of the sick. "Mae, Jess is going home for a bit." The old woman was pushing a tea cart that held soup bowls and a big kettle of broth for those who were strong enough to eat.

Jessica sensed the gazes of the other volunteers touch upon her and then slide away, as if the women didn't know what to say. Or perhaps they worried that her misery would seek their company in the sickness of their own kin.

"I'll watch over Amy," Mae said, "never you mind. We'll manage till you get back." She handed a small, napkin-wrapped bundle to Jessica. "I made you a chicken sandwich. You might not be hungry, but I expect you to eat it. You have to keep up your strength."

Jess was glad that she and Granny Mae had maintained their tentative truce over the past days and nights. Jess had come to rely on Mae's sturdy practicality and unflappable calm in the face of emergencies. When both Bright's and the drugstore had run out of Vicks VapoRub, reflecting a national shortage due to the epidemic, Mae had concocted a reasonable substitute from her own store of essential oils and petroleum jelly.

Jessica believed that Mae had developed a grudging respect for her dedication and hard work. She'd even admitted that not all of Jess's medical knowledge was bunk. At times, she had felt the older woman watching her. She'd known that Mae was looking for a chance to criticize or seize upon what she thought was a mistake. But at least when she'd questioned her, she'd listened to Jess's explanations.

Now, Mae shifted a moist-eyed glance to Amy. "You run along and rest for a while. We'll come for you if there's an emergency."

"I'll give you a ride," Cole offered.

Gripping her chicken sandwich, Jess wavered, then sighed. "All right."

She stopped at the desk to take off her apron and pick up her bag, unwilling to leave the leather satchel behind. As they walked out of the building, Jessica caught Adam's cold glare on them.

Then he made a note on his clipboard.

— — —

"Tell me about my boys. Are they all right? Are they well?"

Emmaline sat across from Tanner Grenfell at her wobbly kitchen table. He made the trip up here to Butler Road every couple of months or so to give her reports about Wade and Joshua. She wasn't sure if it was a kindness or curse, because listening to him only made her miss them more. But she couldn't quite bring herself to tell Tanner to stop coming around.

Green wood in the stove made for a smoky fire. The smell seeped into everything, but it cut the chill. Although she was fairly isolated up here, word of the epidemic had reached her. She would allow no customer through her door who so much as coughed once or looked the least bit sick. But she couldn't afford to stop working completely. Business had dropped off as it was, so today she wore a faded print house dress instead of her faded dressing gown.

"They're just fine, Em, growing like weeds. The schools are closed so they can't catch the sickness there."

"Are they good at their classes?"

"Yes. I know you want them to get their book-learning. I'm not much at helping them myself, but Miss Susannah makes sure they keep to their studies. Since she's been helping at the hospital, though, she won't let me or the kids into her kitchen. We're getting by on my cooking in the bunkhouse." He grinned. "I'm pretty lousy at the stove, too, I guess. Josh says he's tired of bacon and spuds, but we're not starving. And I know she's just being careful."

"She still doesn't know about—well, me?"

"Not as far I know. It's for sure the boys don't."

"Do they ever ask about me?"

He glanced away, plainly uncomfortable. "Not so much anymore."

She propped her chin on her hand and toyed with her package of Lucky Strikes on the table. "After three years I guess they think I gave up on them, just like their worthless father."

"No, they don't. I've told them what you wanted me to, that I'm their uncle and you're in a tuberculosis sanitarium in Colorado." He shrugged. "It leaves the door open if the day ever comes that you want them with you again."

Emmaline straightened. "You know damn well that I want them! I just can't—Tanner, you know better than anyone. You're the one who found me wandering down the street in Parkridge that night, looking for a doctor after Lambert broke my cheekbone. As much as I hated him, when he left us I didn't know what to do."

He held up a hand. "I know, I know, don't get your hackles up. I'm sorry I put it that way. I know you love them." Leaning forward, he put his elbows on his knees and looked into her face. "But it didn't have to be this way. You could have come with me and I'd have taken care of both you and the boys."

Yes, she could have accepted his offer. He was young—about ten years younger than she was—and kind, modest and reserved in his ways. A good man. Even nice-looking. His sandy hair and smoke-colored eyes reminded her of a patient draft horse. But it hadn't mattered. Nothing would have changed her mind.

"Oh, Tanner, we've already talked about this. You did more than enough taking the kids. I don't know what would have happened to Joshua and Wade without your help. But Lambert cheated you out of a lot of money on that phony cattle scheme of his. I didn't think it would be fair to load you down with his wife too." Absently, she studied one of the bare beams overhead. "Anyway, I didn't want to answer to no one after him."

He straightened his long frame and slung one arm over the back of the chair. "I don't have to tell you I wish I'd never met that son of a bitch. He took every dime I had saved, and I was young and dumb enough to let him talk it out of me. But I figure it worked out because I was there when I was needed."

Dropping her gaze, she looked at his mild eyes. "He's in Powell Springs, you know."

"So I heard. If not for Josh and Wade, I'd go after him and beat the shit out of him for everything he did to all of us. He's not such a tough guy, for all that he likes people to think he is."

She heard the bitter edge in his voice and felt a cold shrinking inside. "But you won't, will you? Then he'd find 'em for sure. I don't think he knows where they are now."

"Stop worrying. I said if *not* for the boys. They need to be raised right, and he's not the one to do it."

She relaxed her spine again and let out a breath. "I wish he'd just leave. I don't worry for myself so much, but the kids..."

"I don't think he'll be going anywhere soon. He's digging graves these days for the undertaker, and he brags about how much money he's making at it."

Em shuddered. "God, that would be just like him, that lousy snake. He came up here, but—"

Instantly, Tanner tensed like a startled bobcat. "*Here*? He found you?"

"Yeah, but I showed him the working end of my shotgun and sent him skedaddling. You're right—when it comes down to it, Lambert is really just a yellow-dog coward. I blew off the tree limb over his head, and he took to running."

He started laughing. "I wish I could have seen that."

She went on to describe the rest of Lambert's visit, and the threats he'd hurled from the safety of the blackberry hedge. Tanner laughed. "I guess he might come back, but Lambert never had any truck with the law, at least not willingly. Anyway, I let him know that Whit Gannon is an acquaintance of mine." She didn't tell him that she'd shivered in the darkness for hours after Lambert had gone, trying to regain her composure and courage.

"You be careful of him, just the same. There's no telling what he might do." Tanner's expression sobered a bit. "You've got a lot of spunk, Emmaline."

She waved him off. "Oh, hell, I just do what I need to in order to get by. But this sure isn't the life I thought I'd be living twenty years ago." She looked down at the tabletop again, unable to bear the charity she saw in Tanner's face. If she took it to heart, it would chip away at the fragile wall she'd built around her soul.

Silence fell between them and over the cabin. Outside, a scrub jay, probably the last of the season, let out a harsh squawk in the thinning afternoon light.

Em cleared her throat. "Listen, Tanner, I can't begin to tell you how grateful I am for what you've done for my boys all this time. I...well, I don't expect any visitors this late in the afternoon, so if you'd like..." She let her voice trail off and she tipped her head toward the bed, scented with cheap rosewater. It was the first time she'd made the suggestion to him.

He lurched upright in his chair as if stung by a bare electric wire. Color filled his face. "Oh, Jesus, no, ma'am! I mean, it's not that I don't appreciate—Em, I couldn't do that to you—" He stuttered and stumbled over his words, until she put a hand on his arm.

"It's okay. I only want to thank you." She sighed slightly. "It's all I've got to offer."

Briefly, he covered her hand with his before pulling away. "I'm not worth that much."

She studied him for a moment. "You're worth a whole lot more."

— — —

Jessica and Cole did not speak during the short ride back to her office. Their silence was broken only by the Ford's chugging engine and the creaking complaint of its joints. The single wiper flapped spasmodically over the glass as a spritz of rain dotted the truck's windshield. On the western horizon, a bright band of the day's last sunlight defied the heavy gray sky before full darkness fell.

Cole's gut twisted with feelings of guilt and, vaguely, dishonor. Aside from his failure to enlist in the army, dishonor was an alien iniquity to him. Shaw Braddock would not tolerate any behavior in his sons, other than typical boyish pranks, that would disgrace him or the family name.

This, though—maybe the old man wouldn't see this as shame. But Cole did: he'd told Amy a lie, a big one. He hadn't meant to, but he had, and he didn't know how to undo it.

On top of that, mingled with the guilt, was the fact that she had every reason to believe that he would propose and marry her. But he hadn't been able to find the right moment.

Now fate or God was getting even with him by giving Amy influenza. She was just a sweet, innocent bystander to his fickle heart.

Jessica slumped in the seat next to him as they pulled up in front of the office. Setting the brake, he asked, "Have you got something more to eat than that sandwich Granny Mae gave you?"

She looked down at the small bundle still clutched in her hand. "No. Maybe. Actually, I don't know."

He considered her in the lowering dusk. "Do you have coffee in there?"

"Yes, and Horace keeps bringing me fresh cream."

"Come on, then." He jumped out of the truck. "I might not know much about cooking, but no broncobuster worth his salt can't make coffee."

She sighed. "Cole, what's the point? We have nothing left to say to each other."

He peered into her tired face. He disagreed, but this wasn't the time to say so. There were so many things to be said. "Look, Jess, there's not much I can do right now to help with anything, and I'm just no good at feeling so useless. I'd consider it a favor if you'd let me help you."

Briefly, she closed her eyes, hesitating. "All right." She stepped out of the truck, not waiting for him to help her, and walked across the sidewalk to her office. She fumbled in her pockets for the key, but Cole pulled his out first.

"I've got it." He turned the knob and opened the door for her. Once inside, he locked the door again.

"The cream and coffee are upstairs." Jess flipped on the overhead light. Its incandescent bulb cast harsh shadows on her face, making her look even more tired. Climbing the steps to her apartment, she didn't bother to see if Cole was behind her. It was obvious that she expected him to follow her. Though her skirts carried the hospital smells they'd just left, he detected the faint fragrance that he'd always associated with her—one of dark wood and spice.

It was nothing like vanilla.

In the little apartment kitchen, he took charge. "You have a seat," he said, directing her to a chair at the table. He stoked the fire in the stove, and soon the damp autumn chill fled to the corners of the room. "Where's the coffee?"

She dropped into a chair and gestured in the general direction of the kitchen. "In the hoosier, top right cupboard."

Cole found the coffee, ground the beans, and soon the room was filled with its rich redolence as it perked. Without help, he also located the cups, cream, and spoons. He searched for something to go with the coffee—Granny Mae was right, they had to eat. The best he found was a loaf of bread and a square of butter on a saucer. Jessica hadn't been wrong about her lack of food.

But then as Amy had often reminded him, Jess had never had much talent in the kitchen.

He'd never cared.

Although the bread looked more like scraps by the time he'd butchered it, he was glad for the distraction. But he could feel Jessica's eyes on his back as he puttered.

"Eat your sandwich," he said over his shoulder. "The coffee's about ready."

Satisfied to see her nibbling on the chicken, he balanced the cups, coffee pot, and other stuff to carry to the table. He'd never had much talent in the kitchen, either.

"Sorry about the bread," he muttered, putting it down.

Jessica looked at the uneven hunks he'd sawed off the loaf, then smiled. "It would probably look the same if I'd done it." Mae's sandwich tasted good, but she ate mechanically, simply because she knew she had to.

He poured coffee for both of them. Then he sat down in the chair across from her and splashed a drip of cream into his coffee. "How long before you know…how will we…"

"How will we know if Amy is going to live?" Jessica's interpretation of his stumbling question sounded blunt and clinical, even to her own ears.

He sighed. "Yeah."

"I wish I knew. Some people who ought to die seem to hang on through sheer will or what I can only call luck. Others I expect to improve don't survive. Some people who've been exposed again and again seem to have immunity, but I've had cases from outlying farms that have had no visitors." She put down the sandwich and rubbed her temples. "Talk about feeling useless—that doesn't begin to describe how I feel."

Cole nudged her foot under the table with his boot. "I've never seen a useless person work as hard as you."

"It's not difficult to look busy when you're running around like a chicken with its head cut off."

"So you're not really busy?"

"Of course I am. But I'm scared too."

"You? Jess, I don't think you've ever really been afraid of anything in your life." He said it not as a compliment, but as a statement of fact.

"What on earth makes you say that?"

"You've tackled jobs that would have knocked some men flat on their backs. And you've succeeded."

"Obviously, you haven't listened to some of the things I've told you."

He stared into his cup. "Trust me, I heard all of it."

Suddenly a pocket of pitch exploded in the wood stove, sounding as loud as a gunshot in the quiet room. Jessica flinched.

Cole laughed, startling her even more. "Hey, remember that Halloween night we snuck up to the Leonards' house? You weren't scared that night."

She grinned then, the cloud of doom hanging over her suddenly lightened. "I haven't thought about that in years! You had those firecrackers left over from the Fourth of July. And I was so scared!"

His own grin showed off the dimples that she'd always found endlessly fascinating and attractive. "Amy heard us plotting and made us take her along or she was going to squeal to your dad. We made her the lookout, but she was so nervous and jumpy, I thought she'd get us caught before we even started."

Jess stirred her coffee. "Yes, she never had the heart for adventure, and I think she was all of ten or eleven at the time. When you climbed the trellis and got to the top of the Leonards' roof, even I was sweating. I could see the whole family through the window, holding some kind of prayer meeting in the parlor. Then you dropped those firecrackers down their chimney—"

By this time, they were both laughing, the kind of desperate, happy, hysterical laughter that sometimes overtakes people in their darkest moments. Tears streamed down Jessica's face.

"*Blam, blam, bang-bang-bang—*" Cole imitated.

"Oh, I wish you could have seen them. You missed it all, up there on the roof. They jumped in every direction, knocking over chairs, prayer books flying. Old man Leonard grabbed his shotgun and actually pointed it at the fireplace! Poor Dolly dove under their dining room table with the kids."

They laughed until they exhausted their wind, then drew breath and began whooping again. Cole slapped the tabletop a few times, howling until he'd emptied his lungs. By this time, she had a cramp in her side. Someone watching would think they'd taken leave of their senses.

His face red with the exertion, Cole said, "He was probably expecting the devil to leap out of the flames into their parlor, armed with a pitchfork. But then I got hung up in that rotting rose trellis of theirs while I was trying to climb down. The whole thing gave way. That was when he came outside. He practically yanked the front door off the hinges."

With mock seriousness, Jess said, "I was sure my heart stopped then. At least there was no moon that night, or he would have spotted you, lying there in the flower bed. And Amy, she was hiding in their privet hedge, wringing her hands and crying." She dissolved into high-pitched giggles again.

"Jesus, he would have shot the first thing that twitched. All I could do was stay there and not move a muscle until he went around the house in the other direction."

"Then we *ran*. I didn't know I could move that fast. I had to grab Amy and drag her along or she probably would have hidden in those bushes all night."

"I was scratched up from those roses. They had thorns like arrowheads." He looked at his bare arms, revealed by his rolled-up plaid shirtsleeves. The scars were no longer visible, only the muscle and sinew of a man who'd worked hard for years.

"You're lucky you didn't break your neck."

"We were *all* lucky we didn't get caught. I thought Amy would spill the beans for sure."

"Actually, I thought she would, too. She's such a poor liar. But no one ever found us out."

"I was scared to death they would."

She raised a brow. "You told me you weren't afraid that night."

He waved off the comment. "Yeah, well, I couldn't let you know. I had my sixteen-year-old ego to defend. But old man Leonard would have staked me out in his backyard and let the dogs eat me. He's such a sour crank."

Their laughter finally faded, like a rocking chair that had coasted to a gentle stop, leaving a palpable silence.

"We had some fun back then, didn't we?" Cole said, a bittersweet catch in his voice.

They'd had more than that. They had a history together, one that began in childhood. "We sure did. Before everything got… complicated." She bit on the sandwich crusts, but they'd dried out so she pushed them aside.

"Jess, I wish you had come home to stay when your father died, instead of going right back to New York."

"Sometimes I wish I had, too. I learned a lot in New York, but I'm not certain I'm the better for it. It cost me my peace of mind. I still have nightmares about the things I saw."

His eyes locked with hers, his gaze pinning her to her chair. "No, I mean I wish you had come home—to me."

Jessica's heart squeezed in her chest like a fist. Her throat turned dry and felt as if she'd swallowed a burr. "How can you bring that up now?"

To her utter surprise, he slid off his chair and dropped to one knee beside her. His eyes never leaving hers, he reached up with one work-roughened hand and pushed loose strands of hair away from her face. The backs of his fingers grazed her cheek, and goose bumps bloomed on her entire body, giving her a delicious shiver. Then his hand snaked around the back of her neck and pulled her face down to his. She felt his warm breath, smelled the scent of him, and she was powerless to stop him.

She didn't want to stop him.

His lips touched hers, tentatively, seeking. For that instant, all the years and hurts and betrayals fell away. This was Cole Braddock, the man she'd always loved. She remembered his kiss well, yet it felt brand-new at the same time.

She pulled back, her breath coming fast. "We can't do this," she protested.

"I know." Then he kissed her again.

CHAPTER FIFTEEN

Adam Jacobsen sat at his desk, a sheet of blank paper in front of him. These days, there were no Sunday sermons to compose. Tonight, another writing activity would occupy him.

Outside, the October night had fallen with a clearing sky that made the darkness as black as velvet. His desk lamp provided the only light in the house—he'd come straight to this task as soon as he'd gotten home. Nettie Stark had gone home hours earlier.

He took up his pen, dipped it in his father's inkwell, and with decisive strokes addressed a letter to the lieutenant of his APL platoon. He had a special appreciation of the American Protective League, with its carefully managed organization of captains and companies, lieutenants and platoons. Sometimes he even envied bigger cities and their large financial and industrial employers. Often a majority of the workers were members and reported to leaders at their jobs. Because Powell Springs was a small community, Adam was the only operative in town. His leader, a banker in East Portland, oversaw operatives in other nearby towns as well.

Adam didn't go out of his way to trumpet his association to anyone—an operative was not supposed to disclose his membership or show his badge. But most people around here knew about it, and he was certain this position gave him status that he wouldn't have as a mere clergyman. A minister in the organization might not be common, but he probably wasn't the only one.

Now he sat back in his chair to compose the lines of his weekly report. He generally identified those people he deemed to be unpatriotic—draft dodgers, slackers, or those who did not buy Liberty Bonds or follow the recommended rationing system. He noted overheard conversations that even hinted of sedition or complaints about the war. Anyone whose patriotism was in the slightest doubt was subject to investigation. In fact, he had mentioned Mae Rumsteadt in a couple of previous reports for her dual offenses of refusing to buy bonds and not observing any of the food rationing requirements. Strangers and foreigners were also high on the list of persons to watch, though there weren't any foreigners around here.

He had a sheaf of notes to work with this week, but one name above all others kept coming to mind.

Cole Braddock.

He really had no concrete accusations to level against Braddock. The man's exemption from the draft was a sore point with Adam, but acceptable to the government. There had to be something, though. By his very attitude, Braddock had displayed hostility and contempt for him again and again. Adam disliked him, it was true, but he knew that he wasn't driven by pride, envy, or even personal animosity. No, indeed. There was something unpatriotic about Cole Braddock, and he was going to find it.

Adam always worked for the good of the country. And though he might not be with the Expeditionary Forces, he was still a soldier in God's army.

He sat forward, dipped his pen again, and began writing.

— — —

Jessica pushed Cole away from her. "Stop it," she demanded, her face tingling from the scrape of his beard. "We won't do this!"

He sat back on his heels and looked at her, his eyes dark with an emotion she couldn't identify—stronger than desire, more fierce than lust. His breath came in short, jerky gasps, and her own heart beat like rolling thunder inside her rib cage. With a shaking hand, she pushed her hair away from her face.

"Amy, my sister, *your intended*, is lying in a cot in the high school gymnasium, hanging onto life by a thread, and you—I—" Jessica sputtered to a stop, then finally said, "How dare you?"

Frowning, he stood up. He filled the little space with his presence, and wrath pulsated between them. "Why didn't you come home? I've asked you so many times, but you've never given me a straight answer. You promised you'd come back and marry me. Instead, you strung me along for more than a year, then out of the blue I got that goddamned telegram from you, telling me not to wait any longer. *Why?* And don't give me any of that bullshit about the poor and sick. Were you so busy trying to fix the world's broken heart that you never thought about anyone else's?"

Jessica stared at him. "Out of the blue? *Out of the blue!*" She jumped from her chair and marched to her bedroom to rummage through a trunk. She threw clothing here and there, things she hadn't unpacked, until she found what she was looking for. It was a ribbon-bound packet of letters, on top of which was the wire she'd received from him before she'd sent her own reply.

She pulled it from the stack and stormed back into the kitchenette. He'd taken to pacing the small space like a feral, caged animal, his obvious fury barely contained. She shoved the envelope under his nose. "Here! Does this look familiar?"

He yanked it from her hand. "What is it?"

"It's the telegram I got from *you*. There was nothing in this that would make me want to come home. After everything we'd meant to each other, you can't begin to imagine how betrayed I felt. Then a few weeks later I got a chirpy letter from Amy, saying that you were courting her!" Tears streamed down her face, and angrily, she swiped at them with the back of her hand. "God, Cole, I don't know how you have the nerve to act like the insulted, jilted suitor after that."

He took the message out of its envelope and read it. Then he looked up at her, his baffled expression almost convincing. "I've never seen this before in my life."

"What—what—" Once again, her tongue tripped itself on her frustration and incredulity. She plucked a handkerchief from her skirt pocket and wiped her nose with a savage pinch. "Don't try to hand me that twaddle. You wrote it. It's signed by you. It was sent from the telegraph office here in town. Really, are you going to stoop to a sudden case of amnesia to—"

He shook the buff-colored note at her. "I'm telling you I didn't send this. I didn't write it."

Jamming her handkerchief into her pocket, she snatched back the paper from him and read it aloud. "'Jessica, wanted you for my wife but refuse to wait one more day. I am sorry.' If you didn't send it, who did?"

Cole felt as if he were looking at a mirror image of his life, like that kid named Alice in a book Susannah had read to Tanner Grenfell's nephews. Nothing was making sense, everything seemed backwards. He knew he hadn't sent that telegram, but there it was in black and buff.

"So you got this," he said, taking the paper away from her again. "Then you wired me back telling me not to wait for you."

"What else was I supposed to do?" Her voice had a ragged edge, and she sat down suddenly.

He remembered that April day. Vividly. He'd gone to Tilly's and had gotten so drunk, Virgil Tilly had put him out on the saloon's back stoop with a blanket and a bucket. At least that was where he'd regained consciousness the next day, with a hangover that would have killed a buffalo. It had rained sometime during the night, the blanket was heavy and damp, and he'd been thoroughly miserable. If the hangover hadn't been bad enough, he'd felt as if he'd been kicked in the chest. Kicked in the heart.

"Someone played a rotten prank on us, Jess."

She rolled her eyes. "That's ridiculous. Who would do that?"

"I don't know who or why, but it happened." He saw the pain and certainty of betrayal in her eyes. He could also see that she didn't believe a word he said. "I never should have—never *would* have started courting Amy if you hadn't sent that wire."

"So now it's my fault?" She picked up the dry bread crusts and in a childish fit, threw them at him. He ignored it.

"No, I didn't say that. But I'm going to get to the bottom of this." He folded the message and put it in his shirt pocket. "I need to keep this for a while."

Alarmed, she held out her hand. "No, it's mine. Give it back."

"Don't want to break up a matching set, huh?"

"What is that supposed to mean?" She extended her reach, but he backed up and covered his pocket with his own hand.

"This message and your grudge against me. You want to keep them together and not let go of either of them."

She dropped her arm, stung by the truth he'd revealed to her. "Why do you want it? What are you going to do?"

"I'm not sure yet." He wandered to the window and looked down the street toward the telegraph office. A few possibly guilty parties crossed his mind. Pop—he'd never much liked the idea of Cole and Jess marrying. Jacobsen—maybe, but that didn't make much sense. He hadn't really shown an interest in Jess until recently. "I'll let you know when I learn something."

"This is all so far-fetched, Cole."

"I'm not perfect and I've done some things in my life that I'd give anything to do over," he said quietly. "But I never lied to you. Not before, and not now."

"Maybe not." The vehemence had suddenly drained out of her voice, giving her words a hollow, weary sound. He turned toward her. She looked the same: empty, exhausted. "Anyway, it's water under the bridge, a part of our past. I can't think about this anymore tonight. I came here to rest, then I have to go back."

"Go take your nap. I'll wait for you right here at the table. When you're ready, I'll drive you over."

She shook her head. "That doesn't sound like a good..."

He dropped to his knee again, took her hand, and pressed a kiss into her palm. "Please. Let me do this for you."

Her eyes fluttered closed for a moment and she sighed. Then she gazed at him with that searching look that had always made him feel as if she could see into his heart. "I guess that would be all right. Give me an hour."

"I think you'd better make it two." He squeezed her hand, loving the way it felt in his.

She gave him a small, tired smile. "Okay. Two hours."

He pulled out his pocket watch with his free hand. "I'll be right here."

— — —

Just over two hours later, Cole dropped Jess off at the infirmary. She watched the Ford disappear into the darkness as she stood at the door. In her apartment, she'd slept dreamlessly until she'd felt his hand on her shoulder, nudging her awake.

They'd ridden over here without much conversation, completely avoiding the can of worms they'd opened earlier—the kisses, their suppressed feelings, the matter of the telegram. What if it was true? What if someone else had sent that message? And who on earth would do such a devious, underhanded thing? Jessica's mind whirled with the implications.

Forcing her thoughts to the current emergency, she turned and went inside. The odors that haunted her dreams and clung to her clothing and hair assailed her again. The overall scene was much the same one she'd left. After digging into her bag for her stethoscope, she passed rows of sickbeds and headed straight to Amy. She found Mrs. Donaldson sitting beside her.

"Oh, good Lord, Jessica, I'm so glad you're here. The poor thing, the poor little thing." Laura Donaldson shook her head and wept and wrung her handkerchief as if Amy was already dead.

Alarmed, Jessica took her sister's wrist and peered at her fever-flushed face. Her condition was no better, but at least it wasn't worse. Some people failed so quickly, their lives seemed to drain from them right before Jessica's eyes. "Mrs. Donaldson, would you be a dear and get her a cold cloth for her head? I'd like a moment to examine her."

"Yes, yes, of course!" The woman, whose eyes were faintly discolored from the broken nose she'd recently suffered, jumped off the stool at Amy's bedside.

Taking her place, Jess put the stethoscope against Amy's chest and listened to the sodden, crackling sound of her congested lungs. It resembled the noise of an ice cream soda being sucked up through a straw. With a heavy sigh, she covered Amy's hand with her own. Her sister's hair was a snarl of honey-colored strings resting on the pillow, and faint blue smudges underscored her closed eyes. But she still wore the earrings Cole had given her.

"Oh, Amy," Jess intoned, more to herself.

Amy's lashes fluttered, and she opened her eyes. "Jessie."

It was a pet name their mother had used when she was a girl. No one had called her that in years. Jess's throat tightened and she managed to quell the tears that burned under her lids.

She squeezed Amy's hand. "Yes, I'm here, Amy. I'm right here."

Wracked with coughing and infection, Amy's voice was little more than a croak. "Jessie—I feel so bad—"

"I know, honey. We're doing everything we can to make you better."

"No…I mean I did something…really bad…Promise—promise you won't tell anyone else. If I die—I need you to know—"

Cold, inexplicable foreboding gripped Jessica and sent a shiver through her. "Wh-what did you do?"

"You won't tell…"

"No, I promise. Cross my heart." Jess sketched a quick X over her chest.

"That china dish…the one from England with the bluebirds…Mother's favorite…"

Jessica waited, puzzled. "Dish?"

"I told her…the cat broke it. But it was me—please—don't let her know. She'll be so—" A fit of coughing interrupted her confession.

Jessica couldn't keep the quiver out of her voice. "It doesn't matter. Not now." She knew there was no point in trying to reason with a delirious patient. She should count herself lucky that Amy recognized her at all.

Mrs. Donaldson reappeared with a damp cloth. "How is she?" she whispered. She laid the cloth on Amy's forehead.

"Still with us. It's all I can tell right now. She thinks she's a little girl."

"I know." The woman's mouth turned down and her brows rose and met as her tears began again. "She told me how much she likes Cole, but he doesn't notice her because he's too busy with 'boy things.' Even back then she must have loved him. It's so romantic, so tragic."

Jess shifted on the stool, the guilty memory of Cole's kiss rushing to the front of her mind. But as childish and petty as it seemed, a tart response sprang to her tongue, one she managed to choke back before it escaped.

I loved him first.

I love him now.

— — —

"Damn it, dig faster, men!" Lieutenant Collier screamed.

Shells burst around Riley and his comrades in the cold dawn as a German barrage rained down upon them. They were digging in, stuck here in this apple orchard in no man's land of the Argonne Forest. He and some of the others, including Stoney, Kansas Pete, and Bob Tompkins, plunged pack shovels into the soil. Thank God he'd unbuttoned the top buttons of his coat earlier—the work was hot, made worse by the close-fitting tunic. Dirt flew from their tools and rained down upon them when the shells hit unnervingly, deafeningly close. Time and again Riley had seen the damage that such artillery fire could inflict upon a human body, sending a man's parts in different directions. Under this kind of annihilating assault, the tin helmets they wore might as well have been boat-shaped hats made from newspaper. He dared not take his attention from his task, but he glanced up once. Beyond the heavy pall of smoke, pulverized dirt, and the sweat that blurred his vision, he saw men falling like barley under a hailstorm, mere yards from him. Emerging from the curtain of dust and carbon, Whippy appeared, somehow dodging bullets as if he could actually see them coming at him and knew where to run. He tacked across no man's land, heading toward their dugout, reminding Riley of a football player zigzagging for a goal line. Just to the left of Whippy, a French soldier took a shot in the throat and dropped.

"Whippy," Riley shouted, "come on!"

Another soldier flung up his arms, as if in surrender, and lurched forward, shot in the back.

Dig faster—dig faster—or that will be you.

Riley bent his head and hunched his shoulders. He'd mucked out his share of stables in his youth, and scraped out other holes since he'd gotten here, but he'd never worked a shovel like this before. His heart pounded in his chest with the exertion, but at last they had a decent dugout and flung themselves into it. Fear flooded his veins.

"Gas! Gas!"

Oh, Jesus God, gas again. He scrabbled through the pack hanging from his neck that held his gas mask. He strapped it on just in time to see the ominous, opaque cloud wafting toward them, carried by the concussion of explosions. Over the rim of their ditch, he saw a man not ten yards away, already overcome by the poison that burned out eyes and blistered lungs. The soldier gasped and flopped around like a speared fish. He made that horrible, familiar gurgling sound that for an instant was louder than all the machine guns and bombs. When he turned his head their eyes met—the other soldier's streaming and bloody, Riley's hampered but protected by the eye shield on his mask.

"Whip!" Riley shouted in horror, his voice muffled. Trembling, he stared at Whip where he convulsed on the churned-up dirt. They'd gassed Fournier. The sons of bitches had killed debonair, negligent, cultured Fournier. Someone jerked Riley back down into the ditch, out of the line of fire.

"Goddamn it, Braddock, do you want to get your ass shot off?"

Without conscious effort, Riley pressed one hand to the pocket that held Susannah's photograph, then gripped his rifle in the other and sprang to his feet again. Seized by an unreasoning fury he had never felt before, Riley was determined to kill the bastards who had literally sucked the life from Remy Whipperton Fournier, III.

He leaped from the ditch he'd worked so hard to dig, into the cloud of gas, screaming an inarticulate profanity and firing his automatic rifle as he went. His first goal was to get Fournier. Riley couldn't leave him out there to be used for target practice by the damned Boche. Whip would die with his own men, out of firing range, not shot full of holes. He ran to Fournier and reached down to grab his arm. Blind in his death throes, Whip coughed blood and thrust up a hand. His fist closed around Riley's aluminum identification tag, dangling from its chain, and held on as though it were a lifeline.

"Don't you worry, Fournier, I won't leave you out here!"

He began to drag him back to the ditch. A sudden blow struck Riley in the leg, one that felt as if he'd been hit with a hundred-pound sack of flour. It knocked him off his feet and he found himself sitting beside Whip, stunned and puzzled.

He didn't smell poison gas or the charcoal of his gas mask, but instead the scents of cherry bark and almond.

He didn't see the dead, ravaged landscape of a bombed-out battlefield, but rather the broad, green pastures of Powell Springs.

The last sound Riley heard in the chaos of shouting men and bursting shells was the close-range explosion of the bullet that pierced his thin helmet.

CHAPTER SIXTEEN

"Still no letters from France?" Pop demanded as he presided over the Braddock breakfast table. Most of the early-morning chores had already been finished by the time Susannah rang the triangle.

This morning only the three of them—Susannah, Cole, and Pop—shared the eggs, pancakes, and fried potatoes that she'd cooked. Tanner and the boys were still banished to the bunkhouse for their own safety. Privately, Cole thought that Susannah's precautions weren't of much use; all of them worked together every day. He didn't believe that making them eat in a separate place would do much good. From what he'd seen, anyone could catch influenza.

"No letters from France," Cole replied, avoiding Susannah's hollow-eyed gaze as she handed him the platter of fried eggs. A break in the clouds let sun stream through the windows, harsh and glaring, cutting a slash across the table. "I stopped at Bright's yesterday before I came home, but all we got was the usual—feed catalogs, a couple of stockman's journals."

They'd had no mail from Riley in almost three weeks, and that was not like him. He'd always managed to write at least once a week, depending upon how the fighting was going, although they never really knew where he was. He was permitted to tell them only that he was "somewhere in France." Sometimes all they received was a Field Card, a preprinted post card with general statements such as *I am quite well*, or *I am in hospital*. These were used when soldiers were in battle to avoid revealing any details as to their location. Riley would cross out the lines that didn't apply and sign his name. But they hadn't even received one of these lately.

"Oh, your brother's probably busy giving the Huns what-for. You heard the Allied troops cracked through the German fortifications at the Hindenberg line. By God, I wish I was there." Pop had built a fort of pancakes and eggs, then flooded the whole thing with a river of syrup.

"I'm sure he'll write when he gets a chance," Susannah replied, with forced confidence. "How is poor Amy? She looked so terrible when I saw her." Busy as she was, she still found time to help out at the infirmary now and then.

Cole poked his fork into an egg and watched the yolk run from the center. Susannah was a great cook, but he hadn't had much appetite since learning about that damned telegram. "She's hanging on. She doesn't really know I'm there when I visit."

"And Jessica and you?"

His head came up. Why would she lump the two of them together like that? he wondered. "She's—well, she's tired. She's worried about her sister. How else would she be?" What could he say? That she was beautiful and tempting and elegant and a hundred other descriptions that didn't do her justice? "And I'm just about as fine as you are," he said to Susannah.

She bit her lip and looked at her plate. He felt like a heel for snapping at her but couldn't manage an apology. He hadn't slept much. He'd tossed and turned, and stared at the ceiling over his bed. When he had fallen into a doze, he'd managed to wind his bedding around him like one of the bodies waiting for Fred

Hustad's services. He'd woken up sweating and clammy, his heart throbbing like the high school's bass drum.

A brief, awkward silence settled over them, finally interrupted by Pop, who was yapping on about something Cole disregarded.

He couldn't get that telegram out of his head. He had to find out who'd sent it, had to learn who wanted to come between Jess and him.

When Susannah began clearing the table, Pop heaved himself halfway out of his chair with a dramatic groan. "God, my knees are stiffer than a new pair of jeans."

"Wait a minute, Pop," Cole said, listening for his sister-in-law's footsteps to fade into the kitchen. "I want to talk to you about something."

The old man let go of the chair arms and flopped back onto the seat. "What? That horse with the strangles still giving you trouble?"

"No, she's better."

"I hope so, she's one of our best broodmares. That infection under her jaw could kill her."

Cole didn't need to be reminded. For a while the mare's symptoms had seemed so much like some of the influenza signs he'd seen, Cole had begun to wonder if they were all going to die of the same thing. "She's still on soft food and hot fomentations. Tanner is minding her."

"Then what?"

This was harder than Cole had imagined. "Pop, I know you never much liked the idea of my marrying Jessica."

His father's eyes fixed on him, and he repeated his oft-cited assessment. "Pretty enough. Too smart for her own good."

Cole glanced toward the kitchen and lowered his voice. "Would you—did you ever think of trying to stop us?"

"Stop you? Boy, what are you going on about?"

Cole wanted to avoid the direct question. If he told the old man about the wire Jess had shown him, he'd blab it to everyone at Tilly's and Cole would lose the advantage of secrecy. "Would you have tried to talk me out of marrying her?"

"Jesus H. Christ, I did try! I told you what I thought. Does *anyone* around here listen to me? A man my age ought to get some respect in his own house and—"

This was getting Cole nowhere. Exasperated, he said, "Did you do anything else, like send a telegram?"

Pop looked just as exasperated and completely mystified. He squinted at Cole and blared, "Why the hell would I do that? I live under the same roof with you! Would I ride all the way into town with my joints creaking like a rusted windmill and send you a damned telegram when I could bawl you out to your face for free?" He pushed himself out of his chair again, obviously finished with the conversation. "If I didn't know better, I'd think you were getting addled." He tottered off, muttering and arthritic, to his chair in the parlor, passing Susannah as she returned for more dishes.

Cole checked Pop off his list of possibilities. The old man might be cranky and opinionated, but he wasn't much good at chicanery. Nothing about him was subtle.

"Are you going to eat?" Susannah asked.

He glanced at his half-consumed eggs and pancakes. "Maybe I'll catch something at lunch."

She nodded. Just as she reached in front of him to take his plate, Cole tugged lightly on her sleeve. "I didn't mean to bark at you earlier. We've all been worried about Riley."

She sat down, as if her legs wouldn't support her. Her long, dark ringlets, which curled of their own accord, even seemed limp. "How much more can we take?" She looked into his face, her expression earnest and searching, as if he had an answer. "First the war, then the influenza. Now I don't know where my husband is, and Amy is sick." Her eyes welled up and she rubbed a fingertip over a gouge in the tabletop, as if she could erase the scar.

Cole had been so caught up in his own worries and concerns, it hadn't occurred to him that Amy's illness would come as such a blow to Susannah. "Jess is taking good care of her."

"Oh, Cole, she looks so frail and helpless lying there in that bed. She's my dearest friend. She's been such a good companion with Riley gone, and we spent so much time together after her father died."

It was true. Somehow the two women had become friends just about the time that the family had learned that Jessica would be delaying her return from New York. Although he'd known Amy since childhood, it wasn't until then that he'd really noticed her.

Had Susannah come to believe that Amy was a better choice for his wife? Had she believed it enough to send a forged wire? God, he had to get a handle on this. He was turning everyone into a suspect.

"I don't know what I'll do if she doesn't get better. I don't know what I'll do if Riley—I just don't know..." Her voice trailed off.

He squeezed her shoulder but didn't answer.

Cole himself felt as if he knew less and less with each passing day.

— — —

Jessica sat at her desk in the infirmary, trying to catch up with the mountains of patient notes she'd acquired. Her system of organization was sketchy at best; time and lack of help didn't allow for more. She had three stacks of papers for three types of patients: actively sick, recovering, and deceased. The "recovering" stack contained only a few pages. All three were held in place with fist-size rocks that served as inelegant paperweights.

So far, Powell Springs had lost three hundred people to influenza. In some cities, that many people were dying per day. But this area's wartime population was only about four thousand. And the epidemic showed no signs of peaking yet.

Her hand shook just a bit as she wrote *Deceased* on Helen Cookson's record. Would the day ever come that she delivered the occasional baby into a happy, new mother's arms, or perhaps even discovered a treatment to ease this kind of suffering? Her nightmares of New York's tenements were now interspersed with faces turned nearly black from lack of oxygen and coughing.

Always the coughing.

She had managed to catch another five hours of sleep by taking the empty cot next to Amy's. Even asleep, though, Jess listened for the sound of her cough. As she scratched her pen across the paper she wondered yet again if Frederick Pearson would ever arrive.

They'd had a telegram from him earlier in the week, followed by a letter, saying that he'd gotten stuck in Omaha, where he'd been literally commandeered off the train to help with their epidemic. A public health inspector had boarded during a stop and asked if any doctors were among the passengers. The man whom Pearson had been sitting next to since Chicago had volunteered his identity. He wasn't certain when he'd arrive in Powell Springs—he was in much the same situation as Jessica. Seattle wired her at least once a week, asking when she would be coming. She could not give them a date.

But even if Pearson walked through the door right now, she wouldn't be able to leave. There was too much work for one physician to manage and still do a good job. As it was, she was scraping by with a minimum of sleep and depending on her volunteers to fill in the gaps. Patients had to be fed, washed, dressed, and tended. The laundry problem alone was monumental.

Worse, though she tried not to think about it, the fear of falling sick herself always nibbled at the edges of her thoughts. If that happened—well, it just couldn't.

Just as she jotted a patient's temperature in a file, a shadow fell across her desk. Expecting to see Nettie Stark, Granny Mae, Iris Delaney, or one of her other nurse-volunteers, she was dismayed to find Adam Jacobsen standing there. Their paths hadn't crossed since the night before, when Cole had escorted her out of the building.

And overnight, things between all of them had changed.

His dress was especially crisp and somber. Every hair was in place, as though it dared not defy his comb, and his expression was more serious than usual. "Adam—have you conducted another funeral service today?"

"No, but I have one late this afternoon." He fixed her with a meaningful look over the upper edge of his gauze mask. "How is Amy?" He lifted his chin and gazed toward Amy's cubicle, which was filled with flowers and notes from concerned well-wishers who were able to deliver them. In fact, she'd received more gifts than any other living person in the infirmary.

"She's not really better, but she's not worse, either." Jess put down her pen and folded her hands together in a tight knot. "I'm hopeful that she'll recover. She's doing better than I thought she would."

"That's good news. And how are you?"

"I guess I'm as fine as I can be. All things considered."

"Yes, well, I'd like to talk to you about that. Can you spare a moment?"

Jess didn't like the sound of that. "Of course, Adam. Sit down." She nodded toward the chair next to her desk.

He glanced around at the large, busy room. "If you don't mind, could we step outside?"

"Um, this really isn't a good—you can see I'm swimming in paperwork and…" She gestured at the beds with a wide sweep of her hand.

"Please. I won't take much of your time, and I think this is important." His tone was stern and imploring at the same time.

Jess didn't want to give in, but she couldn't think of another reasonably polite excuse. The one she'd tried hadn't worked. "All right."

She backed her chair away from the desk and stood. As they walked toward the portico, she swore she could feel the heat of his hand on her waist, even though he wasn't actually touching her.

He opened the door for her and removed his mask. They stood at the top of the steps, where the late October air was scented with fallen leaves and woodsmoke. She pulled down her own mask and waited for him to speak.

Adam took one of her hands in his, and she fought the urge to snatch it away from him. "I want to apologize to you for last night."

A crow, black and ominous, lighted on a nearby tree branch and cawed at them. For an instant, she thought that the bird and Adam resembled each other—darkly dressed, forbidding.

She frowned slightly. "For what?"

"I never should have let Cole Braddock take you home. After all, it was so improper, what with Amy sick and the betrothals and all."

Jessica considered him with slightly narrowed eyes, and everything she had always disliked about him came surging back to her mind. "There was nothing improper about it. I was tired and worried, he made the offer, and I accepted it. What *betrothals* are you talking about?"

"Theirs. And I have asked you to be my wife. You can't be seen riding around in Braddock's truck unchaperoned. You should have let me take you home."

Now she did pull her hand away. His proprietary gall and parochial, small-town mind astounded her. "I didn't accept your proposal, Adam."

"But we are as good as engaged."

She took two steps backward. "No, we are not! As thoughtful as the gifts were, a handful of flowers and a box of candy does not constitute an engagement. At least not in this country."

His neck turned as red as a rooster's comb. "Ah. Naturally, you'll want a ring."

Annoyed at his misinterpretation, she snapped, "I do not want a ring. I don't want anything from you."

He flinched, as if she had called him a filthy name. "I can make life easier for you, Jessica." Drawing himself to his full height, he added, "And more difficult for others. I have powerful connections."

She lifted her brows and made an effort not to laugh. "Are you going to ask God to rain toads on me or strike me down with a thunderbolt if I don't agree to this? Really, Adam—"

"That's not what I'm talking about."

"Then what do you mean?

"Cole Braddock has drawn some, shall we say, unflattering attention to himself lately. Attention that people with authority might be interested in."

Jessica's stomach felt as heavy as an anvil. Would Adam actually stoop so low as to bring down the wrath of the American Protective League on Cole? And for what? Her tone cooled to nearly frigid. "Is that some kind of threat, *Reverend* Jacobsen? Because if it is, I do not appreciate it. Would you punish Susannah and Cole and Shaw for business between you and me? And what about Amy? Are you forgetting about her?"

He looked deflated for a moment, as if impaled on the horns of a dilemma. "No…no, of course not."

Fear and anger made her blood sizzle through her veins. "I have work to do. Your 'moment' is up, Adam." She turned and yanked open the door.

"Jessica, wait." He grasped her arm.

Pointedly, she looked at his hand, wanting nothing more than to get away from him.

He released her.

"I'm sorry. Please don't be angry. Don't—don't leave it like this."

She held her grip on the door handle. "Like what? We have nothing else to discuss."

A fine sheen of perspiration broke out on his forehead. "Jessica, please. I have made you an honorable and genuine proposal of marriage. I know the timing isn't the best, but couldn't you give me an answer?"

She closed the door again and crossed her arms over her chest. "Adam, why do you want to marry me? I'm nothing like the kind of woman you ought to consider for a wife. Can you really envision me arranging bake sales or a ladies' aid committee? I can barely boil water. And when it comes down to it, even though we've been acquainted for a long time, you and I really don't even know each other." She refrained from adding that what she did know about him, she didn't like.

Adam looked at the irritated, harried woman on whom he'd pinned his future. Why did he want to marry her? He had two reasons, he realized, neither of which were particularly ethical or romantic. But he dared not reveal those. She would certainly walk away from him for good. So he chose another, one that all women wanted to hear. In its broadest sense, it wasn't a lie.

He swallowed and took a breath. "I want you for my wife because I love you."

— — —

Cole stumbled out of the telegraph office with the rumpled message that Jessica had given him gripped in his fist. In his pants pocket was a wadded note written by Leroy Fenton, attesting that what he'd just told Cole was the truth. Leroy called after him, but he wasn't sure what he was saying. Maybe asking Cole if he was all right.

No, he was not all right.

The afternoon sun, low and blade-sharp, was blinding, but his field of vision seemed to have shrunk to the width of a tunnel. He walked back down the middle of the street to the blacksmith shop, nauseated and light-headed, slogging through puddles left over from the last rain. By the time he reached the big, weathered double doors, his jeans were soaked to the knees and his stomach was churning. With one hand braced on the doorframe, he heaved his lunch into the mud.

Shaking and bathed in cold sweat, he dropped to an old stool just inside, as stunned and winded as if he'd been thrown from a bucking horse. Sitting there, his back against a post and his legs stretched straight out, he reviewed the truth that he'd just learned from Leroy Fenton, and what he'd already known deep inside without proof.

He realized now, with the perfect clarity of hindsight, that sending the forged telegram to Jessica had merely been the last step in what had been a systematic effort to drive a wedge between them. It had worked, too. They had just been unwitting pawns in the scheme.

One thing was certain. Jessica would have to be told, and it wasn't a job he wanted. But it would have to be done. Not now, though. It wouldn't be today.

Not today.

He drew a deep breath and waited for the rubbery feeling in his legs to go away. Then he stood up and walked out to the truck.

CHAPTER SEVENTEEN

Jessica leaned over Amy's cot and put her stethoscope to her sister's chest. Her lungs crackled with rales. But somehow, miraculously, her high fever had begun to drop and was staying down. She was still febrile, to be sure, but after more than a week of illness her temperature now hovered at around 100 degrees. Jess saw this as a first promising step. Amy's recovery would probably be long—she'd read in some health dispatches that those who lived often took as much as a month to begin regaining their strength. Some, even longer. Others were reported to linger in a state of semi-invalidism thus far.

Yet, Amy had never acquired that dreaded, dusky cast of cyanosis. No bluish tinge had marked her as it had others. Remarkably, she seemed to have endured a milder form of this disease. If prayers and good wishes truly had power, they might have worked for her sister. In fact, Jessica had been forced to order that most of the flowers and gifts be moved out of her cubicle. They took up so much room, the nurses had trouble moving around within its tiny confines.

Amy's eyes fluttered open, and she turned her head on the pillow to look up at her. Her hair was a stringy, tangled mess, even though the nurses did their best to brush it out every day. "Jessica." Her voice was soft and weak.

"Amy! How are you feeling, dear?" she murmured, smiling.

"Oh…my arms and legs are so heavy. And my eyes ache." With a sluggish arm, she reached up and patted her chest. "I don't feel like I can get a whole breath."

"No, probably not yet." Cautious optimism seeped into Jessica. These were the first lucid, cognizant words Amy had spoken since Cole brought her in. "But you're doing so much better."

Amy looked around her little cubbyhole, barely moving her head. "I am? How long have I been here?"

Jessica was so grateful for her sister's obvious improvement, their last harsh words were a distant and unimportant memory. "Eight days. You've been very sick."

"Cole?"

Jess sat down on the stool beside her cot, slight unease elbowing her. She hadn't forgotten the feel of his lips on hers again, the rasp of his beard on her cheek. Or his astounding declaration of innocence over that telegram. She forced another smile. "He's been here almost every day."

"He has?" Puzzled confusion crossed her face. "He…I don't remember."

The truth was that "almost every day" had only amounted to Amy's first three sick days. Jessica hadn't seen him since *that* night. He had visited another couple of times, she'd been told, but only when she wasn't around, and just for a moment or two. Though she sometimes heard him working in the shop when she was in her apartment, she never caught so much as a glimpse of him.

"Now that you're better, I'm sure you'll remember his next visit."

"When…when is he coming again?"

"Sometime soon." She wanted to avoid the subject altogether. She patted Amy's hand.

Just then, Granny Mae came by with her cart that carried her soup kettle and bowls. "Well, look who's back with us!" the woman said, her broad smile revealing teeth as yellow as those of an old horse. "Feeling up to some broth, Amy?"

"Broth," Amy parroted.

Jess nodded and motioned to Mae to give her some soup. Mae ladled a small amount into a heavy white ceramic bowl from her restaurant and handed it to Jessica with a spoon. Jess personally dribbled the soup into her sister's mouth, dabbing her lips and chin with a towel. It made her think of feeding a baby bird.

After a several good sips, Jess stood and set the bowl on the upended fruit crate that served as a night table next to each cot. "I think that's enough for now. You still need your rest. Talking can be very tiring for a recovering patient."

"Tired. Yes, I am." Amy's words had a slow, drowsy sound and her eyelids drifted closed again.

Jessica stopped at another couple of sickbeds, then happened to look out the window. Dusk was gathering, and things here seemed to be under control. She could slip away for a few hours to take a bath and sleep, too.

As she tidied her stacks of papers, she was glad that Adam wasn't here tonight, waiting to walk her home. He had done so every night since his awkward declaration. He knew that he'd made her mad, and telling her that he loved her hadn't improved things at all. It rang a false note with her, but she still couldn't imagine why he'd lie about such a thing. Some men would, to take advantage of a woman and gain favors she ought not to give. That hardly seemed to be the case with Adam. During the day when he came to visit patients, he maintained a professional, caring attitude toward everyone, including Jess. He'd made no more mention of his proposal, but apparently was trying to win her over with his attention and thoughtfulness.

His persistence had only become annoying.

For the life of her, though, she couldn't think of a good way to get rid of him without being downright rude. Telling him to take a flying leap would not have bothered her at this point. In fact, she would have enjoyed it; she was tired, overworked, and worried. But his earlier implied threat to report Cole to the American Protective League always put a clamp on that urge. Instead, she'd told him his escort wasn't necessary. He'd insisted that in these uncertain times a woman shouldn't walk alone at night.

She plucked her gray wool coat from the hall tree next to the entrance and pushed her arms into the sleeves. He'd been here earlier and then left to conduct a funeral. Maybe she could slip out and race home before he came back.

Sidling toward the door with her black bag in hand, she peered out through the glass into the fading light, trying to see if Adam was around. Without warning, the door flew open and she saw him standing there.

She leaped back and let out a startled yelp. "Adam! You took a year off my life, jumping in here like that!"

"Oh, sorry. I didn't want you to think I hadn't come to walk you home."

Heaven forbid that she should think that, she thought sourly. She considering lying to him, telling him that she was just going out for a breath of air, but she was carrying her bag. Even if she hadn't been, the excuse would have been pointless. He was like an irritating gnat, one that she couldn't shoo away. She wished with all the energy left in her tired soul that she had never accepted what she'd believed to be his innocent gifts and attention. Coolly, she replied, "Really, I wasn't worried about it." Her lack of enthusiasm didn't deter him a bit.

He grinned broadly, his arrow-shaped nose pointing at the smile. "That's good. I look forward to our little walks. I like to talk with someone who understands what this battle is all about."

He guided her down the stairs. "Which battle do you mean?"

"The influenza, of course." They passed house after house with darkened windows where people would ordinarily be eating dinner about now, their kitchens lit with warmth that spread throughout the homes. Tonight, only random windows glowed dimly, as if from sickroom lamps. Some houses were completely dark.

"What do you think it's about?" she asked, curious to see what he'd say.

"I've given it a lot of thought since this started. I admit I was scared at first, like I told you then. But now I believe it's God's reckoning. Certainly, he's called some of the righteous home. But mainly he's been winnowing out the wicked. That's what the Book of Revelation tells us."

Jessica stopped in her tracks, appalled. "And you think I share your opinion?"

He stopped too, a few paces ahead of her, and turned. The streetlight overhead cast dark shadows on his face. "Well, don't you? You see the hand of God at work every day, casting out those who displease him. Take Nate Pellings, for example. Up to the moment he died I tried to make him admit that he was a miserable sinner for his drinking and gambling. I told him he'd have to pay plenty for all of his sins and misdeeds if he didn't repent. He refused. I presided over his funeral yesterday." He seemed almost pleased.

He was insane, Jessica decided, horrified that he was badgering her patients while they struggled in their death throes. Insane and arrogantly cruel-hearted. Unable to bear his company another moment, she snapped, "I *don't* agree with you at all!"

She sped past him, heading for the sanctuary of her own apartment.

"Jessica!" he called, closing the distance between them.

She almost ran to maintain her lead, so anxious was she to get away from him. But he was taller, and her stride was no match for his longer one. Soon he was beside her again.

He grabbed her arm just as she came abreast of Braddock's Blacksmith Shop. "What on earth ails you?"

She stopped again, pulled up short by his hand. "Adam, let me go."

"Why are you so angry?" he demanded, a frown marking his brow. "You asked me what I think and I told you. Can you honestly say that this epidemic isn't evidence of God's presence on Earth?"

She yanked hard but she couldn't work her wrist out of his grip. "Unfortunately, I can't stop you from coming to the infirmary. But if I were sick and frightened that I might die, you're the last person I'd want to see looming over my bed!" Her breath came fast and her heart raced like a thoroughbred. But anger loosened her tongue at last. "You're like the grim reaper, come to collect souls. All you need is a black hood and a scythe. You don't represent God or heaven or anything having to do with charity or kindness! You're still the sneaky little pip-squeak who tattled on everyone when we were children. Except now your judgment falls on innocent people—the ones you just don't like or who threaten your pompous image of yourself. I cannot understand or conceive of the reasons behind your cruelty!"

He stared at her in the semidarkness, his mouth slightly open, his expression one of astonished, self-righteous fury. "I would advise you to think about what you're saying. And who you're saying it to."

"This from a man who claims to *love* me—more threats. What will you do to me, Adam?" she egged him on. "What will you have done to—"

"Jess, are you having a problem?"

Out of what seemed like nowhere, Cole appeared. Jessica had never been happier to see him. He cut an imposing figure, tall, sweating and damp-haired despite the weather, wearing his leather apron and carrying an iron hammer. She realized they were standing in front of his shop doors and that he must have been inside, working. "Cole—"

"This doesn't concern you, Braddock," Adam snapped.

Cole shook his head skeptically. "Hmm, sounds like it does. You're being jackass-rude to a woman who's an old friend of mine—this is the second time I've had to stop you from manhandling her. It's not how a minister is supposed act, is it?" He knocked Adam's hand away from Jessica's wrist as if it were no more than a flea. Then he added with a menacing tone, "And I've had a bellyful of you myself."

"Jessica, don't let—" Adam began.

Cole turned to her. "Are you about finished here?"

She rubbed her wrist and glared at the man who believed himself to be her fiancé and a spiritual judge and jury. "Yes, I certainly am."

Cole nodded and pushed his chest against Adam's. "You git right now, before I change my mind and teach you the manners you never learned."

Adam's mottled face twitched with defiant anger, his mouth pressed into a tight line. "You'll regret this, Braddock." He added to Jessica, "So will you." Then he turned and walked toward home at a fast clip.

Cole watched him until he was a couple of blocks down the street and said, "Damn, I can't stand that creep." He looked at her. "Are you all right?"

She let her shoulders droop, but fear and anger still hummed through her. "Yes. Thank you for stepping in. I'm sorry you have to keep rescuing me."

"Yeah, well, I hate to say I told you so."

"Then don't," she said flatly. "I've been trying to discourage him for days but he just wouldn't take the hint." She gazed at Adam's retreating back. He was just a speck in the dusky light. "I suppose he has now. But I'm worried about what I might have brought down on us."

Cole nodded. "I always thought he was only a holier-than-thou stoolpigeon. But he's got a mean streak in him a mile wide. I know he's had it in for me for a long time."

A chill, sundown breeze kicked up and caught the front edge of her coat, and she shivered. "You're not the only one on his list."

"How is Amy?" he asked abruptly.

"She's getting better, thank God."

"Good." He gestured over his shoulder. "Look, I've got a couple of things to see to. They'll take me about an hour, but I'd like to come over and talk to you after."

She remembered the last time he'd come over to "talk," and what had happened. "Oh, Cole, I'm not sure. Maybe that's not a good idea."

He looked her straight on. "Look, Jess, this is important. I've been staying away from you while Amy has been sick because I figured you've got enough on your hands. But I learned something you need to know."

She swallowed. "It's not about that telegram, is it?"

"Yes."

"Does it really matter now, after all this time?"

"More than you can guess."

She sighed. "All right." She walked on to her own door.

— — —

A feeling of foreboding settled on Jessica as she tidied the apartment, washed a couple of dishes in the kitchen, and drew her bath.

Since Cole would be here soon, she wouldn't get to enjoy the long soak she'd planned, but at least she'd be clean. Given these busy days, that was good enough. It had to be. As the tub filled, she unwrapped her last cake of Créme Simone and savored its sweet aroma. She'd had no trouble finding the French-made soap in any New York drug or department store. In Powell Springs, Mr. Bright would probably have order to it, and with the war on, there was no telling how long it would take to arrive. When this miserable conflict was finally over—after that he might have less trouble.

After that—

She stopped herself, realizing the direction of her thoughts. She wasn't going to stay here. This was temporary, all temporary. Leaning over the tub, she turned off the faucets, shed her dressing gown, and sank into the hot water. She had no place in Powell Springs anymore, she reminded herself. Despite the chaos of the epidemic, she was surprised by how often she'd thought of herself as home for good.

Though the steam and heat eased the tension from her shoulders, her thoughts marched on. If she had no place here, why then did it feel as if she did? Questions plagued her. She dunked her head to wet her hair, then worked suds into the strands. She scrubbed hard, as if hoping to quiet those questions, but they still bounced around her mind. She suspected Cole was going to tell her something that would upset her wobbly emotional equilibrium. He might have uncovered a clue about the telegram's sender, perhaps forcing her to abandon the grudge he'd accused her of harboring. She'd carried it so long, it had become a kind of shield against him and the world in general. Without it, silly as it seemed, what would she have left? Her last shaky defense would be lost.

Finally, she rose from the water and dried herself. Cole would be here soon, and she didn't want him to find her wearing only her dressing gown. After she worked the snarls out of her hair, she wove it into a braid with clumsy, nervous hands, and put on a simple gray blouse and skirt. She was still standing before her bureau mirror, fiddling with a hook and eye on the neckline, when she heard his knock at the front door.

Making sure the doors to her bedroom and bathroom were closed, she hurried down the stairs. She detected his silhouette through the window and realized he was so familiar to her she would have known his wide-shouldered shape and cowboy hat anywhere.

She opened the door, trying to suppress the leap in her chest and the unwanted flush of pleasure when she saw him. He looked tired, as if he hadn't slept any more than she had. But he was still the most handsome man she'd ever seen, here or anywhere else. He'd washed up, too, slicking back his long hair with water, and changed into a clean shirt and jeans. He carried a napkin-wrapped bundle with him.

"Come in. I don't have anything to eat here, but I can put on some coffee."

"Jacobsen didn't come back, did he?"

She shook her head.

"Good." He offered the parcel. "I stopped by the saloon and asked Tilly to put together some sandwiches. I figured you hadn't eaten."

"I didn't think anyplace in town was supposed to serve food."

"They aren't, but he's got provisions for himself in the back. He had a roast beef and a couple of potatoes."

"Oh, and I still have some butter. Thanks, Cole, I really appreciate it. You're right, I haven't eaten since this morning." She took the sandwiches from him and felt something heavy wrapped up with them. Hefting it a couple of times, she asked, "What else is in here?"

"A bottle of whiskey."

She flushed. "Oh, well, I don't think I should be drinking, especially spirits."

He took off his coat and hat, and slung them on the coat tree by the door. "You might change your mind after I tell you what I've learned."

The sense of foreboding that she'd felt earlier was back, now as heavy as a millstone on her shoulders. "W-what is it?"

"Naw, we'd better eat first."

"All right. Come on."

She led him upstairs to the combination parlor and dining room, and gestured at the table. "Please…sit." While he unwrapped the food, she fetched dishes and silver from the hoosier, along with some of Horace Cookson's butter. "I'm sorry, I don't have much in the way of appropriate glassware." She nodded at the whiskey bottle.

"Don't worry, this isn't what you'd call a high-toned party."

She brought out two plain glasses and filled hers with water at the sink.

"Have a seat," he said, and pushed out the other chair with his foot.

Jessica sat down, and they ate without much conversation beyond the most superficial small talk. She inquired about the farm and the Braddock family. He asked if she thought the worst of the flu epidemic was over.

"I'm not sure just yet," she said, spearing her last piece of potato with her fork. "It *might* be slowing down. I've had fewer cases at the infirmary this week, but I can't say it's a trend. Next week will give me a better idea. You never can tell about these things." She began to describe the possible course of any given epidemic, and cited information she'd received from the East. When he looked at her with his penetrating blue gaze, she realized she was babbling, trying to stave off the inevitable reason for his visit.

He pushed his plate away and, pulling the cork out of the whiskey bottle, poured himself two inches of amber liquid. He bolted half of it, sucked a breath through his teeth, and set the glass down. Then he reached into his shirt pocket. Withdrawing the folded telegram that she recognized instantly, he opened it and put it on the table. It lay between them like a three-day-old fish before he nailed it down with a forefinger.

"I didn't send this to you."

She glanced at it and then busied herself with smoothing the napkin on her lap. "So you've told me."

His eyes didn't waver—she could feel his gaze even though she looked away. "I went to see Leroy Fenton to find out who did."

She forced a small laugh. "Oh, I'm sure poor Leroy wouldn't remember something like that after all this time. He's getting on."

"He remembered just fine. He asked me if *my* memory was giving me trouble." He went on to explain their encounter. "Then he told me who brought the message to him, sealed in an envelope, and paid him to send it."

Jessica leaned forward. "And?"

He picked up his glass and drank the other inch of liquor. "It was Amy."

She jumped to her feet with such violence, she knocked over her chair. "Amy! Cole, do you expect me to believe that? How dare you come here with such a vicious lie about my own sister?"

He didn't raise his voice. He just sat back and looked up at her. "I figured you might say that, but it's not a lie. Trust me, I thought Leroy had lost his marbles when he told me. Then he described that day in such detail, I knew it was the truth. And it made sense. I've had days and nights to think about it."

"It doesn't make any sense at all!" He sat there so coolly, so unperturbed, he could have been discussing the weather. Meanwhile, her breath came in gasps, and blood pounded in her ears. "How can you sit there, calmly sipping whiskey, and tell me this—this horrible *fable*, like you're sitting in the saloon gabbing about the price of oats?"

He frowned. "It's not a fable, and I'm not calm. It's been eating me up inside. I puked when I heard about it, and I don't sleep much at night." Reaching into his pocket again, he produced another piece of paper, one that Jessica recognized as a Western Union blank form. "Read this." He pushed it across the table, and she snatched up.

I, Leroy Fenton, swear that I keyed a message to Miss Jessica Layton, as signed by Mr. Cole Braddock and delivered to me in a sealed envelope by Miss Layton's sister, Amy, dated May 20, 1916.

Leroy's signature and last week's date followed the crabbed, handwritten statement.

"What is this? Did you blab our personal business to him?"

He gave her a sour look. "No, but I figured you might not believe me. All I did was ask him to write down what he knew on this note. At first he didn't want to because I wouldn't tell him why I needed it, only that it was important. In return, I had to swear that this had nothing to do with him, his job, Western Union, or the American Protective League. Thank God, he trusted me."

He stood and came around to right her chair. She stared at him, her entire being pulsing with fury and insult. He didn't move. He simply stared back, held her chair, and waited, silently directing her to return to it. Finally she sat down again, hard, and he went back to his own seat. Lifting the whiskey bottle, he tipped it toward her glass. She nodded, and he poured in enough to give her water a tint.

Raking a hand through his drying hair, he poured another inch of liquor for himself. "But I knew it would be a shitty thing to do, to tell you about this with Amy at death's door. Now that she's getting better, I had to let you know…everything. First of all, it can't come as a big surprise that I'm not going to marry her.

"Next, I want you to understand that I'm going to tell you the truth as far as I know it. I'm not trying to turn you against your sister, but I won't mince words, either, and I'm not going to take the blame for something I had no part of. Our lives have been changed by things Amy did. What you do with the information is up to you."

Jess sat stiff as a broomstick, her lips pursed.

"Like I said, I've had some time to think about this, and I guess I've got most of it figured out. When your dad died, Amy was sort of lost. I know she wasn't especially close to him, but you were gone, and she had to move out of the house she grew up in."

"I had to sell it to pay the property taxes and my father's debts!" She was tired of defending the decisions she'd made.

"Yeah, I know."

She slumped back in her chair and took a swallow of the diluted drink he'd made for her, feeling sullen and put-upon.

"Anyway, she got to be friends with Susannah. And I think Amy genuinely likes her, but I believe her main purpose was to hang around the farm so I'd notice her."

Jess opened her mouth to refute this, but let the words go unspoken. She knew he could be right. Coming from another man, his observation might sound like the basest sort of vanity. But for all that Cole turned female heads wherever he went, he'd never seemed aware of it, or of his own powerful handsomeness.

He continued. "It seemed like more often than not, she'd be in the kitchen helping Susannah and then at the table for dinner. Riley or I would give her a ride back to town afterward. Sometimes she spent the night. She made a big fuss over Pop, and he ate up the attention. And she'd drop little hints about how you were so good at science that you'd never learned to cook or sew or keep house." His expression turned wry. "Pop ate that up, too."

Jess crossed her arms over her chest. "Yes, I'm sure he did."

"Then your letter came, saying you'd decided to stay in New York for a while." He took another sip of his drink. "I can't say I was happy about it, but you already know that. You kept stretching out the time, and when I look back, I realize that was when Amy really started turning up the heat under my skillet."

Jessica's imagination leaped into action. She remembered what she and Cole had once shared. "*Heat*—how? I can't picture Amy...well, I just can't."

He smiled and raised his brows. "My, my, Jess, how your mind works. That's not what I meant. Amy and I have never done anything more than exchange a kiss."

Her face grew hot with the embarrassment of her own mistake and the unwanted images that had flashed through her thoughts. "Your choice of words didn't help." She took another sip of her watered whiskey and her tight limbs began to relax a bit.

"What I mean is that she stepped up her...campaign, I guess you could call it, to catch my interest." He shrugged. "She started fussing over me the way she did Pop. She told me what a shame it was that you put your job ahead of our planned engagement, and that you were dangling me like a trout—"

"She actually said that?" Jess demanded, unable to keep the scorn out of her tone.

"Yes."

"I suppose you agreed."

"Like I said, I wasn't happy about the situation—not happy at all. And you didn't give me a good reason for staying away. At least not one that I could accept."

She began tapping her foot. "Let's not go into that again. And besides, we did not have an 'engagement.' At best, we had an understanding."

He lifted a hand slightly, conceding the point.

"Then your telegram came. I thought of everything that had happened and what Amy told me. You didn't come home and you'd met that man, Andrew Stafford."

"Stavers, and I didn't—"

"Whatever his name was. Yeah, I started to feel like that trout."

She frowned at him, but it wasn't an outright scowl this time. His statement of the facts was beginning to gel in her mind and freeze her heart.

"Riley left to join the army, and Susannah was pretty gloomy. So was I, under the circumstances. Amy became our bright spot. She kept us company." He lifted his shoulders helplessly. "I started courting her. And before I knew it, I knew she was expecting us to marry."

"You didn't waste any time, did you?" she observed tartly. "Did you ever think to write me to ask me about the telegram you received?" Her words still had a sharp edge, but his gaze on her was level and uncompromising.

"A dozen times, but I couldn't make myself do it. Did you think to write to me about the one *you* got?"

She arched a brow and gave him a brittle smile. "Yes, but I didn't think it would be very satisfying. I was so hurt and angry, I just wanted to shout at you. I'm not sure that I'm not still angry."

He drained his glass. "But here we are, Jess. At the end of a long road we never meant to travel, brought here by someone who wanted her own way. And I guess she didn't care who she hurt to get it."

Jess took another drink from her own glass. Tears stung her eyes, and she rummaged through her pockets but couldn't find a handkerchief. She believed Cole, but it was all so hard to accept, so difficult to conceive of treachery like that from her own sister. "I feel like—it's like we're talking about a stranger. This isn't the sister I remember. It can't be. Amy wouldn't do that."

"That's what I thought, too. We were wrong."

"Do you love her?" Her words came out as a whisper.

He closed his eyes for an instant, as if trying to decide which answer was best, a lie or the truth. "I tried to convince myself that I did."

She swiped at the corners of her eyes with her thumb. "It certainly seemed like it. Those new cameo earrings she showed me, the ones she's still wearing, didn't come from a casual friend."

He shifted in his chair. "I bought them for her the day I moved your stuff from the hotel to this office. I...well..."

"Well?"

"I felt guilty because as soon as I saw you at Granny Mae's your first day back, I knew I was just kidding myself. Then when she got sick and I saw her lying there in that cot, before I knew about the telegram, I felt like the biggest heel on the face of the earth. After all, everyone else loves Amy. Why didn't I?"

"Why didn't you?"

"Because I never got over you. And if I'd thought it would do any good, I would have paid the devil an admission price to walk through that hell I traveled, just to get you back."

A flush of annoyance overtook her again. "Really? You didn't try very hard. As soon as you thought the going was tough, you jumped from me to my sister. The damage is done," she said, taking a bigger drink from the glass clasped in her hands.

"Come on, Jessica, how hard did *you* try?" His eyes looked like chips of blue ice. "I don't deny that I've got plenty of regrets. If you can tell me you don't, then you're not the woman I've always believed."

She felt her cheeks grow hot. "Of course I have regrets. But we're not the same people we were before. At least I'm not, and I don't think I ever will be again."

"Because of me."

"Well, no, not completely because of you." The wailing children, their worn mothers, the drunken fathers, the defeated, abandoned old people—their ghosts never left her.

Silence opened between them.

"Maybe we're not the same," he said at last, the hostility drained away. "It could be that we're better."

Her head came up. "Better—how?"

He left his chair and crouched on his haunches in front of her. "We're a little wiser now. Maybe we appreciate each other more." He was so close, he smelled so familiar. She noticed fine lines that fanned out from the corners of his eyes that hadn't been there before, the same strong jaw and broad brow. No one and nothing else had ever filled her heart quite the way he had. Unable to stop herself, she leaned toward him and brushed the backs of her fingers against his hair.

He took her hand and kissed it, lingering over her wrist with his lips.

The feeling, tempting and yet somehow forbidden, nudged the spell that grew around them. "Cole, no." She tried to pull her fingers from his grasp. "We're not going to do this again. You might have reached a decision about Amy, but she and everyone else still think you're her suitor. You have to wait until she's better and then tell her it's over. Otherwise, you're just—just a *philanderer*."

He looked up from her hand, and the seconds passed. Then he pressed his forehead to her knees. "No, I'm not, Jess. I've been bamboozled, and so have you. But I've waited long enough for you—years—and I don't want to wait anymore."

Tears burned her eyes again, and she stroked his hair. Amy, her own sister, had connived and lied to both of them, and the truth was there on the table for her to see. "But suppose that makes our actions no better than Amy's..."

He lifted his head, and she saw the angry, raw flame that burned behind his icy gaze. His voice was low and rough. "Bullshit. You'll just get a nosebleed walking that high road."

Reaching up, he tugged lose the ribbon on the end of her braid where it rested in front of her shoulder. Then he pulled her out of the chair into his embrace. They toppled to the oval braided rug that covered the pine flooring, her skirts tangled around her legs, trapped beneath him and trapping her. His kisses pelted her face like raindrops during a late-summer storm, moist and warm and as welcome.

She wrapped her arms around him, simply unable to resist a moment more.

Anger still twisted through her, fury over what her sister had done, and on a lesser scale, toward Cole for his seemingly effortless recovery from their derailed love affair. Yet, overriding that was the wanting, her desire for him, and the love she'd forced into a corner of her frozen heart. When his lips touched her mouth, her icebound objections and high-minded ideals melted away, freeing that love.

They reached for each other with a restless urgency she hadn't known for over two years. Beneath the fabric of his shirt she felt hard muscle and bone, honed by a lifetime of physical labor. Heat radiated from him.

His chin-length hair fell forward as he looked down at her. "Jessica," he muttered, "Jess, it's always been you." He took her mouth in a kiss that warmed her from within, as if hot nectar had infused her veins. With one hand under her neck, he unbuttoned his shirt. Then he reached for her hand and sandwiched it between his own and his fast-thumping heart. "Always in here."

She couldn't suppress the soft moan inspired by the feel of his warm, bare skin and hard-thumping pulse beneath her palm.

Their previous, interrupted explorations of intimacy now stacked up to create a feverish hunger that was both mature and years in the building. As society dictated, and perhaps despite what Powell Springs might have assumed that long-ago summer when Adam had come upon her and Cole beside the creek, Jessica had maintained her virginity. For twenty-seven years, through youthful temptation, through schooling and her work. She had never wanted or even considered giving herself to any man but Cole.

She had never loved any man but Cole.

His big hand slid up her rib cage and covered her breast, her thin shirtwaist a flimsy barrier, and her body rose to meet his touch.

Jessica knew almost everything modern medical knowledge and experience had to offer about a human body as a machine. How its heart pumped blood, how its organs worked, how it sustained itself and reproduced. But as a vessel of deep, emotion-driven desire, she was unversed.

As Cole's impatient fingers worked at the buttons of her blouse and her combination beneath, his lips and tongue plied hers, hot and slick and seeking. Time and the grim specters of sickness and death receded to a distant corner of her mind, banished by his ministrations. He bent his head to her neck and throat, leaving a trail of warm, moist kisses that focused her senses to an exquisite sharpness. Her head was filled with the scent of him, part male, part whiskey, with a trace of night air that lingered on his clothes.

She traced her fingertips along his face, reading the faint stubble of his beard, the strength of his jaw, the soft skin on the back of his neck that was protected from the weather by his hair. With seemingly no effort, he had her out of her blouse and skirt, and they laid in a heap beside them. He nudged her shoes off as he ran his hands down her legs, pushing her stockings out of his way.

Unfettered by a repressive modesty she would have felt with any other man, she wound her fingers in his hair and pulled his lips to hers again to answer his wordless demand for surrender. Tomorrow and what it might bring didn't matter at this moment—the world could roll on around them. They were stopped in a place that time and circumstances could not reach.

The hard length of him, pressed against her thigh, left no question about his intentions.

Cole unbuttoned and reached into Jessica's white cambric combination. It was silly female underwear that reached her knees, but it obligingly opened down the entire length of her torso. Her smooth body, fragrant with spice and dark wood, was full and womanly.

Outside, within the confines of the shop grounds, Roscoe, Cole's dog, began barking. Cole raised his head, listening for a moment. Roscoe kept up such a furious ruckus that Cole almost interrupted his exploration of her scented smoothness. The dog didn't usually bark like that unless a stranger approached. The doors weren't locked, but the paddock was under this apartment's window. Briefly, he considered going to look. But one look at the softness laid bare before him, and the fire in him raged. He abandoned the idea. The damn-fool mutt had probably cornered some night-dwelling critter. He just hoped it wasn't a skunk.

"No woman is as beautiful as you, Jess," he uttered against her neck. "Not a single one." His hand drifted over her belly and down lower, lower, to the place that even her underwear could not hide from him. She squirmed under his touch.

In one grand sweep, he pulled her into his arms and carried her to the closed room that held the bed. Balancing her, he turned the knob and kicked open the door. A break in the clouds sent a shaft of silver-gray moonlight over the quilt, as if beckoning them to this place. Beyond the window, the streetlight cast shadows on the walls of bare-limbed trees that had shed their leaves.

He put her on the bed and pulled off his shirt while she watched. "Tell me," she murmured plaintively. "Tell me again."

He knew what she meant. Kicking off his boots, he unbuckled his belt and ripped open the fly of his jeans. He shucked the pants, then climbed onto the bed beside her, where she lay with her hair in a cloud of waves spilling over her pillow. "I love you," he said, taking her into his embrace once more. "I have always loved you."

In the midst of everything that had gone wrong with the world—war, disease, loss, and suffering—and between them, his statement was life-affirming to his own ears. A toast to this moment he'd waited for half his life, and a tribute to the woman who had owned his heart for just as long.

The graze of her fingertips along his hip sent blood pounding to every part of his body, and he rolled toward her, putting one leg between hers to give him easy access to her sweetness. Desperate heat and urgency rode low in his belly, demanding satisfaction. But he had to wait, he had to make sure that Jessica was pleasured first.

He ran his hand up the inside of her smooth thigh until he reached the slick, sweet warmth that wept for his touch. At the same time, he took the tight bud of her nipple into his mouth, brushing it with his tongue.

Jessica moaned and arched against him, giving herself to the utter flood of sensation. Their youthful explorations had been nothing like this. The yearning had been nothing like this. Fear of discovery and self-consciousness had inhibited her. Now she felt neither.

Cole groaned against her neck when Jessica reached down to wrap her hand around the hot length of him, and she reveled in his response. All that was female in her surged to life, as if awaking from a years-long slumber. He pushed her hand away and muttered, "Not yet, honey. Not yet."

He played her slick, sensitive flesh with the deftness of the most skilled musician coaxing music from an instrument. Her nerves drawn as tight as the strings of that instrument, each stroke of his hand sent vibrations shivering through her, building the crescendo. He murmured in her ear, only part of which she grasped. When she could stand no more, he pushed on, driving her to a frenzy of sensation that she had never experienced before. She pushed against his hand to meet the waves of spasms that wracked her. Her cry in the darkness was smothered by his kiss.

Shifting his weight, in the moonlight he hovered over her, then covered her body with his own. She closed her arms around him and felt him probe unerringly toward the center of her that even now, still quivered with the aftereffect of her climax.

It took every ounce of Cole's flagging self-control to keep from burying himself in Jessica's welcoming heat. He had thought of this moment a hundred times since he'd first set eyes on her again, even though he hadn't known it would occur. He gave a tentative nudge against her and heard her small, sharp gasp.

"I can't change my mind now, Jess," he warned raggedly.

"No, no—please don't stop."

"I swear I'll try not to hurt—"

But she lifted her hips to meet his, forcing him to become one with her. She closed around him like a warm glove, like a scabbard for a sword, one that would fit no other but the one it had been made for. He withdrew and thrust again, relishing the delicious agony building in him. Jessica's movements complemented his, putting them both on a blade-sharp precipice of desire. At last they were flung into an abyss of emotional passion, of two hearts and souls joined, now and for all time. His release shook him to the core of his being.

He pressed his head to her shoulder, limp and breathing like a winded horse. He felt her smile against his cheek.

"What?"

"You're really quite a man, Cole."

He smiled too. "Was I what you expected?"

She hugged him and he rolled her over so that she lay on him. "Better than I dreamed. And I dreamed about this many times."

"So did I. I couldn't help it, I love you."

She put her hand to his cheek. "Not as much as I love you."

CHAPTER EIGHTEEN

Jessica lay with her head pillowed on Cole's shoulder and one leg thrown over his. She felt she could finally explain to him why she had left the job which, ultimately, had cost her so much.

"I began to realize that I wasn't making any real difference in those people's lives. I kept patching up the same ones, if they lived, and fighting the same problems in others." They had made love once more, and then both had fallen into deep sleep, exhausted and sated. Now the magic of their night together was nearly over. In her sitting room, the clock struck six-thirty. "It didn't matter how hard I worked, or how hard I tried. There were so many factors I couldn't overcome. At first I didn't think I could leave. But then, despite, well, everything, I knew I couldn't stay. There was no joy left in my work. Only a feeling of abject futility. So I suppose I ran away from it." She told him about her month in Saratoga Springs and her self-imposed isolation from the world.

"And now? You aren't still going to Seattle, are you?" He stroked her bare arm and played with her fingers as they spread across his chest.

She turned her face toward the window. "I don't dare think farther ahead than one day. This responsibility I have, taking care of this town, is even less predictable than the duty I had back East.

There, I knew I was battling ignorance and inhumanity. Here my enemy is a mystery, a virtual unknown."

With agonizing reluctance, she disentangled herself from the warmth of his arms, sat up, and perched on the edge of the mattress.

"Jess, wait. Don't go yet." He was too tall for the bed, and yet he looked so right there. It wasn't hard to let her imagination picture him there every night, and waking up with him every morning. Seeing him in the low dawn light, his long hair tousled, his big frame lying back against the pillows, she thought he'd never looked so handsome and appealing.

She sighed. "I have to get back to the infirmary. I have work to do. As long as this crisis lasts and I'm the only physician here, these long hours will go on. Even though the rate of new infections has just begun to drop off, I'm still fighting an uphill battle. And for all I know, it could get worse again."

He sat up too, and began pulling on his clothes. "I guess I've got to go, too. We're wrangling a herd to put on the train late tomorrow afternoon. Will you come to the ranch for dinner after?"

She tensed, pausing with one arm in the blouse she had pulled from the wardrobe. "That's not a good idea, Cole. Not yet. High road, low road—Amy has to face the consequence of her actions and you have to tell her why you're ending your courtship. She's not well enough for that." And Jessica wasn't sure she was ready for whatever might follow after.

He stared at the post on the bed for a moment. "Yeah, I know," he conceded. He stood at the bureau mirror and used both hands to comb back his hair. "At least I can give you a ride to the high school."

"That I accept," she said, smiling. After she'd brushed her teeth and washed in the tiny bathroom, he borrowed her Colgate tooth powder and used his finger as a brush.

In the parlor, she picked up her black leather bag, then they both went downstairs. Cole snagged her coat from the coat tree and held it for her before grabbing his own jacket and hat. They walked outside into the early light and stood for a moment on her stoop. The town was still quiet, and soft mist dampened the air. The last brown leaves lay wet and defeated along the sidewalk gutters, and there was no birdsong to be heard. No traffic rolled past her door, although these days it moved like a wounded animal, even at noon.

Taking her chin between his thumb and forefinger, Cole tipped her face up to his own. "I won't be able to do this when I drop you off. Imagine what those women volunteers would say." He kissed her with all the passion he'd shown upstairs the night before, jarring her resolve to remain professional and preserve her personal ethics about their relationship. His warm breath fanned her face and she felt she could have stood there all morning, letting his lips take hers. The spark of unvarnished joy that he had kindled in her heart last night—the first she'd felt in a long time—burned a little higher, a bit brighter.

When he drew back, she looked into his blue eyes and saw the same raw flame burning there. He was so hard to resist.

"Damn, Dr. Layton, we'd better go before I change my mind about all of this and take you back upstairs."

She laughed. "You mean play hooky? I never did that in my life."

"Maybe you ought to start," he replied. Glancing down, he noticed that one tail of his shirt still hung loose and he tucked it in. Jessica caught herself making the very unladylike wish that she could reach into the front of his pants like that.

They walked to the dew-covered truck parked in the yard of his blacksmith shop next door. Just as he was about to help her in, she heard a male voice.

"Fornicators! Aren't you *ashamed*?"

Jess jumped and was startled to see Adam Jacobsen approach them. His clothes were rumpled, so different from his usual crisp appearance. Where had he come from?

Beside her, Cole stiffened like a wolf confronted by an enemy. "What the hell do you want, Jacobsen? And why is it every time I turn around, you seem to be there, minding everyone's business except your own?"

Adam didn't reply to the questions, but looked them up and down with contemptuous self-righteousness. His hair stuck up in a couple of places and dark circles accentuated the fierce anger in his eyes. "To have fallen so low. I should have known your baser instincts would eventually come out again." He glared at Jessica. "To fornicate with the man who is your sister's betrothed." He spoke in a melodramatic voice that reminded Jess of his father at his most rabid moments in the pulpit. But her hands and stomach turned to ice in the face of this ugly confrontation.

"Watch your mouth, Jacobsen. You're jumping to a conclusion that you can't prove. Just take yourself down the road, or I'll help you on your way," Cole warned.

"And *you*," he went on, pointing at Cole. "Even now, Amy, a fine woman of good character, a shining moral example in this community, is lying helpless in her sickbed, and this is how you repay her trust and devotion?"

Cole knocked away Adam's index finger. "Don't point at me. And mind your own business," he repeated. "You don't know what you're talking about. If you don't leave, I'll forget about that Bible you hide behind and kick your ass up into your skull." He stepped closer to Adam and nudged him with his shoulder, making him lurch backward.

Adam's contorted face flushed the angry red of a throbbing boil. He stepped forward again, his voice shaking with fury. "Don't you threaten me! I'll personally see to it that neither of you can ever hold up your heads in this town again!"

Jessica, unnerved by his behavior, almost expected to see him begin foaming at the mouth.

"To think that I asked you to marry me. You're nothing but an educated tramp!"

Jessica gasped at his vitriolic insult.

"You son of a bitch!" Cole grabbed Adam by his lapel with one hand and pulled back to swing with his other, but Jess grabbed him. He'd put his weight and shoulder behind the punch, but she was able to throw off his aim.

"Cole, no! He's not worth it!"

Adam escaped Cole's grip and danced out of range, his eyes shining with an almost fanatic gleam. "Just you wait!" He turned and walked away at a rapid clip in the direction of his own house. He glanced over his shoulder once or twice, as if to make sure Cole wasn't chasing him.

"Oh, no," she groaned, watching him go. "That horrible man! He'll tell everyone about this."

Cole was flushed too and drew several deep breaths, then locked his fist in his other hand. He watched Adam's retreat. "I know he'll try to make trouble, but what's he going to tell? That he saw me helping you into the truck? We know what happened last night, but he really doesn't. He's just making dirty-minded assumptions. As usual."

"He probably saw us kiss. Maybe. I'm not sure."

He turned to look at her. “Did he really ask you to marry him?”

“Yes,” she said in a weary, disgusted voice.

“And?”

“What do you mean, ‘and’?”

“What did you tell him?”

“I guess I never really refused outright. But I told him I wouldn’t make him a good wife. He had it all planned out—he even expected us to go to heaven together. He assumed I would give up medicine and devote myself to his job. Can you imagine me organizing basket socials and quilting bees?”

Cole released his fist and gave a short, humorless laugh. “No.”

“I told him I couldn’t see that, either. And anyway, I realized you were right about him.” He shot her another I-told-you-so look, which she acknowledged with lifted brows and a resigned shrug. “For some reason, though, he began to assume I’d accepted. That was part of the argument you interrupted last evening. I told him we’re *not* engaged. But I wonder why in the world was he out here at this hour.”

Cole thought for a moment, remembering a couple of things that made cold worry settle in his gut. He nodded toward the passenger seat of the truck and she let him help her in. “Be careful around him.” He didn’t want to frighten her, but he figured she should hear his suspicion. “I think he might have been here, watching, all night.”

She stared at him. “But that’s ridiculous. It’s—it’s creepy!”

“Yeah, well, remember who we’re talking about, Jess. Didn’t you notice he was wearing the same clothes he had on yesterday? And while we were upstairs, I heard Roscoe barking his head off. I think he was barking at Jacobsen. That's why he seemed to appear out of nowhere. He was already here."

He saw Jess shiver. "Watching?"

"Yeah. To see who came and left, and when. Or anything else he might spy." He walked around to the front of the truck and gave the stiff crank a couple of hard turns to start it. When it rumbled to life, he climbed in and fiddled with the choke.

"I'm not afraid of him. He can't hurt me, and I can't let his threats get in my way."

"Just the same, be careful." Looking out the windshield for a moment, he then took her hand where it lay in her lap. "Jess, if anything comes of last night because of him or anybody else, I want you to know I'll be right beside you. I'm not sorry or ashamed about anything we did."

Jess faced him and squeezed his hand. Once again, he knew that she could see the truth of his words because she was looking right into his heart.

For now, that would have to be enough to get him through what lay ahead.

— — —

To Jessica, the following two days passed much the way others had since the epidemic began. A blur of sick patients, dying patients, and convalescing patients gave her the sense of time standing still. Her only real indication of time came from sunrises and sunsets.

She had no idea where Adam was, but she was grateful that he'd stayed away from the infirmary since that horrible morning when she'd last seen him. If anyone noted his absence, it wasn't mentioned.

She hadn't seen Cole, either, but she knew he was probably busy getting the horses ready for the train.

Health dispatches she received from the Red Cross and other sources spoke of the global proportions of the catastrophe, although it was noted that for the most part, newspapers tended to whitewash the situation, if they mentioned it at all. Doctors and nurses were felled as commonly as their patients, and some areas around the country were left to fend for themselves. Some of her volunteer nurses had ended up occupying sickbeds themselves. What would become of Powell Springs if she got sick?

Due to a mix of guilt and lingering anger, Jessica visited Amy's bed as infrequently as possible. At first it wasn't difficult because her sister slept most of the time, and after a couple of brief examinations, Jess was satisfied that Amy was definitely growing stronger. But as she grew stronger, she began to ask questions of the nurses.

The day after her confrontation with Adam, Jessica was tending a patient when she heard Amy ask, "Where is Jessica? Why doesn't she come to see me? Where is Cole?"

She stood on the other side of the sheets that had been erected to create separate patient cubicles. Like a coward, she sped away toward her desk before anyone noticed her presence. But she knew she was only delaying the inevitable. Yes, blood was thicker than water, but Amy's blatant betrayal, masked by what Adam had called "good character" and "a shining, moral example," overrode her filial affection.

Birdeen Lyons tracked her down. Her head was wrapped in a white towel, approximating the look of a British nurse. "Jessica, Amy is asking for you."

Jess glanced up and shuffled the papers on her desk. "Thank you, Birdeen. Will you tell her I'll see her soon?"

The woman nodded and tottered off toward Amy's bed.

Late that afternoon, she was still putting off the visit when Horace Cookson came into the infirmary. Jessica spotted him first, standing just inside the door to the makeshift hospital, unwilling or unable to take another step. Jess hurried forward to greet him. Although he wore his mayor's clothes—the crooked tie, the vest missing one button, the rumpled suit coat, shiny at the elbows—he appeared so much older, so *gray-faced*, she worried that he'd finally succumbed to the illness that had taken his wife and son.

"Mayor Cookson," she said, in a hushed voice. "Are you all right?" The look in his faded, haggard eyes was one of such loss and confusion, it went to her heart. It was a stupid question; of course he wasn't all right. She tried again. "Are you ill?"

He shook his head. "Jessica, is there a room where we can talk?"

"Yes, I sup—" She thought of the cloakroom-turned-morgue, but that was out of the question. "Let's find a classroom." Catching the eye of one of the nurses, she pointed toward the door to indicate that she'd be gone for a moment. She and Horace walked down the hall until they found the empty geography classroom. Its walls were lined with maps of Europe, a world globe sat on the teacher's desk, and the blackboard still bore a reading assignment from the last class that had met there. He waited for her to settle into the teacher's chair, then perched on a corner of the desk, one leg dangling.

There was something bothering him, something besides his recent losses. To interrupt the awkward moment, she said, "I want to thank you for the butter and cream you've been leaving for me. They're a true luxury."

He waved off her thanks. "It's nothing. You know, farmers get to keep enough of what they produce to feed their families, and now, there's just me at home."

She felt so bad for him. "I wish I could have done more. I'm so sorry—"

But he held up a hand. "That's not why I came here, Jessica. Something is going on that you need to know about."

She twiddled with a piece of chalk that lay on the oak desktop, waiting for him to continue.

"Adam Jacobsen asked for an emergency meeting of the town council last night."

The chalk fell from her suddenly nerveless fingers. "Oh?"

"He wanted us to prohibit you from practicing medicine in Powell Springs one more day. At least that was how he put it."

The colored maps on the walls swam before her eyes for a moment. She looked away from them and set her jaw to regain her equilibrium. "Really. And who does he propose to take care of all those people down the hall?"

"He said that Granny Mae could fill in until Pearson gets here."

"Ah, yes, the elusive Dr. Pearson. I have begun to doubt that he even exists." She couldn't keep a tinge of sarcasm out of her voice.

He shrugged, lifting his baggy, unkempt clothes with his shoulders. "Look, I don't know what happened with you and Adam, or anyone else. It's none of my business. Between you and me and the wall, I wish I was back at my farm with the cows instead of doing this job. But he made some pretty harsh accusations, something about moral turp—turpentine? *Turpitude*, that was it."

Insulted and frightened, Jessica felt her face sizzle. She couldn't make herself ask exactly what Adam had told them. "Just what was the outcome of this meeting?"

"We voted against him, of course. We need you here. You're doing a first-rate job."

That he still thought so, after losing his wife and son, was very generous, in Jessica's view. "So I have the support of the town council? They'll defend me against this character assassination?"

"Sure, for what it's worth. There are only two of us, me and Roland Bright. Adam is the other councilman."

Jessica rubbed her forehead with one hand, feeling as if she once again bore the weight of the world on her shoulders.

"I hate to say it—Powell Springs is a good town—but people love this sort of thing. I guess it's human nature. This is bound to get around. Especially now. It'll give them something else to think about besides the war and sickness. There's another thing you should know. Since Adam didn't get his way, he was pretty sore. He threatened to do something else to have you, well..."

She looked up and gripped the edge of the desk hard enough to make her fingertips turn white and pink. "Run out of town on a rail? Tarred and feathered? Or does he want me executed at dawn? What do you want me to do, Mayor Cookson?"

He sighed, as if this was the very last thing he wanted to be dealing with. "I just thought you should know what's going on. Him being involved with the American Protective League and all makes things a little sticky."

She had feared that Adam might cause some kind of trouble. But she hadn't thought it would be this bad. "Thank you for telling me." Rising from the chair with as much dignity as she could muster, she added, "I'm sorry you've been dragged into a personal matter that Adam has decided to make public. I know you have enough to worry about without this. So do I, in fact."

He stood too. "How is your sister doing?"

"She's regaining her strength."

"There are hardly any families who've escaped this—this *thing*. Your sister's recovery is good news."

Jess slanted a look at the weary mayor. "Yes, it is. I can't wait until she's back on her feet again."

— — —

On a siding near the train depot, five livestock cars stood under a gray afternoon sky. Wispy, low clouds grazed the nearby buttes and hills, making them appear close enough to touch. October rains had revived Powell Creek, covering its streambed with swift-running water next to the rails. Cole, Susannah, and Tanner and his nephews all worked toward getting the Braddock horses loaded. They'd been here for hours already, and they were tired and hungry. A sputtering stream of grays and duns jostled for position, hooking their necks over one another's, rearing and balking. At least the end of the job was in sight.

"Damn it all, get that dun gelding up there!" Pop hollered from his saddle on Muley's back.

Cole wished the old man had stayed home. He and Tanner had the situation well under control, and Pop's bawled orders just made the horses more nervous than they were already. Everyone else simply wore harassed expressions. Susannah threw Pop an impatient look.

"I'm going to the depot office," she called to Cole. He nodded and she brought her mare around to the back of the line. She had the manifest and other paperwork that had to accompany the shipment. In the meantime, Cole and Tanner led the last of the animals up the ramp to the railcar and slid the door closed.

Cole jumped down and shifted the ramp out of the way. "God, I'm glad that's over with," he said to Tanner, who nodded.

Tanner turned to the youngsters. They'd climbed onto their own mounts. "Come on, boys, let's get back to the farm. There's still work to be done."

"Aw, can't we stay in town for a while and get ice cream, Uncle Tanner?" Wade asked.

"Not this time, son. It ain't like you two didn't earn it, but everything's closed down because of the influenza. I might be able to rustle up some kind of treat on the stove back home."

Wade and Josh gave each other sidelong glances that weren't lost on Cole. He'd heard that Tanner wasn't much good at cooking.

"I have a better idea," Cole said, untying his own mount, Sage, from the hitching post. "Let's go down to Tilly's for a round or two. It's on me. Pop, are you game?"

"Anytime you're buying I'm game," the old man replied.

Cole chuckled. "You boys wait here for Miss Susannah to tell her where we are. Then go on back to the farm with her. I'll bet she'll find some cookies in the kitchen for you."

"How does that sound?" Tanner asked the kids. Wade grinned, and Tanner ruffled his red hair. "Yeah, that's what I thought."

The three men headed off toward Tilly's. As they rode past the train cars, Cole noticed that his father looked almost pensive. It was most uncharacteristic of him.

"Something on your mind, Pop?"

"Twenty-seven of our best going overseas. They're beautiful, strong horses, every one of 'em," Pop said, glancing back at the railcars. There was a wistful echo of regret in his rusty voice. "I sure as hell hope someone takes good care of them."

Cole gave him a searching gaze. "Yeah, so do I." It was the first time he'd heard his father express concern for the animals that they were sending to Europe. "Men make war on each other. Animals never ask to get involved. Hell, most people don't ask to get involved."

As if deciding that he'd shown an unmanly tenderhearted side, Pop drew himself up as straight as his arthritic back would allow, and the moment was gone. "Well, never mind that soppy stuff. War is men's business and men do what has to be done without a lot of whining. No matter what."

The gibe was not lost on Cole, but he decided not to rise to the bait. It was the kind of response he'd learned to expect from his father long ago.

They passed very few people on the sidewalks as they rode through town. Powell Springs was just a scarecrow flapping in the breeze, a spavined shadow of its former self, hiding from a predator it couldn't see. The only person standing between it and total disaster was Jessica, fine, strong, passionate Jess, who wouldn't let anything get in the way of her cause to care for the people here. Not Adam. Not Amy. Not even her feelings for Cole.

The three men walked into the smoky confines of Tilly's, thirsty and with spurs ringing. It didn't seem to matter what catastrophes or current events rocked the world. The saloon was a constant with its stuffed elk heads and oil paintings, and the proprietor with a towel slung over his shoulder. Only the Olympia Beer calendar changed annually, and the wall posters occasionally, depending upon who occupied the White House in Washington in any given year.

Cole ordered a bottle of whiskey and three glasses, while Tanner and Pop settled at a table. The place was fairly quiet this afternoon; only Bert Bauer and Elvin Fowler were there. Elvin's crutches were propped against the table where he sat. Cole wasn't sure how he had managed to make it into town, although he'd heard that he was becoming one of Tilly's best customers. Poor bastard, Cole thought. He could understand why the man would take up drinking.

He noticed that Tanner stiffened when he saw Bauer, but it didn't surprise him. That grave robber had enough disreputable character traits to offend just about anyone. Cole passed the glasses around the table and poured a shot into each.

"Hey, Shaw," Tilly called from behind the bar. "You're exactly the man we need to settle a bet we've got going here."

"Yeah? What kind of bet?"

"We're trying to decide which is smarter, a pig or a horse. I say a horse, but Elvin is voting for the pig, and so is Bert."

"He would," Tanner muttered under his breath.

"Hell, boys, it's not even a contest. Everyone knows a horse is smarter than a pig!" Pop declared.

"I knew a man who had a hunting pig, once," Elvin said. "That hog could flush out game as good as any pointer. It's their sense of smell."

"I saw one trained at a county fair to choose cards from a deck," Bauer chimed in. "It got the right card every damned time. Show me a horse that can do that." He signaled Tilly for another beer.

"Well, those pigs aren't going to get you home on a moonless night when you're too drunk to find your ass with both hands. A horse always knows his way back. If you break your leg out on the range, no pig is going to give you a ride to help."

"I saw a chicken once that could play a little tiny piano with its beak, and—"

"Damn it, Elvin, we ain't talking about chickens, here. We're talking about pigs and smart horses."

The ridiculous debate began to heat up, and Cole knew Pop was in his element. Everyone had a story to tell, an example to cite. Even Tanner got involved, and he tended to be a quiet man who kept to himself. Cole shut out the braying voices and thought of Jessica, beautiful and fired with passion, lying in his arms.

Tomorrow he would visit Amy at the hospital. Not because he wanted to, particularly, but because he knew he had to. And while he was at it, he'd see for himself her progress. Right now, he tried not to think of the rotten trick she had pulled on them. But it made him wonder if he'd ever really known her at all. Given what he'd learned, he thought she'd be best suited for a snake like Jacobsen. They both pretended to be something they weren't. He drank half of his shot and sat back in the chair to let the tension ease out of his back.

The various merits of pigs and horses were discussed for an hour or so. Lost in his own thoughts, Cole let the conversation flow around him like river water. When he bothered to listen again, he noticed it had switched to baldness.

"Did you ever see a bald Indian?" Pop asked, putting his elbow on the table. "Did you boys ever see a bald Indian?" he repeated to Cole and Tanner. "Nossir! And do you know why?" He didn't wait for an answer. "Because they don't wash their hair. Those chiefs, they're on to something. If you don't want to go bald, don't wash your hair!"

"I don't know, Shaw, that doesn't sound right," Tilly said, flipping his bar towel over his shoulder.

Pop poured another drink and thumped his fist on the table. "Sitting Bull, now there's a good example. They shot him dead but he died with every hair in his braids."

Cole laughed, slapped the table, and shook his head. "That's just a lot of foolishness."

Pop got bristly. "What? You don't believe me? You just take yourself on down to the library and have a look at his photograph hanging there on the wall. Do you think Buffalo Bill would put a Indian in his show that didn't have hair?"

"That's not what I mean," Cole said.

"I've seen that picture," Tanner put in. "He does have braids."

Cole laughed again at the absurdity of the whole thing.

"You're damned right, he does," Pop agreed. "That Bill Cody was a first-rate showman, with Annie Oakley and all."

"Yeah, you tried this trick at home and Susannah got after you for turning the pillowcases gray with your dirty hair. Then she made you scrub your head until it was pink."

Pop scowled. "It's a wonder I have a hair left on my noggin after that."

"You've got plenty."

"Well, women wash their hair and they don't seem to go bald," Elvin pointed out.

"No, and some of them wash it twice a week," Bauer added. "Or even more."

The door to the saloon opened, letting in a gust of damp air and, Cole hoped, a change in this stupid conversation. But when he looked up, he saw Susannah standing there. She still wore her riding skirt and work gloves.

Elvin nodded. "Maybe washing doesn't have anything to do—" Noticing her, he broke off, and no one else said another word.

Two women in Tilly's in as many months. It was unheard of.

But Cole stood, knocking over his chair. Something was wrong. Wrong in every possible way. An inexplicable shiver raced through him, raising every hair on his body. Across the table, Tanner stood up too, suddenly as tense as a spring.

Cole had eyes only for Susannah's chalk-white face. He crossed the few feet separating them. "What's wrong?"

She looked at him as if someone had struck her from behind, a surprise attack that she hadn't yet figured out. Her mouth worked, but no words came out.

"Susannah!" He reached over and gripped her wrist.

Finally, she thrust a crumpled piece of paper at him. With some hesitation, he took it from her and smoothed it out.

It was a telegram. Oh, God, he thought, telegrams had never brought him good news. Never. He read the words twice, then read them again.

> MRS SUSANNAH BRADDOCK
> RTE 3
> Powell Springs ORE
>
> DEEPLY REGRET TO INFORM YOU THAT SERGEANT RILEY BRADDOCK INFANTRY IS OFFICIALLY REPORTED KILLED IN ACTION OCTOBER 11
> M MORRIS ACTING ADJUTANT GENERAL

Cole turned the page over, as if there might some better explanation of the message on the reverse, some proof that it was only a cruel, terrible hoax. But he found nothing.

"Oh, Jesus." Cole's throat was as tight and dry as an old leather glove. His eyes burned as he stared down at the impersonal words printed by the telegrapher. "Jesus Christ."

"Where are the boys?" Tanner asked, and glanced in Bauer's direction.

"At home." Susannah's voice was only a croak. She dropped her head so that the mist on her hair looked like tiny glass beads in the gaslight of the saloon. A choking sob was fighting its way up from her chest.

"Well, what's going on now?" Pop asked. "They didn't give you a hard time at the depot, did they?" Cole looked at his father, who watched them, puzzled and still safe for a moment in his ignorance.

Feeling as stiff and lifeless as a mechanical penny bank, Cole put his arm around Susannah and motioned the rest of their group outside. "We have to go. Right now." His brusque tone left no room for argument.

War is men's business and men do what has to be done.

Irrelevantly, he wondered if Pop's blowhard philosophy would still be the same when he learned that his oldest son had died on a battlefield in France.

CHAPTER NINETEEN

Word of Riley Braddock's death spread over Powell Springs like the dark wings of an eerie, moonless night. Whispered from neighbor to neighbor, through back doors and screened-in porches, it moved along the telephone wire, despite the epidemic that still had most of the town on its knees. The *Powell Springs Star* ran Riley's obituary on the front page. He was the third soldier from Powell Springs to die, although Eddie Cookson, killed by a different enemy, had never gotten out of the Pacific Northwest.

Jessica was checking the inventory of clean linens in a maple breakfront that served as a supply cabinet when Cole walked into the infirmary. She'd already heard the dreadful news about Riley and, not knowing what else to do under the circumstances, had sent an immediate, heartfelt note of sympathy to the Braddock farm.

When she turned and saw him standing beside her desk watching her like a sleepwalker, his pallor, two-day beard, and sunken, bloodshot eyes frightened her. She hurried to speak to him.

"Cole," she said quietly, reaching for his hands.

He said nothing but put his arms around her and rested his head on her shoulder for just a moment. She felt him sigh, and it seemed as if the sorrow of the world was behind it. People nearby gaped and then looked away. Her own heart aching, she hugged him.

Finally he straightened. "How is Amy?"

"She's much better than I ever expected. In fact, I'm planning to release her tomorrow to Mrs. Donaldson."

"Does she know about Ri—my brother?" He couldn't seem to get the name out.

"Yes. Everyone has heard. But how are *you*?"

"I'm—it's not easy for any of us. Susannah hasn't slept in her bed for two nights, not since we got the telegram. She just sits by a window in the parlor, like she's looking for him to come down the road. She cooks, and I help, but none of us is really hungry. We're all having a hard time."

She motioned him into a chair beside her desk and sat down in her own. "I don't suppose you can bring Riley home?" She thought it was unlikely—France was filled with acres and acres of graves.

He shook his head, and he spoke to his knees, not lifting his eyes to hers. "I talked to Horace Cookson. He knows a couple of people in Washington, DC. They're burying the men as soon as possible and pretty close to where they fell. And the horses." His voice faltered, and he swallowed, then looked at her. "God, they're burying the horses…"

"Cole," she whispered, "shouldn't you be at home? Do you need a doctor for anyone? Your father? You could have sent a message—I'd have found someone to give me a ride to your place."

"No, I'm not here for a doctor." He straightened and appeared to recover from his daze. "I have to talk to Amy."

She covered his hand with hers. "Oh, but she understands why you can't visit."

He shook his head and stood up to walk down the sheet-draped aisle where Amy's bed was located. Jess followed, her hands laced tightly together, worry making chills fly down her spine.

Cole rounded into Amy's cubicle and found her sitting up, reading a book. She looked much better than she had when he'd first brought her in. She wore a modest bed jacket and her hair had been braided into two neat plaits, like a young girl's. And except for a slight thinness in her cheeks, she seemed well.

"Cole, oh Cole!" she exclaimed happily. "I'm so glad to see you! But I'm terribly sorry about Riley. It's such a tragedy." She turned her cheek for him to kiss. He ignored the invitation.

He sat down on the stool beside Amy's bed. His head throbbed from the whiskey he'd consumed over the past couple of days, but he was sober now. And determined. "Hi Amy. You're feeling better?"

She put a scrap of paper in the book on her lap to mark her place. "Oh, yes! I'm sorry I scared everyone. Jessica said I was fairly ill for a while. I walked once around the gym this morning. I was a little shaky when I finished, but I'm working to get my strength back. "

"Good."

"Jessica said I can go home tomorrow. To Mrs. Donaldson's, anyway. We'll wait until, well, an appropriate amount of time has passed." She followed this broad hint with a sympathetic smile.

"That's fine. You'll be able to get on with the rest of your life, whatever you decide to do with it."

"What?" She gave him a puzzled look that reminded Cole of the way Roscoe looked when the dog was trying to understand him.

But he was satisfied that she had recovered enough to listen to him. He reached into his shirt pocket and once again pulled out the telegram that Jess had received with his name signed to it. He had whisked it off her table the same night he'd told her who'd really sent it. He also took out the affidavit that Leroy had written. "I have something to show you."

Amy's expression didn't alter. "Oh, Cole, you poor dear. I know how horrible this must be for you, for everyone." Fair or not, he couldn't believe anything she said now, no matter how sincere she might sound. "But really, you don't need to go through the pain of showing me the telegram about Riley."

He unfolded the message and held it up so she could see it. "It's not about my brother. This is the telegram that Jessica got from me a year ago. *Supposedly* from me. I didn't send it."

Her delicate brows drew together and she folded her hands on her book. "I don't understand."

"Uh-huh. Maybe this will help. This," he went on, unfolding the telegrapher's note, "is a statement written by Leroy Fenton that tells who gave him the message to send." He held the pages up to her.

She took them from him and read both. Muscles in her face twitched, and she wouldn't look at him. "You don't believe this, do you?"

He wasn't about to go through another song and dance regarding her snow-white innocence and pure heart. He'd already heard all that from Jessica, before he'd convinced her of the truth. He leaned closer and put his elbows on his knees, forcing her to look at him. In a low, controlled voice he said, "Amy, I'm not going to marry you. I don't love you." She stared at him with her mouth open and eyes wide. "I have always loved Jessica, and you pulled a low-down, underhanded trick on us both. You tried to separate us, and I accept my share of the blame—I never should have started courting you. I wish I had been stronger than that, and because I wasn't, I owe you an apology. But it was only by the thinnest good luck that I learned about your scheme before it was too late. My brother's death showed me that our time on this earth is too damned short to waste on bad decisions. You're free to live your life, but you won't be living it with me."

He snapped the papers from Amy's hands, stood up, and walked away. He came abreast of Jessica, who waited nearby, her face unreadable. Kissing her cheek, he said, "I'll talk to you in a day or so."

Granny Mae, passing them with an armload of towels, gave them a steady look but said nothing.

A high-pitched shriek came from Amy's cubicle. "*C-o-l-l-le!* Come back here!" Every conscious pair of eyes within range turned to stare at him. But he kept walking.

He pushed through the doors and went outside, where Sage waited patiently, tied to the hitching rail. Despite losing Riley, and regardless of all that had happened, a curious feeling of freedom lifted part of the weight from his shoulders. Swinging a leg over his horse, he turned for home.

Inside, Jessica walked to her sister's bed. Now that Cole had confronted her, she felt she should face her as well. She found Amy with one foot on the floor, preparing to rise.

"I think you'd better stay put a while longer."

Unable to argue, Amy fell back, panting from the exertion, but weak enmity narrowed her eyes as she considered Jess. It reminded Jessica of their last hostile meeting in her office, when Amy's influenza had just begun taking hold. Her face was blotchy and wet with angry tears. Jessica almost expected to see her begin gnashing her teeth at her. "You…you must be thrilled. You got your way again, Jessica. I hope you're happy."

Jessica sat on the stool Cole had recently occupied and crossed her arms. "I'm not happy at all. I discovered that my sister, my only flesh and blood in the world, deceived and hurt me. When Cole first told me about what you'd done, I refused to believe it. It seemed impossible that the girl I'd grown up with, the sister I'd worried about and sent money to every month while I was gone, could be so disloyal to me. I would have even paid for your wedding." Her words dripped with irony. "I'd ask you why you did it, but I don't think anything you could say now will help."

Amy struggled to sit up again. "I already told you why. You didn't deserve Cole!"

Had her sister always been such a monster of selfishness? Jess wondered. Had she no conscience at all? "And what gave you the right to decide this? Do you feel no guilt, no remorse?"

Amy gave her a narrow-eyed look. "Did you feel guilty for monopolizing all of Daddy's time?"

It was as if a frighteningly different person lurked behind Amy's mask of pious good deeds. Bitter resentment stirred in Jessica, and though she managed to keep her shaking voice low in this semi-public place, she could no longer contain her anger. "So you decided that you were the one who should marry Cole. You made us both believe that the other had broken off our engagement—"

"You were not engaged. Not officially."

"—despite knowing we'd loved each other since childhood," Jess went on, ignoring Amy's interruption. "You told us unforgivable lies—*us*, people you claim to love. I'm not going to put up with this from you—I won't take it from anyone!" She rose from the stool. "You don't think I deserve Cole? Well, let me tell you something, Amy. I don't think Cole deserves a double-crossing fraud like you."

A quick gasp at the insult set off a mild coughing spell in Amy, but Jessica didn't linger.

— — —

A steady rain lashed the dining room windows at the Braddock farm. Only Cole and Pop sat at the table.

Susannah had gone back to her chair beside the parlor window, and the boys were asleep upstairs. Since Susannah wasn't going near the infirmary any longer, it was decided that their restriction to the bunkhouse, away from the ranch house, could end. They were the only ones who still ate with the gusto of childhood innocence. Cole knew they sensed that something was wrong—the adults were acting funny. Their uncle Tanner had told them that Miss Susannah's husband wouldn't be coming back from the war. But their own parents had left them and they weren't coming back, either. That had been worse.

Tanner sat in the parlor reading a farm journal. Cole had noticed that Tanner had been especially solicitous to Susannah since the news of Riley's death. He liked the hired hand. He did his job, he was quiet and competent, and he was good with those nephews.

Cole picked up his blue enamel coffee mug to go to the kitchen. "More, Pop?"

"I guess." He pushed his own mug toward Cole.

Cole went to the stove and returned with steaming refills. Both men had taken about as much punishment from whiskey as they could stand. Now they were back on coffee.

"I have something to tell you about."

His father gave him a tired, apprehensive look. "Yeah?"

Cole nodded, and explained why he was no longer involved with Amy.

Pop stared at him. "You're sure about all that?"

For the third time, Cole produced his evidence and shoved it across the table. The old man picked up both messages and held them at arm's length to decipher them.

"So now what are you going to do?"

"I'm going to ask Jessica to marry me and stay here in Powell Springs."

Pop closed his eyes. "God, that doctor gal again."

"Come on, Pop, admit it. Amy tried to fool all of us with her underhanded double-dealing. Jessica has never been anything except, well, except Jessica. Amy—" He shuddered. "I honestly don't know who she is. Neither does Jess. And that's not the kind of thing you want to find out after you say 'I do.' "

The old man held up an arthritic hand to concede the point. "Boy, she took us all for a hell of a ride, that's for sure."

"Yeah. Is that what you want in a daughter-in-law?"

Pop sighed and rubbed his white, short-cropped hair, and didn't answer right away. He looked older than Cole could remember, as if his spark, that little internal fire that made him feisty and cantankerous, had been doused. "Sometimes I think I've lived too long," he said finally. "Everything is turned upside down. I'm not sure what a body can count on anymore." With slow, stiff movements, he pulled a small bottle out of his hip pocket and added some whiskey to his cup. "When your ma died, I bulled my way through because I had you two boys to raise, and I knew she'd expect me to do it right." He looked up at Cole. "I've never really been certain if I did that."

Cole fiddled with his spoon, unprepared for this frankness from his father. Immediately, he felt defensive. "Why, because I wasn't the son you expected me to be?"

Pop glared at him. "Did I say that?"

"Sometimes, in so many words."

"How?" he demanded. "How did I do that?"

Cole was in no mood to rehash old arguments and past insinuations. "It doesn't matter now. Let's just say that I often felt like *I* was the one you wondered about." Grief and anger over losing Riley made him say more than he would have ordinarily. "I was the one who didn't turn out the way you wanted."

"Because I wanted you to go to war with Riley?" Pop persisted. He put his elbows on the table and leaned forward a bit. "Well, let me tell you something. I thought it was the right thing to do at the time. Now..."

"And now?"

Cole waited, for what he wasn't sure. Approval, praise, some comment that wasn't laced with criticism. But it didn't come.

He waved Cole off and pushed himself from the chair with a loud groan. "Now I'm going to bed."

Cole watched him shuffle across the floor. Sighing, he stared at the rain-washed windows and at the blackness beyond.

— — —

Early the next morning, Amy returned to Laura Donaldson's house to recuperate. That meant the infirmary would be losing the woman's help, but given her emotional personality, Jess didn't think the loss was that great.

Jessica purposely stayed at her office doing paperwork until she knew that her sister had gone. Their public scene had been ugly, and worse, Jess sensed the subtle division of supporters among the people in the infirmary. Some were sympathetic to Jessica, others to Amy. Jess didn't care who took which side—she found the entire situation embarrassing. If only Cole had waited for a more opportune moment to open this can of worms.

While she sat at the desk in her back room, she caught herself waiting for signs of activity at the shop next door. The sound of hammer on metal, the smell of the forge, the whinny of horses. But there was nothing.

That afternoon after she returned to the high school, she was listening to the sodden lungs of Jeremy Easton, fearing the worst for him, when she heard a commotion outside. She shut out the noise, trying to concentrate on her patient. Laying a hand against his face, she could feel the fever burning within him. Please, she thought, not Jeremy too.

"Well, land sakes!" Granny Mae blurted from across the cavernous room.

Jessica looked up and saw Granny and Iris Delaney at the window. "What's going on out there?"

"I can't tell. But Adam Jacobsen is with a group of people, and they're coming this way."

A cold hand of dread stole around Jessica's heart. Adam had not been seen at the infirmary since the morning he'd jumped out at her and Cole, pointing a finger of judgment at them as if he were an avenging archangel. She walked to the window to stand beside Granny Mae and pulled down her mask, aghast at what she saw outside.

Adam Jacobsen and a ragged band of followers, which included Laura Donaldson, James Leonard, and his reluctant-looking wife Dolly, had gathered on the steps of the high school. James Leonard carried a badly painted sign.

God will judge fornicators

and adulterers!

Through the glass, Jess heard Adam's muted pontificating. "…want your loved ones left in the care of an immoral harlot who masquerades behind her honorable profession?"

A wave of *no*s swelled from the group, like a breeze wafting across a field of summer wheat.

"For all we know, Dr. Layton might have brought this plague with her. We didn't have it until she got here," Adam said.

"Hey, that's right!"

"It's like you said, Mr. Jacobsen. The last days."

"The town council has refused to remove her, refused to admit that I'm right—that she's not fit to practice medicine. Granny Mae can take care of our people. Dr. Layton is not a Powell Springs citizen any longer."

General babbling came from the group, and a couple of people stared at Jessica with angry, spite-filled gazes, making her back away from the glass.

"But we are not powerless," Adam continued, speaking at full volume. "The democratic process that has made us a great nation will let us prevail. Sign the petitions I've given you. Circulate them among everyone you know. If it means going into that saloon that serves demon rum at the end of the street, amen! I know that's where the harlot's fancy man goes to drink, but every signature counts. Do *whatever* it takes. God is on our side!" He pointed to the double front doors of the school. "The harlot is *inside*!"

"Oh, dear!" Iris exclaimed.

"This is horrible," Jessica said, her heart drumming in her chest. "He's inciting them to violence. Cole needs to know about this."

Granny Mae watched the hubbub, her gray bun slightly askew on her head. "Looks like you made yourself an enemy. A dangerous one, too. That little weasel has reported me to the American Protective League twice already."

Jessica sighed and interlaced her hands under her chin, making a steeple in front of her lips with her two index fingers. Why, oh, why hadn't she listened to Cole about Adam? He was not only unhinged, he was as malevolent as a viper. To suggest that she infected Powell Springs with influenza—the man was filled with hate. She almost expected to see Amy in the group, too, except Jess knew that she was still too weak to take part in something so strenuous. And a small part of her heart refused to let her believe that her sister, regardless of what she had already done, would go as far as the people outside.

"I'm going to have to get Sheriff Gannon over here if this gets worse," Jessica said. "Those people could decide to attack the infirmary, and we'll be sitting ducks here with all these patients."

While she waited for the crowd to disperse, Winks Lamont and Bert Bauer came in the back door to collect the two bodies waiting in the cloakroom for burial. Bauer, with his ratlike face, gave Jessica a salacious look that made her cringe.

Adam and his followers finally left, full of righteous purpose, to follow their minister's bidding. Once Jessica was certain they'd gone, she ran back to her office to call Cole on the telephone.

"I'm so glad you're in the house."

"I just came in for a sandwich. I was out in the barn pitching hay. What's the matter?" he asked.

Knowing full well that operators and other parties on the line often listened in on telephone conversations, Jessica hedged. "Plenty. I can't talk about it now. I need to discuss it with you privately."

"Privately—who else is with you, Jess?"

Impatient and frightened, she replied, "Only Birdeen."

A decidedly female gasp sounded that was not Jessica's, followed by a sharp click on the line.

"See?"

"Okay, I'll be there right away."

Jess paced the length and width of her downstairs office, occasionally going to the window to look for both Cole or signs of trouble. She massaged her neck as she walked. After everything that had happened, she began to ask herself, what was the point? Why should she continue to work in medicine?

At last she heard the truck engine and ran to the window. "Thank God," she said aloud, and watched Cole park in front of the shop. She pulled open her front door, and he smiled at her as he approached. Her heart lightened just at the sight of him. Even though he still looked a little haggard, he didn't seem quite as worn out and bedraggled as he had before.

"Jess." He stepped inside and closed the door. Taking her into his arms, he gave her a quick kiss. Releasing her, he said, "Sorry, I guess I'm a little ripe." He smelled of clean sweat and hay and horses, but it was very male and enticing, and a welcome difference from the musty-smelling black suit and scent of hair oil that always wafted from Adam. This close, she noticed Cole was wearing a gun belt with a long-barreled revolver in the holster.

Men in New York didn't wear guns, but things were different here. This was still the Wild West.

"I'm glad you're here."

"I left as soon as I hung up. Are you all right?"

"No." It wasn't like her to be so blunt—people expected to hear that she was fine, no matter what. But she wasn't fine now, and because he was affected by the reason, he needed to know why. "Come and sit. I wish you'd brought that bottle of whiskey." With a last quick look out the front window, she reached over to lock the door. Then she motioned him toward her back room.

He frowned at her obvious nervousness. "What's going on? Sounds serious."

"It is serious."

They settled in the only two chairs left in the back, and she explained what had happened.

His expression turned as dark as storm clouds. "Damn that rotten son of a bitch! I knew should have decked him when I had the chance."

She shook her head vigorously. "Cole, no, you don't understand. We're both vulnerable. If you had hit him, he'd only have more ammunition to use against us. He's going to ruin my reputation for sure. Maybe…maybe even Amy will help him." Her voice trembled for a moment, and tears gathered behind her lids. "Don't think that you aren't on his blacklist too." She propped her forehead in her hand.

He thumped the arm of his chair with his fist. "Oh, *hell*, I wish you hadn't let him come around here."

She rolled her lips against her teeth and looked at her lap, feeling as guilty as a child caught stealing.

Reaching out, he touched her knee. "I'm not blaming you, Jessica. It's just that he wouldn't have had the chance to make this mess if he hadn't gotten so close." He sat forward in his chair. "But what can he do to me? Accuse me of being unfit to raise horses? You're the one I'm worried about."

"He can have us arrested—"

"Oh, brother, I'd like to see him try." He uttered a short bark of laughter. "Arrested! On what grounds?"

"These days, reasons don't matter. The APL encourages people to inform on their neighbors, their friends, *everyone*. It's turned into a witch hunt."

A frantic knocking on the front door interrupted their conversation. Jessica sidled up to the glass to see a breathless Granny Mae. She yanked open the door and let her in. Cole joined them.

"Mae, what's the matter?" he asked.

"Someone is critical?" Jess asked.

Granny Mae waved a hand, then put it on her chest. "Let me get my wind." After drawing a couple of deep breaths, she replied, "That mob—they're on their way—here. James Leonard is leading them."

"What? Why?" Cole asked.

"Did they hurt the patients?"

Mae shook her head. "No. They came into the gymnasium, looking for you. I didn't tell them where you went, but I heard James say they were coming here."

"Is Jacobsen with them?"

"Of course not, that coward," the old woman said.

Just then, the crash of breaking glass sounded in the front. Raised, angry voices, trampling over each other, created the sound of angry, milling wild animals. Jess let out a little shriek.

Cole jumped from his chair and ran to the waiting room, with Jessica fast on his heels. A rock the size of a baseball lay on the floor. He picked it up.

"Oh, dear God. They're attacking the office!" she said.

He looked out the windows and saw some of the people she'd told him had gathered outside the high school. He jammed his hat down on his head.

Furious, he opened the door and faced them. Jessica started to follow, but he pushed her back inside and into Granny Mae, who was behind her.

"There is the fornicator, right here at the scene of the crime!" James Leonard boomed, waving his sign. His wife, Dolly, lurked on the edge of the crowd, looking like a miserable and unwilling participant.

"What are you talking about, Leonard? And what proof do you have to make your accusations?"

He wore a short beard that followed only his jawline and a black felt hat. "Reverend Jacobsen's word is good enough for me."

Cole tossed up the rock and caught it again. "When I report your vandalism and the destruction of my property to the county sheriff, you'll be facing the circuit judge. That will be almost good enough for me. When he sentences you to jail time, I'll be downright happy."

Leonard swelled up like an angry toad. "I didn't throw that rock."

"Really? But here you are, *at the scene of the crime*."

"We want Jessica Layton to stop practicing medicine in Powell Springs and to leave town. She isn't welcome here anymore."

Cole tossed the stone aside and let his hand linger near the pistol on his hip. "Now you listen to me, all of you troublemakers. You get off this property right now, or I swear to God, I'll have Whit Gannon on the telephone so fast you'll all be in a county cell by tonight."

Granny Mae sidled out from behind Cole. He studied the angry crowd and decided that given their rabid attitude, she could be hurt. He put an arm out to block her. But she would not go back inside. She let her sharp gaze fall on each sheeplike follower. "You know, I saw some of you people in the infirmary when you were so sick, we didn't know if you would live or die. Dr. Layton took care of you and your families—wives, brothers, sisters, children—and she never asked for one thing in return. This man," she said, referring to Cole, "carried you inside from the backs of wagons the day we opened for business. He didn't ask for anything either. His brother just died in France, his family is in mourning, and this is how you repay them—with your dirty-minded assumptions?" She made a noise of contemptuous disgust. There was a shuffling of feet and muttering among the rabble. "Now you do like Cole said. You go on home, mind your own business, and stop pestering people who aren't bothering you."

People began to drift away, but Leonard assured them, "We still have our petition. We'll get rid of that woman yet."

The three of them—Cole, Jessica, and Mae—stood on the small front porch until the group had gone.

Jessica spoke first, smiling. "Granny Mae Rumsteadt, you surprise me."

Granny Mae lifted her chin, giving Jess a view of her high-cut nostrils. "I can't abide a bully. Your father and I had our tangles, but he was a good man, Jessica. So is your father, Cole—stubborn as a mule, like me, but good." She smiled a secret smile that made Cole wonder if her comment was more than just a passing remark. "They had some good children." Amy was tactfully left out of the conversation.

"It's not over yet, though," Jessica said.

"Probably not. But it is for now," Cole replied.

"I've got Jeremy to see to. I need to go back to the infirmary."

"Jeremy has the influenza?" Cole's expression was blank.

Jess nodded.

"We'll see to him," Granny said. "I think you've worked enough for one day. If anything happens, we'll send for you."

Cole lifted his hat and resettled it on his head, the adrenaline pumping through him beginning to fade. "Jess, you lock yourself inside. Mae, I'll give you a ride back to the high school. Then I'll come back here and board up that broken window."

He offered his arm to Mae, and she took it as he walked her to the truck.

CHAPTER TWENTY

Winks Lamont burst through the back door of the gymnasium. "He's here! He's here, I seen him myself!"

"What're you trying to do? Wake the dead? Har-har-har!" From her desk, Jess heard Bert Bauer's coarse joke, followed by his braying laughter. She gritted her teeth as she scribbled a note on Jeremy Easton's record. "It better be Jesus you saw, considering how long I been waiting here for you. We gotta get these stiffs in the ground."

Jess took a deep breath and pressed her pen to the paper hard enough to make an ink blot.

"I didn't see Jesus. It was that Pearson fella everybody's been waiting on. He just came in on the train."

Jess jumped to her feet and strode to the cloakroom, where three sheet-wrapped bodies waited. She ought to be accustomed to the smell by now, but it always made her flinch. Winks Lamont's lack of personal hygiene didn't help matters. Bauer's leer she didn't acknowledge at all.

"Winks, did you say that Dr. Pearson is here? You're sure?"

"Yes, ma'am. He's down at the depot, looking for someone to take his stuff to the hotel."

"Did anyone meet him? Horace Cookson? Roland Bright?"

"No, ma'am. Not that I know of."

Untying her apron, she muttered, "Well, for heaven's sake." Hadn't he wired anyone to let the town know he was coming? If he had and no one met the train, Powell Springs wouldn't make a very good impression on the man who had traveled so far to help them.

Since the incident outside Jessica's office the day before, Cole had moved into the shop and had made several trips to the infirmary, still wearing his gun belt, and now, a badge. He'd called Whit Gannon to tell him what had happened, but the sheriff had had to travel to the Multnomah County courthouse in Portland, fifteen miles away. He wouldn't be back for a couple of days. With his own three deputies out sick, Whit had temporarily deputized Cole to act in his absence.

Jessica supposed she ought to wait for him to escort her down to the depot, but she couldn't leave Dr. Pearson just standing around with no one to greet him. She wanted to put him to work as soon as possible. Besides, she had faced the worst neighborhoods in New York City alone, sometimes traveling across the rooftops of the tenements to save time and steps.

She pulled off her mask, sick of wearing the thing and trying to breathe through it. "Iris, I'm going out for a little while," she called to Iris Delaney, as the older woman tended Gladys Zachary, a mother of three whose husband was fighting in Europe.

"Jessica, wait."

Gray-haired, spinster Iris, a bright little bird of a woman with a sweet and cheerful manner, was one of Jessica's favorite volunteers. Always more helpful than hindering, as some of the others were, she did her work and kept her opinions to herself.

Jess began walking toward her, but Iris motioned her toward the front of the room and away from the beds. When she reached her, Jess asked, "Has Gladys taken a turn for the worse?"

"No, she's about the same." Iris lowered her voice. "I haven't had a chance to talk to you since—well, since that horrible exhibition here on the steps the other day."

Jessica tightened her jaw and felt her muscles tense, waiting for some criticism.

"I just want you to know that I think Adam Jacobsen and men of his ilk are shameful. They claim to be good, righteous people, but they're not." Her voice had dropped to a whisper. "I don't care whether his accusation is true or not. It's no one's business what you do in your personal life. Especially when it comes to matters of the heart. It's not a big secret that you and Cole have loved each other since you were children. Life is far too short to live with regret, and sigh over what might have been. Believe me, I know what I'm talking about. Don't let that happen to you."

Jess noticed that her brown eyes sparkled with unshed tears, and she recalled that Iris had had a crush on Roland Bright for as long as she could remember. Why Roland had never acted to make this gem of a woman his own, Jessica couldn't imagine. Impulsively, she leaned forward and gave the older woman a quick peck on the cheek. "Thank you, Iris. Your support means a lot."

Jess slipped on her coat and walked outside into the early November weather, looking to the right and left for anyone who might cause her trouble.

How had things come to this point? she wondered, walking along Main Street. Little more than a month ago, she had returned to Powell Springs for a brief visit with her sister. Since then, she'd experienced pestilence, breathtaking betrayal, and attempted character assassination. She had rediscovered the slim possibility to love again, grieved over every patient lost, and once more witnessed what damage man's inhumanity and intolerance could do to others. As she passed the plate-glass windows of closed businesses, she caught her reflection now and then. She recognized that whatever rest and healthy appearance she'd recovered during her sabbatical in Saratoga had been lost again. Her clothes were wrinkled and she often did her own laundry in her kitchen sink since Wegner's was now closed. The couple had both come down with influenza, although they'd managed to remain in their upstairs apartment, caring for each other.

Her step was not as brisk as it had been when she arrived, but she moved down the sidewalk toward the depot, hoping to find Dr. Pearson and have a chance to greet him properly. Walking along, she saw a pair of young boys coming her way in the street. One of them rode a bicycle, and the other dragged an old stick and looked behind himself to see the track it made in the mud. She thought they were about ten years old.

"Hey, she's that bad woman doctor I heard my pa talking about," one said to the other, pointing at Jessica. He didn't trouble to lower his voice.

The boy with the stick looked up in her direction. "Yeah, I heard about her too. My folks were talking about her and Cole Braddock in the kitchen yesterday morning. My mother said she wouldn't let her take a splinter out of her hand after what she did. She said Mr. Braddock ain't no better. When they saw me, they clammed up."

Jessica's face burned and she kept her eyes trained on the distant wooded hills, but she could feel them staring at her as if she were a bench or some other inanimate object. They certainly spoke about her as if she were deaf.

"Why? What did they do?"

"I dunno, but it must have been bad. I got in trouble just for asking. My dad called her a *hoor*. I asked him if that was some kind of rabbit or a winter freeze. We have hoarfrosts here sometimes. He paddled me for saying the word, so I ain't asking again."

They passed her and Jess swallowed hard, unable to think of anything to say to them until it was too late. Children could be very cruel, she knew, and they usually learned their manners—good or bad—at home.

After their one night together—a night that even now had the power to make her blush with pleasure and modesty—Cole had asked Jessica to stay in Powell Springs. She had put him off, mainly because of the complications of their relationship. But now, despite Iris's advice, how could she stay? Even if she were the only doctor in town, she suspected that she would have no patients. No one would come to her for treatment, thanks to Adam and his hateful petition.

Adam Jacobsen—the very name made her recoil. And to think that he had actually plastered his slobbery mouth on her lips in his uncouth attempt to court her. But she had not once foreseen that rejecting him would turn into this tempest of ruining her reputation and jeopardizing her career.

She wrapped her coat around her more securely as a stiff east wind kicked up. She had to put those troubles out of her mind for now. After all, she was going to meet the man who would provide her escape from this town.

— — —

When Jessica arrived at the depot, she found Frederick Pearson inside, locked in a tense conversation with Abner Willets, the stationmaster.

"Mr. Willets, am I to understand that there is *no one*, not one single porter available in this, this *hamlet*, to take my belongings to the hotel?" Dr. Pearson spoke in a clipped New England accent that no one around Powell Springs had probably ever heard before. He was a tall man, young, who looked and sounded as if he had led a privileged life. His chestnut hairline was beginning to creep away from his forehead, and he didn't appear to have missed any meals. His lofty bearing and well-tailored clothing, however, didn't seem to make an impression on Abner.

"Look, Mr. Price—"

"That would be Doctor Pearson."

Abner continued, unruffled. "In case you haven't noticed, there's a war on. The influenza has knocked this town off its pins, too. I lost my younger porters to the army, and the old one I had is home in bed."

Jessica seized the opportunity to intervene. She crossed the pine plank floor to introduce herself. "Dr. Pearson, I'm Jessica Layton." She put out her hand, which he shook. "I'm sorry no one was here to meet you sooner. Did you wire your arrival information to anyone?"

"There was no time. I just managed to escape the press-gang that practically kidnapped me from the train in Omaha to serve in the hospital there." The tone of his voiced conveyed his indignation and weariness. "I tried to explain that I was expected here. Obviously, that was of no consequence to them."

Jessica nodded. "I suppose I can understand their desperation. I've been caring for the patients here for the past few weeks with no help other than volunteers, so I'm certainly glad to see you. And I'm sure I can find someone to help you with your trunks and such."

"Hallelujah, at last I'll have a passably competent nurse."

Jessica gave him a small, tight smile. "Actually, I am a physician."

Pearson's brows rose. "Really. A *female* physician." His tone made it clear that he regarded such an occurrence as an aberration of nature. She didn't like it, but she was accustomed to it. "And where did you attend medical school?"

"Women's Medical College in Philadelphia."

"Indeed. How unfortunate that you weren't able to attend a larger school. I understand the science courses in these women's colleges don't quite measure up to some of the more established universities, such as Harvard or Dartmouth."

"Yes, Doctor, they do." Already pressured, Jessica's fuse began to shorten. Pearson's blatant condescension was wearing on her nerves like an emery board. "I don't recall that Mayor Cookson mentioned where you received *your* education."

Pearson lifted his chin. "I attended Yale."

Jess smiled. "Not Johns Hopkins? A loss to that institution, I'm sure."

He reddened and tipped her a slight nod, accepting her riposte. For the moment, anyway.

"If you go to the hotel, I'll arrange to have your belongings brought over. It would be helpful if you could come by the infirmary afterward. I'd like you to see what we're doing."

"I shall do that, madam, if you would be so kind as to direct me."

"I'll send a couple of men who are helping there. They'll collect your luggage and then show you the way."

"So I'll have you *and* a staff. That's somewhat comforting news." He looked satisfied.

Jessica gave the arrogant doctor a fixed look. Where did he think he was? "They're not 'staff.' They are grave diggers."

— — —

Frederick Pearson sat on the screeching iron bed, with its faded patchwork quilt, and gazed around his hotel room. If one could call such an establishment a hotel. God, how had he, the eldest son of a fine old family, been reduced to this—this exile? Of course, he knew the answer, but it didn't make his present circumstances easier to bear.

A sharp knock on the door brought him out of his ruminations. Maybe that glorified nurse, Jessica Layton, had managed to accomplish the task of having his baggage delivered. He certainly hoped so. Rising from the chair, he opened the door and found himself face to face with two mud-caked laborers. One was a scrawny specimen, with a pointed face and red-edged eyes that reminded him of an opossum. The other was older, smelled like stale beer and months-old body odor, and seemed to have only two or three teeth in his head when he gaped at him.

"Are you the doc, Fred Pearson?" Opossum Face asked. He looked him up and down, as if deciding whether he had anything of value worth stealing.

"Yeah, that's him. He's the one I seen at the depot," the malodorous cretin confirmed.

"That would be *Doctor* Pearson. And my first name is Frederick, not Fred." Why did he have to keep reminding people of the most basic etiquette in addressing him? "And you are?"

Opossum Face ignored the question and turned to his companion. "See, I told you it was the right room."

"Fine, but I done thought it was at the other end of the hall."

To Pearson the weedy one said, "We got your gear downstairs. You don't travel light, do you, Doc? Whatcha got in them boxes, all your worldly goods?"

In fact, he did. Formal evening attire he would never wear in this village, tennis clothes, golf and riding togs—all to remain packed away. He clenched his jaw, eager to have his trunks brought up and to be rid of these—what had the nurse said they were? Grave diggers? "That is hardly your business. Just bring up the luggage, please."

Opossum Face, disrespectful and cocky as hell, gave him a mock salute. "Whatever you say, Your Highness. The lady doc says you're coming back with us." He and his companion turned and walked back down the hall toward the stairs.

Frederick felt heat rush up his face to his eyebrows at the barbarian's insolence, and he returned, morosely, to his seat on the bed. The pair returned shortly, bumping his expensive leather trunks along the stairs and against the walls with no regard for their contents.

"Will you please be careful with those?" he snapped. "There are fragile items packed in them."

The barbarians ignored him and cursed the luggage like stevedores.

When at last they'd brought everything to his room, the rodent-featured man said, "Okay, Doc, let's go." Once more inciting complaint from the bedsprings, he rose and left with them. They led him through the streets for a couple of blocks to a building that bore no resemblance at all to a medical facility. Then he saw the inscription above the entrance.

Powell Springs Union High School

Pearson stopped at the foot of the concrete stairs. "What is this place?" he asked.

Opossum Face, whose name he'd finally determined was Bert, replied, "It's the infirmary."

"Where's the hospital?"

"Hospital—this is it. People leave here one of two ways, either on their own steam, or out the back door with Winks and me to the cemetery behind the building."

The old sot named Winks nodded in agreement, showing off his three teeth in a half-grin.

Things were growing worse by the minute. Pearson followed his guides up the stairs and through the double doors. They led him to the gymnasium, where he recognized instantly the smell of an influenza ward.

Jessica was leaving Jeremy's cubicle when she saw Frederick Pearson standing in the doorway, still dressed in his expensive clothing, gaping at the room. He took in the rows of beds, the basketball hoops, and the makeshift supply cabinets bearing the signs that reminded everyone they were on loan from Hustad's Fine Furnishings.

"Doctor, I see you found us."

His stunned expression almost made her laugh. "You have no hospital? Even in Omaha they had a hospital!"

"Powell Springs isn't Omaha. It's a small town. Until this epidemic erupted, there were never enough patients to justify a hospital. Because of the emergency, the town council arranged for me to use this gymnasium."

"There are no operating rooms, no laboratory, no orderlies, no qualified nurses?"

Jess intertwined her fingers like a welcoming maitre d', pleased to have the upper hand for a moment. "In your correspondence with Mayor Cookson, did he tell you that we have all those things?"

His mouth was still agape as his head swiveled to inspect his surroundings. “Not specifically, but I was certainly given the impression that Powell Springs is more than the *backwater* it appears to be. In fact, its merits seem to have been grossly overstated. It has none of the modern medical advances I enjoyed on the East Coast.”

“No it doesn’t, does it? I worked in New York for some time, myself. But I’ve learned to adapt. I had to.”

“How are you feeding these people? Bathing them? Managing the laundry?”

“As best we can.” Briefly, she detailed Granny Mae’s cooking and her role as the local folk medicine specialist and occasional veterinary consultant. She also told him about the fire that burned the contents of chamber pots, and the boiling kettles of sheets. “Granny Mae prefers traditional remedies to science, but she has unbent a little. And some of her advice has been rather helpful, although I did draw the line at letting her put sulfur in the patients’ shoes to ‘burn’ the illness out of them.”

He continued to stare in moderate horror. Jessica didn’t want to scare him off, but it was a pleasure to watch his gasbag attitude deflate a little.

“Obviously, this influenza epidemic is an unusual situation. Once it passes”—if it passes, she thought— “things will return to normal.”

“Normal—but what about surgeries, such as cholecystectomies and bowel obstructions? Real emergencies?”

She permitted herself a smile, thoroughly enjoying every moment of this. “Oh, well, those you’ll handle in the back room of the office. There is no operating table, but I’m sure you could order one. My father was the doctor here before his death, and sometimes he performed caesarian deliveries and such on a kitchen table if the patients couldn't travel to him."

Frederick Pearson's face acquired such a scarlet, pinched appearance, Jess thought he looked as if he'd either swallowed a box of alum or was having an apoplectic fit.

"Are you all right, Doctor?"

He uttered an incomprehensible sound.

"I gather that you're not accustomed to a more modest practice style."

"Hardly." It seemed to be the only word he could choke out.

She brightened. "Oh, I just remembered—the medical office does have a telephone. Unfortunately, most other people here don't, and it's only operational during daytime hours."

"Hmm." He managed a very sour smile.

"I'd offer to take you on rounds and update you on the current patient census here, but I'm sure you must be tired after your long trip. Shall we meet again tomorrow morning?"

"Yes—tomorrow. That would be better."

— — —

Frederick Pearson walked back to the hotel with dragging steps and climbed to the second floor where his room was located. Once inside, he planted his generous posterior on the worn cushion of the wing chair, wishing all the more desperately to be delivered from this provincial grease spot on the map.

He was so offended and outraged by what he'd seen and heard so far, he thought his head might explode. Surely, Charon had ferried him across the Acheron into Dante's first level of hell.

He wished yet again that he had never been forced to leave his civilized Connecticut for the savage, gauche wilds beyond the

Eastern Seaboard. He missed desperately the Pearson manse in Hartford, with its large, manicured grounds, its deferential, efficient servants, and other such basic amenities he'd not known since his hasty departure.

He yearned for the pleasant summers spent at the Pearson cottage in Newport, Rhode Island. *Cottage* was the foolish but endearing term for the grand homes of marble and gilt owned by the best families, where he'd enjoyed the convivial company of other summer vacationers such as the Vanderbilts, the Berwinds, and the Astors. The winter season brought concerts and the theater, elegant Christmas soirées, smart dinner parties and weekly salons, and trips into New York City. That life of refined comfort was just a memory now, one that he fervently wished to make real again. And it seemed that the farther west he'd traveled, the more primitive the country became. It wouldn't surprise him to see cowboys and Indians whoop down the muddy street beneath his hotel windows.

He stood and walked to the coat tree that held his jacket. From the inside pocket he withdrew a silver flask which contained the last of the cognac he'd carried with him across the country. Searching the room, he found not so much as a plain drinking glass, so he was forced to drink the choice French brandy straight from the flask. Glum, he flopped into a slick horsehair wing chair that had seen far better days.

Although it wasn't in Frederick's nature to look on the bright side of irremediable situations, he could acknowledge the fact that through his father's political connections, a particular senator had permitted him to be spared from the army and thus the war. So at least he wasn't in some French field hospital, working under even worse conditions than those offered by Powell Springs.

Of course, no good deed went unpunished. To his misfortune, he hadn't realized that in exchange for this boon, he'd been expected to accept the matrimonial hand of the senator's eldest and most socially awkward daughter. So unattractive and lacking in grace was this female—despite a score of tutors, dance instructors, and finishing schools, and an incalculable number of suitors who'd escaped—at age twenty-eight, she remained unmarried. The good senator's wife had even gone so far as to "let slip" the spinster's engagement to him, which of course, Frederick found intolerable. After an ugly scene that had included the renewed threat of military service—as an infantryman—Frederick Pearson had agreed to leave the East for any available position in a faraway American locale.

In his correspondence with Mayor Cookson, he had been led to believe that Powell Springs was a thriving community immediately adjacent to Portland, where timber barons and newspaper tycoons lived in the luxurious style to which he was accustomed. But Willets, the hayseed stationmaster, had told him that the city was a good fifteen to twenty miles west, with not much between but farmland and a few other towns just like Powell Springs. From what little he'd seen, Powell Springs itself was nothing more than a country hamlet.

"'Abandon all hope, ye who enter here,'" he muttered. Then he took the last swallow of cognac from his flask, letting the drops run out onto his tongue.

— — —

Adam Jacobsen sat on a rocker in Laura Donaldson's parlor, facing Amy Layton. He balanced his clipboard on his knee, which held a sheaf of papers. He had made this call to secure the older woman's signature on his petition. She'd given it gladly and invited him to lunch.

"Do you have enough names, do you think?" Amy asked him. Though dressed, she reclined in an overstuffed chair with her feet propped on a needlepoint stool. She wore a large pale-blue shawl draped around her shoulders and looked very much the convalescent.

He tapped the pages of names. "Not yet, maybe, but I'll collect more at tonight's town meeting, and I'm sure those will give us more than we need. Anyway, now that Dr. Pearson is here, it really should be only an administrative matter."

He'd had a visit from Whitney Gannon about the property damage that had occurred at the medical office. Of course, he couldn't condone that kind of violence, and he'd been annoyed that James Leonard had done something so stupid. It would only hurt their cause, not help it. He'd assured Sheriff Gannon that he'd do everything possible to keep his followers from committing further vandalism. In return, Gannon said he wouldn't arrest Leonard, but only fine him with the provision that he pay for the repair. Besides, that office would soon be occupied by Dr. Pearson, and what good would it do to break the windows?

Adam put on an expression of regret. "It's a shame that your own sister, a woman from a fine family, has proven to be so immoral and faithless. This must all be very distressing for you, Amy, especially since you're still recovering from your illness. To discover that Jessica and Braddock have been consorting behind your back while you were in your sickbed—well, I can imagine that it's a bitter blow."

"And the lies they accused me of—sending a forged telegram to Jess to steal Cole away from her." She pressed her palm to her forehead. "You can't begin to know how that crushed me. But then, she was unfair to you, too. I can't understand what happened to the sister I remember. Those years back East must have changed her. She said they did—I just didn't realize how much."

A clucking Mrs. Donaldson walked in just then, bearing a tray of tea and clever little double-layer sandwiches with the crusts cut off. "I've brought you a bit of lunch. You probably don't get many home-cooked meals now, Mr. Jacobsen, since Nettie quit."

"I'm doing the best I can, Mrs. Donaldson, but I appreciate your kindness. Nettie Stark worked for us for so long, I never dreamed she would side against me in this. Being a shepherd for the Lord's flock can be a lonely job sometimes."

Mrs. Donaldson put the tray on a small table between him and Amy, and handed him a plate that held two egg sandwiches and a cup of tea. "Well, don't you worry, you know you're welcome here anytime at all. And I'm sure Amy would enjoy your visits."

Amy adjusted the folds of her woolen shawl. "Oh, I would! I'm afraid I'm not completely recovered just yet, but I know I'll be back to my old self soon. Mrs. Donaldson takes such good care of me." She took the teacup the woman put in her hands and stirred two spoons of sugar into the dark amber beverage. "In fact, if I could get a ride to city hall, I'd like to come to the meeting tonight."

Adam stared at her, surprised. He hadn't even asked her to sign his petition—that would be more than he could expect. "Are you sure? After all, it's your sister we'll be talking about."

She gave him a sweet smile. "Yes, but I can love the sinner without loving the sin, can't I? Isn't that what you would teach us, Reverend?"

Heat rose to his face. Even in her wanness, she was still a lovely young woman. "Well, yes, of course. That's the best way to look at things."

"Besides, I want Powell Springs to remember that this is my hometown, and even though Jessica has let me down, I still care about the people here."

"What a generous, courageous woman you are." He smiled too, and Mrs. Donaldson folded her hands, positively beaming. "I can bring my buggy for you tonight at, say, six thirty? I'll try not to keep you out too late."

"More than one good thing might come from this," Mrs. Donaldson said, still grinning like a matchmaker. "If you really feel you're up to it, Amy."

"I think it will do me good to get out. I've been cooped up for so long."

Adam devoured the silly sandwiches and drank his tea, eager to be about his business. "Well, then. I'll call for you at six thirty. I don't mean to rush off like this, but I have a couple of important things to attend to before the meeting." To Laura he said, "Make sure Amy rests up this afternoon."

Nodding eagerly, she replied, "Oh, yes, I will, I will."

Amy lifted a limp hand and waved. "I'm so glad you stopped by—Adam."

He paused, then reached for her hand and kissed it. "Until this evening, then." Then he walked out into the chilly noon weather.

— — —

Emmaline sat on her iron bed and patted the spot beside it. "Come on, Frank. Come and sit beside me." The influenza epidemic had slowed business to a crawl for the past few weeks, and she hadn't been able to deposit any money in the bank for her boys. Just earning enough to buy food had been a challenge. Tanner had visited to give her an update about the kids and had told her not to worry about the account. There was enough in it for their care. After he'd gone, she'd even found a five-dollar bill that he'd tucked under the sugar bowl on her table. But she worried anyway. So seeing Frank Meadows again came as a relief, even though she still thought he was a little odd.

Huh, as if all her other customers didn't have their quirks. Just so they didn't get too drunk or hurt her, she was willing to put up with almost anything. At least Frank washed.

He smiled and settled next to her, unknotting his tie as the bedsprings sank beneath his weight.

"You haven't been to see me in a while. How are those tractor sales going?"

"What? Oh." He shrugged. "Things have been difficult lately. Farmers aren't much interested in tractors and tillers with their families sick."

"Yeah, I don't suppose so. It's been pretty slow around here, too."

He turned and reached for her, snaking a hand inside her dressing gown to stroke her breast. Then pushing her back on the thin mattress, he kissed her while wriggling out of his own clothes. He flung them over the high foot of her bed, willy-nilly. Usually he was like a fussy old aunt about folding them. Now she sensed an urgency that she hadn't noticed in him before, as if something besides lust had brought him up here. It almost bordered on violence.

"Emmaline, it's been so long," he said next to her ear. He wasted no time on preliminary groping, but instead entered her with a forceful jab that surprised her.

Like a marionette, Em gave the impression of being involved in this moment, matching her movements to accommodate

Frank's thrusting hips, but in reality, her thoughts were far away. That she could separate herself from the grunting, sweating men who paid for her time and body, she saw as a blessing. Without that ability, she'd probably go crazy. So although she might see over Frank's shoulder to his white, flexing buttocks, in her mind she stood in the endless green pasture on the farm where she'd grown up. Above her the sky was deep blue, the way she imagined the ocean might look, and a soft June breeze ruffled the grass around her feet as she—

Suddenly, the door to her shanty flew open so hard the doorknob bounced off the wall behind it. Frank jumped, withdrawing from her, his erection shriveling up like a slug that had had salt poured on it. Irrelevantly, she noticed that although naked, he'd kept his socks on.

"Now there you go, Gannon! Didn't I tell you something rotten was going on up here?"

In the doorway, Emmaline saw that lowdown scoundrel Lambert Bauer. Whit Gannon stood behind him.

"Lambert!" she shrieked, frightened and furious.

Whit, a tall, wiry man with salt-and-pepper hair and a big mustache, looked mortified. His voice boomed up from his chest. "Damn it, Bauer, is this why you dragged me all the way out to Emmaline's place? You told me she was breaking the law—you made it sound like she murdered someone. Em minds her own business and we let her do it!"

"Well, Jesus Christ, Gannon! She's my *wife*! That can't be legal, what she's doing. Are you gonna stand here and tell me there isn't some law about whoring or something you can arrest her for? And what about that son of a bitch with her on the bed, his cock hanging out like—" Lambert pulled up short in his tirade and peered at Frank, who scrambled to cover himself. "Hey—hey now, wait just a minute. I know you!"

Whit took a closer look at Frank as well and immediately looked away, embarrassed. "Look, Bauer, I'm not going to pursue this, and if you make any more trouble for this woman, I'm going to lock *you* up for thirty days. This is my jurisdiction and I don't care what you want to claim. Emmaline is a friend of mine and she doesn't hurt anyone."

"She shot at me once! What about that?" Lambert was nearly purple with rage.

"Too bad she missed. You probably had it coming. Besides, I've been hearing suspicious talk about you and some jewelry you've been using to buy drinks. I think I'll have to check into where you got it." Whit grabbed him by the scruff of his skinny neck and pushed him out the door. With a brief, backward glance he said, "Sorry about this, folks. I didn't realize why Bauer brought me here or I never would have come. Emmaline, you let me know if he pesters you again. I'll kick his ass all the way to the county line." He shut the door behind him. There was a sound of scuffling feet just outside, and then the slamming of car doors.

Em's heart beat like a frightened bird's, and she felt like the wind had been knocked out of her. "Oh, God, Frank. I'm so sorry. That Lambert is no good. He never has been."

But Frank, as pale as milk, was already scurrying back into his clothes. "I've got to go, Em."

"No, please don't leave. I'm really sorry. I'll even let you have it on the house. I feel terrible about this!" Beyond the blackberry brambles, she heard the sound of an automobile engine turning over, then the crunching of gravel under the car's wheels.

Frank had his pants, shoes, and shirt on, half-buttoned and untucked. His tie was looped over one arm, and his jacket hung over the other. If word of this got out, of crazy Lambert Bauer kicking in her door and scaring away her customers, she'd be out of business, and what would happen to the boys? They were all she had in this lousy world, even if she never got to see them.

Frank flung open the door and raced out, not bothering to close it. A moment later, his horse and buggy lurched from her yard at a fast clip.

Emmaline dragged herself up from the bed, and with a hand braced on the doorframe, she watched Frank Meadows's retreat.

Goddamn that worthless Lambert Bauer. If he'd been even half the man he should have been, her kids would be safe and she wouldn't have to worry about doing this degrading work.

For the first time in a very long while, she pressed her face against her arm and cried.

CHAPTER TWENTY-ONE

Jessica leaned toward the mirror over her bathroom sink to pin up straggling wisps of her hair. This morning, she'd had to meet with Dr. Pearson again at the infirmary to discuss the current cases and turn over her notes to him. In a profession dominated by men, she had experienced her share of haughty disdain, but given the circumstances, his was especially galling. His quiet scorn for everything she showed him about the facility had radiated from him. Nothing, apparently, was up to his standards or expectations.

After they'd toured the infirmary, she had brought him back here to show him the office and upstairs apartment, with its two convenient rooms for patients requiring round-the-clock care, such as typical surgery cases or those too ill to return home immediately. There was no doubt that he found it all to be lacking.

When he left, she'd stomped back upstairs for a moment of calm and to start packing her things, still furious with the insufferable man. These were urgent times, times that called for cooperation and the willingness to work toward the common goal of saving lives. Egos and prejudices only hampered those efforts. No, the high school gym wasn't Bellevue Hospital, but they had to make due with the facilities and equipment available.

Walking out into the parlor, she looked around and knew this place, including the office below, would belong to him as soon as she could move out. His name was even on the sign that swung from its iron bracket on the front of the building.

Downstairs, she heard the doorknob rattle and her heart lurched. She had taken to locking the front door at all times now. Images of Adam Jacobsen, his eyes alight with a hateful gleam, or more harassment from his followers crossed her mind. Even people who did not agree with him felt compelled to whisper when they talked about him, for fear of bringing down the tyranny of the American Protective League on their heads. Earlier, Leroy Fenton's delivery boy had brought her another telegram from the hospital in Seattle, asking about her status.

Now a knock sounded.

Jess crept to the landing, but she couldn't see who stood on the other side of the glass from up here.

Another knock. "Jessica?" She recognized Cole's voice and released the breath she'd held, then hurried down the steps. "Coming, Cole!" When she reached the bottom stair, she rushed across the entry to fling open the door. Seeing him there, tall and broad-shouldered, the silver badge pinned to his jacket and a gun belt slung low on his hips, she felt safer. He represented the only security she knew these days. She stepped aside to let him in. He kissed her once on the mouth and then on both cheeks. It was such an affectionate, endearing gesture, she felt her throat constrict with emotion.

"Have you had any more trouble?" he asked.

"No, but I don't feel like I can leave the door unlocked now."

He nodded. "It's probably just as well that you keep it bolted. I went by the high school, but Granny Mae said you came back here. Pearson looked overwhelmed."

Jessica rolled her eyes and sighed. "I don't know how well *he's* going to work out. I'm not sure Powell Springs, even at its worst, deserves him." She nodded toward the back room where coffee was perking on the hotplate.

He followed her and settled in one of the chairs, crossing his ankle over his knee. "Why?"

She checked the progress of the coffee on the work table and swept some stray grounds into her palm that she'd scattered. Dumping them into a wastepaper basket, she brushed her hands. "Aside from the fact that he's condescending and insulting, and doesn't approve of female doctors, I got the feeling that he's going to be a real fish out of water here. He's rather upper crust, from New England, and pretty full of himself. At least that was how it seemed to me."

"Hmm, that should make tonight interesting."

"What's happening tonight?"

"Adam Jacobsen has called for a town meeting at city hall. He wants to formally welcome Pearson and, well..." He looked away for an instant.

She crossed her arms over her chest. "To run me out of town."

He tipped his chair back on its two rear legs. "I didn't hear it put quite that way. But my head's on the chopping block, too. He wants Whit Gannon to take my badge. At least that was what I heard this morning. Hell, he can have the damned thing. It's not like I don't have enough to do."

She threw up her hands. "So Horace Cookson is allowing this even though the influenza is still active and large gatherings have been banned?"

"Horace isn't the same man he was before his wife and son died. I know how he feels."

Jess dropped her hands and let her stiff shoulders relax a little. "Are you going to attend this meeting?"

"Yes, and I think you should too."

Her mouth popped open. "To deliver myself to Adam and his henchmen so they can stone me in the public square without having to come looking for me? Thank you, but no." She turned to the coffee pot and poured two cups, fixing his the way she remembered he liked it.

"That's not what I mean and you know it. You should face him down. He's one man, and a lousy one at that. The reason he has so much power over people is because no one has taken it away from him. You were born and raised here, too."

"I've done the job I promised to do. I filled in until Pearson arrived. Powell Springs has a doctor again and my work is finished."

He let the chair fall back into place and stood to take the cup she offered. "So you won't come tonight?"

She leaned a hip against the work table and sipped her own coffee. "You saw the mentality of those people outside who broke the window. It's not hard for me to imagine that 'meeting' turning into a kangaroo court. Next thing you know, they'll be dunking me in Powell Creek."

He gazed at her for a long minute. In the quiet, she could hear his leather belt creak with his breathing. "I know you have more faith in Powell Springs than that. You've always been a fighter, Jess."

"Maybe. But there are so *many* battles, and I don't want take on every one of them anymore. Some are just too hard to bear." At this moment, she felt almost as defeated as she had when she'd left the East.

He nodded finally, as if he understood what she meant. Reaching out, he tucked a stray lock of her hair behind her ear. His touch made goose bumps rise on her arms. "Then I'll fight it for you. I've lost too much lately to just give up, and I'm not going to stand by and let those sanctimonious hypocrites tear down either of us."

Impulsively, she pressed a quick, hard kiss to his mouth. "I hope you win."

— — —

At six forty-five, most of Powell Springs's citizens who were well enough to attend filled the council room at city hall and spilled out into the corridor. Even Virgil Tilly had closed his place to come to the event. Roland Bright and Horace Cookson scrambled to find every chair in the building, but a lot of people were still left standing.

Susannah and Tanner accompanied Cole, and in a move that both surprised and pleased him, so did Pop. "I'm not gonna have people like Jacobsen and Leonard tarnish our family name. They've got a hell of a nerve, especially Jacobsen. I remember he couldn't even say 'mama' until he was six years old, and he hasn't quit yapping since." This was the most energy the old man had shown since that telegram came. After they learned of Riley's death and Amy's treachery, a lot of the bluster had drained out of Pop. Even trips to the saloon had lost their allure for him.

Cole acted as a spearhead to cut his way through the group, bringing his family close to the front of the room where they could all see the proceedings and hear what was being said. He felt the eyes of others on them and noticed heads bending to whisper as they passed. Looking around, he saw people he'd known all of his life, people he'd done business with, those whose weddings he'd attended and had even shared drinks with at Tilly's. He was counting on that. Maybe they would remember him instead of the man who had come here to destroy his character and attack Jessica and his family.

On one side of the room, James Leonard moved from person to person, papers and pencil in hand, gathering signatures, Cole assumed, for his petition. On the other side, Adam Jacobsen did the same. As seven o'clock drew near, he stopped to talk to a woman who was seated close to the front.

"Oh, good heavens!" Susannah whispered, and pointed discreetly to her left. All four of them turned to look and saw Amy Layton sitting down the row, wearing a shawl and the prim, long-suffering expression of someone who had been grievously wronged. With grave solicitousness, Adam took her hand and bent to speak to her. What now appeared to be Amy's true motive in befriending Susannah had been very hard on the widow. Cole knew she felt almost as betrayed as he did. She had believed that Jessica's sister genuinely cared about her, but she'd heard not a single word from her. Not even after she'd been strong enough to go back to Mrs. Donaldson's had she sent a letter of condolence about Riley.

After some preliminary shuffling of chairs and whispering, the three town councilmen took their seats at the long meeting table. Birdeen Lyons sat at a small desk to their right in her role as recording secretary. It was already hot and stuffy in the room, and the random cough was still enough to make a few people turn suspicious eyes on the possible germ carriers. Some still wore their influenza masks, but many others had abandoned them.

Mayor Cookson rapped his gavel, bringing quiet to the room. "All right, let's get this meeting underway. I'd like to take a moment to welcome Dr. Fred Pearson to Powell Springs. I think most of us will agree that we're happy to see him after so many months."

Polite applause rippled through the group, and people craned their necks for a glimpse of the doctor they'd waited so long to meet. Pearson stood and bowed in all directions, but not even a suggestion of a smile crossed his stern-looking face. "That would be *Frederick* Pearson."

In a town where dress clothing was worn only to church, weddings, and funerals, his expensive suit stood out among the bib overalls and everyday broadcloth and denim.

Adam, looking harassed, dropped some papers and hurried to put them back together. With a glance in Amy's direction, he smoothed his tie and spoke up. "I'm sure Dr. Pearson will be an asset to this community for years to come. I, for one, have sent prayers to God to thank him for sending us this doctor with such fine credentials, and high principles and ideals." This was followed by more applause.

Beside Cole, Pop snorted. "How does he know that?" he whispered.

"Gentlemen," Pearson began, still standing. "I do appreciate your generous compliments and observations of my character. They are most gratifying. And I am sorry to disabuse you of my tenure in Powell Springs, perhaps more sorry than you were to give me a false impression of what this town would be like."

The applause died away to a puzzled silence. Dr. Pearson continued.

"However, now that I have had an opportunity to tour your village, it is obvious to me that Powell Springs's merits were grossly overstated in my correspondence with this distinguished body." He nodded toward the three men sitting at the council table, and his sarcasm was hard to miss. "I would not go so far as to say that I was purposely duped, but clearly the town has a far more cosmopolitan view of itself than is warranted."

People began sputtering with outrage—at least those who could follow Pearson's high-flown speech and flat New England accent. The rest just knew they were being insulted somehow. Cole ducked his head to hide a laugh.

"Exactly what are you saying, Doctor?" Adam demanded.

"What I am saying is that I expected to assume a large city practice with adequate facilities. Nothing I have seen here remotely meets that criteria. There is no hospital, no satisfactory clinic—I suspect that I might even be called upon to deliver a calf or diagnose a colicky sheep. That is, if your folk herbalist isn't too busy making up asafetida charms and running her café. In short, gentlemen"—he turned to face the group—"and ladies, I will stay here only as long as it takes me to find a more promising position in another city. Surely, you can understand that a Yale-educated physician would not want to remain in a place where his skills would not be properly utilized or appreciated." He smiled at last, a most candid smile. "If you will excuse me, I have patients waiting for me in the gymnasium."

He strode out of the room, head up, as arrogant and self-important as a king who had descended from his mountaintop castle to mingle, however unpleasantly, with the great unwashed of his serfdom.

The stunned room flared with a roar of angry voices.

"He'd better sleep with a gun under his pillow tonight," someone barked, and Cole was inclined to agree.

"Have you ever heard the like?"

"Who the hell does that man think he is? Yale—where is that, anyway?"

"If he thinks I'd let him touch a sheep of mine, he's got rocks in his head!"

Weary Horace Cookson stood and banged his gavel repeatedly, calling for order with increasing volume. After three or four minutes, he finally managed to break through the din.

"Everyone sit down and be quiet or I will clear the room right now!" he thundered. At last the noisy outrage dulled to a sibilant buzz. Remaining on his feet, the mayor said, "Now we're in a worse fix than before. We have no doctor and no other on the way. Jessica Layton told me up front that she has a job waiting for her in Seattle. She delayed her move to help us during this influenza crisis."

If ever fate had handed Cole a moment to act, he knew this was it. He stood. "Horace, Jessica might be persuaded to trade working in Seattle for staying in Powell Springs—" He stared pointedly at Adam Jacobsen. "Providing the people who have made it their business to insult her and ruin her reputation stop hounding her and call off their petition drive."

Adam stood. "Mayor Cookson, if I may speak."

Horace sat and waved his assent with no particular enthusiasm. "Go ahead, Adam."

The minister cleared his throat. "Well, this certainly isn't how I expected this meeting to go. It leaves us with the same problem we had before." This time he sought out Cole and glared at him before continuing. "Most of Powell Springs knows by now that Dr. Jessica Layton was recently caught in a morally compromising situation with Cole Braddock. I might remind everyone that Braddock has been almost engaged to Amy Layton, the doctor's sister. A woman of such loose morals does not deserve to be entrusted with the care of our citizens."

Everyone began talking, many of them agreeing with Adam.

While Horace thumped his gavel again, Granny Mae Rumsteadt, skinny and gray-haired, rose like a Fury from her chair several rows behind Cole. "You, Adam Jacobsen, are acting like a witch hunter, not a man of God." She turned and looked at many of the faces around her. "I'm disappointed by every one of you who signed that man's filthy petition. When you were sick in the infirmary, wasn't Dr. Jessica there, tending you, almost every time you opened your eyes? Powell Springs thinks it's too high and mighty for Jess Layton? Well, you saw for yourselves that Dr. Fancy-Britches thinks Powell Springs is too lowly for *him*. Not only that, Amy Layton and Cole Braddock are not engaged."

"Granny, you're out of order!" Adam snapped.

Birdeen struggled to keep up with the flying dialogue.

"Goat turds, *Reverend* Jacobsen!"

Pop and Cole burst out laughing, and so did some others. Several of the ladies present gasped, but Granny Mae wasn't a woman to mince words when she felt she was right. And that was most of the time.

"What proof do you have that any of what you've said about Cole and Jessica is true?" she demanded. "This town has gone to hell in a handbasket, and I'm thinking that people like you, Adam Jacobsen, and you, James Leonard"—she turned to point at the man who'd led the rabble to Jessica's office—"blazed the trail down there."

Adam, his face red with frustration, turned to Horace. "Mayor Cookson, are you just going to sit there and let this meeting turn into a free-for-all?"

The mayor rubbed his forehead. "For God's sake, Adam, Granny, everyone. This isn't a quilting bee where we came to trade gossip. It's a town meeting. We're trying to get serious business accomplished."

"Yes, we are. I will not vote to approve offering this job to Jessica Layton. I saw Cole Braddock coming out of her office at five-thirty in the morning. What do you suppose they were doing there at that hour?"

"What were *you* doing out there at that hour, Jacobsen?" Cole asked. "You looked like you'd spent the night in a hayrick, yourself."

"I was on my way to the infirmary, where I've been comforting the sick." He returned his comments to the assembled group. "I heard them talking—some rather suggestive conversation it was, too. And I saw them kiss."

"Oh, yeah? And I saw your bare ass this afternoon on my wife's bed, Jacobsen, humping away on her. That's lots worse than just talking and kissing on a front porch."

All heads swiveled to see who had made such a crude, monstrous accusation. Bert Bauer stood at back of the room, his shoulder against the doorjamb, and his arms across his chest. Judging by his slurred words, he was liquored up—and mad.

A silence so profound and complete fell over the meeting that Cole thought he heard a horse nickering outside. Jaws hung open and slack, people seemed frozen in place.

Then chaos erupted.

Everyone spoke at once. People jumped to their feet.

"That no-good bastard," Tanner ground out, and Cole wasn't sure which bastard he was referring to.

Adam grabbed the gavel from Horace Cookson's hand and began beating it on the table, his eyes about to pop out of his head and his face gleaming with sweat. "Have that profane, corrupt liar ejected! Throw him out!" he shouted.

A couple of men near Bauer made a grab for him and started to drag him away until he shouted, "It ain't a lie! And it ain't just my say-so, neither. I had a witness with me—Sheriff Gannon! He saw this snot with Emmaline."

Adam, nearing a fit of frenzy, kept pounding the gavel until the handle broke and its wooden head flew across the room.

Whit Gannon, who stood along the far wall, obviously was caught by surprise and looked as if he wished he could be anywhere else but here.

"Is it true?"

"Sheriff, did you see Jacobsen with Emmaline?"

"Who is Emmaline?" This question was asked by several women.

Cole could not believe the drama unfolding before him. He stood to get a good look at Bauer and then turned back to Jacobsen.

"Emmaline is married? To *Bauer*?"

"By God!" Pop exclaimed.

"*Who is Emmaline?*" a woman nearby demanded again.

Mayor Cookson caught Whit Gannon's eye and signaled him to the front. With long, loose strides, the sheriff walked to the council table. Adam eyed him and seemed to shrink in his clothes.

"Whit," Horace said, "is Bert Bauer telling the truth? Did you find Reverend Jacobsen in a compromising situation with Em—that is, Mrs. Bauer?"

"Yes."

Birdeen had taken to scribbling.

"There was no mistake—they weren't just…talking?"

Whit dropped his chin and a corner of his mouth turned down. "Well, no, I didn't hear any talking coming from them." He faced Adam. "Speaking as a witness, I'd say Bauer's description is pretty accurate. Crude, but accurate."

The petition sheets that Adam held fluttered from his hand as he dropped to his chair, chalk-white and perspiring freely.

— — —

As soon as the meeting concluded, Cole ran directly to Jessica's office. "Now, aren't you sorry you weren't there?"

They sat in the parlor upstairs, surrounded by her trunks and cases, and she stared at him. "No—well, yes, I guess I am." She had to laugh. "I'll bet Powell Springs has never seen a town meeting like that one before."

"Probably won't again, either, with two scandals in one night. Plus Whit Gannon took Bauer into custody on a charge of drunk and disorderly conduct, and suspicion of theft over that jewelry he probably stole." Cole leaned forward on the settee. "Anyway, Horace and Roland Bright decided that they will formally ask you to stay in town, permanently, since Pearson thinks he's too good for a bunch of uncultured hicks like us. I suggested that the good doctor might even be interested in taking your spot in Seattle."

"But *I'm* going to Seattle. That's my position, and they're expecting me. I got another telegram from them today." She stood and turned to the box she'd been packing to fold a shawl.

He stood, too, and guided her back to the settee. Then he reached into his pocket and pulled out a worn black velvet box. "Jess, we have to make things right. We were meant to be, you and I. I knew you were supposed to be my wife from the time we were kids. Rough things have happened in the last few years, but we don't have to drag them around with us for the rest of our lives. I made bad decisions, I've lost Riley—I almost lost you. I don't want any more regrets than I already have."

Regrets…regrets…Iris Delaney had mentioned them, Jess herself had thought of them, and now Cole was talking about the same thing. But—

"Cole, things have changed. A lot. What with Amy, and now the lynch mob that has it in for us, what can we do to fix any of that? That won't go away just because Horace Cookson wants it to. He can't order people into my waiting room. Even two boys on the street yesterday called me a whore."

He winced but said, "Jess, you asked me to fight this battle. I did, and we won. The fuss will die down eventually. Besides, those people following Jacobsen and Leonard don't represent the whole town."

She dropped the shawl in a soft heap on her lap. "I guess you might feel differently if you were the one who'd been called names and had your moral character attacked. You know that women, and most especially physicians, are judged by their actions, perceived or otherwise. I…I feel crushed by the disapproval. I won't have any patients here. They'll end up going to Granny Mae before they'll forgive me."

"Well, maybe you could open an office in Twelve Mile. The ranch is about halfway between the two towns."

Her brows rose. "What?"

"I'd even teach you to drive so you could get around more easily."

He dropped to one knee in front of her and held out the black velvet box. "Jessica, I want you to marry me. Right away. No more waiting." He pushed the spring catch on the box and its top flew up.

Astounded, she saw a ring. The setting was of an older style, and the diamond was cut in a manner that made her think of an antique.

He searched her face and gazed into her eyes with a look that shattered her heart. "It was my mother's."

"Oh, Cole..."

"You're right—a lot has happened, good and bad. The only thing I know for certain in this world is that I love you. I always have. I want you for my wife, the way it was always supposed to be."

She put her hand on his arm. "I love you just as much. But the hospital in Washington wants me." Then an idea struck her, a flash of brilliance that she wished she'd thought of sooner. "I know—you could come with me! Seattle is a growing city, you could start a new business up there."

He sat back on his heels and frowned at her as if she'd suggested they drive an oxcart to the moon. "How can I leave my family? Especially now that my brother is gone?"

"But all my education and hard work to get my degree and credentials—with no patients here, I won't be able to use them. And I certainly can't do research. At least I'm needed at that hospital." She gazed unseeing at the pattern in the braided rug under her feet. "Everyone in Powell Springs abandoned me, including my own sister."

"Jessica, you're needed here. I need you here. If you go to Seattle, you'll be running away again, just like you ran from New York."

She pulled her hand away as if he'd slapped it. "That's a terrible thing to say!"

He rose from the floor and sat in another chair, away from her. "I can't turn my back on Pop and Susannah. They're my home, my roots. They're yours, too. So is this town, for good or bad. You and I—together we can face anything."

She put out her hands in a gesture of appeal. "Cole, we can start all over again where no one knows us. I won't have to see Amy every day or those hateful people who've been so cruel, when all I wanted to do was help them get well. Please, come with me."

"So, you'd have to see them. I will too. I'm not ashamed of anything we did. Are you?"

"No, but—"

"And when we're married, there won't be much for any of them to talk about. It'll be pretty dull stuff, especially now that Jacobsen has thrown the mob a new pork chop to chew on."

"Will you at least think about coming with me?"

His gaze was cold and fixed, and she felt him pull back from her. It reminded her of that first day back in town when he'd gone into the café with Eddie. "No."

Her hands closed into two tight fists in her lap and her voice shook with disappointment and anger. "Just once—*once*, I'd like to hear someone who claims to love me say, 'I'd do anything for you, Jessica.' But people keep expecting me to see their side of things and make exceptions for them.

"'I thought you broke off with me so I started courting your sister.' 'I decided you didn't deserve Cole, so I told him you weren't coming back.' 'Whore.' '*Female* physician.' 'You're running away again.' Everyone has an excuse for what they've done to me, said to me. When is someone going to take my side?" she demanded.

He got up and put the ring box on the kitchen table. "Jess, you promised a long time ago that you would come back to Powell Springs and marry me. You promised you would take care of this town and carry on for your father when he died. Not everyone here believes Adam Jacobsen. Even Granny Mae has stuck up for you, twice, against those few. And yeah, there are some crackpots here, just like there are everywhere. You'll find them in Seattle, too, if you go. People who don't think women should be doctors, people who will talk about you. A few who'll disappoint you. But you'll be alone there. No place is perfect."

Jessica watched him put on his hat and sheepskin coat, then he headed for the stairs. He stopped in the doorway and looked back at her. "You made promises here and if you don't keep them, then you're not the woman *or* the doctor that I've always thought you were." He nodded toward the velvet box. "If you decide to stay, put on the ring. If not—well, I'll be next door."

Her eyes smarting with tears, she shot from the settee and said, "You might as well take it with you now." He studied her for a long moment, then walked back to the table and pocketed the small box.

She heard his heavy tread galloping down the stairs and across the floor. The overhead bell rang when he opened the front door and closed it again.

Then he was gone.

— — —

Jessica spent a hard, sleepless night, reliving the scene between Cole and her. He had not only attacked her personal integrity, but her integrity as a physician as well. For a few hours, she wept in great, gasping sobs, punched her pillow, got up twice to tuck in the sheets, and had a glass of warm milk. Nothing helped.

At last, she kicked off the covers, got up, dressed again, and packed the rest of her clothes. Crying and exhausted, she threw things into her suitcases without a care for how they would look when she pulled them out again, wrinkled and crushed. She would get out of this apartment and out of this town as soon as she could possibly manage it. The heavy things like the books she would send for once she reached Seattle. She left a note addressed to whoever read it that told where she was going. And maybe when she got there, she'd write letters to the people who deserved a better explanation for her departure. In time, she might even write to Amy. *Might*. For now, she'd had enough of Powell Springs and everyone in it.

After she washed the few dishes in the sink, stripped the bedding, and straightened the place, she stood at the mirror and put on her hat and coat. Her eyes were puffy from crying and felt gritty from lack of sleep. She couldn't find her gloves, as usual, but those things were the least of her problems now. She turned and took one last look at the apartment where she had spent the last six weeks. Her final glimpse was of the bedroom, where she and Cole had made love, and where, for a few hours, she had at last felt safe from the world and the mountain of crises she'd encountered over the past two years.

The front door key she put on the worktable, letting her fingers linger over it for just an instant before she walked out and closed the door behind her for the last time.

Carrying a suitcase, her doctor's bag, and one satchel, she walked to the train station in the predawn darkness, averting her eyes as she passed Cole's blacksmith shop. She was determined to wait outside the depot, if necessary, until it opened.

But she caught sight of the warm glow of lights from the depot windows. She left her bags outside and opened the door.

"Miss Jessica! This is a surprise." Abner Willets greeted her from his ticket window. She smelled coffee brewing from somewhere behind him. "You sure missed some hot town meeting last night!"

"So I heard. Mr. Willets, I need a ticket to Seattle, please, on the first train available."

The older man looked at her from beneath his eye shade, a slight frown drawing his bushy gray brows together. "You leaving us? I kind of had the feeling that you'd stay since that Pierce fella is going." Abner still hadn't gotten that snob's name correct. If she weren't so miserable, she might find humor in it. "Cole made it sound that way, anyhow."

She swallowed hard. "No, it was always my intention to go on to Washington as soon as he arrived."

"Huh. Well, I guess we'll be without a doctor again, then, since Pierce isn't staying, either."

"What time did you say the train is leaving?" she prompted, trying to get beyond the subject, and the feeling that her heart had swelled to the size of a cantaloupe and lodged in her throat.

He consulted his schedule and looked at the wall clock. "You're in luck. The next one is due in at eight forty-nine. We only get two early trains a week here going to Portland. When you arrive, you'll get your Seattle connection at Union Station." She nodded, and with slightly trembling hands, pushed the fare he quoted her under the brass grillwork that separated them.

He peered at her from under his eyeshade. "Are you all right, Miss Jessica? I know you've had your hands full since you got here."

She managed a wobbly smile. "I *will* be all right, Mr. Willets. It's true, the last few weeks have been a challenge."

He reached under the grill and patted her hand, where it rested on the counter. "We really appreciate everything you did for us. If you're feeling bad about those other sons of—um, troublemakers, just know that. Most of us were grateful you were here."

She tipped her head down to keep him from seeing her tears, then walked to one of the benches to wait for her train.

CHAPTER TWENTY-TWO

Emmaline was sitting at her kitchen table, smoking her last Lucky Strike and deep in thought, when she heard a light knock on her door. Since that horrible day when Lambert had burst in, she kept it bolted all the time. Glancing at her bed to make sure it was presentable—just in case—she rose quietly and tiptoed to the window, hoping she'd be able to see who was standing on her stoop. But the angle wasn't right.

Without making a sound, she picked up her loaded shotgun and pointed it at the door. "Who's there?"

"Em, it's me. Whit Gannon." She must have been buried in her worries if she hadn't heard his automobile pull up outside.

"You got anyone with you this time?"

"No, I'm alone."

Still holding the shotgun by its barrel, she breathed a relieved sigh and opened the door a crack. His snow-frost hair and mustache were a comforting site.

When he saw her weapon, he smiled. "I promise I won't make you use that on me." She heard humor in the low rumble of his voice, but still—

"Are you here on official business, Whit?"

"No, no, Em, nothing like that. I'm not even here for *your* business. I just want to talk for a minute."

Carefully, she opened the door and looked over his shoulder, and to the right and left. She saw nothing but the wet, gray day and the tangle of weeds in her yard. "All right, then. Come on in."

His tall, rangy frame made the little shanty seem even smaller when he stepped inside. "First of all, I'm sorry, again, for that mess with Bauer. I should have known he was bringing me up here on a wild goose chase."

She returned her shotgun to its spot beside the door and motioned him to her table. "I don't blame you, Whit." She smiled slightly. "At least, not all that much. Lambert said he'd make trouble for me."

He settled in the chair opposite the one she took and hooked his ankle over his knee. "Well, I thought you'd like to know that he won't be bothering you again for a long time. Later that night, he confronted the man you knew as Frank Meadows at a town meeting, and I arrested him for being drunk and disorderly, and he had possession of some valuable jewelry he couldn't account for. He was pretty belligerent until he sobered up some in my jail cell. Finally, he admitted that he'd taken it off people before he buried them. He said it wouldn't do them any good where they were going."

She shook her head and picked up the cigarette she'd left burning on a saucer on the table. "God, I can't believe I ever had anything to do with that man."

"I'm going to have a time sorting out who the stuff belongs to. But I did find something on him that I think you can use." She looked at him, wary and apprehensive. He reached into his pocket and pulled out a roll of greenbacks. "There's about a hundred dollars here. I figured you could use it more than him."

She stared at it. "But is this—is this legal? Can you just take it without getting in trouble?"

"No, it isn't, and yes, I can. Like I said before, this is my jurisdiction, and Bauer's in so much hot water, I don't think he's going to make any fuss over this money." He pushed it across the faded oilcloth.

She took the cash and smiled. "Thanks, Whit."

He peered at her playfully. "Why, Emmaline, I didn't know you had dimples," he said.

She ducked her head for a moment, her grin widening. "They only show when I smile."

"Then I'm glad I gave you a reason to show them off. Oh, and in case you were wondering, Frank Meadows's real name is Adam Jacobsen. He was the minister in Powell Springs, but I think a lot of people were happy to see him tumbled off his high horse. He's made trouble for them with the government." He fiddled with the box of matches near the saucer holding her cigarette. "Bauer was the one who ratted on him at the town council meeting, so maybe some good came from that day."

"Jacobsen—he told me he was a tractor salesman. I always thought there was something not right about that. I figured he was married."

"No, not married, but not the honest man of the cloth he pretended to be."

Em's brows rose. "And people think what *I* do is bad."

Whit pushed his chair away and stood up. "Well, I've got to be getting back. That flu business is almost over, but there's always something going on around here. I just thought you'd like to know what happened. And to have a little money for all the trouble that husband caused you. Maybe you can file for divorce and be shut of him once and for all."

She smiled again. "Yeah, maybe I can." She walked him to the door. "You're a good friend, Whit."

He kissed her cheek, tickling her with his big mustache. "So are you, Emmaline. I'll see you one of these nights."

"For you, my door is always open."

— — —

Cole noticed Muley tied up at Tilly's hitching rail as soon as he was within a block of the saloon. Dodging puddles in the afternoon downpour, he supposed that could be a good thing. The father he knew, the one he remembered from just a month earlier, would want to relive and hash over the town council meeting.

Cole just wanted to sit in a corner and get drunk.

He'd barely slept, having spent the night tossing on the cot in the tack room, thinking of Jessica lying in her own bed just next door. A dozen times he'd almost gotten up, put on his pants, and gone over to reason with her, apologize to her, make love with her, chew her out.

There was no question that he couldn't leave his family. Yet the feeling that she'd been right—that no one had really backed her up—had nagged at him throughout the night.

And she had made promises that she hadn't seen through.

But that was because others had failed her. Including himself. He'd wanted her so much that when he thought she'd broken things off between them, he'd settled for what he'd believed was the next best thing—Amy. He'd ignored her hints and flirting for months, but eventually he'd given in.

Late this morning, he'd finally gotten up the nerve to tell Jessica that he'd been wrong and to beg her to stay. When she didn't answer his knock, he'd tried the knob and found the door unlocked. After he discovered that she had gone, leaving no word but an impersonal note saying that she would send for the rest of her things, he'd walked to the side yard at the shop and began chopping wood.

Thwuck! Why hadn't she been willing to listen to his side of the argument?

Thwuck! Why in hell hadn't he seen through Amy's maneuvering?

Thwuck! How could he lose the same woman twice in his life?

Wood chips flew around him, some narrowly missing his eyes, and by the time he stopped, drenched with sweat and muscles screaming, he swore he'd chopped what must have been an entire cord of alder for the forge. He'd hoped he could work off the ache in his chest and the utter emptiness he felt, but he realized he could chop wood until doomsday and the desolation would still be there. But at least he'd realized what he must do.

When she finally arrived in Seattle and he had an address for her, he'd take a trip up there and ask her to forgive him. He owed her that much.

For now though, a bottle of whiskey would have to do. He planned to buy one and take it back to the shop so that if he passed out, Virgil Tilly wouldn't put him out in the rain again. When he reached the door and pulled it open, the familiar smells hit him in face—tobacco smoke, beer, that spicy sausage that Tilly kept in the back, wet clothes, pickled eggs. Inside, as he predicted, the old timers were all stirred up over last night's doings. They greeted him and went back to their conversation, everyone speaking loudly due to their failing hearing.

But Pop, he noticed, was sitting at one of the corner tables by himself, not really participating that much. His oiled black duster hung from one of the nearby pegs along the wall and dripped into the sawdust covering the floor. Cole lifted a hand in greeting and went to sit with him for a minute.

"I'm glad to see you out again, Pop. I figured this weather would be hard on your joints and you'd want to stay next to the fire at home."

The old man flexed his gnarled hands. "The rain don't help much, but I wanted to get in on the jawboning about last night." He gave him a smile Cole didn't often see these days. "That Jacobsen—didn't Bauer take him down neat as you please? Like nailing a squirrel at two hunnerd yards—*bam*, right between the eyes. Who would've thought he was diddling Emmaline?"

"Yeah, I have to admit I wasn't sorry to see that happen." Cole smiled just thinking about it.

"And the poor woman, married to that bastard, Bauer—she must have been the family he claimed he was looking for when he first got here. I heard Gannon asked Winks about the jewelry Bauer stole off those dead people. Winks is practically wetting himself over it because Bauer's trying to pin part of the blame on him. I know Winks, though. He's got a smaller brain than a turkey, but he wouldn't do that." He got quiet for a minute and looked at the whiskey glass in front of him. "To rob a person who's already been through hell...God, I can't think of it." He shook his head.

Cole knew it wasn't local folks Pop had in mind.

He pulled himself from his ruminations and said, "You know, you did yourself proud at the meeting last night."

Cole looked up, surprised. "Yeah?"

Pop nodded. "And me, too."

He sat back and gaped at his father. He couldn't remember ever getting a compliment like that from him. He signaled Virgil Tilly to bring him a bottle and a glass. The least he could do was share a drink with his father before he left. "Thanks, Pop."

"Well, I guess your doctor gal has got herself a job now that snooty Pearson pretty much told us to suck rotten eggs."

Cole waited while Tilly delivered his bottle to reply. "She left."

"Left!" he barked, his eyes wide.

He put up a hand to get the old man to lower his voice.

"What do you mean, 'left'?" He didn't whisper, but the rest of the customers went on without paying them any attention.

Cole told him part of what Jessica had said last night, that she'd predicted she'd have no patients and that Powell Springs would never forgive her.

"Do you know how to find her?" Pop asked, pouring himself a drink from Cole's bottle.

"Not yet. But her note said she'd send an address to forward the rest of her stuff to as soon as she has one."

Pop fixed him with the same hard stare he'd used on him and Riley when they were boys. "When she does, you'd better go up there and bring her back."

"What?" Cole couldn't believe his ears. Of course, that was his plan, but he hadn't announced it. "You never liked her!"

"Didn't say I don't like her. Said she was too smart for her own good. But she didn't get into that fix here by herself. Weren't you with her?"

Cole glanced away, feeling heat creep up his neck.

Pop lifted his glass briefly. "Well, there you go. If that doctor gal is the one you want, prove it to her. Make her believe you. This town isn't going to hold a grudge against her. She's a good woman."

"I thought you liked Amy." Cole poured a stiff shot for himself now.

"Bah. Too sweet to believe. No one is that perfect and nice without a reason. Turns out I was right."

He almost laughed. His father was clumsy when it came to expressing his feelings. But Cole heard his support beneath his bluster, and that was good enough for him.

— — —

With her damp handkerchief wadded up in her fist, Jessica watched the landscape slip past the window of her train. Now and then the rain let up enough to let her see acres of farmland, tall stands of timber, and the last of autumn's colors in the trees. But it all went by in a blur, none of it really holding her attention. She kept her face turned to the glass, trying to hide from the curious stares of others.

The train car swayed and clacked over the rails, carrying her farther north to Seattle. Some passengers wore the familiar gauze masks she'd grown so accustomed to. She'd worn hers for a while, but it made it so difficult to wipe her streaming nose that she'd given up and removed it. A few sitting near her eyed her with misgivings, but she couldn't bring herself to tell them she wasn't sick with influenza.

She was only crying.

The tears would come in waves, as did the relentless questions that kept nagging at her. The aching emptiness in her, though, was constant.

Had she made the wrong decision to leave Powell Springs? Had she run away again, as Cole had said? And if she'd made the right choice, why was she so miserable? Leaving New York had not felt like this.

She glanced around, wishing that she could be one of these people with their faces buried in books or chatting with companions, going about their business. One man held a copy of an area newspaper with today's date, November tenth, and she noticed distractedly that not one mention was made on the front page of the carnage the Spanish influenza had wrought. People were still getting sick, still dying, and she knew that although the West Coast didn't seem to have suffered the staggering number of cases the East had, the epidemic wasn't over.

Turning back to the window, she saw a deep river gorge below the trestle they were crossing. But it was Cole's face that kept coming to her mind's eye. The memory of Cole's touch on her bare skin, holding her hand, the warmth of his body through his shirt.

More questions plagued her. Could she have faced the small, angry group in Powell Springs with him standing beside her to give her strength? Did she owe it to her own townspeople to stay and care for them, instead of leaving them to haughty Dr. Pearson?

Very worst of all, despairing though she was—had she broken her own heart this time?

"Olympia!" the conductor announced in a booming voice. "Ten minutes to Olympia, Washington!"

Her nerves as frayed as an old rag rug, Jessica jumped at the intrusion.

"Excuse me," she said, flagging down the gauze-masked conductor. "How much farther to Seattle?"

He consulted his big railroad pocket watch. "That would be about another three hours, ma'am, counting the stops." She nodded her thanks, and he moved down the aisle, continuing his blaring announcement.

Three more hours of this. Maybe at the station in Olympia, she could get off the train for a few moments to wash her face in the ladies' room and collect herself. She just had to.

It sounded like a monumental task. She had never felt more scattered or alone in her life.

— — —

The next afternoon, Cole stood at the forge in the shop, pumping the bellows until the embers glowed red with a heat that could incinerate a steak in sixty seconds. In the stall, Mr. Bright's beautiful chestnut Morgan, the one he used for his grocery deliveries, stood waiting for a new set of shoes.

He didn't really want to be here. But the only temporary escape from heartache he knew, besides alcohol, was work. Backbreaking, constant labor that made every muscle scream for mercy and would let him fall into bed and into a sleep that came close to death. Last night, he'd ended up bringing his whiskey back here and leaving it, corked, on the shelf in the tack room. Only about two inches were missing from the full bottle, and those he'd shared with Pop. Getting drunk wouldn't have changed anything—he'd have just felt worse today.

And he felt bad enough as it was.

1918 was not turning out to be a good year for anyone, but Cole felt like the Braddocks had had more than their share of misery. The only thing he could say—so far—was that by the grace of God, or luck, or whatever made the world turn, the entire family had escaped the influenza epidemic, and not many could claim that.

Suddenly, over the sound of his own tools, he heard the fire bell ringing. It was located next to city hall, and when it rang, everyone who could was expected to drop whatever they were doing to run and help. Cole bent to put down the tongs he held and in his haste touched his shoulder to the forge. Swearing, he looked down to see a one-inch triangular piece of fabric burned right off his shirt and an angry red mark beneath. Granny Mae's sovereign treatment for burns was urine. Huh, he'd like to hear Granny Mae tell him to pee on this…

Still cursing and trying to see how bad the burn was, he walked to the double doors. Just as he reached them, he heard an odd whooping coming from the street, as if it were New Year's Eve. From the train station a steam whistle blew, continual, long sharp blasts that carried all the way down here.

God, what was going on?

People opened their doors, and from the shops that had reopened, customers and proprietors poured onto Main, all looking to see what the hoopla was about. Then he saw Leroy Fenton's bicycle boy peddling up and down the street, waving a piece of paper and shouting at the top of his lungs.

"It's over! The war is over! Armistice! The fighting stopped at eleven o'clock in the morning in France. The war is over!"

"Well, I'll be damned," Cole said aloud and laughed. He leaned against the doorframe and watched people hug and cheer. Now and then he looked down at the burn that was beginning to blister. Pulling off one heavy leather glove with his teeth, carefully he tore open the hole in his shirt for a better view. God, he was getting to be as clumsy as Jeremy. At least the kid had survived his injury and the influenza. "Oh, hell," he muttered.

"Do you need a doctor?"

Cole's head flew up and he saw Jessica walking toward him, carrying her doctor's bag. She looked as tired and worn as he felt, but she was smiling, and though her skirts were wet and dirty from the street, it was as if the sun had come out. The pain of his burn forgotten, the pain of everything forgotten, he opened his arms to her.

Jessica dropped her bag in the mud and ran the last few feet right into his embrace. He rained kisses on her, inhaling her fragrance. Holding her face between his hands, he asked, "Jess, is it really you? Are you home?"

"I'm home, Cole. I was an idiot. I never should have gone. You were right, this is where I belong, with you, the love of my life. I got off the train yesterday in Olympia and exchanged my ticket to come back. I had to spend the night in Portland to get my connection, and the station master there said I'd be home by morning. But the train was late—Union Station was mobbed with people celebrating the good news."

He looked down at her, and saw the love in his heart mirrored in her eyes. "It doesn't matter. You came back. You're here. The war is over. This is a great day!"

"It's a *wonderful* day."

He picked her up and whirled her around, laughing again. "Wow, just wait till Pop hears about this."

EPILOGUE

"Jessica? Are you ready?" Susannah stuck her head through an opening in the door and whispered to her. Jess stood in a small side room off Mayor Cookson's office.

Nervous, she nodded. In turn, Susannah nodded to the small assembly behind her, then slipped in.

"Do you have everything you need? A handkerchief?"

Jess took a deep breath. "I'm fine." She reached out and grasped Susannah's hand. "I want to thank you for doing this, for being my witness. I know the timing isn't the best, considering everything. But you look beautiful."

"I am *honored* to be your witness," she replied. "This is the way things were always meant to be, you two together. I hope you'll be as happy as Riley and I…were." She swallowed and her eyes were bright with standing tears. Jess squeezed her hand. "Here's your bouquet. I ordered it from a florist in Portland. The conductor held it the whole fifteen miles out here to keep it from being crushed."

Jessica took the arrangement and smiled. "Pink roses."

"That's what Cole told me to get. He said they're your favorites."

She nodded, amazed that he'd remembered.

This wedding had been cobbled together in a week's time. Jessica was not getting married in a white gown, but under the circumstances, they'd done well enough. Granny Mae had done all the cooking for a feast that would be held in the town council meeting room.

Best of all, Cole Braddock stood on the other side of that door.

Sometime during the past week, Amy and Adam had left town in the middle of the night on a train headed east. That was all anyone knew. She had left no letter for Jessica, who'd decided it was just as well. Maybe someday, after enough time had passed…

Frederick Pearson had indeed traveled north to take Jessica's place at Seattle General Hospital. Whether Dr. Thomas Martin, the chief of staff, would keep the odious man was another issue. But not her concern.

Right now, Mayor Cookson was ready to officiate at her wedding to Cole, and that was all that mattered.

She smiled at Susannah again. "All right."

Susannah opened the door to Mayor Cookson's office, and the first person Jessica's eyes fell upon was Cole, dressed as handsomely as she'd ever seen him.

Waiting for her.

Waiting to take her home.

THE END

HOME BY NIGHTFALL

by

Alexis Harrington

An Excerpt from CHAPTER ONE

Meuse Valley, Northern France
July 1920

Although he had no memory of it, he had arrived here in that ambulance.

Leaning again on the hoe handle, he heard a motor start up, then saw a car with the Red Cross emblem on its side pull out onto the road. Obviously, it had been visiting this farmhouse. It moved away slowly, and the man at the wheel eyed him, but too much distance lay between them for either to really see the other. Finally, the car rounded a bend in the road and disappeared.

"Christophe! Viens.Prendsdéjeuner.Ne le laisse pas refroidir."

His French was not as fluent as a native's, but he understood that Véronique was calling him to lunch and to come while it was still hot. Turning, he saw her standing in the doorway of what had been a bigger farmhouse. The rest of the structure had been blasted away by a shell during the war. Both he and Véronique had to be careful when they worked the tract—unexploded shells lurked in the soil, as unstable as nitroglycerin. An old farmer farther down the valley had hit one with a shovel last spring and was killed. Another casualty of war, one claimed after the Armistice.

Waving to Véronique, he put down the hoe and reached for his crutch, a crude, homemade thing, and hobbled his way across the field toward her. She was a pretty woman, not yet forty years old, and despite losing her whole family to the Great War, she managed somehow to maintain a generous, hopeful heart.

"*Viens. Manger,*" she repeated when he reached her. The sun gleamed on her russet hair, the long part that hung out the back of her kerchief.

"*Parlesanglais, Véronique.*"

She gave him a mulish look. "*Non.*"

"*Oui, anglais.*"

With an exasperated sigh, she said, "Come to table."

"Close enough." He gave her a smile and a peck on the cheek. She smiled, too.

The single room that remained within the stone walls of the farmhouse was cramped but clean, and the roof didn't leak. He hoped that when his strength improved, the two of them would be able to sort through the rubble of stones outside and rebuild a room or two. Though a relief group formed by the Society of Friends had offered to move them to a village with new housing, Véronique had refused to go. This land had been in the Raineau family for generations, she was the only surviving member of that family, and she was not about to leave it. She had, however, accepted basic furniture—a table and chairs, and a bed—vegetable seeds, and the gardening tools they'd provided. When a skinny milk cow wandered onto the property, now seeming as rare as a diamond, they'd captured it and let it graze on what weeds and other scrub it could forage. But if they couldn't find a way to breed it again, the cow's milk would dry up.

A small pot of rich potato-and-leek soup waited on the table, with a round of crusty bread and a bottle of wine. How she worked such magic at her stove with so little, he didn't know. New shops in the nearby village carried staples, but money was still in short supply.

He pulled out a chair and sat down, his injured leg protruding stiffly. Véronique sat across from him, whispered a blessing in French, and crossed herself, the signal that they could begin eating.

The soup was warm and tasty, and his appreciative noises made her smile again. "The Red Cross was here today?" he asked in French. Christophe knew the term *Croix Rouge*. "I saw their car leave."

She paused, her soup spoon on the edge of her plate. "While you were working?"

"Yes."

"And they saw you?"

He shrugged. "I'm sure they did. We watched each other."

"It was a man and a woman. Americans."

"I hope they'll bring help. We should need it." He corrected his linguistic blunder. "We *need* it." He knew that volunteers from the American Red Cross had come around before, checking on all those who had returned to the area after the Meuse-Argonne Offensive. The organization had been part of a relief effort as well. "Did they mention the sheep from Algeria that have been promised?"

"No."

"What did they want, then?"

Véronique was a forthright woman, direct and unsparing of her brandy-colored gazes. But now she glanced away. "They asked about you."

He'd been pouring a glass of wine and stopped. "Me—what about me?"

"They know you are American, too. They are curious."

Abruptly awash with a formless, uneasy dread, he put down the bottle.

"They wanted to talk to you, but I told them you were gone to the village. I was afraid they might upset you with their questions."

He shook his head, puzzled. "I do not understand '*détresse*.'"

She touched his arm to make him look at her, and put a hand to her forehead. "*Affliger.*"

Distress. That he did understand. He felt safe here with Véronique.

"They asked where you are from, how you came to be here."

He tore a piece of bread from the round loaf. "What did you tell them?"

"The truth. I pulled you from that wrecked ambulance beside the road. You were the only one still alive. The driver and the other man—" She shuddered. "The shell destroyed them." She paused. "It has been almost two years. You still remember nothing?"

"No."

"They asked if you had identification. But you did not, and I told them so. To me, you are Christophe. That is all I know."

— — —

ABOUT THE AUTHOR

Photograph by Elena Rose Photography, 2011

Alexis Harrington is the award-winning author of a dozen novels, including the international bestseller *The Irish Bride.* She spent twelve years working for consulting civil engineers before she changed track and became a full-time novelist. When she isn't writing, she enjoys jewelry-making, needlework, embroidery, cooking, and entertaining friends. She lives in her native Pacific Northwest, near the Columbia River, with a variety of pets who do their best to distract her while she is working.

Charleston, SC
28 December 2011